BERTRAM *of* BUTTER CROSS

A WESTERN LIGHTS BOOK

BERTRAM *of* BUTTER CROSS

JEFFREY E. BARLOUGH

GRESHAM & DOYLE

BERTRAM OF BUTTER CROSS
First Edition / August 2007

Published by Gresham & Doyle
Los Angeles, California

Cover: *The Enchanted Wood* (oil on canvas)
by Elizabeth Adela Stanhope Forbes (1859-1912)
Private collection / Bonhams, London / Bridgeman Art Library

To learn more about the Western Lights series visit
www.westernlightsbooks.com

Library of Congress Control Number: 2006927744

ISBN: 978-0-9787634-0-4

Text set in Garamond Antiqua
Printed in the United States of America
on acid-free paper

To my Uncle
FRANK S. ZIZDA

CONTENTS

PART ONE

PART TWO

PART THREE

PART FOUR

PART FIVE

PART SIX

I spit into the face of Time
That has transfigured me.

YEATS

BERTRAM *of* BUTTER CROSS

PART ONE

THE FIRST CHAPTER

SOMETHING IN THE WOOD

IN the springtime of our grandparents — that is to say, when our grandmothers and grandfathers all were very young — there occurred in the town of Market Snailsby, in Fenshire, a mystery of singular character and incident. More precisely, it was the unraveling of this mystery that occurred, for the mystery itself had been a staple of popular legend for a good many years, during which time it had resisted all solution. This is the story of the working-out of that mystery, and of what was discovered in Marley Wood, and who discovered it and how, and what came of it all in the end.

Market Snailsby was one of those long, lazy, meandering sorts of towns that are often met with in the marshlands. Its quaint old houses and ancient cobbled streets were scattered in profuse array along the banks of the River Fribble near its junction with the River Lour. The Fribble was rather wide for a Fenshire river, but not very deep, and navigable only by the lighter barge traffic. It was a good eel-river, though, and a fine one for fishing, and of much benefit to the towns-people. There was a beautiful old stone bridge crossing it, at a point midway between the Market Square and the Church of All Hallows. On the other side of the bridge, on the river's south bank, stood the pretty little ivy-covered posting-inn called the Broom and Badger. It was here at the Badger that the drivers of the mastodon trains used to put themselves up, after putting their teams out behind it on the broad, open stretch of meadowland that was Snailsby Common.

In those days, teams of enormous shovel-tusker mastodons — southern cousins of the more familiar red thunder-beasts — were employed in many districts for the clearing of the coach-roads. These creatures, with their broad, elongated, scoop- or shovel-like jaws and tusks, had proven themselves to be ideal instruments for the necessary logging and digging. The roads often followed the course of ancient trackways that thunder-beasts of every stripe had been traversing for centuries. At the time of my story, teams of shovel-tuskers were in operation even in so wild, remote, and lonely a region as the fens. Like most everyone the inhabitants of this wilderness needed their coach-roads; although identifying trails of sufficient substance amidst the miry bogs and reedy marshes of Fenshire and Slopshire was rather a knottier proposition than in most counties of the realm.

It was late in the afternoon one day — a day, aptly enough, towards the end of springtime — when a fast-trotting mare, a golden chestnut with a flaxen mane and tail, was seen drawing a shay-cart in the Tillington Road, some miles to the north and east of Market Snailsby.

Occupying the seat of the cart were two figures wrapped up in cloaks and mufflers. The one handling the ribands was a steady-eyed woman of about forty with a head of dark curls, bunches of which could be seen spilling out from under her bonnet. Her name was Jemma Hathaway. Miss Hathaway was a substantial citizen of Market Snailsby, of a family that had long been prominent in the town; indeed there had been Hathaways in the area since long before the granting of the town charter. Beside her sat a snub-nosed, ruddy-cheeked young girl called Molly Grime. Like Miss Hathaway, Molly was dark-headed and not unhandsome, although her hair was considerably tamer and hadn't the slender threads of gray that had begun seeping into her companion's. Molly, too, was of a family long-established in Fenshire, if one of lesser eminence: for she was a maid-of-all-work, whose services were in demand in the home of Miss Hathaway and that of a neighbor, one Sir Hector MacHector of Mickledene Hall.

In the box behind the women rode a third and uncommonly patient passenger — a dog. He was a rather active, alert, high-spirited sort of dog to be lounging in a shay-cart watching the dreary flats of Fenshire pass him by. He was one of that dappled breed — short white coat sprinkled over with black spots — known familiarly as a *coach dog,* from their frequent use as guards upon the mail coaches. This particular coach dog's name was Snap, and he was a valued member of the household of Miss Hathaway and her brother Richard. Like his brave fellows he guarded the mail, if only after a fashion — once the postman had delivered it, he guarded it. He was much beloved by his mistress and master, and much indulged; although to the two cats of the household he was rather less precious. To annoy him the cats had taken to calling him a "plum-pudding dog," which is a far less imposing title than coach dog.

Miss Hathaway and her companions had traveled that morning to the distant hamlet of Tillington, to visit a friend who had taken to her bed, and now were making their way home. The hour was late, the air was cold, and the warm blaze of the kitchen fire in the Hathaway cottage was on the minds of all. Only their cook and housekeeper, Mrs. Rudling, and the two cats would be on hand to greet them, however, Miss Hathaway's brother having left several days before on a trip to the county town of Newmarsh; but he was expected home within the week.

The chestnut drawing the shay-cart was another of the prominent Hathaways of Market Snailsby. Her name was Rosamond, but to most she was known simply as Rosie — a plain enough name, and a common one, too, for such a pretty pacer, and as fine a mare as could be found in any neighborhood. She was the joy of the stable and the apple of the eye of Mr. Richard Hathaway. Plain "Rosie" though she might be, she was in most every other regard anything but plain or common. Her esteemed position in the animal family at Mead Cottage had never been challenged, by either Snap or the cats; nor was she above reminding them on occasion that her given name was *Rosamond,* which to Rosie was as grand and noteworthy a name as any horse had ever had, whether Pegasus, Bayard, or Roan Barbary.

For some two hours now the shay-cart had been rattling along in the road. On the travelers' left stood the winding river — looking its usual drab and monotonous self, like the sky above it and all the flat, fenny landscape roundabout — while on their right loomed a darksome wood. That wood was Marley Wood. A vast and seemingly impenetrable fortress of evergreens and oaks, it stretched like a great, bosky belt across the whole of middle Fenshire, isolating Market Snailsby and the boggy wastes of Slopshire to the south of it from the more prosperous towns in the north.

As they were passing a spinney that adjoined the eaves of the wood, something caught first the eye, and then the ear, of Miss Hathaway.

In her eye — in a corner of it, actually — she detected a flash of movement in the spinney; in her ear, seconds later, the ring of childish laughter.

Alarmed at the thought of a child's playing so near the wood, and so far from town, she brought Rosie to a stand and called out to the unknown small one.

"Hallo! Hallo there! Can you hear me? What are you doing there?"

No response.

"Who can it be, ma'am?" Molly wondered.

"I've no idea. There are no farmsteads in the area, and we've seen no cart or wagon stopped along the road. How can the child have gotten here?"

Another call to the spinney — same result. The eerie quiet of the place brushed the faces of Miss Hathaway and Molly like the prevailing wind, which in Fenshire is a chilly northwester.

"'Tis awful brisk, ma'am, and be growin' brisker," Molly warned, rubbing her hands. "And the dark be drawin' on soon."

"Hallo — you there!" Jemma called again. "This is Miss Hathaway, of Market Snailsby. What is your name? And where are your parents?"

At last came an answer from the spinney, although it was not the one she sought.

Ha, ha, ha, laughed the spinney. *Ha, ha, ha!*

"I shall see who it is," Miss Hathaway declared, with a determined chin; and handing the reins to Molly she jumped lightly from the cart.

"D'ye think it wise, ma'am?" questioned the maid. "For 'tis Marley Wood there, ma'am — *Marley Wood!*"

At that moment two small children came stealing forth from the spinney. They halted at its edge and peered curiously at the women and at Snap in the box.

"Hallo! What are you doing there?" Miss Hathaway exclaimed. "You must be careful — this is not a place for playing in. You musn't tarry longer, for the night is fast approaching. You should be off home! Come, children, we'll take you there."

To her surprise the two merely looked at one another and giggled. Snap, catching their scent, barked at them from the cart, as though urging them to heed his mistress's words. Miss Hathaway repeated her admonition, but it only set the little ones to giggling again; then they drew back into the cover of the thicket.

"Children! Children, come here! *Children!*" cried Miss Hathaway.

Come to her they did not; came instead the scrunch of tiny footsteps on the crisp snow of the spinney, retreating hastily in the direction of Marley Wood.

"Did you see them, Molly?" Miss Hathaway asked.

"Ou, aye, ma'am. A darlin' small girl and boy, the pair of 'em well-garbed for the season."

"Do you know them?"

"No, ma'am."

"Nor do I."

Miss Hathaway paused as she debated what she should do. Should she go in search of the children? Or should she leave it alone, trusting that their parents or guardians were somewhere about?

But who could those parents or guardians be? Market Snailsby was not so big a town, so that most of the young folk in it were known to the grown-ups by sight. And who would be out here this late in the day, allowing their offspring to play so near the treacherous wood? Why, the very idea of it, in the opinion of Molly Grime, was a boggle and a bafflement!

Having resolved that no harm should come to the children if she could prevent it, Miss Hathaway thrust her hand under the seat and drew forth a gleaming blade. It was one of her brother's cutlasses, one light enough for her to wield effectively, and which, for safety's sake, she carried with her whenever she was on the road. For no one in Fenshire who had a whit of sense went unprovided when so far from the security of town.

"Ye'll not be chasin' after 'em into the wood now, ma'am?" said a disbelieving Molly. "No, ma'am, not into Marley Wood! No, no, ye shouldn't go a-trampin' about in there — "

"I shall, if I have to," said Miss Hathaway as she removed her cloak, and made a few practice lunges with her sword at an unarmed shrub hard by. "But they still may be hanging round the spinney. Keep a watch on Snap and Rosie now, like a good girl."

As she turned to leave there was a yelp from the box, and Snap the coach dog, far from pleased at being left in the care of Molly Grime, came bounding after her.

Brave-hearted Snap! Guardian of the mail he was, but more even than that he was guardian of his mistress.

"I'll see you safely through," he vowed, his tail furiously a-wag, "and as for the brats, I'll nose 'em out in a trice!"

And so the two of them set off for the spinney, Miss Hathaway
with her blade in hand and Snap eagerly sniffing the ground before
them.

Molly, having watched them out of sight, uttered a groan, and
mumbled something to herself about "not borrowin' trouble." Then,
finding herself suddenly bereft of companionship, she began casting
nervous glances about her, at the darksome wood and the dingy river,
and at Rosie standing in the traces, and in such wise maintained a
worried lookout. She was none too happy about Miss Hathaway's
decision to go after the children, and even less happy about her own
lonely post in the road. But she put a maid-of-all-work's stoic face on,
and bided a while — that is to say, she waited.

Into the spinney plunged Miss Hathaway and Snap. After a little
searching through the tangle of tree and scrub, however, it became
clear that the children were not there. And so, together, mistress and
coach dog strode on into Marley Wood.

Having breached the gloomy stronghold, Miss Hathaway felt the
weight of it pressing on her almost at once. It was like stepping into
a vast, secret world of dimness and enclosure. Soaring evergreens grew
thickly round her on every side, with here and there a menacing oak,
its skeletal trunk and limbs like the hand of a buried giant thrusting
up from below. Silence ruled, apart from the twittering of a few small
birds, and the groaning of a branch amidst the mass of timber from
the occasional breeze that penetrated. A feeble light was struggling to
pierce the timber-tops, the snow and ice clinging to the trees doing
little to reflect it; so that the deeper into the wood she and Snap went,
the darker it became.

Glancing round her at the looming pines and sinister clumps of firs,
behind which anything might be lurking, the consequences of her decision were brought swiftly home to Jemma. Steel or no steel, she
understood that in obeying her impulse she had embarked upon a
risky enterprise. Everyone knew the reputation of Marley Wood; from
their nursery days all in Market Snailsby had been warned against its
perils. Oh, if only her brother Richard had been there to help her —
or to stop her!

Gingerly she picked her way through the frosty maze, the nose of
Snap and a broken trail of footprints serving as her guides. The tracks
appeared to lead towards a wall of fir-trees which lay directly ahead.

Could that be where the children were hiding, Jemma wondered? But *why* should they be hiding? And what business had they in this evil place to begin with?

All at once Snap let out an excited bark and dashed through the wall of firs. A moment later the soft beat of hooves was heard behind it.

Perhaps it was a pony ridden by the children? Perhaps that was how they had come to be out here? Perhaps Snap had found them!

Silently Miss Hathaway stole forward towards the trees, her cutlass at the ready, her eyes alert for the slightest movement, her ears for the slightest sound.

"Snap!" she called softly. "Snap, are you there?"

She was answered by an odd, funny, choky sort of noise. She identified it as the voice of Snap, but so strangely altered as to be almost unrecognizable. Never before had she heard him make such a noise.

"Snap, what have you found? Is it the children?"

It was especially dark there because of the overhang of the dripping, ghostly pines, and impossible to discern anything more than a few feet in front of her. Abruptly Snap's funny noise was transformed into a yelp — a very frightened yelp — and then the coach dog himself came charging out of the trees, his tail and most everything else about him quivering with alarm.

"Help!" he cried. "Help! help! help!"

Whatever it was Snap had discovered behind the wall of firs had given him a raging case of the jim-jams. Indeed, he was so shaken by it that it seemed he might shake off all his spots on the spot.

Miss Hathaway recalled one other time when she had seen him in such a state. It was the day a marsh devil had come slinking over the bridge from south of town, and made its way upriver as far as Mead Cottage. The marsh devil, known more properly as a *dirk-tooth*, was a kind of saber-cat. A savage and powerful beast, it was the most common species of giant cat in the marshlands, and was known to hunt in the wood.

A stab of fear went through Jemma, as she wondered if it might not be a marsh devil hiding there amongst the firs. Or perhaps it was something worse; for the reputation of Marley Wood was just that — *the worst*.

Marsh devils, flat-head boars, and spotted lions roaming its murky aisles, and winged teratorns its tree-tops, all of them seeking prey! It was no wonder so few in Fenshire now dared brave the dangers of the wood, even when well-provided with cutlass and claymore.

But what of the children, Jemma thought? Had they fallen victim to the slavering jaws of the monster? And what of her and Snap? For surely they would be next . . .

Came then another sound from behind the firs, a sound like hooves crunching snowy turf.

The marsh devil! But how could that be? For marsh devils were cats, after all, and cats, as everyone knows, had no hooves —

Something stirred back of the nearest tree. Miss Hathaway looked very hard at it, trying to make it out in the dimness. It was not so much the sight, as the *sense* of something there — a vague impression of something standing behind the tree, something tall and strange and oddly shaped, eyeing her stealthily and coldly through the branches.

A shiver raced down her spine. Against her better judgment she raised the point of her sword until it touched a limb of the fir-tree. Ever so gently she parted the branch from its fellows. As she did so there was a rush of movement, and a face leaped into the gap between the branches.

It was an ugly face, as faces go. It was a face with two angry, staring eyes in it, and a pair of lips drawn back in a hideous scowl, teeth bared and nostrils blown wide, the whole of it pasted onto a human head and framed by a tumbling mass of orange hair. But there all resemblance to humanity ended, for the head was perched atop a grotesquely long, sinewy, and altogether unhuman kind of neck, round which the orange hair streamed down like a waterfall.

She saw the head snake its way towards her through the branches, saw it push its face right up to hers; and stopping there, its eyes mere inches from her own, it glared at her and growled.

Miss Hathaway's breath went out of her in a single, horror-stricken gasp, and she reeled back, exclaiming — *"Good heavens!"*

But it was only a gasp, and only a glimpse; then the face was gone, and the air rent by a blood-curdling scream — a wild, ear-splitting, unearthly wail, like the cry of an anguished spirit — that erupted behind the tree.

So shocked was Jemma by all of this that the cutlass dropped from her hand. In desperate haste she knelt to recover it, deciding in that instant that, children or no children, the better part of valor this day was retreat.

On hearing the frightful cry the valiant Snap had answered with some cries of his own — such gallant and bravely-warning yaps and yelps they were — and then promptly turned and bolted, calling over his shoulder to his mistress to *follow, follow!*

They made a fiend of a dash for it, Snap at full gallop and Jemma trailing him on the run. Back through the frosty maze they sped, back the way they had come, back, back towards the spinney and the comforting dullness of the marshes.

They had made it nearly to the edge of the wood when something gripped Jemma from behind, and caught at her throat as if to strangle her. In a panic she took it for the thing from behind the tree. But it turned out to be nothing so monstrous as that, merely a drowsy limb that had snagged her bonnet and threatened to rip it from her head, the bonnet-strings acting as a noose. She recovered quickly enough; and then the misty gray light of Fenshire was all about her once more, and she and Snap were out of the wood and through the spinney and hurrying towards Molly and Rosie and the safety of the shay-cart.

Only too glad to have escaped with her whole skin, Miss Hathaway prayed that the children had escaped too; for in her heart she knew there was little she could have done for them. Out of breath she flung her blade into the cart, just as Snap leaped into the box. Then she sprang onto the seat and without a word to Molly snatched the reins and whip from the poor bewildered girl's hands.

"Gee-up!" she cried to Rosie. "Gee-up, Rosie — *gee-up!*"

The chestnut, sensing that something was very much amiss, responded at once; and so off they dashed, hooves drumming, wheels churning, sod and gravel spraying, cart and harness jingling and jouncing as they flew along. Fortunately that stretch of road had some of the firmest ground in the neighborhood, and as a consequence Rosie was able to work up a rattling good pace.

Despite the unsettling nature of her experience, Miss Hathaway was determined that she would find out who the two children were and to whom they had belonged. *Had* belonged — for she had to admit it, she was convinced that the pair of them had met a grisly end behind the wall of firs. Indeed, how could it have been otherwise?

They had been traveling at Rosie's lively pace for some little while, speeding towards Market Snailsby and the kitchen fire and home, when Miss Hathaway abruptly drew rein and halted at the roadside.

"What is it now, ma'am?" Molly asked; for since fleeing Marley Wood her mistress had offered her not a word of explanation.

"There is someone there," Jemma said.

She had spied something near the wood — the trees bordered the road very closely there — and then an unmistakable sound broke upon her ears and those of Molly.

Ha, ha, ha was the sound. *Ha, ha, ha!*

"'Tis the childhers — the darlin' girl and boy!" Molly exclaimed. "Well, I'm fair amazed at it."

Indeed she was, as was Miss Hathaway; and so it was, and there they were — two tiny, laughing faces peeping out from some brambles round the eaves of the wood.

"Children, you must come here!" Jemma called to them, and rather sharply, too. "Children, it's dangerous to be playing there!"

Snap barked, and sent a deep-voiced howl rolling towards the wood; Rosie tossed her mane and shuffled her feet. Again the children merely laughed. They pointed small fingers at the shay-cart and its passengers; then, smiling and giggling, they scampered off.

How could the children possibly be there, Jemma wondered? How could they have escaped their grisly end? What was more, how could they have kept pace with Rosie and the flying shay-cart? The crunch of hooves on snowy turf — perhaps it *had* been a pony there in the wood? Perhaps that was how they had trailed the cart for so many miles?

But what of the snake-necked thing that had growled in her face?

Molly meantime had been urging her mistress to drop all thought of the children, for this day at least. There was something not right about them, she declared, something unnatural — something *spookish*. It was an assessment with which Jemma, in the end, found herself reluctantly agreeing.

Nothing nearly so exciting happened for the rest of the drive. Miss Hathaway remained absorbed in thought for the better part of it, happy to know that the children were alive, but troubled, too. She had made up her mind to ask the vicar about them at the first opportunity, when the outposts of Market Snailsby hove into view round a bend in the river. Moments later the early lights of the town were seen glimmering in the distance.

Most likely the vicar would know to whom the children belonged, Jemma thought. He knew all the families in the parish, all the yeoman farmers and the husbandmen on their smallholdings, and was conversant with the fen-slodgers, those citizens of stout heart and sturdy constitution who lived by fowling and fishing on the marshes. Yes, more than likely the vicar would know whose children the two were.

The lights of Market Snailsby looked particularly inviting in the fast-gathering gloom. It was nearly the dinner-hour, and Mrs. Rudling would be concerned about her tardy wayfarers on the road. A heavy fog had begun creeping down upon the countryside; already the dismal flats and marshes across the river had been swallowed up by it. But it mattered not, for there on the travelers' left was Mickledene Hall, and beyond it Mead Cottage — sights for which Miss Hathaway and Molly gave grateful thanks, and which meant only one thing . . .

Home!

THE SECOND CHAPTER

OUR HUNTING FATHERS

IN the morning, bright and early, as the story-books say — well, early at any rate, for it is rarely bright on a Market Snailsby morning — Rosie found herself hitched again to the shay-cart in preparation for a drive into town.

Miss Hathaway, having passed an uneventful night, had largely recovered from her scare; and with the cheery bustle now of breakfast round the kitchen fire, and the company of Mrs. Rudling, Snap, and the cats, she began to wonder if she might not have — how shall I put it? — *imagined* certain details of her foray into Marley Wood.

It had been the stress of venturing into that dreaded domain, cutlass in hand, to brave the unknown, which had triggered an excessive rush of imagination; or so she tried to convince herself. It was a pleasant enough thing to wish for, I suppose, and a salutary one. But the arrival in the kitchen of Molly Grime, fresh from Mickledene Hall — Molly Grime, who could bear witness to certain particulars of yesterday's adventure, and her mistress's response to them — was sufficient to dispel the cloud of wishful thinking, and allow Jemma to see her pleasant thing for what it was: a pleasant fiction.

After breakfast she and Molly took their places again in the shay-cart, and out through the gate and into the Tillington Road they went. As they rattled along they saw Oldcorn House passing by them in the mist, and Water Street where it descends to the river, and the imposing red-brick mansion known as Goose Stacks (so called because it had been built by a man named Goose with a fondness for chimneys). A little farther along, at the crossing of Widemarsh Street, the Tillington Road ended and became the High Street; and down it the shay-cart rolled on its way into town.

Market Snailsby was a town neither very large nor very small, and it was very much a Fenshire town. Nearly all of its houses, cottages, and shops were antiquely picturesque. They had walls of clean white plaster striped with black oak timbers, and doors deep-set like monks peering from under their cowls, and casements a-burst with latticed panes. Most had the high, bell-shaped gables, steep-pitched roofs, and flaring eaves so common in the marshlands, features which lent them a certain dreamy or fanciful appearance. The roofs were mostly of tile or reed-thatched, and snugly overhung the walls and windows like the brows of sleepy hounds. As well there were a few houses of brick like Goose Stacks, and some quaint old cottages made of the same smooth cobbles that formed the town's streets and lanes.

Market Snailsby being a river town, it had a river wall running along a part of it, where anglers young and old could be seen fishing of an early morning. From Widemarsh Street down to the bridge-end, and a little beyond it, the prime angling-posts already had been claimed and lines dipped into the Fribble by the time Rosie and the shay-cart rattled past. Tiny ones on tiptoe could be seen peeping expectantly over the wall, as their elders smoked and chatted amongst themselves in that easy way Fenshiremen have done since before Adam of Eden-shire was a pup, or so the saying is.

Molly, having been set down in the Market Square, went at once to the old Market House where she was to do some shopping for Mead Cottage and for Lady MacHector of Mickledene. The Market House, which occupied the center of the Square, was a Snailsby land-mark — a round, gabled, weather-vane-topped structure of open arches and oak pillars, under which the tradesmen and farmers of the town were wont to display their goods. It was here that Miss Hathaway was to return and collect her once the church clock had sounded the hour of ten.

Meantime Jemma had driven on to the vicarage in Holy Street. Beside the vicarage stood the Church of All Hallows, with its lovely old porch, and its tall steeple rising above the trees. This steeple was another landmark of the town. It was one of the finest steeples in the marshlands, and the loftiest object to be seen for miles around — when there was no fog, of course, and if one excluded the soaring pines of Marley Wood.

She found the vicar standing under a plum tree at the side of the house, thoughtfully surveying his garden. At the moment his garden was awash in snow; but a little snow in springtime did not deter him from working out his plans for the coming season as regards his herb beds, his roots, and his roses. Mr. Ludlow was a hard-working, open-minded, forward-looking sort of man — qualities not often associated with country clergymen in a place like Market Snailsby. He had shown himself to be a good, steady vicar, one who knew how to fill a pew, how to entertain guests and talk easy small-talk with wives, and put others at their ease regardless of their station.

"Ah, good morning, Miss Hathaway, good morning! Will this winter never end? Will the sun never shine?" he smiled, extending his hands in welcome to his visitor.

"It will shine, vicar, have no doubt of that — some day. In any case we have had one or two moonlit nights of late."

"Ah, so we have, indeed."

The air was decidedly brisk there in the garden, and in the town, and in Fenshire generally, and as the vicar and Miss Hathaway talked together their lips emitted a visible steam.

Mr. Ludlow was a big, bluff, strapping sort of country clergyman, with a bold forehead and thick, dark brows, a long nose, a substantial jaw, and a smooth chin. Truth be told he more resembled the farmer his father had been than he did a vicar; and so it was only natural that he should take an interest in his garden. But Mr. Ludlow had other interests as well, as for example his wine-cellar, his pipe, his books, his sporting paper, and his daily morning's ride on the Snailsby gallops, all of which he was exceedingly fond. Mr. Ludlow was fond of his wife, too, for the most part, and if there had been any infant Ludlows at the vicarage I'm sure he would have liked them just as much.

Another interest of the vicar's was his pet glyptodont — a peculiar, tortoise-like creature with a shell of bony armor and a furry snout, which the vicar had acquired in its infancy, and which in the interim had grown to about the size of his drawing-room sofa. The glypt had strayed from her enclosure in the early hours — the gate had been left ajar — and was at liberty somewhere in the neighborhood. Mr. Ludlow inquired of Miss Hathaway if by chance she had spied Hortense in Holy Street, or in Vicar's Walk, or in the churchyard? (The casual observer will be forgiven for mistaking "Hortense" for Mrs. Ludlow, for it was not she who was meant but the glypt). Miss Hathaway answered by saying that she hadn't seen the animal, but that she was sure it hadn't traveled far. Then, keen to get to the point of her visit, she described for Mr. Ludlow the boy and girl whom she and Molly had encountered in the Tillington Road, and asked him if he knew whose children they might be?

A look of concern came into the clergyman's face. "Strange — very strange," he murmured. He gave his chin a thoughtful rub, and after a few moments' pondering declared that he had a notion or two as to the identity of the small ones, and assured Miss Hathaway he would look into the matter that very day.

The vicar agreed with her that the children's playing round Marley Wood had been decidedly unwise. The wood was a frequent haunt of creatures of every ilk, he said — beasts and monsters mostly, and other nasty things, whose far-off roarings were often heard in Market Snailsby in the night. All of this Jemma well knew; although for the time being she refrained from telling him of the snake-necked nasty thing that had growled in her face. In point of fact she had told no one of it as yet, not even Molly or Mrs. Rudling. If Richard had been at home, however, she likely would have confided in him at once, for she and her brother were the nearest friends each had in the world since the loss of their parents.

Mr. Ludlow stated he would be glad once the new road through Marley Wood had been cleared, as it would mitigate the danger somewhat, while providing a shorter and more convenient route to towns such as Ridingham and Newmarsh. Its aim was to bring the lonelier districts of south Fenshire and Slopshire into closer touch with the north, improve trade, and speed the mails. Of course the dangers of the forest could never be eliminated *in toto*, and it would be chiefly the mastodon trains, with the vans and coaches traveling in their protective company, that would ply the new route. But it would greatly lessen the time required for the journey, and put Market Snailsby more firmly on the Fenshire map by making it easier for people to get there.

Beyond these, the vicar had his own reasons for desiring improved trade with the north.

"For you know, Miss Hathaway, the wines we get round here are not of the best. Oh, good gracious, no. One must travel to Ridingham or Newmarsh to find a decent bottle. How I look forward to tasting an Ogghops sherry again! And as for Ayleshire wines — well, everybody knows that Ayleshires are the very finest in the realm. I've but one Ayleshire claret left in my cellar — *one!* Oh, and some Nantle port will be very nice — "

"Really, vicar, there's more to Ridingham and Newmarsh than the vintner's stores and the wine-vaults," Jemma exclaimed.

"Of course, of course, you're perfectly right, Miss Hathaway," said the vicar, nodding and chuckling at this little extravagance of his. "I'm afraid I've had wine on the noggin of late, you know, for my cellar is close to running dry. Your brother has been to Newmarsh recently, has he not?"

"Yes. In fact he is there now, at the Municipal Library."

"Dear me! I wish I'd known. I should have asked him to look out a few bottles for me. That new bogberry wine we had last night was just awful."

"Perhaps he can help you out next time. He'll be returning for another week in the summer," Jemma informed him.

"He is still researching that treatise of his?"

"Yes, although he has gotten a trifle behindhand with it of late. He too will be happy to see the road put through. It will hasten the drive and spare him a deal of bother."

"Oh, indeed," the vicar said brightly. "To travel by coach all that long way round Marley Wood — all those miles and miles — requires an investment of considerable time and effort, not to say expenditure. As a result most of our trade remains with our locals here in the south by way of the Fribble and Lour, and the Drovers' Road. But Snailsby market-days aren't what they once were, Miss Hathaway, as the both of us can attest. With each passing year they draw fewer and fewer. The new road will allow trains and coaches from the north to cross the wood directly. I dare say it will do our town and tradesmen a power of good."

The clergyman went on a little more in this vein, as he was wont to do, and concluded by marveling at the pluck and determination of those who had come before them — those sturdy citizens of yore who had raised a town in the midst of the marshes, and made it what it was today.

"Did you know, Miss Hathaway, that Fenshiremen — our ancestors — years and years ago used to hunt not only in the marshes, but in Marley Wood?"

"Yes, I've heard something of that."

"In bygone days Snailsby townsfolk weren't so fearful of the world. What was a marsh devil or the occasional spotted lion to such sportsmen as our forefathers were? Mind you, there wasn't so much farming carried on then. For our ancestors, the chase — scouring the wood for venison and swine — was part and parcel of their lives. For Man cannot live by bread and eel alone! What I've come to admire the most, I suppose, is their boldness, their courage in the face of adversity. I have been reading something of those early families, you know, in the volumes of the Fenshire Historical Society."

"Have you, now?"

"Oh, indeed. Take for example the family de Clinkers, now long extinct. First and foremost amongst them was the renowned Godfrey de Clinkers, who some three hundred years ago built himself a hunting-lodge in Marley Wood. Can you imagine it, Miss Hathaway? The risk, the peril, the hardship of constructing a mansion inside the wood — the very audacity of it! Ah, such colorful lives they had in the old times. I remember hearing about the lodge from my father, years and years ago. Although I don't know of anyone who's actually seen it, if it still stands, for no one but a hare-brain would venture into the wood nowadays — too many nasty things afoot there! The bravery, the sheer cheek of these stout ancestors of ours never fails to astonish me. Their adventures make for very cozy reading by a late night's fireside, that I can tell you."

Miss Hathaway was seized with a temptation, if only for a moment, to pour forth the tale of her own adventure in Marley Wood, but her concern at being labeled a "hare-brain" got the better of her.

Food, drink, leisure, a relaxing read by a cozy evening's turf-fire — the good things in life — these were very important to Mr. Ludlow. He had a small private income to augment his clergyman's salary — a mere two hundred a year was hardly a comfortable living — and was not so much in want as were others of his brethren round Fenshire. (As for his fellows in the county of Slops, well, there were scarcely any in Fenshire so badly off as *that*). He had a fine church with a landmark of a steeple, and a snug home and garden on glebe-land, and a gentle and very useful spouse, and a pet glypt, and at Snailsby vicarage enjoyed the kind of life most any clergyman would have murdered for.

But to return to the children. Mr. Ludlow voiced his suspicion now that the two could be the offspring of one Hester Pippins, a young woman with whom Miss Hathaway was not acquainted. It was this Mrs. Pippins whom the vicar intended to visit later that day. She had lost track of her husband, he said, and was not so responsible a parent; moreover he had had trouble with her children recently in the matter of their catechisms.

"The pair are a trifle undisciplined," he explained, confidentially of course.

Further, he believed that there were relations of this Mrs. Pippins at Beeworthy, near Tillington, and that she may have journeyed there in the past few days to see them.

"Although there are Pippinses down in Slopshire as well, round Shroud and Monkston-in-the-Mire — fen-slodgers, you know," he went on. "Half-wild they are, some of them. A mixed and motley group to be sure, but not the sort for her to be calling on — and not by way of the Tillington Road. No, my guineas are on Beeworthy. She may have traveled there by coach, or more likely in some obliging farmer's wagon, for Mrs. Pippins has no horse and less money. Not to worry, Miss Hathaway, I shall winkle it all out this afternoon."

Though satisfied to a degree by the vicar's assurances, Miss Hathaway remained skeptical. For some reason, call it intuition, she didn't believe that the two children who had laughed at her and Molly in the Tillington Road had anything to do with any Pippinses.

How had the children come to be out there, and alone? And how had they kept pace with the shay-cart if Mrs. Pippins had no horse? To these and other like questions Mr. Ludlow shook his head and admitted that he had no answers, but he promised he would winkle some out. Likely he would have had no answer either for the snake-necked thing behind the firs, or the weird, unearthly wail, had Miss Hathaway chosen to tell him of them.

They went inside now to escape the cold, and fell to chatting for a time about the weather, and the vicar's garden, and parish affairs, and this and that, until Jemma took her leave — the clock in the church tower was striking ten — and went off in search of Molly Grime.

Moments later Mr. Ludlow set forth on a little search of his own, for Miss Hortense the glypt. He found his ungainly pet blissfully a-snore by the watermeads of the Fribble, where she had been grubbing for dainties amongst the sedges. Gently he awakened her, and led her back to the vicarage. It was a task requiring no small amount of patience, for glypts, with their heavy armor and their four squat, stumpy legs, like drawing-room sofas are not known for their speed.

Once home he returned his pet to her enclosure, by which time it had nearly gone eleven. Noting this, the vicar went next in search of his wife and his morning's tea and buns, although not necessarily in that order.

THE THIRD CHAPTER

CLOVER AND CORNEY

HAVING collected Molly and the stores she had gathered in the Market Square, Miss Hathaway turned Rosie and the shay-cart into the High Street and off they clattered in the direction of home.

As they drove along Jemma found her glance straying across the river to the vast, dreary expanse of fenland away to eastward. As for the river itself, it was host this morning to some lazy traffic — a couple of barges being towed by horses making use of the path on the south bank. Over everything lay a typical Fenshire garnish of gloom, a fragrance of fog, a chilly dusting of snow. Such a misty, marshy old river town Market Snailsby was, Jemma mused, and a shivery one, too!

She was looking forward to returning home and getting on with her chores for the day. Mead Cottage had belonged to her late parents, and was the only home she and her brother had ever known. But their parents had been taken from them too soon, and now the house was hers and Richard's alone. The thought of it always saddened her, and she tried not to dwell on it too often, or too deeply. Then she caught a glimpse of Rosie's bright eye, and observed the tossing of her shapely head and yellow mane, and at once her spirits were lifted. Rosie was very much her brother's horse, and the sight of her never failed to put Jemma in mind of him. She would be very glad to have him back at Mead Cottage once more, and hoped that his researches in the library were progressing satisfactorily.

Even more, perhaps, she was looking forward to his counsel as regards her adventure in Marley Wood.

As she drove in through the gate, Jemma wondered if her friend Ada Henslowe might have come round for a visit; but alas there was no sign of Spinach, Ada's stout little riding-horse, either in the drive or in the yard. Miss Henslowe, who lived at the opposite end of town, was a frequent guest at Mead Cottage. She and Jemma had known one another since they were children. Like Miss Hathaway, Ada was an accomplished hand at the pianoforte — or, more correctly, an accomplished pair of hands — and together the two friends, ofttimes joined by Richard on his violin, had passed many a musical hour there in the house by the Fribble.

While Jemma was busy liberating Rosie from the traces, Molly took some of the stores inside to Mrs. Rudling, then hurried off with the rest to Mickledene Hall. A short while later Miss Hathaway was passing through the stable-yard, when she came upon a cat sitting on the dwarf wall. The color of the animal's fur was identical to that of the lumps of snow that had collected on the wall, and it was only by means of her soft *miaow* that Jemma had been alerted to her presence.

"Well, hallo there, Clover!" she exclaimed, scratching the little cat briskly about the chin and ears. In response the dainty Clover bumped her head against Jemma's hand and broke out in a spate of purring.

Clover was a shy little creature — a gentle, quiet soul. Ordinarily she hid from human strangers, like many of her kind, and sometimes even from those she knew. But she knew Miss Hathaway well enough that she had no need to hide, and even had called out to her.

It is an established fact that cats are able to recognize those who are in sympathy with their kind and those who are not, for they are on the whole rather more discerning creatures than most people would have you believe. Their arithmetical skills, too, are highly developed. It has been shown, for example, that cats are able to count; for if there are too many persons in a room most any cat will bolt, and if too few, will search in vain for its absent friends.

But Clover, being a shy little cat, did not count as well as many of her fellows. She had big green eyes and a pink nose, and her coat was as winter-thick as it was winter-white. Her face shone with an innocent and a trusting expression, like that of a kitten new-dropped into the world, though she had already several springtimes under her collar.

"Now, then, I wonder if Corney is here?" said Miss Hathaway, thinking aloud.

Corney was Clover's master — Mr. Anthony Oldcorn, the Hathaways' elderly neighbor and a family friend of long standing. Corney lived at Oldcorn House, the next on the south side, and like Clover and Miss Henslowe was a frequent visitor at Mead Cottage. He greatly enjoyed the company of the Hathaways, just as Clover, shy creature though she was, enjoyed the company of the Hathaway cats.

Behind the stable-yard was a kind of gazebo standing atop the bank, on a little height above the Fribble. It was here in this favored retreat that Richard and Corney often met to prepare their rods, lines, and hooks for a morning's angling in the stream. On a board affixed to one of the pillars was an inscription — SACRUM PISCATORIBUS — which as any schoolboy knows is old Roman for "sacred to fishermen." To Jemma it was yet another reminder of her brother, and of how eagerly she looked for his return. But it was with a degree of anxiety, too, that she looked for it; for the journey round Marley Wood was not only a lengthy one, but a perilous one as well for coaches traveling alone.

As she neared the house she spied the figure of the postman striding up the drive, letters in hand. Round the neighborhood young Mr. Murcott was known familiarly as the "postie," for so he was called by Sir Hector MacHector, the Hathaways' substantial neighbor on the north side, whose family seat, like Mead Cottage and its gazebo, overlooked the river.

Mr. Murcott was the son-in-law of Mr. Samuel Travers, landlord of the Broom and Badger, the pretty little posting-inn where the mails were delivered and sorted. Needless to say, Mr. Murcott owed his job to this family connection. In those days there were no regular mail deliveries in most of south Fenshire; one had to call for one's letters at a posting-house or other like establishment. But in Market Snailsby the townsfolk had the services of a son-in-law to distribute the mails; and so no one, especially not those living on the outskirts of town, begrudged Mr. Murcott his small share of nepotism.

Snap, having gotten wind of the postie's arrival, came bounding round a corner of the house. He came not to challenge, however, but to greet; for unlike many of his brethren, Snap, being a coach dog, was a friend to postmen. Having received a warm welcome from Mr. Murcott — who really was a very decent and hard-working young man — he went off again after some squirrels he had been chastising in the back-garden.

Some bits of bread had been left out for the squirrels by Mrs. Rudling, who had a soft spot in her heart for the creatures. But to Snap these *shade-tails*, as squirrels are known in dog society, were little better than thieves, and it was his bounden duty to oust them. As usual, however, the squirrels, full of cheeky energy, had been giving him fits — taunting him, and calling him "booby" and "pudding" and a "weak sister" and the like, and flicking their tails at him with a frenzy.

"Kuk kuk kuk!" they could be heard jeering. *"Kuk kuk kuk!"*

The squirrels had all the advantages of the high ground, where they could sit and hurl insults at him for hours. And being quicker and more agile on the low ground, they had the advantage of him there as well; and so it was a hopeless endeavor for poor Snap. Far be it from the proud coach dog to shirk his bounden duty, however.

"Move along there!" he cried, advancing upon the marauders with battle in his eye. "Move along, I say!"

But squirrels have their own way of laughing, which most people don't know of; and the squirrels were laughing now.

Because Snap, whose other duty it was to guard the mail, had relinquished that task in favor of disciplining the shade-tails, it was left to Miss Hathaway to step into the breach. Little Clover, observing from her perch on the dwarf wall, shook her head and sighed.

"Poor pudding dog," she murmured. "Such a simple fellow. Ah, but what else can one expect of him? Heigh-ho!"

Waving her good-bye to the postie, Miss Hathaway strode towards the house. Mead Cottage was a lovely mix of plaster and timbering and hardy Fenshire brick, with lead-latticed windows below and little dormers in the sloping roof above, capped off by a trio of chimneys. From the stable-yard a gravel drive ran beside the house and out to the gate in the brick wall that enclosed the front-garden. The wall allowed for some safety and privacy, and made for a very cozy atmosphere, even in springtime, when the lawn and shrubberies were dusted with a snow that seemed in no hurry to be leaving.

Clover knew that her master was inside the cottage, for she had followed him on his walk from Oldcorn House. Seeing Miss Hathaway approaching the steps, she dropped to the ground and, racing after her, darted past her heels and into the house just as the door swung magically open.

In the passage Jemma discovered a crab-tree stick in the umbrella-stand, and a coat and cap hanging on the wall, and recognized them at once as Corney's. He had come for tea and a chat with her and Mrs. Rudling. Mr. Oldcorn was a widower who lived alone, and in consequence was more than a little glad of his neighbors' company.

Miss Hathaway dropped her letters on a chest in the passage, and went on into the kitchen, which was the *de facto* center of activity of the house. Mrs. Rudling was just laying on the tea and sundries, and the clink of spoons and rattle of china sounded very pleasantly in Jemma's ear. Spick-and-span was the cook and housekeeper of Mead Cottage, and spick-and-span was her kitchen, its neat rows of copper and pewter gleaming in the gray light of the latticed windows.

"Hallo, Corney!" Jemma sang out in welcome to their guest.

The elderly gentleman sitting at the table rose to his feet. He was a spare, shy, quiet sort of person — not unlike his cat — of some sixty-odd years, with a kindly, cultured face. His hair, or what remained of it, was splashed with silver and neatly combed. Fen-born and fen-bred, Mr. Oldcorn was a gentleman of small fortune who had once been a magistrate, and who had since retired from the fray to his modest home beside the river. He had been a jaunty fellow in his youth, but the years had gradually eroded him. Some remnants of his youthful self still lingered, however, in the smartness of his wearing-apparel, and the care with which he selected it. *Very particular about his togs our Mr. Oldcorn is*, was the general remark heard about town in this regard.

The old gentleman politely returned his neighbor's greeting.

"Good morning, my dear," he said, his smile revealing two rows of widely-spaced, peg-like teeth. "Tell us, have you heard the news?"

"What news is that, Corney?"

"He's gotten it this morning from Mr. Haggis," hinted Mrs. Rudling. "Haven't you, sir?"

"What's he gotten from Haggis?"

"Haggis" was one of the gillies, or manservants, of Sir Hector Mac-Hector of Mickledene Hall.

"Riders," said Corney, his eyes shining. "Riders in Marley Wood!"

Mystified, Jemma glanced at Mrs. Rudling. The housekeeper — she of the pleasant apple-face, and hair as frosty-white as Clover's — smiled and nodded in reply.

Corney meantime had resumed his seat, which was the signal for little Clover to spring into his lap and settle herself there.

"Riders, and ghostly lights," the old gentleman went on eagerly. "It was the evening before last. You'll recollect, Jemma — it was the night the moon came out."

Miss Hathaway sat down in the chair opposite him, under the big smoked beams of the kitchen ceiling. One of the two Hathaway cats, Gerald by name, not to be outdone by a visiting feline, promptly bounced into her lap, and sat peering across the vast expanse of table at Clover. Gerald was a gray tiger-tabby, and very much the kitchen cat, having passed the better part of his life within its cozy compass. In this he was quite unlike his brother Herbert, who was something of an adventurer, and who spent much of his time on patrol seeing that all was shipshape and in proper order in the neighborhood.

"Who saw these riders and these ghostly lights?" Miss Hathaway asked.

"It was Haggis himself," Corney replied.

"Did any others at the Hall see them?"

"Likely not, for it was well past midnight. Haggis wouldn't have seen them either, had he not been restless and unable to sleep from an indigestion."

"And who should be galloping about Marley Wood in the middle of the night?" Mrs. Rudling wanted to know. "Somebody daft, I'll warrant."

"It was more than a somebody, I'm afraid — more like an entire string of riders, or so Haggis claims. Mind you, I'm not suggesting that we doubt his word, for he's rather a down-to-earth sort of chap, being an outside man and all. He's not a crank."

"Perhaps he dreamed it?" Jemma suggested.

The old gentleman shook his head. "I doubt it. I heard his testimony myself. His voice had a most sturdy ring of conviction in it."

"What of Jorkens, then? And what of Sir Hector?"

"They feel as I do, that what Haggis saw was no dream. Oh, I do wish your brother were here! Likely he'd have some idea who these riders might be."

Miss Hathaway had an idea or two of her own as to who the riders might have been, but almost immediately she put the both of them out of her head. She refused to believe that two small children — Pippinses or no — could have been galloping about Marley Wood in the dead hours of the night. Why, it was too absurd even to think of!

She stirred some milk into her tea. "So what is your view of it, Corney?" she asked.

"I have yet to formulate one, I'm afraid. A ghostly gleam of lights in the wood like lanterns flashing — the distant rumble of hoofbeats — the sound of men calling — for it was the faint shouts of the men that drew Haggis to his window — "

"You say Haggis heard voices as well?"

"Indeed, and the baying of hounds."

"Hounds, too!" Jemma exclaimed.

"Yes. Likely it was a hunt of some kind."

"But there's none as hunts in Marley Wood," Mrs. Rudling pointed out. "None by day even, and sure none by night!"

Miss Hathaway's interest quickened. Men shouting, lights flashing, hounds in full cry — most certainly *not* the doings of two small children. As for the hunting angle, well, she was in agreement that no one hunted in the wood nowadays; but that had not always been the case, as the vicar had lately reminded her.

No one but a hare-brain would venture into the wood . . .

There had been no hunting in Marley Wood, not for a few hundred years at least. Not since those bygone days when their gallant forefathers — such bold spirits! — had scoured the wood for venison and swine. Not since the days of Godfrey de Clinkers.

Supposing, however, that a few anonymous hare-brains had decided to take up hunting in the wood, and at night. What might they be after? Flat-heads? Marsh deer? Or perhaps a hideous, orange-haired, snake-necked monstrosity of a thing that liked to growl in people's faces —

"Who do you reckon these hunters were?" Jemma asked, a trifle uneasy at the memory of her experience.

Corney shook his head again, saying he did not know, and drank a little from his cup. "This tea really is quite splendid, Mrs. Rudling," he said.

"Thank you, sir," beamed the housekeeper.

"I'm sure it's very good tea," said Clover, glancing round at her hosts, "but haven't you something for *me* today? For I am a guest here, too."

"Tut, tut," sniffed Gerald. "Don't bother, dear — you'll not get any grub out of them that way. You'll need to do a little buttering up beforehand."

It was about this time that Snap, tired of being harangued by shade-tails, and knowing there was company in the house, trotted up to the door and demanded admittance. In the kitchen he went immediately to the hearth-rug and stretched himself out full-length there, looking as pleased as Corney to be in the presence of Jemma and the others.

The elderly gentleman took a biscuit from the tray. "So I'm afraid that's all I know of the incident. Whoever these men on horseback were, they were not from Market Snailsby, of that I'm convinced, as is Sir Hector. Strange, is it not, to be having moonlit nights in the midst of this dirty weather?"

"It is," nodded Miss Hathaway.

"As for myself I haven't a clue who the riders might be. Some stray sportsmen out for a moonlight gallop, perhaps? Country yokels from parts unknown?"

"Weren't anybody sane, that's for certain sure," declared Mrs. Rudling. "Must be crackers to be a-tearing through Marley Wood — and in the night-time!"

"Indeed," said Jemma, gazing with a reflective eye on nothing in particular. "For as I've heard the vicar say — and quite recently, too — there's many a nasty thing afoot there . . ."

THE FOURTH CHAPTER

MR. BLATHERS EXPATIATES

CORNEY, still musing, helped himself to a bit of seed cake. The cake, like the biscuit and the tea, was splendid, for which Mrs. Rudling was properly flattered.

"And what of Richard?" Corney asked. "When do you expect him home?"

"In another few days," Jemma replied. "He is still in Newmarsh, at the library in the Shire Hall, pursuing his researches."

"That treatise of his concerning the late Sir Pharnaby Crust and his music?"

"Yes."

Corney nodded. "A useful composer, of whom regretfully little is known, and the only one I ever heard of to have sprung from Fenshire. I'm afraid that ours is a county not known for begetting useful composers. Musicians, yes, for you and Richard are both highly accomplished in that regard. But composers — well, they're hardly thick on the ground in these marshes."

"Sure, it's 'cause there's not much ground for 'em to be thick on, sir," remarked the housekeeper.

"The records in the library, which have only recently come to light, should be of immense help to him in his writing," Jemma said. "There is much private correspondence, as I understand, and a host of other documents touching on Sir Pharnaby's personal affairs — of which, as you say, little is known."

"He will be returning by way of Dragonthorpe?"

"Yes. It is his usual route."

As everyone did who had business in the north, Richard had the lengthy drive round Marley Wood to contend with. One did have some small choice in the matter, though. One could book a seat on the Tillington coach, which skirted the wood round its eastern edge, or on the Dragonthorpe ditto to the westward — either way, a journey of some ninety miles all told. The road through Dragonthorpe was the busier of the two, but the more tentative as well, particularly at this time of year, when it was beset by melting snows and incursions of the marshland. Unfortunately the two rivers, the Fribble and the Lour, were of little help in reaching Newmarsh, as neither flowed to the northward or had any tributaries that did so.

"He will need to return again in the summer, when he expects to finish the book," Miss Hathaway continued. "There is a publisher in Ridingham he believes will take the manuscript. Otherwise he intends to approach his old music tutor at Salthead, in hopes the university press there will bring it out."

"I wish him the best of success. To have such a work published would be an admirable feat, concerning as it does a topic so obscure as Sir Pharnaby Crust, Fenshireman. I wonder if the learned professors up at Salthead have ever heard of Sir Pharnaby, or even of our little county in the marshes? For we are so removed from the world here."

"Matters might be worse, sir," remarked the housekeeper, with a knowing glance, "as we could be removed to Slopshire, after all."

"No argument there, Mrs. Rudling!" Corney laughingly agreed.

The conversation having turned to universities and professors as it had, it turned next and rather naturally to the subject of Corney's son. Young Philip Oldcorn had gone up to Fishmouth with the goal of becoming a solicitor, and was presently a student at Clive's Inn, the great legal university and center of the law. Fishmouth was the seat of governance of the sundered realm, and anyone wishing to make his way in the worlds of politics and lawyering had to go up there.

"He has obtained for himself a clerk's position with Marrowbone, Marrowbone, and Cleaver. Indeed, it was Mr. Tots Marrowbone himself who recommended him," said Corney, who was not above a little boasting when it came to his son. Phil was the old gentleman's only child, having arrived rather late in the lives of Corney and his wife, and to the considerable surprise of both.

"Is it a respectable concern, this Marrowbone and whatsit?" Jemma asked. "For I'll admit I know little of solicitors and the law, nor does Richard, apart from what we've gleaned from Arnold Inkpen in the matter of our father's will."

"Oh, indeed, it's a most respectable house, and well-connected, too. Mr. Tots Marrowbone is the senior member and oversees the parliamentary interests of the firm. I had the pleasure of meeting him once when I was in Fishmouth attending to a J.P. matter. His influence is said to extend to the very highest levels of government."

"Then I say, well done, Phil! That's most encouraging, Corney — he'll make a fine lawyer, I'm sure. Of course, we hope he'll settle in Market Snailsby once he's passed his examination. Now, then, where has Herbert gotten to?" Jemma said, her thoughts abruptly shifting from young Philip to the gray tiger Gerald lounging in her lap, and thence to Gerald's more venturesome — and absent — brother.

Mrs. Rudling informed her that Mr. Herbert Hathaway had graced the kitchen with his presence earlier that morning when he had taken his breakfast, then had trotted off in the direction of Mickledene Hall. Since then no one had seen him. Snap, raising his head, turned an inquiring eye upon his mistress, as though asking if she wanted him to hunt up the fellow? Evidently she did not; and so he laid his head again between his paws and resumed his ease.

"Ah, and there's even more news," spoke up Corney.

"Yes?"

"It's said that Mrs. Chugwell is on her way, and will be arriving shortly to prepare for the season's operations in the wood."

"That's good to hear. We shall all be very pleased when the job is done."

"The team has been wintering at Deadmarsh, as per usual, and is to follow along presently. Word has it that Mrs. Chugwell and her son will be undertaking an inspection of the road first thing, to examine its condition since the last year's recess. I believe there is to be an official escort — Shand the fen-reeve, and Mayor Jagard, and Sir Hector and the gillies. And they'll be sword-in-hand every one of them, that I can tell you, for you know in that wood things can leap upon you unawares."

The truth of his statement Miss Hathaway appreciated only too well. Mention of the wood made her a trifle uneasy again, following as it did on talk of mysterious riders and their hounds giving chase in the eerie glow of the moon.

"Answer me this, Corney. What would you say if I were to tell you that I, too, have seen riders in the wood? Or at the very least that I've heard them — or heard one of them?" Jemma asked.

A sudden hush fell over the group.

"Ma'am?" returned the housekeeper, pausing in her work to stare at Miss Hathaway, as if she had not heard her aright.

Another pause of silence followed, one long enough that even the cats and Snap took notice of it.

"I should say that you must tell us of it, my dear," Corney answered at last.

And so she did. Her audience listened with rapt attention (all but the animals, of course, for the cats already had had most of the story from Snap). Unfortunately neither Corney nor Mrs. Rudling had the slightest inkling as regards the identity of the children. Their views concerning the wood and its reputation accorded with those of the vicar; and as for the horrid, snake-necked thing with the shower of orange hair, well . . .

"This is a remarkable tale," Corney said, slowly and thoughtfully, "although it sounds nothing like mounted riders hunting by moonlight with lanterns a-swing. And there's not a marsh devil or spotted lion in what's left of Christendom that resembles this monster you describe."

"Ah, sir, and a *monster* sure it must be!" said Mrs. Rudling, looking very worried. "For I've heard nowt of any giraffes being seen round these marshes, nor in the wood either, in all my lifetime."

"There have been no giraffes since before the sundering — apart, I think, from a group I once saw in Crow's-end, at the zoological gardens there."

"It was no giraffe," grunted Snap — who of course had first-hand knowledge of the thing behind the firs —"but what it was I'll not say, for I don't know exactly myself. It was like nothing I've ever smelled."

"Poor pudding dog! You were very brave," Clover said, sympathetically.

"Tut, tut — let's not be exaggerating," sniffed Gerald. "Probably it was nothing more than his shadow."

"But your mistress saw it, too," Clover pointed out.

At that moment came noises of arrival on the front steps, which drew Mrs. Rudling from the kitchen. Jemma thought it might be her friend Ada, but her hopes were quickly dashed. Into the room stumped a little round man with a shiny dark head and an inquisitive, bird-like gaze. He had a small, sharp beak of a nose and a pursed lip, which combined with his horn-rimmed spectacles lent him a passing resemblance to an owl.

"I say, it's Blathers!" Corney exclaimed.

Mr. Blathers it was indeed. He was an old friend of Richard's, and a confidant of Sir Hector MacHector's. Like Corney he had come for tea — or, in his case, cocoa — but unlike Mr. Oldcorn he was surprised to find that Richard was not there. It had quite slipped the mind of

Mr. Blathers that his friend was from home. But he seemed not the least bit crushed by the news, and was more than happy to join the party. He had come, he said, to show Richard his new magnifying spectacles, which he drew from his coat-pocket and proceeded to show the others now in his stead.

Years of bachelor regularity had left their mark on Mr. Blathers, in all the little habits of his daily round, in his regular adherence to a diet of milk and vegetables ("purifiers of the blood," he called them), in his clean-shaven, ruddy appearance, even his clothes. He invariably wore black, with a white collar *sans* neckware, and so was often mistaken for a clergyman — something he found endlessly amusing, for religion's hold on him was tenuous at best. Some in town thought him a crank, some a meddlesome busybody, others merely an eccentric; but mostly they held him to be a decent fellow, and generally harmless.

Having passed his new spectacles round the table and enlarged upon their qualities to the full, the visitor drew up a chair, the seat of which he proceeded to rub briskly with a handkerchief, before applying his own seat to it. Next he filled a pipe and lighted it, and soon was puffing away like the proverbial house afire. All the while he was keeping up a running conversation in his rapid, quick-spoken way, as much with himself as with anybody else present. The cats and Snap were noticed to be observing his performance with more than casual interest; for animals seemed always to be fascinated by the odd, busy being that was Mr. Blathers.

"His flow of speech is quite remarkable," commented Gerald.

"What's he gibbering about now?" Snap wondered.

"The spookies in the wood," Clover explained.

"Ah, yes — the ghostly lights in the wood," said Mr. Blathers, as if on cue. "I've heard something of them myself. Had it from Haggis while on my morning's walk. It was outside the Corn Exchange, as I recollect. Or was it the Mudlark? Funny thing, memory. Haggis was most insistent he hadn't been hallucinating, and I for one believe him. It was towards the morning hours, he said, and the moon was out. Funny thing, the moon. If you ask me it has something to do with de Clinkers and that lodge of his in the wood."

Here Mr. Blathers paused for a moment to catch his breath, removed his spectacles, polished them carefully with his handkerchief, and then replaced them on his nose, before running on again.

"Ah, yes — the lost hunting-seat of de Clinkers! Our holy man at the vicarage hasn't the monopoly on county lore he has on his holy books. Humph! Well, I've gathered a few facts myself about that lodge. Did you know, for instance, that it had doorknobs shaped like human hands? Windows opening onto blank walls? Staircases leading up to air and then down again? And there were other queer things besides — concealed panels — secret chambers — elaborate bogwood carvings — locks and bolts of peculiar construction — and a clock that strikes thirteen!"

Time for another catch of breath, and for Mr. Blathers to blow his nose — once, twice, three times — into his pocket-handkerchief, before going on again.

"This de Clinkers was a strange egg, or so the story is. And strange eggs are something I should know about, for that's what most round this town think of me! Well, I don't care a hang, and neither do you. Ah, a thousand thanks, my good lady, for the cocoa." (This last to Mrs. Rudling). "Of course old de Clinkers was an odd stick. Who else but an odd stick would build a house in the wood? Bow-hunting for deer, and spear-hunting for swine — hunting for flat-heads, no less! No such types around nowadays; everybody is so very *civilized*. Humph!"

To all of this Jemma and Corney and Mrs. Rudling could do little but nod their agreement, the flood of words spilling unchecked from the lips of Mr. Blathers like the Fribble overflowing its weir.

On the odd chance their visitor might have some information that could be of service, Jemma related for him — when she could get the words in edgewise, and only after gaining his strictest confidence — the particulars of her adventure in Marley Wood. As her story unfolded, Mr. Blathers's face exhibited mounting excitement. His brows flew up into his hair, his eyes behind his horn-rims bulged, his jaw fell. By the end of it he could scarcely contain himself; he was like a roaring tea-kettle about to burst from the hob.

"Jumping cats!" he exclaimed. "And she says it with her head on. Well, this beats everything. A snake-necked horror roaming through Marley Wood! Never heard of such a thing, and neither has our holy man, I'll be bound. If I ever saw it myself I'd be scared blue, and that's the truth. Funny thing, truth. Never heard such a story in all my life. Hardly scientific, though. By ginger, this beats everything — past, present, and to come!"

As if to vent the rising steam of his excitement, Mr. Blathers suddenly sprang to his feet and raced round the table, then raced round it a second time, before throwing himself down again onto his chair. Snap glanced up in alarm at this strange behavior, but a look from Jemma assured him that all was well.

"And so whose nippers can they be?" said Mr. Blathers, hurrying on again. "For I know Hester Pippins, and they're not her nippers, I don't believe. Humph!"

"I thought not," said Miss Hathaway.

"So if not her children," Corney wondered, "then whose?"

"Some country clodpoll's," opined Mr. Blathers. "Some low-brow without an ounce of gray matter, to be letting nippers run free in the wood. A little tap on *that* fellow's geranium might prove instructive."

"It's just as I was saying about the riders, Mr. Blathers," spoke up Mrs. Rudling. "Daft, the lot of 'em."

As no one knew whose nippers the children they might be, or had any prospect of knowing within the next hour or two at least, the conversation returned to the subject of Mrs. Chugwell and her impending arrival, and the soon-to-follow inspection of the new road with Mr. Jagard, Sir Hector, and the rest.

Mr. Blathers, hearing the name of the Right Worshipful Mayor of Market Snailsby uttered in his presence, made a face as if he had just swallowed a large bug.

"Mr. Walkadine Jagard is a great puffed head," he declared. "Everybody knows it. Speaks in riddles, makes promises he never keeps, and has an easy answer for every question. Humph! No sincerity there. Funny thing, sincerity. Too much pleased with himself, that's my view — too highflown for marsh folk."

"It goes with the title of Mayor, I think, Mr. Blathers," Jemma observed dryly.

"Damned flashy togs, too," complained the little man in black. "Well, the fellow's a clothes-horse. Rather too gaudy for my taste — something a trifle *chichi* about him. Not quite genuine, like the man. Not quite Fenshire!"

"If I remember rightly, his grandfather on his mother's side was a native of Foghampton," said Corney. "They are rumored to be a family of some account there."

Mr. Blathers winced. *Foghampton!* Well, that explained it. *I'd not give a pennyworth of punch for Foghampton.* He opened his mouth as if to speak again, but reconsidered and instead jammed a piece of seed-cake into it. Immediately his face relaxed, and a warm glow of satisfaction came into his eyes. He took a whiff at his pipe, then thumped the table with his fist and loudly proclaimed his approval of all cocoa, cake, and marsh tea — past, present, and to come!

Mrs. Rudling accepted the compliment with her usual modesty. Then, taking up her cloak and bonnet, she announced that she was off to Mickledene on an errand, and that Molly Grime, newly returned from that locale, would see to their needs in her absence. Before she left, however, she apologized to Jemma for neglecting to mention that Miss Henslowe had sent word and was expected for dinner. The news gave Miss Hathaway much joy, and Molly, too, as it meant there would be duets galore at the pianoforte that evening.

After the housekeeper had gone, Mr. Blathers resumed his lengthy expatiations upon whatever topics happened to strike his fancy. Meantime he had donned his magnifying spectacles and was making a close examination of the knotholes in the kitchen-table, and the big green eyes in the head of Clover, and the black markings, one by one, that adorned Snap's coat. This latter activity, however, caused the poor coach dog such distress that he could hardly stand it, and, tearing himself from the hearth-rug, he fled the room in a panic.

The gray tiger Gerald, concerned that he would become the next object of Mr. Blathers's researches, vaulted from Jemma's lap and scampered after the pudding dog. Almost at once a combined fit of hissing and barking erupted in the passage. The suddenness of it caused Mr. Blathers to lose hold of his spectacles, and they went crashing to the floor, shattering one of the lenses.

"Oh, Lord, sir!" Molly cried.

"Goodness, I'm terribly sorry, Mr. Blathers," Jemma said.

Mr. Blathers made another face.

"Drat the luck!" he exclaimed, gazing in startled surprise on the disaster. But it did not affect him long, thereby giving view to another of his oddities — his wonderful equanimity. Quickly resigning himself to the situation, he shrugged and shook his head, and returned the spectacles to his pocket. "Help for spilled milk there isn't any, I'm afraid. Funny thing, spilled milk. No matter. Speaking of which, perhaps I'll take a little more milk in my cocoa — a little more juice hot from the kine! A thousand thanks, my good young woman — "

A short time later the sound of a pianoforte could be heard in the drawing-room — it was Miss Hathaway, readying her fingers for the evening duets to come. Her visitors listened from a couple of chairs nearby, Mr. Blathers working hard at his pipe and Corney musing from under half-shut lids.

As she played through her exercises, Jemma found her thoughts wandering from the music to her late adventure in the wood, and then to ghostly lights in the night-time and the shouts of riders and the baying of hounds. No stray sportsmen out for a moonlight gallop, of that she was certain!

And she wondered what might happen next that would shine some further light, as it were, on these mysteries.

PART TWO

THE FIRST CHAPTER

BY CLOPTON STAIR

BESIDE Clopton Stair, which lay at the end of Fore Street, on the river's south bank, Mr. Ingo Swain was attending to his traps.

Mr. Swain was an eel-trap man; that is, he caught eels for his living. As you know the Fribble was a good eel-river, and in the waters round the foot of the stair Mr. Swain maintained a line of cage traps made of wicker. These contrivances, variously termed "eel-pots" or "eel-baskets," were shaped like large bottles or jugs, and strung together at intervals along a rope. Once baited they were dipped into the river from the low pier beside the stair, where they lay submerged, waiting for Fribble eels to enter.

In form Mr. Ingo Swain resembled one of his traps, for he too was bottle-shaped — a copious, drooping bellyful of a man, like an enormous teardrop astride a pair of ridiculously short legs. His clothes had been assembled from an untidy jumble of materials, all of them frayed and dirtied. Numerous small oddments and articles of his profession hung from them, here and there, so that he clanked and rattled a little as he walked. On his head he wore a grimy cap, on his chin a grimy stubble of whisker. The flesh of his face was thickly veined, and daubed with mud, and the eyes under his heavy brows were as round and shining as those of the eels he snared for his livelihood.

Mr. Swain had his traps laid at three places in the town — at the pier beside the stair, round the stone bridge that spanned the Fribble, and downstream by Snailsby Mill. It was his habit to inspect them twice daily for tenants, and having extracted such beauties as had been snared in the interval, to set them again with fresh bait.

"And what's that you bait 'em with, Mr. Swain?" said a small voice at his elbow.

The voice belonged to a tow-headed little scrub of a little girl in a beaver bonnet. She was dressed in a warm woolen frock and a plaid coat, button boots, and mittens, and had been peppering the eel-trap man with queries for the last half-hour.

"Sprats," grunted Ingo, as he hauled up the next trap on the line. "Sprats they be baited with today."

A brief pause of thought by the child.

"What's sprats, Mr. Swain?"

"Sprats be little fishes. These eels, ye see, they likes their dainty little fishes. But 'tain't all they'll take, for they likes their bit o' chick now and then, and their bit o' rabbit in season. Fresh — always needs to be fresh! And these eels, they likes their earthworms, too. Rare greedy for 'em they are."

"They're peculiar traps," the child remarked. "Tell me, did you make them?"

"Aye, and right fine they be for ketching," nodded the eel-trap man. "D'ye see the bottom o' this pot here? Well, 'tain't a pot-bottom at all, but an open door into a kind o' funnel, as invites yer eel to wriggle in an' shelter. And what happens then, ye'll be asking? Well, there be this crown o' spikes, here at the narrow end o' the funnel, as traps yer eel inside. And at t'other end o' the pot be this hinged lid, by which ye removes yer beauty and places yer bait."

"And the bait be sprats?"

"The bait be sprats."

"Where do you get sprats, Mr. Swain?" the little girl asked, after another pause.

A trace of annoyance crossed the face of Ingo.

"Why, sprats be taken from the river, child. And as for the pots, well, ye places yer bait at close o' day, mostly, for yer eels, ye know, be nocturnal creatures."

"What's nocturnal?"

"Nocturnal's night. 'Tis the time yer eel likes to be on the move. In the daytime, ye see, these eels be mostly retired to their burrows. They bean't much for stirring in the light, unlessen the water be low, and the weather warm — which bean't too often in these fenny parts."

"Eels may be fine for some," declared the child, "but I think they're horrid. I'd rather eat a fish."

"But eels be fishes too, child," Mr. Swain pointed out. "Lookee, now, see what's been ketched here in this pot. See this fellow here — a great, shiny, freckled beauty!"

So saying, he dislodged the slippery-skinned eel from its prison-cell, and lowered it writhing and squirming into a sack he carried with him.

The little girl stuck out her tongue. "Ugh!" she cried. "I'll certainly not be eating *him*. He's uglier by far than most."

"Why, Miss Sukey Elizabeth Shorthose, ye'll not be needing to eat that fellow. He be meant for Joliffe o' the Mudlark, away there down the road."

"Does Mr. Joliffe like eels?"

"'Tain't for him as sich; 'tis for his customers, child — for his bill o' fare. The Broom and Badger bean't the only eating-house in this vicinity, ye know. 'Tis the Mudlark, in point of fact, as has stood at the waterside much the longer."

"How much longer?" the child asked.

The eel-trap man turned from his pots with a sigh. "Lord bless us, but ye certainly does ask a rare mort o' questions for sich a tiny sprat."

"I'm not a tiny sprat."

"Ah, but ye are, child."

"But I'm *not* a little fish. My mother says I'm a little human person."

Mr. Swain exploded in a laugh that shook his great heavy belly, and the boards of the pier besides.

"So what else be in yer mind today, child?" he asked, once he had recovered from his good humor.

Truth to tell Mr. Ingo Swain led a rather solitary existence, and, though he was loath to admit it, secretly welcomed company — even the company of so curious and bedeviling a little human person as Miss Sukey Elizabeth Shorthose, who, truth being told again, was wont to be bedeviling most anyone in the town upon whom she happened.

After a few minutes spent watching him inspect the next couple of pots, both of them void of catch, the child said —

"Tell me, Mr. Swain, something about the pig-faced lady."

The eel-trap man started at the request. Glancing at her over his shoulder, he fixed the little human person with a suspicious eye. "And what pig-faced lady might that be, then?" he asked.

"The one who was lost in the wood. Did you know her, Mr. Swain?"

"What pig-faced lady as was lost in the wood?"

"The pig-faced lady with the scarlet kerchief on her head. The old lady they called Mother Redcap."

The brow of Mr. Swain visibly darkened. He let fall the trap he had in hand, and looked very hard and sharp at Sukey.

"And just how would ye know about *her*, child?" he demanded, sternly.

"From Jayne Scrimshaw. I've heard her speak of the pig-faced lady who lived by the mere. But there's more to tell, I'm sure. Jayne says she was a hag and a witch, and other things besides."

Mr. Swain licked his lips and frowned. Hitherto he had been most patient with little Sukey Elizabeth Shorthose. How far to pursue their conversation now, he wondered — a conversation which had taken so unexpected and so unpleasant a turn? Its subject was not one that Mr. Swain enjoyed either thinking or speaking of. The subject of witches always made him uncomfortable, and that of Mother Redcap even more so.

"Bothersome!" he muttered under his breath.

"Oh, please, Mr. Swain, I promise I shan't tell," begged the child. "Was she a hag and a witch, and other things besides?"

"Aye, 'tis likely it were so — but mind, child, I bean't one to be accusing," said Ingo. "I never knowed the old trot myself. It were many, many year ago that she were lost — fifty year and more now. I were just a young sprat like yerself then."

"Was that before you were in quod, Mr. Swain?"

Again the eel-trap man was taken off his guard by her question. He paused for a moment to scratch his cheek with a grimy fist, and collect himself.

"And who was it as told ye *that*, child? Jayne Scrimshaw, I do suppose!" he retorted.

It was well known that Mr. Swain on more than one occasion had passed some of his idle hours in the town lock-up, on account of some tippling and rowing and other like indiscretions of which he had been guilty now and again.

"It wasn't Jayne Scrimshaw as told me that. It was my mother," said Sukey.

Mr. Swain regarded her thoughtfully from under the heavy penthouse of his brows.

"Well," he grumbled at length, "'twas long afore I were 'in quod,' as ye've so delicately phrased it. Long, long afore."

"Was Mother Redcap ever in quod?"

"Never as I knowed of, though there be some as said she'd earned it," he answered, in a voice barely above a whisper. "'Twas these same gossips as called her witch, but the truth o' *that* I never knowed, and never cared to know. A smoke-dried, skinny old hag she were, or so they said — aye!"

"With a pig face?"

"With a pig face. As to witches, well — at the least a trader in potions and remedies she were, and herbs and barks, and toadstools. And more'n likely a river-worshiper she were to boot. All them Celts, ye know, was river-worshipers."

"What are Celts, Mr. Swain?" the child asked.

"What be Celts? What be Celts? Well, never ye mind now, Sukey Shorthose, for I've not the time to go into it with ye. As for the Redcap, well — well, 'tis best ye refrain from speaking o' pig-faced ladies in general, or so be my advice. And 'tis partickler best that ye not to be speaking o' *her*, not with Jayne Scrimshaw, and not with no one, if ye cares to prosper."

So saying, the eel-trap man glanced uneasily round him at the pier and stairs, and up and down the bank, and across the dreary stream to Goose Stacks and the river wall and the rest of the town on the opposite shore. From far off in Holy Street the church clock of All Hallows could be heard striking the hour.

"Whyever not should I speak of her, Mr. Swain? Can she hear us?" Sukey asked.

The eel-trap man responded with an impassioned fluttering of his hands. "Sh-h-h-h!" he warned, clamping a grimy thumb to the child's lips. "Or sure 'tis woe betide ye, child — for ye scarce knows what ye be saying!"

"But what happened to Mother Redcap?"

The eel-trap man scowled. "What happened to her? Why, I'll tell ye what happened to her, child, if it'll serve to stifle ye. The Redcap, as likely's been a stiff'un these many a year — or so 'tis hoped — well, up and off she tramps into the wood one morning for her herbs and her toadstools, and never after was spied again by living eye. 'Tis thought sure she's cold as mutton now, for a twisted old crone she were already in those days — aye, and a ripe and rotten old age it were, too. Most likely it were a marsh devil as gobbled her, or a flat-head maybe, or a teratorn as plucked her off to Slopshire, or something other as prowls the wood as fell upon her, and stripped the meat from her ancient bones!"

The eel-trap man gave a little shudder at the thought of it — in fact it was rather a large shudder, for Mr. Swain was rather a large man — one that set his arms and legs to squirming like the eels in his sack. The effect of his words on little Sukey was considerable, but, unfortunately, it was only temporary.

"Hark to me, child. My advice to ye is never to speak o' the Redcap," he warned. "The old trot may be a stiff'un, but that don't mean she can't hear."

"What's a stiff'un, Mr. Swain?"

"Why, a stiff'un's a dead 'un, child," said Ingo.

"A dead one, Mr. Swain?"

"Aye, dead. As mutton."

Little Sukey screwed up her brow in puzzlement. "But how can she hear us, Mr. Swain, if she's a dead one?"

Mr. Swain had by now arrived at the last of his pots, and the last of his patience.

"Why don't ye go home to yer mother?" he growled, in rather a louder tone than previously.

For once the child kept silent, although go home to her mother she did not. And when Mr. Swain, having concluded his inspection of the pots, took up his sack and trudged up the sedgy bank to the road, little Sukey was there again at his elbow. She was curious to know what he did with his eels once he'd "ketched" them, but, in view of his present mood, was hesitant to ply him with any further queries.

They had scarce gone a dozen paces when she experienced an odd sensation, and, if his countenance was any judge in the matter, so too had Mr. Swain.

It felt as though the earth had quivered underfoot, much the way the boards of the pier had quivered under the weight of Ingo when he laughed. The body of the eel-trap man wobbled unsteadily on his short little legs. Again the ground shook — and again — and again — four, five times it shuddered beneath his boots.

From out of the chill and misty air came the distant sound of a trumpet-call.

Little Sukey glanced away to eastward, to the far edge of Snailsby Common, where a long row of trees was standing tall and dark above the mist. Beyond them lay Ten Acre Meadow. As she watched, the tops of the trees at one point were thrust violently aside, and a gigantic form came plunging through them.

"Look there, Mr. Swain!" she exclaimed.

The eyes of Ingo followed her gaze, to the spot where a steely-gray monster larger than a house had burst from the timber. It had a huge shaggy head and ears, and a great long snout armed with shovel-like jaws and tusks, and a curling trunk. This trunk the creature on a sudden lifted into the air, and from its gaping mouth came flying the roar of another trumpet-call.

"It's a tusker, Mr. Swain!" Sukey cried out with glee. *"It's Ranger!"*

More precisely, it was a shovel-tusker mastodon, which with every *thud!* of its massive, pillar-like limbs was causing the ground under the snow-spattered Common to tremble.

Straight towards them across the Common the tusker jogged, its head bobbing, its belly heaving and swaying, its silver harness jingling and jangling. It covered the distance in less than no time and, striding up to them, came to a majestic stand in the road. Majestic indeed was the picture presented by the steely-gray giant, and a lofty one, too, soaring as it did to a height of some twenty feet above the amazed eyes of Ingo and little Sukey.

Two persons occupied the cab astride the thunder-beast's mighty shoulders. One of them, the driver, was a genial young fellow with a shock of dark hair; the other was a plump, matronly woman, of middling age and ample girth. Even from their considerable elevation the resemblance between the two was plain enough to identify them as mother and son.

"Hulloa there!" the young fellow called down from the cab-window. "Hulloa, Miss Sukey! Hulloa, Mr. Eel Man!"

Then it was the tusker's turn. Lifting its trunk and parting its enormous jaws, the monster blared forth another greeting — one that likely could be heard across the entire length and breadth of south Fenshire, and for which the eel-trap man and little Sukey were obliged for the moment to stop their ears.

The child's response to the thunderous salutation was a whoop of delight.

"Hallo, Matt! Hallo, Mrs. Chugwell!" she exclaimed, waving to the newcomers on high. "And hallo to you, Ranger! Welcome back to Market Snailsby!"

THE SECOND CHAPTER

PHANTOM RIDERS

JUST then a smart little gig came wheeling up the road from town. The driver, a chipper young gentleman in knee-smalls, reined his horse to a halt in the shadow of the tusker — it was a figurative shadow at best, as there was no sun to cast it — and raised his hat and eyes to the travelers.

"Good day, Mrs. Chugwell. And a good day to you as well, young Matthew," he called out, straining for a view of the pair riding overhead. "We are most happy to see you, and are quite at your service."

The matronly woman of ample girth, otherwise Mrs. Chugwell, smiled upon him from the window of the cab.

"Good morning, Mr. Inkpen. My gracious, isn't the spring lovely this time of year? We simply adore it. We have come these many miles from our camp over to Deadmarsh, and are bound for the Badger, as you may have supposed. Your Mr. Travers is such a dear man for an innkeeper, and his wife a worthy soul."

"True enough indeed. I have myself just come from that fine establishment, and can report that all is in order for your arrival."

The chipper young gentleman addressed as Mr. Inkpen, Christian name Arnold, was the town solicitor. He was a decent enough fellow for a lawyer, and so boyish-looking that the graybeards of the place still thought of him as the younker they remembered from long years agone. True, he had still his younker's sticky-out ears; but his manner now was all briskness and efficiency, and his wardrobe as smart as his gig.

Mr. Inkpen was another of those in the town who was eager to see the new road cleared. His family were on intimate terms with Mayor Walkadine Jagard, who, not surprisingly, was a great proponent of the enterprise. More trade, more visitors to town, more notice in the shire — it was the same view as that espoused by Vicar Ludlow and a host of others.

"For we in Market Snailsby are rather isolated by our fens, and by this wood," the lawyer had been heard to remark, as had Corney, and the vicar, and that same host of others. "But business will be much improved once the north of Fenshire is within easy reach."

From her lookout Mrs. Chugwell called down to say that she and her son had come to inspect the new road, and to draw up their plans for the season's operations. Already the time was growing short, for the winter had been a lengthy one, and they were keen to be about the job.

This Mrs. Chugwell, as I have hinted, was a lady of generous proportions. She had tiny, twinkling eyes and a nicely got-up face, genial and dimpled like her son's, a couple of chins, and hair piled atop her head like a wavy gray sea. She was dressed rather fashionably for a mastodon driver, her tastes running more to cashmere, striped velvet, and other fine materials — with a liberal garnish of ruffles, bracelets, and earrings — than to your driver's usual cords and tops, box coat, and glazed hat. A casual observer might have mistaken her for some lordly gentleman's wife, a mistress of the manor, or a wealthy dowager, and never guessed at the truth.

Her son Matthew, by contrast, was a slim, wiry replica of her late husband. It was Mr. Phrank Chugwell, a native Fenshireman, who had acquired and superintended the team of shovel-tuskers, and greatly expanded its operations, before perishing in a riding mishap some years ago. Upon his demise his widow had assumed command of the team; but as the duties attendant thereof were not so congenial to her — they did not accord well with cashmere, velvet, and other fine materials — she had early on entrusted the day-to-day charge of the tuskers to her son. His was the responsibility to manage the beasts, hers to negotiate terms for the agreements that employed the team in its clearing and mending operations in Fenshire and the neighboring counties.

"And where are the rest of your — er — ah — creatures?" inquired the attorney, his eyes filled to overflowing with the colossal, steely-coated bulk of Ranger, which towered above him like a castle keep. "For it seems to me there were more of you last year."

As indeed there were. The other members of the team, Mrs. Chugwell informed him, were prepared to leave Deadmarsh just as soon as her inspection of the road had been completed. In their absence Mr. Angus Daintie, her son's able young assistant, had been left in charge at the camp. This was to be the team's third season in Marley Wood, and it was anticipated that a fourth yet would be needed to push the road through.

"Then we shall all celebrate in the autumn of next year," said Mr. Inkpen, nodding his appreciation, "by which time Newmarsh and Ridingham will be as near to us, in a coaching way, as Dragonthorpe and Stoke Moreton are today."

"Bravo, Matt! Bravo, Mrs. Chugwell!" applauded Sukey, with a little wave of her bonnet.

It was then that Mrs. Chugwell, peering down at her from the vast height of Ranger — surely the largest and most awesome of thunderbeasts ever to have stamped foot in Fenshire — inquired of Miss Shorthose if she fancied a ride to the Broom and Badger today?

Well, the answer to *that* was hardly in doubt.

"Oh, yes, please, Mrs. Chugwell!" the child exclaimed, brimming over with enthusiasm.

And so the operation commenced. First the mighty Ranger was directed to ease his stupendous self down onto his knees and elbows — slowly — gingerly — carefully — his hind limbs first, and then the fore — at which point Matt let drop the cord-ladder from the cab, and little Sukey sprang aboard it.

"Brace up, now, Suke," he called to her.

"All right, Matt."

So saying, the child set her teeth, took firm hold of the ropes, and in a flush of excitement scaled nimbly up the ladder and through the door of the cab. There she was welcomed by Matt and his mother, and settled down with them for the final leg of the journey, which, admittedly, would be a short one — down the length of Fore Street to the pretty little ivy-covered inn at the bridge-end.

"Where we shall be just in time for lunch," Mrs. Chugwell noted, with a crinkly smile.

Meantime the cord-ladder had been drawn up and the door clanged shut. At a word from Matt the tusker rose again to his full and altogether dizzying height. The cab swayed briefly from side to side as the ground fell away below. Came another trumpet-blast that split the air, followed by a sudden lurch forward, and away they went, the massive, tree-like limbs of Ranger *pound-pound-pounding* the earth of Fenshire as he thundered off.

Mr. Inkpen raised his hat in farewell, and sat watching for a time as the mastodon lumbered down the road; then, nodding briskly to the eel-trap man, he swung his horse about and followed after. Passing the visitors at the Broom and Badger, he continued on his way over the bridge to the other side of town, bent no doubt on some important matter of lawyering.

Mr. Swain meanwhile had been left standing in the road, alone with his thoughts — he was, as I've said, a solitary sort by nature — and his sack of eels. Though relieved of the burden of Miss Shorthose and her queries innumerable, he found himself burdened still with the products of her visit — with the uneasy glances he began casting about him once the lawyer had gone, and the uneasy thoughts that were crowding in again upon his brain, thoughts of a smoke-dried, skinny old pig-faced crone of a hag who had vanished in the wood, and of whom he had been so uncomfortably reminded by little Sukey.

Keen to be about his work again, he was trudging along towards the bridge to inspect his second line of traps when a small boat came gliding up, and a voice hailed him from the thwart.

The voice belonged to the oarsman, and the boat's sole occupant — a short, square, burly little bulldog of a man. He had a rusty beard and whiskers like copper wool growing from his jaw, and hair so fiery red, and brushed up so stiff and straight, it was like flames licking at the top of his head. Through the narrow windows of his spectacles shone two of the fiercest blue eyes ever seen in Christendom.

"G'day tae ye, Mr. Swain! Hae ye chanced tae hear the word o' late?" said the bulldog.

"What word, Mr. Haggis?" growled Ingo, a trifle unhappy at being interrogated again so soon.

"Man, man," sighed the fierce-visaged Haggis, "hae ye no heard o' the lights in Marley Wood? Nor o' the ghaistly cries o' the hoonds in the nicht?"

Haggis it was indeed, one of the gillies of Sir Hector MacHector, returning from a morning's errand for the Laird. He drew his boat in closer, and propping himself on one oar sat staring fiercely and bluely at Mr. Swain.

"What lights? What hounds in the night?" said Ingo, curling his eyes round his shoulder for an uneasy peer at the gillie.

Mr. Ingo Swain, I must confess, was a little afraid of the dark — an odd affliction for a man who made his living catching eels — and could not suppress a shiver, much like that he had felt at the mention of Mother Redcap. He almost dreaded to hear what Haggis had to say, for anything having to do with Marley Wood boded naught but ill to any man.

"Hoot, toot, Mr. Swain! 'Twas this past week, at dead o' nicht, whan the bright moon be oot — sae rare! — that I spied the lights i'the wood. Like Devil's lights they were, an' voices heard in their company — the shouts o' mony men, an' the hoofbeats o' their ghaistly steeds, an' the baying o' hoonds, an' the blast of a hunting-horn. 'Twas a meet i'the wood — hunters in full halloo — hunters, Mr. Swain, on the dash through Marley Wood in the nicht-time!"

The eel-trap man felt his heart give a thump. Sooth to say he had heard tales before of these ghostly lights in the wood, and of the phantom riders and their hounds. He had thought it all superstition, or at most the ravings of susceptible townsfolk in a heavy drunk. He recalled that the riders were said to appear only when the moon was out, which was not so often in the south of Fenshire. The extent of Marley Wood was considerable — a vast, far-spreading domain it was — and Market Snailsby adjoined but one short stretch of it. The nearest large pack of hounds, he knew, was over at Huntwhistle. Perhaps some bold Master from that place had taken an interest in the wood and chosen it for a meet.

But in the night-time?

Like most Fenshiremen Mr. Swain didn't care for woods in general, and that of Marley in particular, where unseen horrors lay in wait to snare the unsuspecting traveler. Like those other Fenshiremen, he preferred the winding streams and rivers and the broad, open expanse of flat-land that was the marshes. Given a choice he would sooner have braved the chilly mists and fogs, the sodden trackways, the islands and thickets, the miry bogs and sedgy banks, than the stifling closeness of the wood.

"Mayhap 'tis auld Godfrey de Clinkers, woken up after three hunnerd years tae hunt in the wood agin," Haggis suggested, "or sae there's some as do suppose."

"Swamp-lights," the eel-trap man muttered in explanation — wishing, hoping, praying that it were so — "'tis naught but swamp-lights, Mr. Haggis."

"Swamp-lights, Mr. Swain — i'the wood? Havers, man, tisn't that ridiculous!" laughed the gillie, firing another blue glance at him.

It was ridiculous, and Mr. Swain well knew it. Swamp-lights — the elusive "will-o'-the-wisp," or *ignis fatuus* — were thought by some to be caused by noxious vapors arising from the marshes. But they were seen almost exclusively in the summer, and never in Marley Wood.

"Mayhap then they be the flamin' souls o' suicides?" the gillie suggested. (Canny Haggis! He knew how such ideas would work upon the mind of the impressionable Ingo). "Or the ghaists o' puir folk drowned i'the marshes? Or the glowin' een o' marsh devils? Marsh devils, man! And what o' the calls o' the riders, an' the cries o' the hoonds? An' what o' the hunting-horn? Na, na, man — there be na sic swamp-lights as they hereaboots!"

"Not marsh devils," prayed Mr. Swain under his breath, for of all things on earth it was the dreaded cats he feared the most. "Not marsh devils — man-killers, confound 'em — Lord bless us, a plague of all marsh devils as keeps watch in the wood!"

"Na, na, ha' done wi' talk o' marsh devils, Mr. Swain. Dinna fash yer breeks o'er it, man. 'Twas juist a bit o' fun on ma part," laughed Haggis; then, beginning afresh — "What think ye now o' Herne the Hunter? For hae ye never heard, Mr. Swain, o' that legend o' Windsor Forest of auld?"

Mr. Swain had not heard of that legend, and was not sure that he wanted to; but that would not deter Mr. Haggis from improving the eel-trap man's education.

"A wood demon was Herne, wha led a ragin' host o' spirits o' the damned on raiding parties, mounted upon ghaistly steeds, and 'companied by specter-hoonds — by ma certie, a muckle great horde! Unco' cruel an' bluidy was this Herne, an' immortal too — spared frae earthly sufferin' an' death — an' could appear an' vanish frae sight o' men whaneffer an' at his ane choosing. Aye, an' 'tis mortal doom awaits ony folk wha crosses his path. 'Twas said this Herne gained his mighty powers frae a bluid-pact atwixt himsell an' the Devil."

"The Devil *you* say," Mr. Swain nearly retorted, but caught himself in time. "Well," he offered in place of it, "this bean't Windsor Forest, Mr. Haggis, and Windsor Forest did perish in the great sundering, as likely did this Herne fellow, if ever he lived — aye, immortal or no!"

"Ye may think as ye will, Mr. Swain," said Haggis, with a grim, sly turn of his head. "Howsomeffer, I wadna be ower hasty wi' ma judgment till the Laird has looked intae the matter, as he'll be aboot soon eneugh."

It appeared that the testimony of Haggis had been corroborated by others, who had seen and heard similar things on that same moonlit night, as the gillie now informed Mr. Swain. Of course this left the eel-trap man in an even worse state than before; and as he watched Haggis dip his oars into the river and glide slowly upstream towards the Hall, a chill wind blew up and stung him in the face.

Returning to the business of his occupation, a feeling of loneliness crept over Mr. Ingo Swain as he trudged along, clanking and rattling, towards the bridge. Again he was seen casting nervous looks about him, and now and then a furtive glance across the river at the long curtain of Marley Wood rearing up behind the town.

Before him, in the mixed slush and snow and gravel of the road, lay the trail of prints left behind by the feet of Ranger. Each impression was nearly the size of a kitchen copper, and large enough to wash several children in. A powerful thunder-beast like Ranger, he mused, certainly should be proof against any horror that might be encountered in the wood; and so it occurred to him that perhaps Mrs. Chugwell and her team might discover what was going on in there, as regards the ghostly riders and their hounds, once they had set about their work.

Then again, perhaps they might not.

At all events it was not Mr. Swain's problem to puzzle out, for he was an eel-trap man, not a ghost-trap man; and if indeed it was demons and spirits of the damned that were flitting about Marley Wood in the unholy glare of the moon, then even the might and power of an entire herd of Rangers would be useless against them.

THE THIRD CHAPTER

W E follow Mr. Haggis now as he pulls for Mickledene Hall, the home of Sir Hector and Lady MacHector, a short distance upstream of town.

The Hall was a handsome, picturesque pile of brick and timber draped in ivy, of turrets ancient and venerable, of high Fenshire gables and flowing eaves, and a tiled roof boasting a display of chimney-work rivaled only by that of Goose Stacks. There was a fine old porch at the front, and stables and kennels at the rear, and a coach-house for the Laird's gig and rustic wagonette. Like its neighbor, Mead Cottage, the Hall at Mickledene stood beside and a little above the river, its windows affording airy views of Fribble, fen, and fog — and, of course, Marley Wood.

As he drew near it, a shrill drone of pipes reached the ears of Mr. Haggis. Bagpipes that would be, of the Highland variety, sounding out the music of the Gael — the *pibroch* of the MacHectors. The piper was no other than the Laird himself, who could be seen standing on the little bridge over the stream that flowed through his waterside garden. He had the bag of the instrument cradled in his arm, his lips to valved tube and his fingers to chanter, and was blowing right lustily, as was his habit. When not piping full blast in his garden, the Laird might be found at the river wall in town, or in the common-room of the Broom and Badger, filling the air with his music of the "black sticks." For although the Laird of Mickledene was devoted to his pipes, the Lady of Mickledene was not; and as a result the knight was obliged to pursue his hobby mostly out of earshot of his wife.

Mr. Haggis knew better than to disturb the Laird when at his recreation, so he hauled his boat ashore and strode quickly round to the Hall. Searching for Lady MacHector, he found her in the drawing-room.

This drawing-room was a fine apartment, and a spacious one — a high, oak-ceilinged, lattice-windowed, wainscoted-and-tapestried sort of drawing-room, full of cumbrous, old-fashioned furniture upholstered in shades of yew and vermilion. Stags' horns, foxes' heads, fishing-rods, coats of arms, tartans of the Clan MacHector, halberds, cutlasses, and claymores adorned its walls, a rich array of carpets its floor. It was, all in all, a thoroughly manly and MacHectorish sort of drawing-room for the Lady of Mickledene to be receiving callers in.

A log-fire was crackling and snapping in the big cobblestone hearth, beside which the lady was entertaining her guests — well, one of her guests, at any rate. This was a taut, small woman with shiny eyes, a long thin blade of a nose, and a face bleached a ghostly white by the exuberant application of powder. She was wrapped in charcoal-colored tweed, the better perhaps to highlight the interesting pallor of her features. In one of her hands she held a tea-cup, and very properly, too, with the little finger extended. This specter, who went by the name of Locket, was acting as housekeeper and nurse to the MacHectors' neighbor over the road. Mrs. Locket was often at the Hall, chiefly for the purpose of exchanging gossip with Lady MacHector.

The neighbor across the road was a Mr. Jervas Wackwire, of Wackwire House. Mr. Wackwire was an antique specimen of a widower — a meager, moldy old man, bald of head, frowning, side-whiskered, pinch-lipped. For the last few years Mr. Wackwire had been a captive of the wheeled chair in which he was presently sitting, some few miles from Mrs. Locket and Lady MacHector (I exaggerate as regards the distance, but not by much). The chair had been rolled to the very farthest corner of the apartment, and placed before one of the windows there. The view from the window was intended to occupy the old man's muddled senses, thereby freeing Mrs. Locket for her morning's tea and conversation with Lady MacHector.

Mr. Wackwire had suffered an irreversible erosion of the brain, and as a result was no longer capable of speaking sensibly. When he did speak, it was in clipped, hurried phrases, the meaning of which was a mystery to all but Mr. Wackwire himself. It was for this reason that a nurse of Mrs. Locket's competence and character had been engaged to look after him.

Mr. Wackwire spent the better part of his days — every one of his days now, every week, every month, every year — sitting stiffly in his wheeled chair and staring at the world through uncomprehending eyes. One of the duties of his nurse was to take him out of the house now and then and air him, as it were, like the meager and moldy old suit to which he had been reduced. And as Mickledene Hall was so very convenient, she usually took him there, only to cast him aside while she indulged in tea and gossip with Lady MacHector.

As much or more as her reputation for chit-chat, Mrs. Locket was known for her addiction to odd hats, an example of which lay on the chair beside her. A flat, flounderish thing with a low crown, it was her hat *du jour*, and could as easily have been mistaken for a bad pancake as a woman's fancy *chapeau*.

Such was the scene in the drawing-room when Haggis stumped into it. Pausing at the threshold under the Gothic arch of the door, he signed to Lady MacHector that he had returned from his mission for the Laird, and was at her dispose if needed.

Mr. Wackwire, catching sight of Haggis from the angle of a rheumy eye, raised a withered hand and in a thin voice commanded him to — "Get me a lobster!"

The gillie — whose ruddy countenance in jest had often been likened to a lobster's — was mightily offended. He glared at Mr. Wackwire; then, recollecting the state of the old man's senses, he quickly cooled, and shrugged off the meaningless request.

"*Auld nutter!*" he grumbled under his breath.

"What was that, Haggis?" said Lady MacHector, glancing at him from behind her tea-cup.

"'Twas but naught, m'lady. By yer leave, m'lady?"

The lady graciously inclined her head, giving Haggis leave thereby to step to the fire and warm himself.

"Pray, do forgive him, Mr. Haggis," said Mrs. Locket, with a smile of condescension at the antique specimen, "for as you know, Mr. Wackwire is no longer in his right wits. His attacks have left him unable to phrase his speech correctly. Really, one hasn't the least notion at times how to take him; he simply *refuses* to make himself understood. He is a positive cipher, to be sure."

"The poor man," sighed Lady MacHector. "He was a very fine old gentleman for a neighbor, once. It pains me to the quick to see him in such a state, as it does the Laird. I am afraid there is no hope for him."

"It is the wish of Providence, my lady," explained the nurse and housekeeper.

"Oh, I think not, Mrs. Locket," returned Lady MacHector, with a doubtful frown. "At least I certainly hope it is not. For no Providence I hold to would condemn such a fine old gentleman as Mr. Wackwire was to such a life."

Her words seemed to kindle a response in the old man. The head of Mr. Wackwire turned slowly round on his neck, his eyes hunting for his nurse, whom he commanded to "bull's-eye that mush faker!" — by which he appeared to mean Haggis.

Mrs. Locket smiled again. Mr. Haggis, not so forgiving this time, glared at the moldy old suit from his place at the fire.

For the most part Mr. Wackwire seemed to recognize Mrs. Locket, or just barely; at the very least he seemed to understand that it was her job to attend to his needs. Never once, however, had he called her by her name, but instead would address her by any of a number of colorful substitutes — "Tula," "Mrs. Lightbody," "Quince," "Jane-a-Dandy," "Dr. Sirloin," "Biddabadda," and other like disconnections as happened to tumble from his tongue.

He also on occasion would call her "darling" — a thing Mrs. Locket found particularly disturbing, and which was immediate cause for her to wheel the moldy old suit out and air it.

"You were saying, my lady?" smiled the nurse, turning again to her hostess.

"It's celery sticks at midnight!" proclaimed Mr. Wackwire from his wheeled throne, with a defiant gesture at the ottoman hard by.

Nurse and hostess traded glances with one another, and with Haggis; then Mrs. Locket shook her head gently, took a little smiling sip of her tea, and resumed her chat with the Lady of the house.

As you may imagine it was rather difficult to hold a conversation with Mr. Wackwire directly, and so Lady MacHector by default held it with Mrs. Locket — as indeed most everybody did. It was all very practical and understandable, and relieved the nurse of a good deal of boredom, not to say vexation.

For her part Lady MacHector enjoyed her little chats with Mrs. Locket, who had no shortage of news on offer, much of it conveyed to her by the peddlers, washerwomen, and tradesmen's boys who regularly turned up at the Wackwire door. Lady MacHector was a handsome woman, like her house, and in surprisingly good repair for an old Laird's wife (which was not such a surprise, after all, considering that she was a good deal younger than her husband). She had large and lovely violet eyes, rich, dark hair, and a voice that rang very pleasantly on the ear. She was partial to flowing gowns that fit rather more loosely than otherwise, so as not to betray her gently-expanding figure —

though it was still a handsome and an elegant figure for a lady of her years and station, have no doubt of that.

Having warmed himself sufficiently, Haggis was about to quit the apartment when another of the gillies entered it. A dour, dish-faced sort of gillie was Mr. Jorkens, with his broad chin and heavy gaze, and his hair neatly slicked with pomatum. A former outside man who had come inside, he was serving as butler and steward at the Hall. His attire nowadays was in every way exceedingly neat and proper, in mighty contrast to that of the groundsman Haggis, who remained an outside man looking in.

Mr. Jorkens claimed to have news that no one else at the Hall had possession of; and so he offered it now to Lady MacHector and Mrs. Locket, and to Mr. Haggis, too, if he was so disposed.

On that same evening when Haggis had reported his ghostly lights and riders in the wood, said Mr. Jorkens, a servant from one of the neighboring houses, trudging homewards alone, had been accosted by a stranger near the cleft tree at the top of Water Street, on the very edge of the wood. This stranger had carried a lantern in his hand, and that illumination, combined with the weird light of the moon, had revealed to the astonished servant a man dressed all in green, and in the style of a bygone age. He had a bugle-horn hanging at his side, and slung across his shoulder was a quarterstaff, a deadly weapon employed by park-keepers in fabled days of old.

This curious tale excited the interest of the listeners at once.

"How very odd! Who could it have been?" Lady MacHector asked. "There are no park-keepers in Marley Wood. And we've had no fancy-dress parties of late that might explain it."

"Nane, m'lady," agreed Jorkens.

"Was the man sober?"

"The servant, m'lady?"

"The servant, and the park-keeper."

"Sober sae far as I ken, m'lady. 'Twas Mr. Bunting as spied the keeper, an' a muckle great sober-sides he is. As tae the park-keeper's state, howsomeffer, he couldna swear. Right churlish he was, though, this park-keeper, an' wi' a lunge of his staff told Mr. Bunting tae gang aboot his business, or be sufferin' a thwack o' the pate."

"Dear me!" Lady MacHector exclaimed.

"Aye, m'lady. Then, said Mr. Bunting, the park-keeper he vanished awa' intae air, as if he'd never been. Like a ghaist, m'lady!"

"Goodness!"

"Some cracked rustic, my lady, to be sure," nodded Mrs. Locket, with a knowing air. "Some drunken beer-swiller out for a tramp, or one of these fen-slodgers whooping it up in the town. For it's well-known, my lady, that people *will* go off their heads in moonlight."

"Stew a lop from that order-taker!" barked Mr. Wackwire from his distant seat.

This helpful suggestion notwithstanding, Mrs. Locket went on to wonder if it might not have been an April Fool's prank — someone "hunting the gowk," as it was known there at the Hall? But as Lady MacHector quickly observed, several weeks already had passed since the first of April; for it was then that her husband the Laird had claimed his "gowk," or cuckoo, for the year — namely Mr. Erskine Joliffe, landlord of the Mudlark inn and public house.

This Mr. Joliffe was perhaps the only person in town who didn't care to see the road put through Marley Wood. Amongst other reasons he feared it would attract too many visitors — and of the wrong sort — to Market Snailsby. Now this might seem an odd view for an inn-keeper to espouse, someone whose income relied on the patronage of customers. But this Mr. Joliffe was a more than usually independent sort of gentleman for a landlord. If customers came in, he prospered in his till; if customers did not come in, he prospered in other, more private ways. Mr. Erskine Joliffe was a thoughtful, contemplative man, who preferred the solitude and serenity of his beloved marshes to the contentious world of commerce in which his fellow townsmen were mired. And it was precisely for this reason that he had been chosen for the Fool's Day prank.

The prank had consisted of the town's physician's dashing into the tap-room of the Mudlark and requesting a glass of "pigeon's milk" for his deathly-ill patient, ostensibly a guest at the inn. Mr. Joliffe had spent upwards of an hour seeking the needed remedy in the town — without success, I might add — until, spying a calendar in one of the shops, the date *April the First* had leaped out at him. To his credit Mr. Joliffe had seen fit to celebrate his gowking with a hearty laugh and a fill of his pipe, together with a round of drinks for Sir Hector and Dr. Chevenix, the aforesaid physician and fellow-prankster.

As for the park-keeper in green and his menacing quarterstaff, an explanation other than April the First would have to suffice.

The talk had reverted to gossip, with some minutes passing by, when Mr. Wackwire suddenly became very agitated and, aiming a trembling finger at the window before him, cried out that there was "a devil cat in the pokie-pat!"

Lady MacHector and her guest sprang from their seats in alarm. The gillies, both of whom had quitted the room shortly before, now came charging back into it, Haggis with his sword drawn and Jorkens brandishing a claymore he had scooped up in the passage.

As it turned out the "devil cat" was no slavering monster of the dirk-tooth variety, but a small black feline of the domestic sort, who had parked himself on the window-stone outside. He had a snowy chest and muzzle and four white paws, one of which he was washing with a pink tongue.

"Herbert Hathaway, you run off home this instant," commanded Mrs. Locket, whose face, had it not already been ghostly white from powder, would certainly have gone so. "Frightening Lady MacHector that way — frightening Mr. Wackwire that way — frightening all of us that way, to be sure!"

Indeed it was only Herbert, the more adventurous and independent of the Hathaway cats of Mead Cottage, on his daily circuit round the neighborhood. Of course he took no notice of Mrs. Locket; he hardly ever took any notice of her, except when she threatened him with one of her hats. Herbert generally took no notice of anything with two legs unless some culinary reward was in the offing.

"Take that malt and lather it!" cried Mr. Wackwire, meaning Herbert.

As if on cue, a fluffy-tailed squirrel leaped from behind a sofa onto the window-seat and began barking at young Mr. Hathaway.

"Kuk kuk kuk!" the squirrel cried, flicking her tail at him with a frenzy. *"Kuk kuk kuk!"*

Herbert paused in his washing long enough to sniff curiously at the window, and to hiss at the squirrel a time or two, before resuming his ablutions.

"Dear me," exclaimed the Lady of Mickledene. "Whisk! Little one, what are you getting up to there? For it isn't polite to bother the cat."

The squirrel was the cherished pet of Lady MacHector, who did not care much for cats, domestic or otherwise, although she did not hate them, either. But little Whisk, following the example of Herbert and Mrs. Locket, conspicuously ignored her.

To add to the excitement, a scraping rush of paws was heard in the passage and a small terrier came bounding into the room. Quick as a flash he was at the window, and there commenced an excited yelping that sent old Mr. Wackwire into a dither, Whisk flying for safety, and Herbert packing.

"Begone! Begone!" cried the little terrier, his feet barely reaching to the sill. "Begone, cursed cat, from my lady's window! Come on, some of you, and after him!"

"Thrasher! Ha' done, sir, ha' done! Hoot, toot, man, ye'll be raisin' the vera Devil himsell ane o' these days, an ye're no canny," said Mr. Haggis, rushing to collar the dog. "Dreadful sorry I am, m'lady — "

The terrier was Sir Hector's prized favorite amongst the dogs of his kennel. A fussy, bossy little creature was Thrasher, and an accomplished ratter, who on account of his master's partiality had appointed himself chief of dog society in the neighborhood. To keep watch and ward at the Hall was his charge, one he took as seriously and with as much pluck and determination as any small terrier could.

More confusion followed, until Haggis succeeded at last in hustling the little bossy-boots from the room, with grateful thanks from Lady MacHector and Mrs. Locket, and a demand from Mr. Wackwire to "sign the gazettes, and pay dittoes to the cadge-men!"

Upon his return, the gillie found Mr. Jorkens in further conversation with Lady MacHector and the nurse. He was telling them of a legend he recalled hearing, many years ago, about an ancient park-keeper in green who was said to haunt Marley Wood. What was more, he declared, Sir Hector and he, with the aid of the dogs, were intending to have a scout round the top of Water Street for evidence of this ghostly woodsman, just as soon as the Laird was done with his piping.

Hearing this, the fiery Haggis made pledge to accompany them, as he had something of a vested interest in moonlight phenomena. He then surprised the others with a little news of his own, saying that he had spied Mrs. Chugwell and her son arriving in Market Snailsby that morning, on purpose to inspect the new road. The team of shovel-tuskers was to follow soon from Deadmarsh, at which point the season's work would begin in earnest.

"Aye, an' 'tis aboot time," declared Jorkens. "'Tis a bluidy great shame, Mr. Haggis, whan Fenshiremen be afeart tae gang intae a wood, for thought o' wha' may be astir there. Tae be 'feart o' bogles — 'tis a sorry, waeful thing. 'Twas no the way i'the auld time."

"Say nae mair, Mr. Jorkens," Haggis agreed, with a sad shake of his head, "say nae mair, for I ken that right weel."

A sly joke then passed between them, that perhaps the churlish keeper in green had been none other than Mine Host of the Mudlark, Mr. Erskine Joliffe, endeavoring to frighten his fellow-citizens and prevent the road from being cleared, and thereby preserve the serenity of his reedy fens and lonesome marshes.

"Na, na, 'twasn't Joliffe, I dinna believe," opined Jorkens. "'Tis no vera likely — he disna hae the brains for it. Mair like 'twas some loon wi' a taste for the whiskey."

"Brains?" said Mr. Wackwire, catching at the word. Smilingly he extended a quivering hand to the others across the room. In the palm of that hand were the remains of a muffin given him by Mrs. Locket. It appeared to be an offer to partake. "Please? Please? Brains?"

"Crack-brains, *I* call it," Haggis whispered to his compatriot, who silently nodded his agreement. "The auld nutter be mair than a few tiles short of a roof, an' no likely tae be makin' up the difference."

"Addle-pated, he is," sighed Jorkens. "Daft to the bane."

"Aye. 'Tis all marigold tea wi' him now."

"A sad case, Mr. Haggis. Vera sad."

The gillies then took their leave of Lady MacHector and her guests, and withdrew through the arch into the passage.

"Now, pray continue, Mrs. Locket," they heard their mistress saying as they exited. "What other news have you of town?"

"Much news, my lady, and more to be sure," replied the nurse, eagerly, "though I should like to find out if Mrs. Chugwell has bought a new hat for the season. For you know, my lady, she *is* something of a fashionable woman herself. Very stylish is our Mrs. Chugwell — for a mastodon driver!"

THE FOURTH CHAPTER

SQUATTERS AT THE LODGE?

WHEN Sir Hector MacHector returned to the Hall with his black sticks, his day's piping done, he returned with something else besides — a paunchy gentleman of about fifty, with copious jowls and a mustache of the walrus type, and a wide-awake clamped to his head, who followed the Laird in at the door. This gentleman, who had trotted up on his horse while Sir Hector was still at his music, was Mr. William Shand, the fen-reeve. Mr. Shand had heard something of the menacing park-keeper and his quarterstaff from the town gossips — those same known to Lady Mac-Hector and Mrs. Locket — and had ridden forth to consult with the Laird. Learning of Sir Hector's plan to search the top of Water Street for clues, the reeve had volunteered to join him.

They entered the drawing-room where Lady MacHector was holding court. The Laird of Mickledene was an imposing figure of a man — a tall, comely gentleman in splendor of plaid and furze-cloth, lean and nimble of frame, but rock-solid, with a back as straight as an arrow, and a head topped with a crown of white hair as smooth and glossy as cream. His brow, like his frame, was unusually tall, and in its shadows lurked a pair of eyes whose gaze held a glimmer of mischief in it. One had the feeling that here was a man of stern resolve who nonetheless took pleasure in all the little jests of life. He was a gentleman of parts and accomplishments, who was known and respected throughout the south of Fenshire by every kind of folk, and whose opinion was regularly sought on matters of importance. With his quiet assurance, his pride of bearing and his graceful presence, he was the very picture of a Laird of the Clan MacHector, and a Knight of the sundered realm.

His friend Shand, his size and appearance notwithstanding, was, like the Laird himself, a first-class horseman. He had just come off the gallops, where he had spent the morning exercising his hunter. It was a favored habit of his, something he often did in the company of Vicar Ludlow and one or two others of a horsy persuasion. By trade, Mr.

Shand was a brewer; and so a very popular fen-reeve was he, having been elected to the position by town meeting every year for the past seven running. In his office as overseer he was charged with superintending the common lands of the parish, which included within its bounds the town of Market Snailsby and the neighboring hamlets of Pitchford, Strood, and Shipton-on-Lour.

With the return of the Laird preparations for Water Street quickly went forward. Having laid his beautiful silver-mounted pipes aside, Sir Hector changed into his riding-habit and clanked out into the yard to the stables to see to his horse and his groom. This groom had been a very famous whip in his day, one who could drive a four-in-hand with uncanny skill, and who had retired to a comfortable existence amongst the stableflesh he so admired. To him was entrusted the task of equipping the Laird's favorite road-horse — a clean, alert little gelding with clever eyes and an easy, supple walk. The gillies meantime had been assigned a pair of sturdy cobs for their own employment.

In the stables the men found themselves the objects of attention of Mr. Herbert Hathaway, who lay dozing atop the corn-bin. Evidently Herbert had not abandoned Mickledene, but instead had repaired to the calm and quiet of the barns for a spell of meditation. His curiosity being attracted now by the arrival of Sir Hector and the others, he sat up, yawned, and blinked his eyes at them. Truth be told Herbert's curiosity was attracted by any and all matters arising within the bounds of his daily circuit; and it was with considerable interest that he watched the saddles and bridles being fitted on, and the girths made tight, as the horses were readied for their little excursion.

In the course of these activities, some mention was made by the horsemen of Mrs. Chugwell and her pending survey of the new road. Mr. Shand declared that he was looking forward to the adventure, and to obtaining a glimpse perhaps of the ancient hunting-seat of Godfrey de Clinkers which lay buried in the wood.

"Hum! An' what's that ye're sayin' there, Willie, aboot auld de Clinkers?" inquired the knight. "For dooms me, man, there be no a body alive in Snailsby, nor elsewhaur either, has spied the hurley-hoose i'the wood."

"Ah, but then you wouldn't know, Sir Hector," said Mr. Shand, with an air of polite apology. "When the road-clearing was halted last year, Mrs. Chugwell and her workers were, in my estimation, already very near the site of the old lodge. For I saw a map once — had it in my study in fact, for the longest time, though I seem to have mislaid it now — and am fairly convinced, based on my recollection, that the road will pass very close to the lodge, or what remains of it. Now if there *are* squatters in Marley Wood — these riders and park-keepers and such — they could very well have made their camp at the lodge, as it is the only habitable dwelling in the neighborhood."

"Aye, 'tis likely, I jalouse, but only an it remains 'habitable,' as ye ca' it, Willie," Sir Hector pointed out. "For 'tis hunnerds o' years auld the noo, an' wi' no a body tae keep it frae fallin' tae pieces, a muckle great ruin it must be."

"True, Sir Hector. But it was a stout and commodious structure in its day, having cost de Clinkers a mint of money to build, not to say a few lives. There is a woodcut drawing of it which I have seen in a book at the vicarage, and a mezzotint as well, which hangs upon a wall of the Municipal Library in Newmarsh."

"Aye, an' a lonelier hoose couldna be fancied. An' what sort o' men might they be wha be squattin' there? For I dinna b'lieve that gentlemen frae Huntwhistle or ither fine sportsmen be fules eneugh to be keepin' hoose i'the darksome wood. Nor ha' they need tae be."

"Some old tramp fellows, perhaps, Sir Hector?" the reeve suggested.

"Gangrels and scaff-raff, then, think ye? But an 'tis true, then 'tis oor duty tae oust 'em — 'tisn't that sae, Willie? Forasmuch as auld de Clinkers an' his wife were o' this parish, an' the land on whilk the lodge were built be parish land."

Mr. Shand appeared a whit troubled by the Laird's remarks. Although he liked his job as fen-reeve well enough, he didn't particularly relish the thought of having to enforce local ordinances in a place like Marley Wood. He was a brewer, a man of conviviality and compromise, and not accustomed to having such things as phantom riders on his patch.

"If we must," he said.

"An' what o' the hoonds, sir?" queried Haggis, with a fierce brushing of his beard. "For I dinna believe there be mony an auld tramp fellow or whateffer as will be keepin' a pack o' foxers."

"Nor horses either," added Jorkens. "Na, na, 'tis no sae vera probable."

A puzzled look came into the reeve's face. "Hounds, Mr. Haggis? What hounds be these?" said he, glancing from gillie to gillie, and then to Sir Hector.

It appeared that this aspect of the story had escaped the ears of Mr. Shand, and so he had a full account of it now from Haggis. Some "old tramp fellows" the riders most probably were *not*, the brewer was obliged to admit, but more than likely well-armed sportsmen hailing from parts unknown. Such indeed was the general consensus, arrived at after a period of discussion, during which the old groom could be seen chewing on a straw and nodding and chuckling to himself at the lunacy of the times.

"An' can ye be sure, gentlemen, 'tis no auld de Clinkers himsell i'that wood?" he wondered aloud. "For as tae squatters an' sportsmen an' ithers o' that ilk, it disna seem ower likely."

"Hum! Well, 'tis true, Steenie, I'll no be brushin' aside auld de Clinkers mysell," acknowledged the Laird, "but 'tis no sae likely either, wad ye no say, whan the man be stane-cold deid these three hunnerd years the noo?"

"As you yourself have stated, Sir Hector, no one alive has ever visited the lodge," said Mr. Shand.

"An' returned tae tell of it," Haggis added.

"Its position, however, remains only a guess on my part; my recollection of the map may have failed me. But as that corner of the wood lies within the fringes of this parish, I suppose we are obliged to look into the matter."

But the reeve showed little enthusiasm for the task. Searching for clues in Water Street was one thing; searching for squatters in the beast-haunted wood was quite another. But of course they would be traveling under the escort of the mighty Ranger; and so, after a little reflection, some of Mr. Shand's uneasiness left him.

"Whate'er be gaun on in there, 'tis naething tae the gude, by ma certie," declared Haggis.

"Naething indeed, Mr. Haggis," agreed Jorkens.

"Hum! An' what o' the twa bairns i'the wood? The bairns o' Miss Hathaway an' oor Molly?" said Sir Hector.

"Bairns? Do you mean children?" blinked Mr. Shand, not comprehending. Could it be, he wondered, that something more had escaped his ears?

Aye, children they were indeed, nodded the Laird — two small children to be precise, to all appearances lost, whom Jemma Hathaway had encountered on her recent drive from Tillington. This item of interest the Laird had received from Molly, of course: had received it, but had not given it so much thought until now. Altogether he found it difficult to connect the lost children with ghostly riders and the mysterious park-keeper in green; nonetheless his intuition told him there *was* a connection there.

"A wee-bit lass an' laddie they were, but oor Molly didna ken their faces," Sir Hector related. "'Tis a mystery wha they be. But maist everything aboot the wood be a mystery."

"It all sounds *rummy* to me," yawned Herbert from his place atop the corn-bin.

"As well it should," snorted the gelding, with a toss of his shapely head. "It will come to nothing, you'll mark my words, sir. Ghostly riders indeed!"

"I wouldn't know a ghost if I saw one," Herbert admitted, after a moment's reflection. "But neither would I know a park-keeper, I don't suppose . . ."

"Perhaps we've a regular family of squatters on our hands, then, what with these children and all?" suggested the reeve.

"An' likely as daft as auld Jervas Wackwire tae be squatting there," said Haggis. "O' that, sir, I've no a doubt."

"Aye, juist as I've no a doubt as tae Mr. Wackwire himsell," said Jorkens, laying a finger to his nose in sign of confidence. "For an ye'll recollect, Mr. Haggis — 'tis tae be celery sticks at midnicht!"

"Perish me, but there's na gainsaying that, Mr. Jorkens."

"Hum! An' by St. Poppo, 'twill be midnicht indeedy, ma gillies, an we dinna hurry it up the noo," Sir Hector urged, as he put boot to stirrup and leaped astride the gelding. "An' sae let's awa' for Water Street yont an' larn the troth o' the matter. We'll gang thegither, ma men, an' take na risks. Aye, tae Water Street — an' keep yer whingers an' yer claymores close tae hand!"

His companions chorused their agreement, and mounting to their steeds they followed him into the gravel court and out through the gates of the Hall. Once in the road the riders swung their horses' heads towards town, their destination the cleft tree at the top of Water Street, their goal to prove the ghostly park-keeper less than ghostly.

The chilly air sprang at them as they trotted off, Sir Hector in the advance, sitting tall and arrow-straight in the saddle like the Laird and Knight that he was. Behind him rode the gillies, both of them keeping a sharp alert. Lastly came Mr. Shand, his jowls bouncing like the brim of his wide-awake, but a determined figure nonetheless. No more than a stone's throw from the gates, horses and horsemen vanished into a mist and were gone.

Meantime young Mr. Herbert, his meditations complete, had eased himself down from the corn-bin and strolled out into the yard. Having been driven from the Hall by the combined efforts of Thrasher, Whisk, and Mrs. Locket, and having nothing now but the old groom to occupy his attention, he paused to sniff the air a bit and look about him. *What to do*, he wondered, *what to do?*

It was a problem that had taxed the mind of many a small cat in many a stable-yard, in Fenshire and elsewhere, on many a day.

"Oh, hang it all! Whatever's the use? I'll be off home now, I suppose," he decided at length. "What a nuisance that little bossy-boots of a Thrasher is."

And so off home he went, slipping quietly across to Mead Cottage — *his* destination the kitchen, his goal to pass some time in the company of his brother Gerald and Mrs. Rudling and the hearth-fire.

Young Herbert Hathaway was a fortunate small cat, as small cats go. He did not trouble himself over ghostly park-keepers, or little lost children in a wood, or horrid, snake-necked monstrosities that growled in people's faces. And with such blissful ignorance he was, like most others of his species, more than content.

PART THREE

THE FIRST CHAPTER

MISS HENSLOWE INQUIRES

MORNING found Miss Ada Henslowe jogging her horse past the vicarage on her way into town.

Miss Henslowe had enjoyed a fine supper at Mead Cottage the other night as the guest of her friend Jemma Hathaway, and in the course of it had learned many an interesting thing about Miss Hathaway's drive from Tillington in the shay-cart.

Afterwards Miss Henslowe had apprised her friend of some further particulars she had gleaned concerning the mysterious riders and their hounds, and the ghostly park-keeper in Water Street, whom Sir Hector and Mr. Shand had taken it upon themselves to investigate. There were some in Market Snailsby, she declared, who considered these troubling apparitions to be just that — apparitions, manifestations of a spectral presence, demons from the infernal realm. And then of course there were others, people like Dr. Chevenix, Mr. Blathers, and Mr. Shand — rationalists all — who favored a more earthly explanation. Although how anyone could be so idiotic as to have chosen Marley Wood for riding in, Miss Henslowe could scarcely fathom.

There had been Henslowes and Hathaways, both of them families of account, dwelling in Market Snailsby since round the year dot. The Church of All Hallows, which Ada was passing now, was brimful of plaques and other memorials celebrating these past generations and their good services to town and county. There were hardly any in Fenshire whose lines of descent from their ancestors were so clear — those same sturdy ancestors for whom Vicar Ludlow had professed such admiration, and who in bygone times were known to have scoured the wood for venison and swine, and Devil take the danger!

Miss Henslowe lived in Short Street. It was, as the name suggests, a street of no very great dimensions, but it had some fine, gabled houses in it, and the street was a clean street. It lay a little distance beyond the vicarage and grammar school, on the road out of town — that is, on the coach-road running due southwesterly towards Stoke

Moreton and Dragonthorpe. Miss Henslowe's cottage stood near Blossom's Court and the old cherry gardens, directly across the river from Snailsby Mill. It was just past the cherry gardens that the looming fortress of Marley Wood had been breached by an opening — it was the entrance to the new road.

Like her friend Jemma, Miss Henslowe in years was just to the back of forty; and yet her hair was as soft and golden, her smile as fresh, her eyes as clear, and her step as lively as in her childhood days when she had skipped her way along Holy Street to school. She was a light-hearted woman by nature, who, like Jemma and Richard, had been left her home by her parents. Her chief interests were knitting, painting, and gardening. Nor were her skills at the pianoforte to be sneezed at, and a part of the attraction of Mead Cottage was the making of some lively music in concert with the harmonious Hathaways.

As she was riding along, she spied the vicar walking his pet glyptodont by the watermeads of the Fribble. Ordinarily, glypts preferred a warmer clime — their ancestors came not from Market Snailsby but from much farther south, in that shadowy realm of lakes and lagoons that bordered the sundering zone — but they had learned to take what came their way in a sundered world. Now, what was the name of that trader who had convinced Mr. Ludlow that he simply must have one? Miss Henslowe searched her brain for it. Such a curious name it was — Pickleheap, she thought, or something like it. She remembered, he had been a pushy kind of chap, sharp-nosed, with horn spectacles. *My good friend!* was how he had addressed the vicar, despite having never set eyes on the reverend gentleman before in all his life. She supposed it was simply his way of getting people to like him.

Mr. Pickleheap had been traveling with a mastodon train as it rumbled through Fenshire, and the vicar, his eyes drawn to the inoffensive-looking little creature in its wire-and-wicker cage, had been struck at once by its novelty. He had heard of these glyptodonts before, he told the trader, but never had he seen one; and so the deal, like the vicar himself, was struck.

At first Mr. Ludlow had been much taken with his new pet; but now that it had swelled to the size of his drawing-room sofa, he and his wife were wondering how much more yet it had to grow. It was well-known that the clergyman made frequent use of the glypt as a footstool, on those cozy evenings when he was at his reading; indeed, this had been one of the creature's many virtues as trumpeted by Mr.

Pickleheap. But most footstools of Miss Henslowe's acquaintance did not require so much care and looking after, nor had they any need to be taken for walks round the watermeads of the Fribble.

In the meantime a farm wagon had come rattling across the stone bridge from the Drovers' Road. It drew up at the spot where the vicar was standing, his arms folded and his eyes on Hortense while she grubbed for dainties amongst the sedges. Seated in the wagon were a couple of gingery-whiskered young men, who looked to be exact duplicates of one another. Miss Henslowe recognized the pair at once — they were the Doughty brothers, respectable yeoman farmers from out on the marshes. Free unattached bachelors both, they were decked out in their best fustian, with belchers at their necks, leather leggings, and hobnails. On their heads they wore identical large hats, impossibly tall as to crown and broad as to brim.

Miss Henslowe spurred her horse on, and as she came within earshot could hear the brothers inquiring of the vicar if he had seen anything unusual of late in Marley Wood?

No, the clergyman replied, he had seen nothing unusual there.

Well, had he heard something, then, the brothers asked? Something like the baying of hounds, perhaps?

No, Mr. Ludlow replied again, he had not — but he *had* heard tell of both, he said, and thought it all most strange. Whereupon he proceeded to tell them all he knew; for the brothers, spending as they did most of their time on their lonely farm, had heard only rumors, and were keen to find out what they could while in town.

Needless to say the loamy pair were agog at the news, and wondered if perhaps a horde of marsh devils had taken to prowling the wood; but the vicar answered that he didn't think it likely.

"But there bean't any such vasty packs o' hounds round hyar, sir," the brothers replied, with identical perplexed countenances. "The nearest be them over to Huntwhistle. And o' course there be Lord Cratchley's pack at Wickham Wheepers. And as for Sir Hector's kennel, well, they bean't *his* dogs, that's sure."

"Strangely, it is only on these bright, moonlit nights we have had that these oddities appear," the vicar remarked. "Now, why should this be so? And why should we endure so much fog and cloud all the year, when the sun never shines, and yet have such lovely evenings at times? I dare say it's a puzzle to me. But Marley Wood has a reputation for puzzles, one that stretches back centuries, and which I have been reading something of recently. Ah, well, I suppose it all comes down to the same thing in the end. *Omnia exeunt in mysterium . . .*"

The respectable yeoman farmers were left scratching their identical heads, for neither of them understood pig Latin let alone its ancient original.

The vicar went on to describe for them how he had been spending his evenings of late by his snug fireside, researching the annals of the Historical Society — researching, no doubt, with his glass of wine at the ready, his pipe in his lips, and his feet propped comfortably on the back of his dozing glyptodont.

"Now, then," he continued, "as regards the hounds, I dare say Lord Cratchley may have — "

"'Tis the evil goblin-hounds o' legend!" the brothers suddenly exclaimed. "Oh, aye, sir. 'Tis the black dogs — the dreaded bogeys — lusting for human souls to devour. 'Tis a sign, sir, that evil days be at hand."

The vicar paused, believing this explanation to be more than a little dubious — not to mention uncomfortable — and preferring instead some more rational interpretation; the which, however, he had to confess he was, um, er, unable to produce at the moment.

The brothers were likewise amazed to learn of the ghostly park-keeper who had popped out of a shrubbery at the top of Water Street. Miss Henslowe, who had by now joined the group, declared that she too had heard of this antiquated figure with his lantern and his bugle-horn, and his quarterstaff for cudgeling with, and from no less a witness than the servant Bunting himself.

Bunting reported that the park-keeper had warned him off and told him to beware the wood, before evaporating into empty air. In truth it had sounded like the tale of a man shaken out of a dreamful sleep, or out of something worse — a liquorish stupor. On its own merits the sighting would have counted for little, but the man Bunting was reckoned a reliable fellow, and his testimony, in conjunction with that of others who had since come forward, reporting a similar experience, warranted serious consideration.

"But of what use is a park-keeper in such a place?" Ada wondered. "He wouldn't last a day in that wood, quarterstaff or no."

"Hundreds of years ago such a man would have been indispensable to a stag-hunter like Godfrey de Clinkers," the vicar noted.

"Hundreds of years ago perhaps. But who would be stag-hunting in Marley Wood these days, vicar — and by moonlight? It's rather difficult to understand."

"Ah, such color and variety the world had in those old days," the clergyman sighed. "Our ancestors at their birthing must have been apportioned an extra share of cheek, or so it has always seemed to me."

"This day and age most folk don't care to tread the woodways, even by daylight, sir, lessen they be well-prepared," said the brothers, their hands reflexly gripping the hilts of their cutlasses. "But by night — oh, aye, 'tis a fool's errand to be hunting in Marley Wood."

"My thought exactly," concurred Miss Henslowe.

"Lessen they be from Slopshire, o' course — not much brain there!" the brothers quipped, the one with a loud chuckle and the other a knowing wink, at the expense of their less fortunate countrymen to the southwards.

"And as the coaches and carriages on the road do not drive by night," Ada observed, "they cannot be travelers of any sort with which I am acquainted."

"Nor I," said one brother.

"Nor I, neither," chimed in the other.

"Perhaps it's the man in the moon, then, for he is the only one known to be out on such evenings," the vicar suggested lightly.

"Or footpads — highwaymen, sir!" speculated the first brother.

"But there is no highway in the wood — not yet, at any rate," Ada pointed out.

It was all so very strange, this vanishing of the overcast on those curious, moonlit nights when something was astir in Marley Wood. For the most part the clearing remained limited to the skies over the wood itself, and over the roof-tops of Market Snailsby, and did not extend much beyond them to the fens roundabout. For whatever reason the fair Diana only rarely showed herself out on the marshes.

"We must see what Phoggie Finlayson has to say about it," declared the Doughtys, in reference to a fen-slodger well-known about town for his perspicacity and his interest in civic affairs. "Oh, aye, Phoggie will know."

So resolved, the brothers bade their farewells to the vicar and Miss Henslowe and clattered off towards the Market House, where they had butter and cream to sell, and where they hoped to learn more about the odd events of recent days and nights.

Because Hortense had not yet exhausted her search for dainties, the vicar was obliged to remain a while longer, which gave him an opportunity to discuss the odd events in some detail with Miss Henslowe.

"You have heard Miss Hathaway's report of the two children in the Tillington Road?" he said.

"Yes, I have."

"I'm afraid my interview with Mrs. Pippins produced little of significance. She hasn't traveled to Beeworthy this year, and so they were most definitely not her children there in the road. Unfortunately I've been unable to winkle out anything more than that."

"It's just what Jemma expected you'd find," Ada told him. "She doesn't believe that the children had anything to do with any Pippinses, as she phrased it."

The vicar's face registered surprise. "Indeed? Well! At any rate I've made some additional inquiries, but they too have led nowhere. I must conclude that the children are the offspring of strangers. Fen-slodgers, perhaps, a family with whom I've yet to scrape an acquaintance — "

"But slodgers from where, vicar?" Ada inquired. "For Tillington and Beeworthy are some distance away, and there is no village or farmstead in the area where the children were seen. And there is the question of how they managed to keep pace with the shay-cart. Jemma believes they must have had a pony; she may have heard its hoofbeats in the wood. Somehow the children were able to follow along, and rather briskly, too. For Rosie is a real clipper, you know, and to judge by Jemma's account they were making quite a good rattle of it in the cart. And still the children caught them up."

The vicar shook his head, answers again failing him. Miss Henslowe was about to ask him his opinion of the horrid, snake-necked thing behind the firs, when she suddenly remembered that he had been told nothing of this little item; and so she held her tongue. Her friend Jemma, understandably enough, was not keen to be joining the local hare-brain set, or the crank set either for that matter. As yet she had confided in only a few close friends. Although others besides Haggis now had seen the mysterious lights in the wood, had heard the fiendish cries of the hunters, the yelping of the hounds, and the blare of the hunting-horn — and some even had glimpsed a ghostly park-keeper in green — only Jemma Hathaway had reported coming face-to-face with a hideous, snake-necked monstrosity with a tumble of orange hair.

At any rate, no one as yet had *admitted* to it . . .

Miss Henslowe told the vicar that she was bound for Mead Cottage now and would relay his news regarding the children, or lack of it, to Miss Hathaway. Mr. Ludlow in his turn asked her to offer his apologies to her friend. He had hoped to winkle something out for her, he said, he really had, but, sadly, he had failed.

And so they parted, Miss Henslowe riding on through the cobbled High Street, and the vicar left to loiter by the Fribble while Hortense pursued her browsing.

The snow was fast disappearing all over the banks of the river now. There were only scattered patches of it remaining here, and a few faint traces of it there. Spring was coming at last to the fen country! Soon Mrs. Chugwell would be making her inspection of the new road, the thought of which caused the vicar to stop a moment and consider, much as Mr. Swain had done before him.

Who knew what Mrs. Chugwell and the others might find there in Marley Wood? Perhaps they would stumble across some answers to these mysteries that had arisen. The vicar, stout horseman that he was, already had decided he would join the survey party — the Chugwells and Ranger, Sir Hector, Mr. Shand, and whoever else cared to brave the perils of the wood. For he had to admit it, he was most curious to know what was lurking there in those grim and shadowy forest aisles. Perhaps he might learn something that would be of value to the members of the Fenshire Historical Society . . .

Mr. Ludlow had taken his horse onto the gallops that morning, as he often did, and along the way had caught sight of the mighty Ranger grazing upon Snailsby Common. What a picture it had been — the steely-coated mastodon swaying gently to and fro, like the oceangoing vessel he resembled, a-sail in all his grandeur upon the broken green and snowy sward of the Common. Even from a distance the vicar had been greatly impressed, as indeed he was every year, by the awesome magnificence of the shovel-tusker.

Surely whatever was lurking there in the wood was no match for such a creature! For as Mrs. Chugwell and others of her profession were fond of boasting, there was nothing in a sundered world that could stop a thunder-beast — and a mighty tusker even more so.

THE SECOND CHAPTER

MOTHER REDCAP

MISS Henslowe arrived at Mead Cottage to find Jemma in the kitchen with Mrs. Rudling and Corney. Gerald and Herbert were there as well, both of them having found comfortable places to lounge in, as was Snap, who lay dozing on the hearth-rug. The coach dog's senses had been alerted as soon as Ada rode into the yard, but, knowing that she was often at the cottage at that hour, he did not bark or otherwise disturb the cats' restful state of mind.

Advertising her presence with a cheery "Yoo-hoo!" in the passage, Ada discovered that the talk that morning had been concerned largely with the Chugwells and their coming activities.

"They are about to undertake their inspection of the new road," Jemma was saying as her friend strolled into the kitchen.

"Which, conveniently enough, begins very near my house," Ada said brightly. "Hallo, Corney. Good morning, Mrs. R."

She sat down with Jemma and Mr. Oldcorn at the big table by the fire, where the hot tea, biscuits, and seed cake were in plentiful supply.

"They need to see how the road has borne the winter snows, and then will chart the next stretch to be cleared," Jemma explained. "Mrs. Chugwell estimates they are already more than half-way through the wood. Both Sir Hector and Mr. Shand have volunteered to join them on the survey."

"And I hear they intend to investigate the odd happenings in the wood as well," Ada said. "Whether they'll find any trace of your two children, however, I won't venture a guess. Oh, by the by, Jemma, the vicar has told me it's just as you thought — they've no connection whatever with Mrs. Pippins. Mr. Shand and Sir Hector are concerned we may have squatters on parish land. Speaking for myself, if there are any squatters in Marley Wood they're more than welcome to it."

Molly Grime, who had been at her work in the passage, entered the room now and declared that she thought the wood to be "bogled and bedeviled," rather like the mind of their old gentleman of a neighbor over the road, Mr. Wackwire.

"Have ye not heard his latest, ma'am? 'And 'twill be celery sticks at midnight,' says Mr. Wackwire. That an' more, as my own ears have been witness to. Some of what I've heard from that old man's lips, and from Mrs. Locket's — well, ma'am, 'tis enough to make yer heart leap through yer hat, justabout."

"Mrs. Locket has a very active imagination," said Miss Hathaway. "What's more she has a nose for gossip, and has been known to exaggerate on occasion, and to be subject to flights of fancy. As for Mr. Wackwire, well, the poor man can't help it. His mind is gone."

"Ou, aye, that's for certain sure, ma'am — 'tis near spookish at times," averred Molly.

"And as regards Mrs. Locket," spoke up Ada, "do you recall, Jemma, her reaction to her first glimpse of the lady Hortense? She raised the alarm that a 'sedge-monster' had invaded the town, and that the watch should be called out to protect the citizens. Sedge-monster! It was only Hortense browsing at the waterside. The vicar had left the gate ajar, and she had taken advantage of it."

"Poor Mrs. Locket. Well, I suppose she has a difficult life," sympathized Corney. "It can't be easy looking after old Wackwire, and with not a relation of his in sight to offer aid."

"And o' course a body can't tell what Mr. Wackwire is saying, or wanting, most times," declared Mrs. Rudling. "Sure, sir, it must be fair maddening."

"Aye, 'tis to be celery sticks now, Mrs. Rudling!" Molly exclaimed.

"Of course we don't begrudge Mrs. Locket her flights of fancy, or her occasional liberties," said Jemma, "for I would imagine that caring for Mr. Wackwire is rather a chore."

"Exactly," nodded Corney, who, being not a young man himself, was well aware how great a challenge it was for his own housekeeper to care for *him*. "As for my situation," he smiled, touching on that subject, "it is not so easy either, I don't believe — and I've still half my senses."

"It's a jolly good job Mr. Blathers isn't here, Corney, or he might challenge you on that point," Jemma laughed.

Her remark triggered a burst of merriment, one in which Mr. Oldcorn participated as freely as the rest. He was as unsentimental a man as could be for a gentleman of his age and station, and did not shrink from a little humor at his own expense.

"D'you fancy another cup o' tea, sir?" the housekeeper asked him.

"Thank you kindly, Mrs. Rudling."

"So, do you think they'll find the old hunting-lodge this season?" Miss Hathaway struck in, addressing the whole group. "I hear that Mr. Shand reckons it to be very near the place where the work left off, and that the squatters may have established their camp there."

"Oh, no, ma'am, that I can't see," opined the housekeeper, with a frowning shake of her head. "Squatters in Marley Wood? 'Twould be worse than daft. Sure, there be too many monsters for any sane bodies to be camping there!"

Scarcely had the housekeeper uttered these words, than she and the others found their glances straying in Jemma's direction — even Snap, who looked up in response to the momentary quiet — although no one was so graceless as to mention snaked necks or tumbling masses of orange hair.

It was Ada who finally broke the silence. "I quite agree. Besides, what would be the point? There are far more congenial places to hold a meet."

"Perhaps that is the point," Jemma suggested.

"How do you mean?"

"Well, you know, dear, perhaps it's a manly sort of thing. A gentlemanly challenge. A test of nerve, of valor. An opportunity for bolder spirits to risk everything for the chase, including the privilege of having one's brains dashed out, or the flesh ripped from one's carcass."

"Or perhaps these squatters are enchanted, and can't be harmed by the creatures of the wood. Perhaps they've claimed the protection of Mother Redcap?"

Miss Hathaway's face brightened at mention of the name. It was a name she had not heard spoken, or even had thought of for that matter, in many a long year. "Oh, Mother Redcap," she echoed. "The old recluse my parents used to talk about. It's a pity, Ada, that we are too young to remember her."

"Ah, sure, the Redcap," Mrs. Rudling was heard to murmur. Immediately all eyes sought her out; embarrassed, the housekeeper whisked round and made herself suddenly very busy at her chopping-board.

Her actions prompted Ada to ask, innocently enough —

"Did you know her, Mrs. Rudling? For it was so very long ago that neither Jemma nor I could possibly have — "

"Well, Miss Ada — if you must be asking, 'tis of a certain age I am," the housekeeper replied, without looking round, and without the least pause in her work. "And so is our Mr. Oldcorn, I'll warrant — for I've heard nowt to the contrary!"

The ladies shifted their attention to the gentleman in question.

"Well — um — indeed," he conceded, a trifle taken aback, but with a glint of amusement in his eye. "It seems that Mrs. Rudling and I, being of a certain vintage, as she says, do have our memories of Mother Redcap — from our *childhood* days, of course. Is that not so, Mrs. Rudling?"

"Very early childhood, sir," amended the housekeeper.

"Indeed. Very early. Although I've heard it said, Mrs. Rudling," Corney added, with a smiling glance at Jemma and Ada, "that we may 'grow young again in the youth of those about us.'"

"Oh, Corney, you are such a gentleman!" Ada exclaimed. "And we thank you very much for it. Don't we, Jemma?"

"If I remember rightly, Mother Redcap was an herbalist — a 'white witch,' as they say," her friend recalled. "At any rate that is how my parents spoke of her. Rather an ugly duckling she must have been, too, from what I've gathered. She went off one morning to search for roots and mushrooms round the eaves of the wood, and never came back. That was some fifty years ago, was it not?"

"Indeed," Corney answered, with a pause of thought — not so much at the memory of those fifty years agone, but at the speed with which they had flown past him. "No trace of her was ever found. After a few months, when it was clear she was not going to return, the parish took her ancient cottage in charge. It was in bad repair and eventually was pulled down, for safety's sake, as it was thought to be in danger of collapsing."

"Where was her cottage, exactly?"

"Just outside of town, by Goblin Mere, on the way to Yocklebury Great Croft."

"Ah, I remember now — such a lonely spot. There are a couple of ruined stones there, and some shattered timbers, but little else to mark it."

"The mere has had many unpleasant associations. Even today it is a place where few people care to go. Yet there are hardly any now who remember the old woman who used to live there, or even have heard of her."

"I remember, when Richard and I were very small, we were driven out there and shown the spot by our father. Yes, yes — the house of the old pig-faced woman, beside Goblin Mere! I'd completely forgotten. It wasn't far from the derelict windmill, as I recall . . ."

Ada paused with her teacup half-way to her lips, and stared at Jemma.

"Why, that is near *my* house," she said.

Corney nodded. "It lies at the end of the long meadow, past the entrance to the new road. But Mother Redcap aside, the mere has always been a haunted place. As children we used to hurl stones into it to frighten the resident goblin."

"Has anyone a clue what became of Mother Redcap?"

"None. Although there seems little doubt she met with a mishap. Most likely it was a marsh devil. As I recollect, several of the creatures had been seen slinking about the mere and the cherry gardens in the days before she went missing. All business in the town had come to a stand, and the parish watch was on the alert. Of course the search for her necessarily was limited, taking place as it did only round the eaves of the wood; no one dared to venture inside. I remember our old vicar chastising us for being unchristian, but really — the woman kept to herself most of the time, and showed little interest in others. And they in their turn showed little interest in braving the wood to find her."

"Had she any relations? Did anyone ever inquire after her?"

"No. You see, she was not from these parts. She was from somewhere down in Gloamshire, I believe. She never divulged anything more than that, and no one cared enough to ask."

"Had she any friends in town?"

"Very few. Oh, she was not an unfriendly person, and not in the least standoffish; just a trifle odd. She had strange ways — foreign ways — Gloamshire ways, I suppose. I can see her now — a tiny, dried-up, wrinkled old woman, nearly toothless, with a huge stoop in her back. Not exactly an oil painting! Of course the gossips called her a witch; but the gossips will call any scatty old lady a witch who lives on her own and takes an interest in simples and mushrooms and the like. Although she did have a bit of a temper, I know . . ."

"I had the strangest dream once," Ada remarked. "I dreamed I saw a figure crawling along the ground with a sack over its head. When the sack was removed I saw that it was Mother Redcap. She had a scarlet kerchief on her head and a redcap mushroom in her hand. When I asked her what she was doing, she said she was filling the sack with lies. I must admit, I never understood that dream."

"Nor I," said Jemma. "Really, dear — the tales you come up with!"

"Well, you know, at least my tales haven't any wild-eyed, snake-necked things in them that growl in people's faces," Ada laughed.

The silence that attended her words was palpable. Mrs. Rudling swung round from her chopping-board and stared at her in surprise; Corney cleared his voice and looked politely askance. Even Snap opened a lazy eye. It was an uncomfortable silence, too, especially for Ada, who discovered that her remark was not so joking a one as she had intended.

"Oh, ma'am!" cried a distressed Molly; and putting a hand to her lips she scurried back into the passage.

Miss Hathaway had found her experience in the wood extremely troubling; and so Ada made haste at once to apologize, and to assure her friend that they would get to the bottom of the mystery, with or without the aid of Vicar Ludlow and his Pippinses. Perhaps the coming work in the wood, she suggested — the presence of the Chugwells and their drivers, not to mention their stupendous mounts — might clear not only the new road, but some of the fog from the mystery as well. For now, however, a change of topic was in order.

"And what of your son, then, Corney?" Ada said brightly. "What news of Phil?"

In a glow of pride Mr. Oldcorn offered some words on the progress of his offspring, who had been diligently attending to his studies at Clive's Inn, and his clerkship in the very respectable house of Marrowbone, Marrowbone, and Cleaver. He finished by saying that he expected his son would be down for a few weeks during the long vacation.

"Ah, sure, sir, we'll look forward to seeing the young man again," smiled Mrs. Rudling.

"And once he has completed his terms and is enrolled as a solicitor, he can move home for good and give our Mr. Inkpen a run for his ducats," said Ada.

"I think it more likely that Arnold will take him under his wing, and offer him a position as junior partner," Corney hinted. "For he desperately needs the help, or so he has told me — in the strictest confidence, of course."

"'Inkpen and Oldcorn, Solicitors.' It has a distinct ring to it. You should be very happy, Corney. Still, it's not so good a ring, I don't think, as Marrowbone, Marrowbone, and Cleaver."

"Goodness, miss, but it does sound like a gang o' butchers, to be sure," exclaimed the housekeeper.

"Well, need I remind you, Mrs. Rudling, that we *are* speaking of lawyers here?" Ada returned.

Her quip inspired a fresh round of hilarity, one to which Mr. Oldcorn again seemed not the least averse.

"And what think you of 'Dodger and Fleece,' Corney?" said Miss Hathaway, joining in the merriment.

"I believe that to be a Nantle firm," her neighbor replied, trying to keep a straight face — with miserable success.

"But a respectable firm, do you think? And with a ring to it?"

"Oh, very much so."

Mr. Oldcorn was big-hearted enough, and good-humored enough — and, more importantly, just mischievous enough — to enter into the spirit of the ribbing, despite his own son's enrollment in the profession under siege. After all, hadn't the old gentleman himself been a magistrate once, and a witness to every crafty dodge and long-headed maneuver known to learned counsel?

"Oh, I say, we are naughty, aren't we?" Ada laughed. "Please say you forgive us, Corney."

To his credit Mr. Oldcorn did not reproach them for their naughtiness, as he couldn't himself resist having a bit of fun at the expense of the wily practitioners of the law.

"Also in Nantle, as you may have heard, can be found the eminent firm of Maule, Pick, and Slaughter," he said.

"And what of Clippurse and Gouge?" Ada asked. "Eminent — or respectable?"

"Eminent — *and* respectable," said Corney. "Very."

"And Long and Causley?"

"Ditto."

"Cookham and Edam?"

"Ditto, ditto!"

"And what of Snare, Gypsum, and Flam?" Jemma chimed in.

The merrymakers might have been a trifle embarrassed, I think, had the town solicitor chosen that moment to stroll into the kitchen, and overheard these aspersions cast on his honorable profession. Indeed, such a thought may not have been so far from their minds, perhaps, for when Snap abruptly sprang to his feet and dashed into the passage, barking excitedly, it claimed their attention — and that of the cats — as forcefully as if Lawyer Inkpen himself had appeared in the doorway.

"For the love of Henry, can't a fellow have a little peace?" complained Herbert, with a grumpy look round. "What a nuisance! That pudding dog will be the ruination of himself. Always making noise. How very inconsiderate of him."

"As sure as eggs is eggs, brother," Gerald yawned, "there's not a truer statement been made in this house today. But what can he be enthusing about? Another visitor?"

"Maybe it's that man Blathers and his spectacles."

"Or some peddler on the tout for a sale."

And still Snap continued his barking.

"Oh, for heaven's sake," Herbert griped, covering his face, "that dog's got no more sense than a ham-bone."

Came then a subtle shaking of the ground underfoot — a steady succession of tremors, one following quickly upon the other, and each more powerful than the one before it. The truth flashed upon Corney at once.

"Thunder-beast!" he exclaimed.

Excited, slightly alarmed, and feeling perhaps just slightly guilty — for it had crossed their minds that it really *was* Arnold Inkpen, come for a visit — he and the others hastened into the passage. They found Snap and Molly standing at the drawing-room windows. Both the tongue and tail of the coach dog were going at a furious clip.

What the two had sight of in the windows was not an attorney, thank heavens, but something even more imposing — a gigantic shovel-tusker mastodon. The creature was parked in the road just outside the gate, its head and shoulders towering above the lowly garden wall of Mead Cottage.

It was none other than the mighty Ranger, with young Matt Chugwell at the reins. Already the cord-ladder had been unfurled from the cab-door, and a gentleman in a greatcoat and hat was making his way down it.

Recognizing the traveler at once, Miss Hathaway gave a joyful shout —

"It's Richard!"

THE THIRD CHAPTER

THE RETURN OF RICHARD

MR. Richard Hathaway it was indeed, home from New-marsh and his researches in the Municipal Library. He had been to the library often in recent years, in pursuit of the elusive Sir Pharnaby Crust, Fenshireman, and musician and composer *extraordinaire*. But how came he aboard a shovel-tusker?

He had secured a berth in the western coach — the "High Flyer," by way of Dragonthorpe — and had been set down as per usual at the Badger. There he had run into young Matt, who had offered him a lift to Mead Cottage. Matt and Richard were old friends, the Hathaways having become acquainted with the family through Matt's late father, the industrious Phrank Chugwell, who had been known to their parents. Mrs. Chugwell had been out visiting in the town when Richard arrived, in part to avoid another tedious encounter with Mayor Jagard, who had been sighted in the area. Fortunately it was the amiable Mr. Shand, who as fen-reeve and way-warden was the officer responsible for the road-clearing, with whom Mrs. Chugwell conducted her business, and not the insufferable Mayor of Market Snailsby.

Richard was welcomed at the gate by his sister and an exuberant Snap and the others. In the kitchen the cats peered at him from under drowsy lids, saw who it was, yawned, and went back to sleep. Both knew they could elicit his patronage at any time by means of a little flattery, or the strategic brush of a trouser-leg; for he was a dreadfully soft touch for a master. Besides, tawdry shows of enthusiasm or sentiment were not for them. Such displays were for unruly creatures like Thrashers and pudding dogs, and not for so splendid and dignified a species as theirs.

"How was your journey?" Ada asked, once the traveler had surrendered his coat, hat, and carpet-bag to Molly Grime, and everyone had settled themselves again by the fire.

"Exhausting," Richard replied. "We were stopped for a number of hours at Dragonthorpe, owing to rumors of a marsh devil that had been circulating in the town. But in the end the watch turned up nothing — a false report, evidently. Some near-sighted old dear, perhaps, who'd spied a squirrel in her garden and gotten the jitters. And so here I am, little worse for the excitement."

"Well, we're very glad of that," smiled Jemma. "And we are happy there was no marsh devil."

Mr. Richard Hathaway was the veritable spit and image of his sister, from his steady gaze and youthful looks to his curly dark hair into which the gray was stealing, slowly, strand by strand, as if the very grayness of Fenshire itself were seeping into it. One respect in which they differed, however, was in Richard's love of pipes, one of which he filled now and lighted. He was a confirmed pipe man; whole vast clouds of smoke trailed him wherever he went. Smoking aided his concentration, he said, and helped to keep the chill off. When he and his friend Blathers would get to puffing away there in the kitchen like a couple of lime-kilns, or a pair of infant Vesuvii, poor Mrs. Rudling was left with little recourse, in the defense of her nostrils, but to fling wide the casements and expel the suffocating fumes to the atmosphere.

"Now, then, you'll want to hear all the news from town, I'm sure," Ada began. "And there has been quite a lot of it while you've been away. In fact Market Snailsby is positively bubbling over with news these days."

"What news is that?" Richard asked. He had eased himself back in his chair with his arms crossed and his long legs stretched out before him. But although he made a show of listening, he seemed strangely preoccupied. Both Ada and Jemma noticed it — in the frequent glances they saw him cast about the room, for example, as if he were looking for something he could not find, or was expecting to appear at any moment. They traded puzzled looks with Mrs. Rudling. Perhaps there was something lacking amongst the tea-things; but no deficiency could they identify. Even Corney recognized that something was amiss.

"What is the matter, Richard? What *are* you looking for?" Jemma asked, unable to restrain her curiosity.

"Where are the children?" was her brother's interesting response.

"Children? Which children?"

"The two who were peeping in at the windows when we arrived at the gate. I saw them from the cab. Have we other visitors?"

Another exchange of glances. Jemma asked for a description of the children, something of their appearance, their expressions, their clothing. To her surprise — or, perhaps, to her lack of it, for she had half-anticipated his response — the description corresponded exactly to that of the pair in the Tillington Road.

"Shouldn't they be in school?" Richard wondered. "They seemed old enough. Who are they? And where have they gotten to?"

Without another word Jemma drew on her coat and hat and went outside, accompanied by Ada, to have a look round the front-garden. It did not take long to find them, even in the mess of snow and slush that was late springtime in Fenshire — traces of tiny footprints. The two were soon joined by Richard, who had received no explanation from either his sister or her friend; nevertheless he entered cheerfully into the spirit of the exercise.

The trail of prints led to the gate, where it was quickly lost in the muddied confusion of the road. Across the way, however, some faint tracks could be glimpsed, here and there, in the snowy meadow that stretched off towards Marley Wood.

And it was directly towards the wood that the tracks appeared to lead.

Evidently the children had arrived at Mead Cottage before Richard had, and had left once he had gone into the house. Probably they had hidden themselves round back in the interval, as Snap had not detected them. There was little the dog's keen senses could do at present, however, given the conditions and the good start the two had gained.

"Very curious," Jemma said.

"Yes, it seems they were," her brother remarked.

Out of the wood the children had come, peered shyly in at the cottage windows, and then back into the wood they had scampered. Nowhere, though, could the searchers find evidence of the pony tracks that would have been expected. If it was a pony that had brought the children all that distance to Market Snailsby, then it had been left in the wood.

"Dashed odd about those two — and dashed odd about this little hunt of yours. Now, then, sis, won't you tell me what it's all about?" Richard asked, after they had returned to the kitchen.

Briefly Jemma outlined the situation for him, relating all that had transpired in the Tillington Road and in Market Snailsby in the days since he had left for Newmarsh. As she poured out her story, a look of astonishment came into his face. His eyes grew progressively wider, and the kitchen air progressively smokier, as each new detail was laid before him. And as his wonder increased, so too did his restlessness. By the time she had finished he had slid forward in his seat and was balancing himself on the edge of it, all the while plowing impatient fingers through his hair and exclaiming — "Good gracious! Goodness me! Matter of fact! Well, I'm jiggered!"

"My reaction exactly, when I first heard of these things," Corney said.

"We know that the children are real, at any rate, as they've left us their footprints to see," Jemma concluded.

"Unlike this ghostly park-keeper of Bunting's, and the phantom riders and their hounds?" said her brother.

"Exactly. No trace of them has been discovered, either at the top of Water Street or round the eaves of the wood. Or so our Molly learned yesterday at Mickledene."

"Aye, 'tis true, sir," the maid declared, with a vigorous nod.

"Both places were searched by Sir Hector and the gillies and Mr. Shand, but they found nothing apart from a single, broken trail of hoofprints. Some wild horse, I should think."

"Nothing more?" Richard said.

"Nothing. No evidence of a horde of riders, or hounds, or a staff-wielding park-keeper."

"So what are we to make of these many reports?" Ada asked. "For I've heard from Mr. Ludlow today that Mrs. Crumbey and her little daughter, who live behind the vicarage, last night saw the park-keeper round the edge of the wood, and were threatened by him in the same manner as Bunting and the others. And then he vanished into air!"

"Perhaps it's magic," suggested the housekeeper, thinking aloud.

"Magic, Mrs. Rudling?" blinked Corney.

"Yes, sir, magic — conjured out of that same air by two bedeviled children."

"Ou, aye, something spookish they were!" averred Molly.

"Well, I suppose it *could* be magic . . ." Richard mused, scratching his head and smoking.

"But magic went out years ago," Jemma remarked, "or so your scholarly friend Mr. Blathers never fails to remind us."

"Oh, but I've heard of bedeviled children afore, ma'am, in my girlish days," said Mrs. Rudling. "For my grandmama did tell me stories of such conjuring."

"Conjuring by Mother Redcap, perhaps?" Ada suggested.

The housekeeper paused a moment, her brows tightly knit. "Oh, I shouldn't think so, Miss Ada. Not *her*. And not after these fair many years."

"I agree, it's quite impossible," said Corney, "for she was already an old woman when she disappeared. She couldn't possibly be alive today, either in the wood or elsewhere."

"What's this about Mother Redcap?" Richard asked.

After he had been briefed on the subject of their earlier discussion, he spent a further few minutes absorbed in thought, in generous collaboration with his pipe.

"Squatters, I should say," he declared at length. "If Shand believes it's so, and Sir Hector as well, then I'm inclined to their view. It's a fair enough assumption. Whatever the reason, it would appear that some strangers have chosen Marley Wood for hunting in. As for the absence of tracks — well, I'll admit, it's rather a mystery."

"I don't believe in squatters," Ada said firmly. "They would be prey to every creature that stalks the wood. How they should last more than a day in there I haven't a clue."

"Then what are we left with? Supernatural visitations? Magical children? Collective lunacy?"

"Consider your marsh devil at Dragonthorpe, Richard, and how it affected the people there," said Jemma. "It was but a single animal — and only a rumor of one at that! And what of that creature I confronted when I followed the children into the wood?"

"Which you are never to do again, sis, unless I am at your side," Richard admonished her. "It's far too dangerous, even with a good cutlass in hand, to challenge a — a — well, whatever the dash it was."

"Awfully plucky of her, *I* thought," said Ada.

"I was only trying to save the children," Jemma explained.

"But you can't save them if you are slaughtered in the attempt by a wood monster," her brother pointed out.

"At least you've taken my story seriously, and haven't numbered me with your collective lunatics. That's something!"

"Never, sis. Besides, it would appear our Snap here saw the monster as well, and his witness is as good as revealed truth."

"Revealed truth — or is it *dog*ma, in this case?" said Ada, cracking wise.

"My thanks to the both of you," Snap said with a yawn. He had resumed his winking and dozing on the hearth-rug, now that the thrill of his master's return had subsided, but had been keeping a flop-ear to the conversation.

"I believe I'll look in at the grammar school on my way home," Ada said, "and have a little chat with Alice Pingle. I'll inquire if any of her pupils have been excused from their lessons today."

"That's a capital idea," Richard nodded.

"I should have spoken to her after my talk with the vicar. But I assumed he already had questioned her about the children in the Tillington Road."

"Logic suggests that these are not Market Snailsby children, or slodger children either, for that matter, otherwise the vicar should have known them."

"You're probably right. But I shall make the attempt in any case. After all, one never knows."

"Then you'd best keep an eye open for our fair Mayor," Richard advised her. "He was on parade this morning when the coach drew up. Mrs. Chugwell had managed to clear out beforehand, but poor Matt was not so lucky. You know how Jagard annoys them with his bombast."

"Yes, you mustn't allow yourself to be drawn into a conversation with him," said Corney. "He can be quite the bore when he's rattling on about himself or his stables. As you know he fancies himself a great judge of horseflesh — which is rather a lark if you've seen that new hunter of his. So beware!"

"No matter what the subject is, he can turn it to himself in a trice. And you know how he 'dresses at' people, as though he simply must outshine them in every way, even in personal attire."

"Well, he has nothing to fear from Ada Henslowe on that score," Ada laughed, "for if he dressed like me he'd look ridiculous."

"He has always been that way, although perhaps a little more so since he gained higher office," Corney noted.

"I reckon this to be the fifth year of his glorious Mayoralty," said Richard, "and as no one else covets the job, I suppose we're stuck with him. As for what functions of significance he may perform for our little borough, I am wholly without an inkling."

"But surely a town needs its mayor?" said Ada, drawing on her gloves.

"Indeed it does," Jemma smiled, "but there's no need to be chatting with him. Good luck, dear. Let us know what you find out at the school."

"If I learn anything of interest I'll come round again in the afternoon. If you don't hear Spinach's hoofbeats in the drive, you'll know it was a wash-out."

"And stay clear of Jagard. You'll never be rid of him once he has you by the ear."

"Right. I'll see my way out, then. It's good to have you back with us, Richard."

After Ada had ridden off, the conversation underwent a slow and inevitable decline. The clock in the passage was sounding the hour, the cats were winking and stretching, and Snap had gone off in search of squirrel raiders when Corney at last took his leave. Richard got up and escorted his good friend and neighbor to the door. He then returned to the kitchen and with a brisk clap of his hands declared it was time to unpack his things and sort out his notes.

"I believe I'll have a change of togs," he said, then abruptly wheeled round, snapped his fingers, and exclaimed — "But first I must say hallo to our Rosie!"

So off to the stable he went, to pass a little time with the apple of his eye, and upon whom he had not laid that eye in almost a fortnight. On his return to the house he stumped upstairs to his bedroom, mumbling to himself something about rods and flies, and how he hadn't cast a hook in so long a time and was keen to get to the river again, the Fenshire weather permitting.

At the grammar school Ada learned from Miss Pingle, the pretty young schoolmistress, that only a single child had been absent that day — a boy, who had been quarantined for the measles at a farmstead westwards of town. Dr. Chevenix had seen him the previous afternoon and made the diagnosis. As for the children in the Tillington Road, Miss Pingle already had told the vicar that they were no pupils of hers. Perhaps, she suggested, they were visitors to town, and were lodging with their parents at the Broom and Badger?

Miss Henslowe thought this a possibility worth investigating, so she swung Spinach about and trotted him over the bridge to the inn.

The Broom and Badger was an ancient and a homely specimen of a posting-inn, in the full Fenshire style, with its tall gables, its latticed casements peeping from under the brows of a mossy roof, and its outdoor settle and horse-trough fronting the road. Hanging from a gibbet-arm above the entry was a board of painted wood depicting a plump little badger-wife, almost as homely as the inn itself, sweeping away the dust with a birch broom.

The fancied resemblance of the badger-wife to Mrs. Kitty Travers, the helpmate of the sober-eyed landlord, had been much remarked upon by the town wags. Fortunately for the wags, the character and temperament of Mrs. Travers were less in accord with a badger's than her likeness otherwise might have suggested.

Miss Henslowe found the landlord in his tap-room, but her inquiry turned up nothing of interest. There were no children at the inn, Mr. Travers informed her; further to that, he didn't believe there were any strangers in the town with children such as those Ada had described. It was a poor season for visiting, he explained. Things would be better come summertime, and better still the next year, of course, once the new road was in operation.

So Miss Henslowe thanked him for his trouble and set off for Short Street.

Hard by the Market Square her luck ran out. A strutting little bantam of a mustached gentleman stepped forth from the Guild-hall and, veering directly into her path, brought Spinach to a halt with a raised arm and a lofty halloo.

The gentleman was dressed to the nines in an outfit of very smart appearance — coat of cinnamon cloth with velvet facings, gaudy cravat, laced canary waistcoat, knee-shorts of powder-blue, and mahoganied top-boots. Crowning the tiptop of this magnificence was an elegant high hat, set on his head at a rakish angle. In one gloved hand he carried a fancy walking-stick, which it was the gentleman's habit to tap upon the ground when speaking, to give emphasis to some important point he had to convey.

"Ah, my dear Miss Henslowe, and how are you this morning?" he exclaimed, with a grand sweep of his topper. "And how have you been keeping yourself?"

"Very well, Mr. Jagard."

"And how has that charming mother of yours been keeping herself?" (The Mayor smoothing and smoothing his mustaches with a lordly thumb and finger).

"My mother has been dead these three years now, Mr. Jagard," Ada replied. "You were at her service in the church, as I recollect."

"Ah! Indeed. Of course, of course — remember it now. Sorry to hear. Well, well! So many details to keep track of. And how has this horse of yours been keeping himself, eh?"

"Spinach has been keeping himself very well, sir."

"Been keeping him in his bran mash and his oats, have you?"

"When I am able, sir."

"Ah! Indeed. Been tucking in his feed, has he? Well, well, he seems a serviceable little nag, if a trifle stoutish in the legs." (The Mayor tapping his stick upon the ground). "Free from vice, is he? Well, one can never tell. What do you call this color, then, eh? Motley? Skewbald? Ragged liver? And just look at that nose — nose-*bag*, more like. Well, well! And what have we here? What do you call this short, square paint-brush of a thing hanging here — a tail? And this ratch down his face, a blaze? Oh, and I don't care for the look of that ewe-neck — "

Hearing this litany of slanders directed against his person, Spinach cocked his ears, threw back his head, and snorted loudly —

"*Bother it!*"

The Mayor, unheeding, continued his inspection. "Rather a slow goer, I should think," he remarked, taking a brisk turn or two round the aforesaid little nag.

"He can go eight miles an hour in harness," Ada said brightly.

"Love you, dear!" Spinach exclaimed, batting his eyes at her.

"You see that he gets plenty of stable rest, do you?" inquired Mr. Jagard.

"Of course," Ada answered.

The Mayor sighed, heigh-ho, and shook his head with the topper on it. "Pity! For you know, Miss Henslowe, nothing ruins a horse so much as rest." (Down went the stick again).

"Pity *you!*" Spinach grunted, with a little sidling move towards the offender.

"He seems a trifle restive," Mr. Jagard observed. "Give us a look at his feet. Ah! Perhaps he requires the services of a smith?"

"Beef-brain!" snorted Spinach, dancing a little closer. "I'll show you feet, I think — "

The Mayor laughed softly, with an easy nonchalance, and patted the horse's shoulder.

"Ah, well! More's the pity. But we can't all be born thoroughbreds, now, can we, old fellow?"

"Nincompoop!" Spinach retorted, with an impatient jerk of his head.

How little the Mayor comprehended his reputation in horse society in the town!

"Spinach is in every way a thoroughbred to me, sir," Ada declared, trying not to draw the Mayor overtly into conversation, but resolved nonetheless to defend the honor of her stout little riding-horse.

"Ah! Indeed. Well, naturally. Full of spirits he is, too, I'm sure. Well, I suppose it's all that's left to him."

"Numskull! Ninnyhammer!" thundered Spinach.

"My hunter is doing rather nicely himself. Do you know him, Miss Henslowe? Jokester he's called, by Prince Padraic out of My Blue Lady. Why, he's as good as any three of these ordinary nags rolled into one." (Stick tapping again — three times).

"I'll roll *you* into one," Spinach warned.

The Mayor smiled suavely. "He's a great humorist is our Jokester, as you might suppose, always full of tricks. Not unlike myself in that regard! And he's a fast trotter to boot, very good in deep ground, and steady at his fences. Why, he can bound over a gate like a buck, and swims like a soap-bladder."

"Indeed?" said Ada, feigning interest.

"Oh, yes. Do you know, we give him a white radish twice a week. It's a delicacy for him, but of course we think him well worth it. After all, he's more than three times any of these trotty little cobs, now, isn't he?"

"*'Ware heels!*" Ada cried, as she felt Spinach give a plunge underneath her and lash out with his hooves. Fortunately for Mayor Walkadine Jagard, the aim of Spinach was a couple of atoms wide, thanks to the slippery cobbles of the High Street.

The Mayor went to recover his hat and stick — both had gone flying in his haste to get clear — and on his return was offered the sincerest of apologies by Miss Henslowe.

"No need, no need," the Mayor smiled, flicking a gob of mud from his topper. "Full of spirits, he is — well, it's just as I told you! Yes, I know a horse when I see one, Miss Henslowe. And a Fenshireman, you know, is nothing without his horse."

"And some even less," Spinach huffed. "White radishes indeed!"

"He's hardly ever brained anyone," Ada said in her horse's defense. She nearly added *who didn't need braining*, but had sufficient command to restrain herself. Truth be told she was hankering to be off home, and so was Spinach. But how to disengage herself from Mayor Jagard without giving offense, warranted or otherwise?

"I rejoice, and thank my stars every day I have such a fine, intelligent animal as Jokester," the Mayor sighed; and shaking his head in wonder at his good fortune, he placed his high hat *sans* mud back on the top of it.

"Bother your Jokester," Spinach grunted, peevishly — "and bother you besides!"

"I dare say you'll have noticed, Miss Henslowe, how a gentleman's horse will mirror the qualities of the gentleman himself?" Mr. Jagard remarked. (Tap! Tap!)

No, Ada replied, she had never noticed any such thing.

"Indeed? Well, well! And so how are you filling in your days, then? And how is that charming little mother of yours?"

This last query brought the discussion to a swift and a convenient close. Seizing her opportunity, Ada hastily excused herself and trotted off towards Short Street and home.

"Extraordinary happenstance!" boomed the Mayor, staring after her in surprise. "It seems our Miss Henslowe would be rid of me. Imagine that! A remarkable case. The poor woman must be sorely troubled." So saying the Mayor plucked forth his yellow gold watch, which dwelt at the bottom of a very yellow waistcoat-pocket. "Ah! Well, well — just look at the time. Lunch already!"

And striding off towards the bridge, stick in hand, he set course for the Broom and Badger, to inflict himself again upon Mr. Travers and the unsuspecting company of the inn.

THE FOURTH CHAPTER

ROUND THE TOWN

AS we follow in the steps of the Mayor, we see him stroll across the bridge to the Badger; then we see him pause in his stride before the house, and consider for a time; and then we see him pass the Badger by. Having refreshed the folk there with his presence already that morning, he has decided upon a change of venue; and putting on a brisk pace he fares instead to the Mudlark, where he will take his lunch in the company of Mr. Erskine Joliffe in the pleasing atmosphere of his ancient inn beside the river.

If the Mayor had kept to his intent and looked in at the Badger, he would have found the sober-eyed landlord and a host of the regulars in attendance there — Dr. Chevenix, Mr. Blathers, Lawyer Inkpen, and Mr. Ingo Swain amongst them. (The latter had brought some eels for the kitchen, and was waiting to be compensated for his trouble). The Mayor would have found them down in the tap-room of age-blackened oak, a warm fire hissing and crackling, and the company gathered in an attentive circle round Mrs. Nan Chugwell of Deadmarsh.

The good lady had seen her way clear to return — once the coast *vis-à-vis* Mayor Walkadine Jagard had itself cleared — and was regaling her audience with tales of her adventures since she had last visited their small corner of Fenshire. The crowd was hanging on her every word, and no one would have been happier than Mrs. Chugwell herself (aside perhaps from the landlord and his wife) that the perambulating Mayor had chosen to pass the Badger by — if, of course, they had known of it.

Shovel-tuskers and their drivers were a busy lot in those days, and their services were in fierce demand. Together Fenshire and Slopshire comprised the chief stamping-grounds, as it were, for the Chugwell team, and had so for quite a few years. There were many localities in these shires where the clearing of roads was a difficult business, owing to the uncertainty of the ground, to the scarcity of gravel beds and good alluvial soil, and to the wandering beasts of prey that ofttimes interfered with the work. But there was nothing under heaven — not a marsh devil, spotted lion, or short-faced bear — that could stop a thunder-beast, of whatever stripe; so that the road through Marley Wood was, for the Chugwells, simply another problem to be solved, another job to be completed.

Throughout, her audience marveled at the confidence exhibited by Mrs. Chugwell, who, as you know, was about the least likely-looking person in the world to be a mastodon driver. She had donned one of her prettiest frocks, and had had her hair "done up" in the town, and her cheeks rouged and powdered. She was, in short, about as pleasant, as fashionable, and at the same time as dignified a matronly woman of ample girth as one could meet in a month of Sundays.

In the early years Mrs. Chugwell had confined herself chiefly to the preparation of the meals for her family and the drivers. As a cook she had been a killer; but her amiable disposition had proved such an asset, that her husband had engaged her as his ally in their negotiations to broker new contracts for the team. The untimely death of Mr. Chugwell had thrust his widow into that position of authority she now held. As a result, thanks to the efforts of her son and Angus Daintie, she had been given free rein to focus her powers on the superintendence of the business, and had left her cooking days behind her.

"You must tell us of the short-face you ran upon at Threep," invited a gentleman amongst the listeners.

"Yes, yes, indeed you must, Mrs. Chugwell. Tell us of the short-face," enthused another.

"And the mylodon outside the Ring o' Bells at Ogghops," urged a third fellow.

"And the teratorns over to Paston Meadow," clamored a fourth.

Each of these requests the good lady very graciously fulfilled. In the course of her work Mrs. Chugwell had encountered nearly every size, shape, and species of wild creature known to prowl a sundered world. She had been aboard ship as well, and in sailing the long coast had beheld those far-famed demons of the deep, the mighty toothed whales called zeugs. More astonishing yet, she claimed to have seen imperial mammoths in the snowy wastes north of Saxbridge town. Although a few of the so-called "dwarf" mammoths were known from the southern islands round Nantle, the imperial species remained, in the popular imagination at least, an unverifiable legend.

And yet Mrs. Chugwell had seen them!

They dwelt, she said, amongst the glaciers, in a vast, frozen country where hardly anyone dared go, and where they had been spared the depredations of humankind. Mrs. Chugwell had seen woolly rhinoceroses there, too, and musk oxen, and snow-footed reindeer, and other ice-bound creatures, all of them living out their lives far removed from the sight of man.

"Aye, but sich things be not so troublesome in Fenshire," spoke up a thin, creaky little bald man, with a mustache on his lip and a patch on his eye. "The troubles in Fenshire be marsh devils, Mrs. Chugwell — spotted lions — flat-head boars — and ghosts in Marley Wood."

"Aye, that's telling it, Phoggie!" chorused some of his fellows.

"Sich be the dangers in that wood. Are ye sure, now, they'll not be troublesome once the road be cleared?"

"Well, sir," said Mrs. Chugwell, her face radiating that confidence all had wondered at, "marsh devils and spotted lions I know something of, ghosts I do not. You shall have your road, gentlemen, and a fine, wide road it shall be, too, and a straight one, with lots of verge. Think of it, gentlemen. Trains and coaches speeding through the wood from Market Snailsby to Ridingham — in under four hours!"

"Under four hours!" echoed her listeners, nodding and smiling at one another, their eyes aglow with admiration for this unlikeliest-looking fashionable lady of a mastodon driver.

"By ginger, that's a notion worth two," declared Mr. Blathers. In his excitement he turned his chair around and straddled it, adjusted his horn-rims (the better to see Mrs. Chugwell by), and tossed up a huge cloud of smoke from his pipe. "Ah, yes, a remarkable claim, and a remarkable number. And she says it with her head on! You, my good lady, are a remarkable woman. Is she not remarkable?"

"Remarkable!" applauded her admirers.

"Indeed," smiled a chipper young man with sticky-out ears — it was Lawyer Inkpen. "Mrs. Chugwell, as I have told you and your hard-working son, we are all of us greatly in your debt. Though that is but a figurative expression, of course, as the parish rates and the county-wide subscription and the excise have, to this point at least, admirably rewarded you for your services."

"Aye, she's cleared half the road now, and half the ten thousand pounds to boot," nodded the creaky little bald man.

"It's a hatful of money, but a hatful well laid out," stated the landlord.

"You shall have coaches galore plying your new road," Mrs. Chugwell promised them, "and so you need no longer be strangers to the north country. No more the long way round, through Tillington or Dragonthorpe. No more the endless weary hours, the insupportable conditions, the breakdowns in the miry ruts and the dangers attendant therein. No more bogs and marshes, gentlemen!"

"No more bogs and marshes!" they marveled.

"I see we shall have to change our notice there," said Mr. Travers, by which he meant the small signboard that hung on a wall of his taproom, and which read as follows —

☞ LETTERS DISPATCHED AT 8¹/₂ EVERY MONDAY AND THURSDAY MORNING BY THE WESTERN COACH, BY WAY OF DRAGONTHORPE, LOCKSLEY, RIDINGHAM, AND NEWMARSH.

"No more bogs and marshes?" echoed Mr. Swain, who appeared a trifle confused. "Well, how can it follow? For Lord bless us, there be little else but bogs and marshes in this county."

"Aye, and besides, Phoggie won't take to it," chuckled one wag, "for Phoggie's one as calls a bog and a marsh a home. Ain't that so, old glossy-pate?"

The creaky little bald man, who went by the name of Phoglander Finlayson, shot out of his chair. Mr. Finlayson, as you know, was a fen-slodger, a denizen of the marshes — one of those sturdy souls who lived by fowling and fishing, and who knew every firm tussock path, every sluice, every dyke, every bog, and every thicket in the country roundabout. But as he dwelt not far from Market Snailsby he considered himself a townsman, too, and unlike many of his fellows took a lively interest in civic affairs.

"I bean't for bogs and marshes, George Crumpler, when they sink roads and livelihoods!" he retorted, staring down his opponent with his single eye like a Cyclops, before resuming his seat.

"Ah, well, sir — perhaps you should speak to Mr. Erskine Joliffe as to the advisability of *that*," suggested Mr. Blathers, with a wry smile.

As you'll recollect, Mr. Joliffe was that single man in town whose wish it was that Market Snailsby should remain the serene, unspoiled, untroubled little backwater that it always had been — in brief, that it should remain free of new roads. Mr. Joliffe had gained a reputation as a dissenter in the matter of the road-clearing ("anything for a quiet life" was his motto, which he had posted on a signboard in the tap-room of *his* establishment, and which he entirely lived by), and was not looking forward to the rise in traffic. He was sure that society in the town would become irreparably unstitched by trains and coaches speeding between Market Snailsby and Ridingham in under four hours.

"Now, then, we all know Mr. Joliffe's position," said Dr. Chevenix, a neat, dapper little man with silky gray eyes and a clipped mustache.

"And as a citizen of this town he has a right to his opinion," noted Mr. Inkpen. "But there is little doubt this new thoroughfare will be a boon to us all. Bogs or no bogs, marshes or no marshes, we must re-join the wider world. We are Fenshiremen, after all — and Fenshire-women too, by your leave, Mrs. Chugwell — and Newmarsh is our county town. How many of you in this room, may I ask, have visited our county town in the past year?"

Two raised their hands — young Mr. Inkpen himself, who was a frequent traveler on lawyerly concerns, and Mr. Blathers.

"And Ridingham?"

Again Mr. Inkpen and Mr. Blathers.

"Do you see? We are hopelessly isolated here," the attorney went on. "The contact will do us a wonder of good. You do know how we are viewed in Newmarsh, do you not? 'Yokels' they call us there, and 'bumpkins,' 'wet-shods,' and other things far worse. That is what they say about us in Newmarsh. That is how we are portrayed in our own county town! And so how are we to dispel this false view, gentlemen and lady? Do you know how *I* should dispel it?"

"Bring a suit in law for defamation," suggested Mr. Blathers, with satirical amusement.

"*Tee-hee!*" somebody snickered.

Lawyer Inkpen shook his head — a surprising denial for a gentle-man of his profession.

"I think not," said he, waving aside the recommendation, and the snicker. "Knowledge, gentlemen and lady — knowledge! We shall dem-onstrate to the worthy citizens of our county town that we are *not* yokels or bumpkins — certainly not wet-shods — by encouraging them to visit us, thereby improving trade and communication, and allowing them to know us better. That knowledge, gentlemen and lady, is how we shall dispel this false view."

Dr. Chevenix touched a finger to his mustache, a mischievous smile playing across his lips. A small, delicate man, the doctor looked and acted vaguely French, despite his claim of descent from certain Hoddinotts of the old Welsh marches.

"Perhaps, Arnold," said he, "we should not wish for *too* many to be thronging in. For if the Newmarshers begin visiting in their hordes, then surely they'll come to see us for what we really are — hobnails and chaw-bacons!"

This remark produced some huge guffaws amongst the professional men in the audience, but not a titter amongst the rustic majority, who could be seen scratching their collective heads in puzzlement. At this juncture Mrs. Travers — the plump little badger-wife of the inn-sign — came trotting in with Mr. Swain's reward for his catch of eels. The eel-trap man nodded his thanks, slipped the coins into his pocket, and departed the house, rattling a little as he went.

Mrs. Chugwell had informed her listeners that tomorrow was the appointed day when she and her son were to inspect the new road. If all went as planned, the shovel-tuskers and their drivers, commanded by Angus Daintie, would be sent for at once to begin the season's operations.

"Aye, but what of the ghosts, then? What of the hunters and their specter-hounds, and the devilish park-keeper? Will you oust them for us, Mrs. Chugwell?" one of her listeners wanted to know.

"Aye, for they need to be kept down," said another.

"Send 'em packing!" urged a third. It was young Mr. Murcott, the postie, and son-in-law of the landlord.

"There are no ghosts in that wood — scientifically speaking," said Mr. Blathers. "That is my declared view of it, and that will be Dick Hathaway's view as well, as soon as I tell him of it. Humph!"

To underscore the firmness of his opinion — and his general disdain for popular superstition — Mr. Blathers took out his handkerchief and very publicly blew his nose in it.

"But Sir Hector found no tracks where the keeper was, and but a few hoofprints round the wood," Mr. Travers pointed out.

"Nor any sign of hounds, either," his wife added. "It's for sure unsettling, Mr. Blathers, for what can they be but ghosts and demons that leave no trace?"

"Aye, Kitty is right. The people are full of vague fears, and Sir Hector's search has done nowt to reassure them."

"If it bean't ghosts and demons in the wood hatching some plot agin us, then I don't know what it be," declared Mr. Finlayson.

"Although I abominate all ghosts and demons," stated Lawyer Ink-pen, calmly, "I should hesitate to render a judgment at this time. An absence of evidence is not necessarily evidence of absence."

"I have traveled much throughout these towns and counties," said Mrs. Chugwell, "and never once have I spied either ghost or demon."

"Ah, but my dear lady," Dr. Chevenix returned dryly, "have you looked for them?"

"I have not," answered the lady, with a crinkly smile. "But just the same, neither have they looked for *me*."

"It's squatters in that wood, sure as you're alive," was the opinion of Farmer Dillweed, a lanky old yeoman with a great white shaving-brush of chin whiskers, "and with no more brain than a stone to be squatting there. Real queer potatoes they must be."

"Aye — nut hatches!" nodded Mr. Murcott.

"There may be marsh devils, and teratorns, and flat-heads in that wood — and perhaps other things besides, as I've lately learned," said Mr. Blathers, a trifle mysteriously; but not a word of Miss Hathaway's secret did he divulge. Then, to clarify, he added — "I refer to other things of a beastly nature, not a ghostly."

"True, sir; but it's said that nowt, beastly or otherwise, can stop a shovel-tusker. Isn't that so, Mrs. Chugwell?" said the landlord.

To no one's surprise, Mrs. Chugwell expressed her wholehearted agreement with this view; at which point a waiter entered to announce that the good lady's early dinner had been laid on in her private room.

"It's spitchcock today — fried eel — courtesy of Mr. Swain," Mrs. Travers informed her. "He is our eel man, as you know."

The Broom and Badger was justly famed for its cheesecakes, nappy ales, and cream of pumpkin soup, but it was known almost as well for its spitchcock and eel-pies and other like delectables. Mrs. Chugwell found the dinner entirely to her taste, and was assured by the landlady that young Matt would receive his share just as soon as he returned. He was out on the Common at the moment, parading Ranger before some of the town children. The shovel-tusker was far and away the grandest and most magnificent thunder-beast ever to have rumbled through those parts, and his arrival each year always constituted a spectacle.

Meantime Dr. Chevenix had taken up his bag and excused himself, saying he had a call to make on that antique specimen of a widower, Mr. Wackwire. As he was climbing into his dog-cart, the doctor spied

Mr. Erskine Joliffe outside his inn a short ways up the road; and so he prodded his horse in that direction, intending to have a little chat with the meditative host of the Mudlark and subject of the recent gowking.

The innkeeper, clad in his usual tweeds, was standing with his arms folded and his pipe in his lips, admiring the view across the Fribble. The Mayor had taken his leave of him, and Mr. Joliffe had come up for some air. It was fresh air, it was cool air, it was Fenshire air! It was calm and peaceful outside his inn, and the voice of the river murmuring at his feet sounded very sweetly in his ear. It was but one of the many voices in that marshy landscape that Mr. Joliffe so treasured.

Having exchanged a few minutes' pleasantries with Mine Host, the doctor swung his cart about and resumed his errand. Over the bridge he went, and through the town and out of it. On every side of him the trees were shedding small tears under the influence of spring. As he came near Mead Cottage he slowed his horse and drew rein; for there, stretched out at his full leisurely length upon the garden wall, was a drowsing Herbert Hathaway.

As the dog-cart came alongside, Herbert opened his eyes and voiced a greeting. The doctor and Herbert were kindred spirits of a sort. In their own ways both were enamored of the wild, mysterious, lonely beauty of the fens. "There's nothing in this busy world worth taking seriously" was Herbert's motto, and, in the doctor's view, a very tempting one it was, too.

Truth be told, Dr. Chevenix had found himself in something of a quandary of late. He had been thinking that, if he had it to do over again, he might have sided with Mr. Joliffe in the matter of the new road. Purely and simply, the doctor believed he had made an error. Business might be business in the view of men like Arnold Inkpen; but was it not the case as well that Market Snailsby was Market Snailsby?

What need was there to "rejoin the wider world"? For what was there in Newmarsh or Ridingham, or in Fishmouth for that matter, to compare with the serenity of these marshes?

"Ah, what, indeed?" smiled Herbert, gazing round him with a blissful eye. "Anything, my dear doctor, for a quiet life!"

PART FOUR

THE FIRST CHAPTER

TELLS OF MARLEY WOOD

DAWN, and the citizens of Market Snailsby are still largely abed as a party of riders makes its way across the bridge into Holy Street. It is a small party, as parties of riders go, being possessed of only five mounts; but it is an impressive party all the same, because the mighty Ranger is numbered amongst the five.

All along the route, yawning, blinking faces appear at windows, and shivering figures in doorways, to watch in silent amaze as the parade passes by. Mostly they are watching Ranger's majestic figure, as it goes sweeping past them with its long, rolling stride, like an ocean galleon under sail through the dim and misty streets. With every step the giant takes, the ground underfoot quivers a little; so that if the citizens still abed have not been alerted to his presence before he thunders past, they most certainly have afterwards.

Ranged ahead of the tusker are four men on horseback. Riding point on his favorite gelding is Sir Hector MacHector, resplendent in full riding-dress with silver buttons, baldric, and jabot. With one hand on the pommel of his saddle and the other holding the whip and reins, he stands as straight and tall in the stirrups as the twin feathers of his Balmoral bonnet. Behind him ride the gillies on their sturdy cobs, and Mr. Shand on his hunter. Men and mounts alike are fitted out with a splendid show of arms — dirks and cutlasses, claymores and falchions, and deadly short swords or "whingers" of bladed Scotch steel.

Occupying the cab atop Ranger's shoulders are Mrs. Chugwell and Matt, Vicar Ludlow, and Mr. Richard Hathaway. Security in their airy perch is guaranteed by Ranger himself; but that has not kept young Matt from packing a trusty sword or two, and Richard his best cutlass. Mr. Ludlow, avid sportsman though he was, never carried steel out of deference to his vocation. But though no one but a hare-brain would be fool enough to brave the wood nowadays — or so he had informed Miss Hathaway — this road survey of Mrs. Chugwell's the vicar considered a special case; so that, for today at least, he had suspended his usual objection to wood-braving.

Having left the vicarage and the Church of All Hallows behind them, the party made steadily for the edge of town, passing Short Street and the cottage of Miss Henslowe along the way, and Blossom's Court and the old cherry gardens. A little farther on, past the town limits, an avenue of recent construction appeared which diverged from the main track. Into this the riders directed their mounts.

Upon their left rose a sinister object, black and grim, bearing a shaft and crossbeam, and chains creaking in the morning air. It was the old town gallows, with its rusted gibbet-irons — deserted now, but a place where once, in ruder times, crowds had gathered to see thieves and pickpockets launched to their just rewards. Beyond the gallows lay a dreary meadow, stretching off towards another deserted place — the dismal black pool known as Goblin Mere.

Directly ahead of them stood the towering curtain of Marley Wood. Unlike Miss Hathaway, who had found herself immured in a gloomy maze of dimness and enclosure, the riders, upon their approach, found something rather different: a cleared path leading straight through the wood. It was the new road, the fruit of the past seasons of labor by the Chugwell team of shovel-tuskers and their drivers, wood-cutters, and navvies. Some ghostly wisps of fog could be seen drifting across its surface, which was sprinkled here and there with a few late patches of snow. Above it hung a narrow gray ribbon of sky, lighting the way between the packed masses of timber which bordered the road on either side.

So into the wood they went, Sir Hector and the other horsemen keeping a careful watch below as the Chugwells set about their examination of the road and its verge. Stumps of trees which had been grubbed up in prior seasons, and whose boles and branches had been used to construct the roadbed, could be seen scattered about the underwood. It was in fact a plank road that Ranger and the horses were traversing, the planks having been hewn from the trees that had stood there, then laid side-by-side and embedded in pitch, and buried under a layer of crushed stones, gravel, and asphaltum. It was a signal improvement over the miry coach-roads that circled the wood to the east and west, one made possible by the shorter length of the new thoroughfare and the firmer ground upon which it lay.

The vicar was enthusiastic in his praise. "Beyond question, this will be the finest avenue in the marshlands," he exclaimed.

"I agree, it's capital," nodded Richard. "What a marvel it will be when it is done!"

"No more bogs and marshes, gentlemen," smiled Mrs. Chugwell, in gracious acceptance of the compliments. "So I have promised you, and so you shall have it."

For several hours the party made sure and steady progress. Mile gave way to mile, as Sir Hector and his fellows, their eagle-eyes roving into every nook and corner, kept alert for the marsh devils, spotted lions, and flat-head boars that prowled the forest aisles, and the winged teratorns that haunted its upper terraces. All about them small birds were twittering and cooing, woodpeckers were knock-knock-knocking, and squirrels were leaping and barking — signs of a benevolent nature that accorded well with the pleasant jingle of harness from horse and tusker, the squeaking of saddles, and the *trit-trot, trit-trot* of iron shoes.

Less pleasant were the menacing roars, bloodthirsty shrieks, and sinister howls that periodically rang out in the wood, at times far off in the distance, and at other times uncomfortably near at hand. Often the voice of a marsh devil was heard amongst the bestial choir, which caused the horses to shy a little and toss their manes, and snort fiercely into the air. Even the mighty Ranger became a trifle restive, lifting his trunk and swinging his huge, long-jawed head from side to side as he probed for clues with his delicate senses.

Even worse were the vague forms and stealthy shapes that were seen slinking about the trees, or striding through the shadows of the underwood. Often this was accompanied by a feeling of eyes watching from afar — any action on the part of the watcher being restrained, no doubt, by Ranger's colossal presence. It was clear to everyone that the dim and gloomy forest aisles were teeming with savage life.

In proof of this — as if further proof were needed — were the frequent sightings of dead animals, lying either in the road itself or along the verge. Most often the remains were those of some unfortunate herbivore; occasionally, however, the carcass of some larger, more fearsome beast was encountered. Each new discovery served as a reminder to the travelers of the potent dangers that surrounded them. Deep, ancient, and mysterious was Marley Wood, and full of secrets!

As they proceeded they would sometimes run across a snarl of timber where a tree, either from age, disease, fire, or other cause, had collapsed onto the roadbed. The location of each was duly noted by Mrs. Chugwell; whereupon Matt would give the order, and Ranger would slip his long jaw and tusks beneath the fallen giant and with a mighty heave send it flying from the roadway, as easily as a deal in a timber-yard. Then they would resume their trek, the rhythmic *pound! pound! pound!* of the tusker's feet and the jingle of harness joining in concert as they drove ever deeper into the wood.

As the time passed Sir Hector and the other horsemen gradually be-came conscious of something in motion behind the trees on their right hand. Curiously, whenever the men would rein in their mounts the movement would cease; when they spurred their horses on again, how-ever, it promptly resumed. They scoured the dimness with their eyes, trying to spot their elusive shadow but never finding it. They were left with the uncomfortable sensation that they were being followed, that their every thought, every action was being carefully scrutinized.

High up in the cab, too, the feeling was palpable.

"What *is* it out there?" Richard wondered aloud. "For, dash it all, it has been trailing us for these several miles now. I don't mind saying it's giving me a case of the jitters."

Young Matt shook his head. "I don't know what it is, sir, but it does seem to be dogging us. I've caught a glimpse of — of — well, of *something*, I believe, now and then. At first I thought it was a horse, but now I'm not so sure. What do you think, Mother?"

"My gracious, I simply cannot tell, although the fact that it is there can scarcely be doubted," the good lady replied. "Whatever it may be, however, it's for certain neither a ghost nor a demon, that I'll warrant. What do you say, vicar?"

"A horse — bearing one of our phantom riders, perhaps?" Mr. Lud-low suggested.

"A rider very likely, but hardly a phantom. For I've never known the wild horse that would trail an armed party and a tusker for mile upon mile on its own account."

"I thought perhaps it was carrying someone, when first I saw it, but now perhaps not. More than likely it was no horse at all," said Matt.

"If not a horse, then what?" Richard asked. He was thinking of his sister's encounter with a certain snake-necked monstrosity, which, for the time being, he was bound to keep a secret.

"As I did not see it myself, sir, I cannot offer an opinion," said Mrs. Chugwell. "Although we have had such an experience before, have we not, Matt?"

During each of the prior seasons, as her son now explained, there had been reports by the workers of strange flittings in the wood, and tracking movements, and a sensation of eyes watching from a distance. It was observation not so much by beastly eyes, most felt, but by eyes possessed of a certain intelligence. The spy had never revealed himself, but a common finding had been the presence of a horse's hoofprints in the areas where the team had been at work.

The young man's story was interrupted by a sudden flash in the air overhead. A huge, feathered shape with wings outstretched went gliding across the ribbon of sky. The creature was perfectly black save for its head and neck, which were dyed a brilliant crimson.

"Teratorn!" Matt exclaimed, craning out the cab-window. "And there — look there — another!"

The raised hands of Sir Hector and his fellows indicated that they too had spied the winged ill omens of the air, which were hovering at a level just above the tree-tops.

"They'll not be so brazen as to attack with Ranger on the watch," Mrs. Chugwell assured her guests. She called down to the horsemen — "Let us move along, gentlemen. For we must complete the survey and return the many miles to town before nightfall."

Everyone was very much aware of that, and so they pushed on with renewed firmness and resolve, despite the danger lurking in the sky above their heads. The winged ill omens, meantime, seeing that they were outmatched, soon drifted off in search of other prey.

Not long after, horses and tusker were brought to a halt by a stand of trees that barred the way ahead, marking the point where the last year's work had left off. Here the road ended for the present, and the new season's operations soon were to begin. Somewhere beyond the stand of trees — many, many miles beyond it, on the far side of the wood — lay Ridingham; but it would be late next year yet before the road reached it.

Thus far this plank road of Mrs. Chugwell's had borne the Fenshire snows rather nicely. True, there had been those few fallen trees, and some places where the roadbed needed strengthening, owing to a general looseness of the ground; but for the most part the survey members were delighted with what they had seen.

They were stopped now, of course, and could proceed no farther. The cord-ladder had been unfurled from the cab, so that the passengers might descend for a time and stretch their legs. It was at this juncture that Sir Hector, having alighted from his gelding, called attention to a trail of prints in the soft earth at the roadside. The tracks were relatively fresh, and had been made by a single horse which had crossed the road at that point before returning to the sinister domain beyond the verge. Interestingly, the animal had worn no shoes.

Was it simply a wild horse, Richard asked himself — or a mounted rider? One of the ghostly horde, perhaps — or a stray sportsman from parts unknown, as Corney had suggested? But the ghostly riders, as Sir Hector reminded everyone now, had left no trail to follow. The horse that had left these tracks might be unknown to them, but it was no phantom.

Mr. Shand suggested that it belonged to one of the squatters, and, if so, then perhaps the ancient lodge of de Clinkers lay somewhere close at hand.

But it was the road, not ancient lodges, that was the chief concern of Mrs. Chugwell and her son. The two now commenced a brief inspection of the way forward of the terminus, and in consultation with their charts began to outline certain improvements to their plan for the coming season. Meantime the reeve, in mental consultation with his missing map, was attempting to work out, with the aid of a compass, the direction in which lay the lost hunting-seat of de Clinkers. In this effort he was joined by Sir Hector and the gillies, Vicar Ludlow, and Richard.

It was not long before the eerie sensation of unseen eyes watching was upon them again, and upon the animals, too. The mighty Ranger could be seen turning his head this way and that, and shifting his great weight from foot to foot, while the horses, their ears cocked, nervously sniffed the air and pawed the ground with their hooves.

What was it? *Where* was it? Round which tree or shrub were the stealthy eyes peering?

"There!" Haggis abruptly whispered, his attention fixed on a point in the darkness beyond the verge. "'Tis there, by ma certie. A shadow moving atwixt the trees!"

"Na, na," Jorkens answered back, "'tis ower there, Mr. Haggis — ower there!" And he indicated a spot some distance removed from the first.

"Hoot, toot, man," returned Haggis, with a fierce glance, "are ye blind? 'Tis *there!* Aye, 'tis plain eneugh — or sae it did seem — "

"I don't know where it is," said Mr. Shand, looking very pale and sober under his wide-awake, "but I know it is there somewhere. We are being watched, of that I am certain."

The Laird, sweeping the area with his commanding gaze, voiced his agreement. "Aye, 'tis right y'are, Willie. Hum! An' an unco' devilish thing it is, too."

"What d'ye take it for, Laird? A marsh devil?" Jorkens asked.

"Na, na. For the horses, man, they seem no sae mich afeart o' the thing, as boggled by it," Sir Hector replied. "D'ye no see that?"

"Aye — so it is, Laird."

"I agree," nodded Mr. Shand, "for my hunter there knows a marsh devil when he smells one, and he's not smelling one now. It is something else, in my estimation. A flat-head, perhaps?"

"No sae vera probable, Willie, nor a short-face either, for sic a monster hard by wad ha' driven the nags tae bolting, sure. Belike 'tis some lesser creature," said the Laird.

"Or something the like of which we know nothing," was Richard's thought, as his mind turned again to his sister's story. He pointed his sword in the direction favored by the burly little bulldog. "I am inclined to Haggis's view — I think it is *there*. And I for one should very much like to know what it is."

"Then we maun gang thegither an' oust it," said Sir Hector, in a determined voice, "for sure 'tis been fashious for a wee while the noo — whateffer it be."

The way was too thickly crowded with trees to allow for Ranger to pass, but not so the horses. Quickly Sir Hector, the gillies, and Mr. Shand mounted to their saddles. Richard, wanting very much to join them, to his disappointment was obliged to stay behind — for to accompany them on foot, even with his good cutlass at the ready, was to invite disaster.

Leaving the light of the roadway behind them, the riders plunged into the heavy gloom of the firs and pines. The air in the wood was cold and dank, and had an earthy savor. Here and there thick drifts of snow stained the forest floor. In some places the ground was tough and hard, and clattered under the horses' feet; elsewhere it was as soft as sponge cake. The thoughts of the men were trained upon their errand, however, as they made cautiously for the place where Haggis had spied his shadow atwixt the trees.

A sudden exclamation from Mr. Shand drew their eyes to something lying upon the snow nearby. As they gathered round it they saw that it was another carcass, that of a stag, or what remained of it. Like the hoofprints, it was relatively fresh; what had caught the attention of the reeve, however, was the broken shaft of an arrow that was sticking out of it.

"Squatters!" he whispered.

"Ma certie, 'tis plain as a packsaddle," nodded Haggis.

Someone had been bow-hunting in the wood, and quite recently, too. So much for the ghostliness of *that* hunter! Moreover, the stag had been butchered where it lay — hardly the work of a marsh devil or some wandering scavenger.

The horses, which had been sniffing curiously at the remains, all at once lifted their heads. Again there had been movement in the wood; again the watchful, unseen eyes were upon them. As the men readied their weapons, a slight noise reached their ears — the sound of hooves crunching snowy turf.

"Dooms me, ma gillies," whispered Sir Hector, "but 'tis frae the clumber pine ower yont that the gangrel be spyin' on us."

"That tree there?" said Mr. Shand.

"Aye, Willie. D'ye no see him keekin' round it?"

It was true. From behind the bole of the tree a figure could be seen peering, its eyes studying them from the shadows. Still as a stone it stood, almost like a shadow itself; but there was no disputing its reality.

"*There!*" whispered Haggis.

"No a doubt aboot it," Jorkens declared.

"I see it, too," nodded the reeve.

All looked to the Laird for guidance. He did not take long over his decision.

"Calmly, ma men," he said. Speaking softly to his horse, he nudged the gelding forward with his heels. The horse did not particularly relish the thought of challenging whatever was hiding behind the clumber pine; but, like the gillies, he trusted wholly and completely in the leadership of his master.

They had advanced but a few paces when the figure suddenly withdrew behind the tree. Moments later a drum of hoofbeats was heard retreating into the wood.

"We maun gang after him, an we're tae fathom it oot," urged Sir Hector. "But be ware, men — an' be canny."

Behind the tree they discovered some fresh prints identical to those Sir Hector had found at the roadside. Hoofprints they were, made by a horse without shoes.

For some minutes the men gave chase, losing the trail in the gloom and finding it, and then losing it again, and finding it again. After a time it became unclear just which trail they were following; for in the interim other tracks had begun to appear, laid down at different times, that crossed and re-crossed one another, and made a general confusion of the matter. Some looked to be days older than the rest, while the freshest prints — those they thought marked the retreat of their spy — had all but disappeared.

It seemed they had lost the trail for good.

With the menacing forest close about them on every side — the dim and shadowy corridors, the echoing beastly roars, and the ever-present threat posed by the dread Carnivora — no one was keen on remaining any longer, now that their hope of finding the spy had evaporated. So they wheeled their horses about and started to pick their way back through the maze in the direction they believed the road lay. The horses, like the horsemen, were very glad of this decision, for they too were anxious to return to the safety of the road and Ranger.

Sir Hector was mentally reproaching himself for not having brought a good trailing-hound or two, when the voice of Haggis jarred him from his thoughts.

"Perish me, Laird, but 'tis a thing suspect ower yont!"

Away to their left lay a clearing of sorts — a rarity in the wood — one which they had passed earlier while trailing their spy, but had given no mind. In this direction Haggis now spurred his horse, to the general surprise of his companions. But the sharp blue eyes of the gillie had descried something of importance, and so the Laird and the others turned and followed after him. Not far from the clearing they rejoined the burly little bulldog where he had pulled up and was awaiting them.

What the gillie had espied was a pair of stone columns, standing some ten feet apart, and partially concealed by the thick overhang of the trees. Each was topped by a couchant marsh devil, wrought in the

same stone as the columns but heavily eroded. The columns themselves were cracked and moldering and splotched with lichens. Between
them hung two tall gates of hammered iron adorned with many a
flourish and scroll, all of it decayed and rusted. Hoofprints similar to
those the men had been following showed in the earth hard by.

The gates had been latched shut but were not locked. But it was
what lay beyond them that claimed the chief of the men's attention.

Peering through the ironwork their eyes traveled down a lengthy
causeway of boarded planks, which stretched across a wide ditch to a
second pair of gates. Behind the gates a block of buildings could be
seen in the clearing beyond the trees.

"Gate piers topped by couchant devils," murmured Mr. Shand, "and
a railed passage ahead, spanning what likely was a moat, with a stout
and commodious mansion beyond it — all of it just as in the mezzotint
in the library at Newmarsh . . ."

"Aye, that lost map o' yers looks tae ha' been right handy, Willie,"
nodded Sir Hector, with quiet excitement. "'Tis the auld hurley-hoose
i'the wood — by St. Poppo, man, 'tis the secret lodge o' de Clinkers!"

THE SECOND CHAPTER

...AND WHAT WAS DISCOVERED THERE

ALL was still and silent behind the gates, as Sir Hector and his companions searched the dimness with their eyes, trying to make out what they could of the lodge beyond the causeway.

The tall trees appeared to surround, but had not entirely overgrown, the ancient hunting-seat; thus most of its fabric stood exposed to the gray Fenshire light. It consisted of a number of wings of varied styles and heights, all grouped round a central courtyard. Their fronts, some of which jutted out at odd angles, faced onto the court, while their conjoined backs formed the protective, castle-like exterior of the lodge. The building material looked to be chiefly fieldstone and brick, with a smattering of timber. So much the observers were able to discern from their vantage-point, but no more, their view of the structure being impeded by the heavy overhang of the trees.

The ditch that encircled the compound had once contained water, but was filled now with a sticky morass, the remains of centuries of decay of needles, cones, leaves, dead bark and boughs of trees, and other debris. Likely it had been some hundreds of years since the moat had been dredged, and it looked it.

Sir Hector and his companions put their heads together. It had just gone afternoon, by the Laird's watch, and there appeared to be plenty of time left for the return to Market Snailsby. The Laird reminded the others that, so far as any knew, no one alive had set foot in the lodge of de Clinkers, and sae was it no right and proper the noo that they should be the first? But it was Mr. Shand — he who had joined the survey not only to inspect the road, but on the odd chance that the lodge might be discovered — who sounded a hesitant note. What if the squatters were there, he worried, and in their numbers? Had he and the others ample force to repel them? To this the Laird replied that he did not know, but hoots, man, was it no their bounden duty tae look intae it? It was an answer with which the amiable brewer, in his capacity as fen-reeve and overseer of the parish lands, had little choice but to agree.

The gillies meantime offered to fetch any others amongst the party who might wish to view the lodge, and in so doing thereby increase the size of their forces; and so off they rode. They returned shortly with Richard Hathaway riding awkwardly "pick-a-back" on Haggis's cob, and Vicar Ludlow on that of Jorkens. Both men were eager to examine the storied lodge of de Clinkers, and had seized the opportunity at once, leaving the Chugwells to their professional researches in the company of Ranger.

Straightway Sir Hector drew the latch and opened the gates. The rusted, drooping forms creaked and jarred noisily on their hinges. Directly within stood a small gate-house, vacant and forlorn, its windows gauntly staring like the eye-holes of a skull. The causeway before them was railed on both sides, and overhead as well. Men and mounts filed across it in haste; and passing through the inner gates, which too were unlocked, they emerged into the light of the clearing.

Strange, the vicar thought, for squatters not to have secured the chief portal of their hideaway. The causeway appeared to be the sole means of access to the lodge. Almost at once the answer came to him — what need was there for securing? What need to guard against human encroachment in a place like Marley Wood? What need for locking gates where there was no one to invade one's privacy?

They were now in the courtyard of the lodge. Like the gate-house it was deserted, and eerily quiet save for the clink of their horses' shoes on the paving-stones. They spent some minutes observing the various features of interest that presented themselves to view. The design of the lodge was highly irregular, with its riot of gables fancifully carved in the old Dutch manner, its nests of chimneys twisted and turreted, and its many windows, some with antique-fashioned casements, others tall and gracefully arched. The walls and what could be seen of the roof were, like the gate-piers, heavily stained and mottled. To no one's surprise, much of the lodge looked a woeful ruin; from its crumbling stonework to its pitted façades of brick and timber, it was like some gloomy architectural leviathan that had begun to shed its skin.

The once proud and flourishing hunting-seat of de Clinkers was more like the ghost of a house than a house. A time-eaten ruin, a bleak remnant of a vanished age was the Laird's "auld hurley-hoose i'the wood." Yet in spite of it all it remained possessed of a weird, romantic sort of beauty — a beauty which was not easily defined, and whose effect was not easily shaken off.

Richard noted how closely the buildings resembled those in the mezzotint in the library at Newmarsh, that same to which Mr. Shand had made reference. He and Sir Hector then gave voice to a wish, were it in their power, to turn back the wheel of time and observe the lodge as it had been in its vanished youth, when Godfrey de Clinkers was there; to see the revels of the sportsmen, the merry gibes, the wassail and the mirth, the feasting, and the preparations for the chase; nor were Vicar Ludlow and Mr. Shand long in seconding the motion. So mournful a picture did the lodge present now, so strange and so silent, so much *of another world,* that they half-expected a ghostly park-keeper in green to step out from the shadows and accost them for trespass.

There seemed to be no one about the place, no sign of hounds in the kennels or horses in the stables, which looked as dreary and empty as the gate-house, and likely had been so for a very long time. And so where were the squatters keeping their animals? Perhaps, the thought crept upon Sir Hector and his companions, there were no squatters at the lodge at all . . .

And yet — here and there, amidst the mud and slush and cracked stones of the courtyard, were the traces of hoofprints. The gillies were the first to call attention to them, and to note their similarity to the tracks they had been following in the wood and had seen outside the gates. Someone had visited the lodge recently, but just who it was they had no means of knowing. The feeling of unseen eyes upon them had all but evaporated since they had crossed the causeway; indeed, they felt safer there in the courtyard, hemmed in all round by the sheltering walls of the lodge, than they had at any time in the wood.

They left their horses in the yard and mounted the steps of the nearest wing. As they approached the entrance, Mr. Shand gave a little start and pointed to the handles of the double-doors, each of which had been fashioned in the shape of a grotesquely-carved human hand.

"Dear me," blinked the vicar, "how very strange."

"Outlandish!" proclaimed Jorkens.

"An interesting feature," commented Richard, who had heard something of the lodge's architectural peculiarities from his friend Blathers.

Leering at them from over the entrance was a sculpted horn-player, and beside it a gargoyle with its nose struck off. Flanking the doors were two uncomfortably-realistic portrayals in stone of slinking cats

— a marsh devil on the left, a spotted lion on the right. The doors themselves were composed of two large oak panels hung on ornamental hinges, with locks and fastenings of an unusual design.

But as was the case with the gates, the locks were not in use. Seeing this, Sir Hector strode boldly forward and, grasping the carved hands in his, threw open the doors.

Inside was a foyer, or vestibule — very tall, very cold, and very dark. Again, as in the courtyard, the visitors were greeted by silence.

"By rights we should be considered intruders," Richard remarked, glancing round, "but after so many years the title has reverted to the county and parish, I suppose."

The vicar nodded. "Yes, it is in Mr. Shand's bailiwick now."

Sir Hector drew their attention to a pair of standing brass candlesticks on a table, and the tinder-box beside them.

"Ye'll note, ma men," he observed, "that the mutton-fats there be o' recent usage. 'Tis a sign the hurley-hoose be no sae lonely after a'."

Throwing open another double-door — it too had human hands for handles, but of the skeletal kind — they entered a chamber very long and lofty, which looked to be the great hall or banqueting-room of the lodge. It was a considerably brighter apartment than otherwise would have been expected, owing to the line of windows that ran down one side of it — very high windows they were, stretching from wainscot to rafters — and a series of skylights in the pitched roof.

The visitors' eyes were drawn at once to the wall upon which the gray light in the windows was shining. This wall consisted of a single, massive decoration in bog oak — in essence a sort of sculpted tapestry. Like the windows it extended the full length of the hall, the figures in it projecting in high relief from the black, peat-stained wood out of which they had been carved.

"Ah, marvelous, marvelous," the vicar exclaimed, rushing at once to examine the work. "What lovely reliefs — what glorious craftsmanship — extraordinary detail — this is something the Historical Society will be most interested in, surely — "

"It looks to be a hunting scene," Richard observed.

"Aye, Dickie — 'tis the hunt of auld de Clinkers, I jalouse," said Sir Hector. "'Tis he himsell at the heid there, vera probable, an' his gillies wi' him, an' ither gentlemen o' rank an' skill, a' ridin' tae hoonds. 'Tis a right bonny piece o' work, o' that there's na gainsayin'."

A glorious work it was indeed, in its depiction of an armed party of horsemen and the hounds sweeping by at their feet. In the van, as noted by Sir Hector, rode a stocky gentleman of middling height, with a broad face and eager eye — most likely Godfrey de Clinkers himself. His right hand was raised in sign to his followers, all of whom looked more than ready to be following him. The entire work was beautifully detailed, with each figure, whether man or beast, fully rendered and life-sized. It was a celebration of the chase — the *raison d'être* for which de Clinkers had erected his hunting-seat — showing the great man himself leading his friends and servants on an excursion in the wood.

In the mid-portion of the sculpture, shown running along on foot, was a long, lean man bearing a quarterstaff and bugle-horn — a park-keeper. The fashion of his attire, like that of the horsemen, was some several hundred years out of date.

"Yes, yes, a magnificent work," enthused the vicar.

The others nodded their concurrence. Even the gillies, who were largely ignorant of art, seemed moved by it.

"And to have wrested it out of bog oak!" Richard exclaimed. "What a wondrous achievement."

"Oh, indeed," nodded the vicar. "The artisans who executed this piece were divinely gifted. The modeling of the surfaces — the expressions on the faces of the hunters — well, it's really quite extraordinary. And the sheer scale of it!"

"I agree, it's capital."

After another few minutes spent admiring the carving, the visitors turned their attention to the great hall itself. The furniture, all of it rustic and old-fashioned, was arranged neatly about, a dining-table with leather-bottomed chairs occupying pride of place in the center of the room. At the farther end of the hall stood a huge stone chimney-piece, with its garnish of andirons, oak settle, and screen. The floor of the apartment, which was composed of glazed tiles, had been recently swept, most likely with the broom that stood in the chimney-corner. On the whole this part of the lodge looked to be in exceptionally fine repair. There was little doubt about it — someone had indeed taken up residence in the ancient hunting-seat of de Clinkers.

But who?

Richard and the vicar exchanged glances. Perhaps this was where the children were living? But if so, then someone else was living here as well. Someone was keeping the hall clean and tidy — hardly the work of youngsters, more likely that of a maidservant or housekeeper perhaps.

Richard smiled at the thought. Here they were in the storied lodge of de Clinkers, deep within the treacherous, beast-haunted wood, and what were they musing about? Children, maids, and housekeeping!

"Hum! 'Tis no what I'd looked for tae find," declared Sir Hector. "'Tis a boggle, it is — eh, Willie?"

"It certainly hasn't the *appearance* of squatters — too tidy for a pack of old tramp fellows," the brewer admitted. "To think of it — the legendary hunting-seat of Godfrey de Clinkers — here in the flesh!"

Their uncomfortable feeling of being spied upon had abated, yet still the visitors found they were being watched, if only by the gallery of portrait-paintings that were ranged about the wainscot. Eyes stared out at them from the proud faces of men and women of centuries past and done. Most of the images were full-length, the gentlemen sporting huge, full-bottomed perukes and plate-armor, the women in lace and ruffs, and every one of them faded to yellow with the years.

"I dare say this is he," said the vicar, gazing up at the stout figure of a man posed rampant-guardant against a woodland landscape. "Yes, here is Mr. Godfrey de Clinkers himself. And here beside him is a picture of his wife, the lady Isobel."

His was a face like that the old Romans used to stamp on coins; hers a laughing, good-natured countenance with full lips and an impish eye. The similarity of de Clinkers's image in oils to that of his carved representation in bog oak was unmistakable. Here was the face of a great man, a bold man, an eccentric man — the face of a man with cheek enough to have erected a hunting-lodge in Marley Wood. There were none such as he left in Fenshire nowadays, that was for certain!

"He perished in a riding accident, as I recollect, at the age of fifty-eight," noted the vicar. "His horse fell and crumpled him. Game to the last! As for the lady Isobel, she suffered from a diseased heart, I believe, and died of water on the chest. There were no heirs, and no claimants."

"None at all?" said Richard.

"None."

And still more eyes were watching them, too — eyes that belonged to the many trophy-heads which were on show about the room. Heads of elk and stag, wolf and fox, bison, tapir, flat-head boar, marsh devil, spotted lion, and short-faced bear hung from rusty fastenings. *Flat-heads and short-faces, marsh devils, spotted lions!* Even Sir Hector and the gillies were astonished by it.

"Such colorful lives these ancestors of ours must have led!" the vicar exclaimed.

What fear had such men as de Clinkers of the world? Devotees of the chase, they had scoured the wood not only for venison and swine, but for dirk-tooth and the mighty lion as well. It staggered the brains of modern-day Fenshiremen to think of it.

The visitors had been making a slow, steady circuit of the hall, the interest of each shifting variously from the oil-paintings to the stuffed heads of game, empty suits of armor, and other relics on display there, when a sudden shout was thrown up by Vicar Ludlow.

"Oh, my gracious heavens!" he cried, falling back a step or three.

At once the others rushed to his aid, their eyes tracing the clergyman's horrified gaze.

"Perish me!" burst out Haggis.

"God o' Grace!" thundered Sir Hector.

As for Richard and Jorkens, both were too shocked — or too sickened, more like — to contribute aught but a few startled gasps.

There on the wall, amongst the stuffed trophy-heads of deer, bison, and boar, hung the stuffed head of a man, staring at them in wide-eyed surprise.

The image burned itself into the brains of the visitors, and brought to the fore thoughts of their morning meals, which seemed poised to reappear at any moment. But then —

Slowly, slyly, Sir Hector MacHector, Laird of the Clan MacHector and Knight of the sundered realm, began to laugh.

His companions regarded him with disbelief.

"Laird?" questioned Jorkens.

"Why, dooms me, men," chuckled Sir Hector, "d'ye no ken the humor of it? 'Tis naught but paint an' plaster! An' d'ye no see it be the man himsell?"

The Laird nodded towards the head — a sculpted and painted plaster head, as the others now saw — and then at the picture of Godfrey de Clinkers hanging nearby, of which the head was the dead image, so to speak. The sculpted head of plaster on the wall was a portrait of de Clinkers himself, made up to resemble one of his trophies.

"Well, I'm jiggered," Richard exclaimed, vastly relieved. "This de Clinkers chap was a dashed peculiar fellow — but a capital one!"

"Dear me," gulped the vicar, a trifle embarrassed by his outburst. "Dear me — oh, I say — such colorful lives they had in the old days."

It was a view with which the plaster head on the wall, had it the gift of speech, doubtless would have agreed.

But the relief of the visitors was short-lived. Almost at once they heard a noise behind them — a noise like a rustle of movement, followed by what sounded like a yawn.

Instantly on the alert, they wheeled round *en garde*.

"Whisht!" Haggis whispered, darting his glance about the chamber. "Wha's yon?"

"There is someone else in the lodge," said Richard.

"Aye, Dickie, o' that ye're right eneugh," nodded Sir Hector. "An' 'tis no sae far awa', either — 'tis right bluidy here i'the hall! Can ye no feel it?"

"I can — whoever the dash it is!"

"Ower yont it is, Laird," said Jorkens, his eyes clamped on the far end of the hall where stood the huge stone chimney-piece and its garnish of andirons, settle, and screen.

The gillies had drawn their whingers, and Sir Hector his claymore, and Richard his sturdy cutlass, and the reeve his sword, and the vicar his brow — and in such wise they crept, step by cautious step, towards the chimney.

"The settle there, I think," Richard nodded.

"Aye!" whispered Jorkens.

It was one of those grim-looking, high-backed, ancient kinds of settles that are often encountered in old houses. It stood with its tall back to them, and was shielded in part by the ornamental screen.

"Easy the noo, men," warned the Laird as they drew near it, "an' above a', be canny."

They had closed to within a few yards of the target, their blades outthrust and gleaming in the light, when a small face with two sleepy eyes in it peered round at them from the settle.

"My very word," the vicar gasped.

The face belonged to a rumpled small boy with a thatch of straw-colored hair. He yawned, rubbed the sleep from his eyes, and glanced inquisitively at the strangers who had intruded upon his nap.

"Where have they gone?" the boy asked.

"Goodness me, that's the very chap," Richard said. "That's the little fellow I saw peeking in at the windows of Mead Cottage. I'm certain of it. And there was a little girl with him."

Sir Hector, having determined that there was no significant threat to their persons, sheathed his weapon and dropped to one knee at the child's side. He looked curiously into the face of the rumpled small boy; the small boy looked curiously into his. In all probability the child had never before seen a Laird, and Sir Hector did not wish to frighten him.

"There, there, ma wee young mannie," he said, in a soothing tone. "MacHector's ma name t'ye — the MacHector o' Mickledene Hall, Fribbleside, tae be precise. An' what might ye be called, laddie?"

"My name is Bertram," the child replied.

"Hum! An' a bonny name it is, friend Bertie, an' a gentle one forbye."

"And who are these others you've asked after, my boy?" the vicar inquired.

"Who are *you?*" the child shot back.

"Why, I am Vicar Ludlow of Market Snailsby, and this is Sir Hector MacHector, as he himself has just told you. These others here are our friends."

"Who is the large fat man?"

"That is Mr. Shand. He is our fen-reeve, and as such has charge of this property. And this is Mr. Richard Hathaway. We have only just arrived here. And what is the rest of your name, then, Bertram?"

"The rest of my name?"

"Yes. Is Bertram your Christian name, or your family name?"

"Bertram is my name."

"I see. And where do you live?"

"I live here."

"Aye, but for certie ye've no lived here a'ways," smiled Sir Hector. "Whaur bide yer ane folk, then? Whaur be the home o' yer clan an' family?"

The question seemed to puzzle the rumpled small boy.

"Where do your parents live, Bertram?" the vicar said, by way of translation.

"In Butter Cross," the boy replied.

"And where is that, exactly?"

"I don't know."

"Is it very far off?"

"I believe so."

"How came you here to the lodge?"

"Sarah showed it to me."

"And who is Sarah?"

"Sarah is my friend."

"And when was it that your friend showed you the lodge?"

"I can't remember."

"Where are your parents now?"

The boy thought for a moment, then gave a little shrug of his shoulders.

"Are they stopping in Market Snailsby?" the vicar asked.

The child thought again, and shrugged again, and in general looked about as rumpled and drowsy as any rumpled small boy could after being roused from his nap.

"The boy's parents may be lodging in town, perhaps at the Broom and Badger," said Mr. Shand.

"I'm not so sure of that," spoke up Richard, "for Miss Henslowe has made some inquiries, and heard from Travers that there are no guests with children staying at the Badger. And as for the Mudlark, well, I am fairly certain Joliffe has no guests at all."

"Judging by the boy's garb, I'd wager he belongs to a slodger family — Butter Cross or no Butter Cross," said the vicar.

"But what would a slodger child be doing in Marley Wood?"

"Ah. Well, perhaps he has gone missing from his home?"

"But if a child had gone missing, even a slodger child, surely we would have heard of it?"

The vicar, thinking for a moment, was forced to agree. "True, sir. We have had no report of a lost child. Dear me, this is all very strange. And who can these others be whom he's asked after?"

Amidst the feathery litter of ashes in the hearth were a handful of glowing embers — evidence that someone earlier had prepared a fire, for the child's comfort no doubt, but that it had gone out while the boy had been sleeping. Someone as well had piled a stack of fresh turf and timber beside the chimney-piece. Undoubtedly this someone was one of those whom the boy had asked after.

Richard turned to Bertram, who was making himself comfortable again on the settle, fluffing up his little pillow and preparing to resume his nap.

"Your friend Sarah who showed you the way here — is she a little person like yourself?" Richard asked.

"Yes."

"Is she the little girl who was with you the other day when you looked in at the windows of my house? Do you remember that? Mead Cottage it's called, in the Tillington Road, at the very edge of town."

"Yes. It seemed such a nice house, and we were curious to know who lived there. But she's gone off now, I suppose. I've not seen her since the morning," said Bertram, with another yawn. He seemed to be losing interest rapidly.

"We must look for this little Sarah. I dare say she can't be far off," the vicar urged. "We dare not leave these children here on their own."

"Likely she has charge of a horse or pony," Richard reminded him.

"Ah, indeed — I'd nearly forgotten. That *will* make matters more difficult. How dangerous it is for children to be galloping about the wood! How can they have survived? And yet there was no sign of the stables being in use — "

Richard was stroking his chin and wishing mightily for his pipe and some tobacco, the better to concentrate with. He turned a thoughtful eye again upon the boy.

"You asked us, Bertram, where 'they' had gone. Whom did you mean?" he asked.

But the child was too sleepy now, or too unconcerned perhaps, to answer. He had dropped his head onto his pillow and drawn his little blanket up, and was keen to be napping.

"We must search as many of the buildings as we are able," said the vicar. "If we can't find this little Sarah, we may at least return the boy to town with us. My wife and I will look after him until his parents have been identified. He looks to be in need of some tidying up. Just look at that hair! And those clothes — "

"'Tis slodger garb, I jalouse," nodded the Laird.

"Decidedly rustic," said Mr. Shand.

And so it was agreed, the vicar being deputed to remain with Bertram for the nonce while Sir Hector and the others carried out the search. But no trace of a little girl or her pony did they find.

What they did find was a host of additional curiosities, all of them lending further support to the accounts of Mr. Blathers. There were, for example, a number of strange doors. There was a door that opened onto a brick wall, and a door that opened onto another door, and then

onto a third door, which in its turn opened onto a full-length portrait
of a surprised Godfrey de Clinkers in his night-dress, a taper in one
hand and a sword in the other. There was another door that led into
a closet, which was not so strange but for the fact that the closet turned on a pivot and, when activated, discharged the unsuspecting victim
onto a loft in one of the stables.

There were a variety of clumsy staircases, hewn mostly from whole
logs. One led up to a painted archway on a wall, and another to a gallery with no floor. There were old, disused clocks with human faces,
and mirrors with sculpted hands and heads peeking from behind them.
In a niche in a wall they found a row of books, bearing such titles as
How to Waste Time and *The Answer to Everything* — books whose
secrets would never be divulged because they were made of plaster.
There was a window with the painted face of a marsh devil in it; a
turnspit in the shape of a smallsword in the kitchen fireplace; a long-
case clock showing thirteen hours; a portrait bust of de Clinkers with
his wig back-to-front; and more — all of them serving to mark the
famed builder of the lodge as an eccentric of grand proportions.

As they went along they called out repeatedly for Sarah, but received no answer. They found a couple of small beds suitable for children, however, and a wardrobe containing some children's clothes of
the same rude design as Bertram's. And they found toys as well — peg-
tops and hoops, shuttlecocks, and some ragged dolls.

In a small chamber which looked to be a kind of study or work-
room, not far from the great hall, they came across an ancient folio
volume — an herbal — lying open on a reading-desk. Some articles of
needlework lay nearby, along with a frame for working embroidery,
a spinning-wheel, a smoothing-iron, a lute, and a long-stemmed pipe of
the churchwarden variety. There was a little table to play cards at, and
a pack of cards and a cribbage-board on the table, and a few cookery
books and a volume of children's verses on a shelf, and some other
books besides. And there were some more brass candlesticks showing
signs of recent use.

In the old stone kitchen where the turnspit like a smallsword was,
they discovered a kettle on the hob, a roasting-jack, some jars and a
spice-box, a hand-mill, and a chopping-board. And there was a dresser,
too, bearing some old trenchers and porringers, all neatly stacked, and
some pewter mugs and goblets. And in the adjacent scullery they discovered the remains of three meals.

The remains of breakfast, perhaps, for Bertram, Sarah, and — whom?

Someone had been attending to the creature-comforts of the children. Someone had been reading about herbs in the study, and someone had been sewing, and someone had been smoking, and someone had been playing cards, and someone had been keeping the great hall and its neighboring apartments clean and tidy.

And someone had brought down a stag with an arrow and butchered it.

"By ma certie, Laird," said Haggis, running a fierce hand through his beard, "'tis no natural for bairns tae be dwellin' in sich a place. Whosomeffer he be as holds 'em here, 'tain't right or proper, by ma reckoning."

"A squatter — or an abductor?" wondered Mr. Shand. "For surely it is against their will that these children are kept here."

Sir Hector nodded gravely. "Aye, 'tis likely, Willie, or sae it seems tae me. Howsomeffer, it looks tae be but one man as keeps 'em here — an' one man be no sae formidable 'gainst five blades o' steel. We'll ha' na trouble wi'the gangrel, an we find him."

"The boy looks to be in good health, and not particularly afraid," Richard observed.

"Aye, Dickie. But still, 'tis no right or proper thing tae be keepin' the bairn frae his clan an' family."

"Perhaps this man *is* their family? Perhaps, Sir Hector, this man has taken up residence here, and Bertram and Sarah are his children?"

It was a possibility that none of them had considered, except perhaps Mr. Shand, who had wondered aloud if a family of squatters might not have overrun the lodge. It had not occurred to them that an old tramp fellow might have offspring.

But how to reconcile this with Bertram's claim that it was little Sarah who had shown him the lodge?

Sir Hector glanced at his watch. He saw how much more time now had passed since they had left Market Snailsby, and how much less of it remained for the journey back.

"The hour be late the noo, an' we maun ride," he announced. "As for the bairn, 'twad be wiser, d'ye no agree, tae bring the lad wi' us, an' sort the matter oot i'the town? For we've naught but whim an' fancy tae guide us here."

The others paused to consider.

"I suppose it would be wise, for safety's sake," nodded the reeve. "Meantime Mrs. Chugwell and her son will be wondering what has become of us. We must for certain be clear of the wood before dark."

"But if the child truly belongs here, we shall have hard work to explain ourselves," Richard observed.

It was a point upon which all were agreed; but they were agreed as well that they had little choice but to take Bertram with them. It was left to Sir Hector, with his calmness and assurance of manner, and air of quiet authority, to break the news to the dozing boy.

"Come awa', then, ma wee young man," he said, gently. "Ye need ha' no fear tae trust us, but we maun remove ye the noo frae this muckle hoose tae the safety o' town. Market Snailsby that town be. There, there — dinna let it fash ye. Forgie us, laddie, but 'tis the best for ye, till matters be sorted oot. 'Twill be na mair than a wee-bit while, sure! Sae up wi'ye, ma man, an' be joco."

At first the boy refused. He did not care to leave what he claimed was his home, he said, or to leave the others. In reply Sir Hector told him once more that it was for his own good that he pay a short visit to the town. The urgings of Vicar Ludlow, joined now with those of the Laird, went far to further the cause. Soon the child was teetering on the brink.

"Come awa', laddie, come awa'!" Sir Hector exhorted him. "For we maun make haste."

"Tell me, young Bertram," smiled the vicar, "do you know what a shovel-tusker is?"

The boy nodded.

"Ah, very good! Well, did you know that there is a shovel-tusker in the road not far from here? Do you know that road — the fine one being put through the wood? Well, Mrs. Chugwell and her son are building that road, and they are waiting for us there with their tusker. His name is Ranger, and he is something to behold. He is huge and gray and shaggy — a most impressive fellow altogether! — and there is a cab on his shoulders for riding in. How would you like to ride in that cab all the way to town, as the guest of Mrs. Chugwell?"

The idea appeared to fire the boy's interest, and spirited him up considerably.

"Oho, ma laddie!" Sir Hector exclaimed. "An' had I ma pipes the noo, I'd play 'em tae ye. D'ye ken the pipes — the black sticks — ma braw wee man?"

The difficulty resolved, they departed the lodge and were soon outside the gates of the causeway. There Bertram was accorded the rare privilege of riding with Sir Hector on his gelding; and when all were safely mounted they trotted off through the wood to the road.

Bertram was mightily impressed by the sight of Ranger, and wasted no time scampering up the cord-ladder to the cab. Soon after, with the horsemen again riding ahead, the party set off upon the road. It was a relief to escape from the gloomy maze of the wood, the gray ribbon of sky seeming as bright as sunshine by comparison. Moreover, with the survey completed they were able to travel at a swifter pace than before. As a result the time went rapidly by; but as it did so a familiar feeling began to steal upon them — the feeling of invisible eyes watching from afar.

They had not found little Sarah in their search of the lodge. Could it be her eyes that were watching them? Could it be Sarah and her pony who had been tracking them all the day?

Following his initial excitement at seeing the tusker, Bertram had taken to yawning again, under the influence no doubt of the rhythmic lurch and sway of the cab. Soon he was lost in a comfortable slumber in the arms of Mrs. Chugwell. The good lady had not had a rumpled small boy asleep in her arms for many a season, not since her son Matt had filled that role; and she found it not an unpleasant thing in the slightest.

"Butter Cross, Butter Cross," she heard the vicar murmuring to himself. "Now, I wonder where that is?"

"Butter Cross?" she repeated.

"Ah, yes — yes — Butter Cross, Mrs. Chugwell. The young man there claims it is where his parents reside."

"Butter Cross," smiled the mastodon lady, who from her occupation knew more than a little about geography, "is a small market-town not far from Salthead, many leagues to the northwards. It has a fine market cross, round which food used to be left for the Salthead people to take, years ago, when the plague had swept over that city."

"Ah, I see. That is most enlightening. Thank you, Mrs. Chugwell. So the boy hales from a town a considerable distance from here. I dare say that will ease the search. For we don't have many visitors from such far-off places . . ."

The night was setting in when at last they emerged from the wood. What a joy it was to be clear of that dreadful, dark domain! Spread before them was the broad, open, welcoming country of the fens, with its reedy marshes and waterside meadows, and the distant lights of Market Snailsby peeping through the mist.

They had just passed the old gallows and its creaking gibbet-irons, and were congratulating themselves upon their success, when a hideous scream rang out behind them in the wood.

It was a weird, wild, unearthly kind of sound, something between a howl and a wail. For a long time it hung trembling on the misty air. As if in answer to it Ranger lifted his great heavy ears and trunk, and the horses snorted and tossed their manes. It was the cry of some predatory beast, surely; but no beastly marsh devil or spotted lion ever was born that had given utterance to such a sound, for there was something undeniably human about it, too.

It was a sound that sent a chill through all who heard it — all, that is, but the rumpled small boy in the arms of Mrs. Chugwell, who had sat up and was listening intently, and looking back at the wood with a wistful, yearning gaze.

And as the weird, unearthly cry faded and dwindled away, he sighed.

THE THIRD CHAPTER

AN IMPOSSIBLE CHILD

ALREADY a week had passed since the encounter with the children in the Tillington Road, and now one of those very children was lodging with Mr. Ludlow and his wife amidst the cozy comforts of the vicarage. For both Jemma and Molly had identified young Bertram as one of the two they had seen that day — one of the two who had laughed at them from the spinney, and whom Miss Hathaway had followed into the wood, where she and the valiant Snap had run bump into something the like of which they had never before bumped into.

On the second day after the return of the survey party, a group of interested persons was assembled in the parish rooms. They had come to learn more about the child who had been found alive and living in the storied lodge of de Clinkers. Present to aid in the effort were some of those who had found him — Sir Hector MacHector, Vicar Ludlow, Mr. Shand, and Richard Hathaway. The gentlemen were seated round a table beside the boy, who himself sat facing the group of interested persons on a little raised chair, alone, like a prisoner in the dock. The vicar's wife had stationed herself nearby, however, so that she might keep an eye on the lad, and cheer him along with a string of encouraging nods and winks; for having no children of her own she had found much to busy herself with in this rumpled small child of somebody else's.

The boy's rustic attire had been exchanged for a nice little turnout of jacket, clean white shirt, and trousers and waistcoat all-in-one. He had received a bath and had had his hair clipped, and so was a rather more presentable child now than the one Sir Hector and the others had discovered in the great hall of the lodge. *He has a charming little face, if a trifle pale,* thought Mrs. Ludlow. *I suppose it comes from living in that dreadful wood. But what a good boy he is — such a respectful little dear!*

Despite the improvements to his person, Bertram continued to insist, to the Ludlows and their household and everybody else, that he be permitted to return to the lodge and to his mysterious friends who lived there. Evidently the magic of Ranger and the ride in the cab had worn off; nor, it seemed, were the joys of Market Snailsby and its marshes sufficient inducement to the child to remain.

Mayor Jagard was the first to question him, something he had made vastly clear to everyone was his privilege and duty as chief townsman of the parish. To this point the Ludlows had been able to wring from Bertram very little in the way of useful information; thus it was up to the child now to explain himself, publicly, the Mayor contended, and to provide some clues as to his identity and origin so that he might be restored to his family. The search in town had turned up nothing; there were no visitors from Butter Cross or Salthead stopping there, nor had any of the locals misplaced a rumpled small boy who corresponded to Bertram's description.

The strutting little bantam of a Mayor, supplied with a nice little turnout of his own — it was canary and crimson today — strolled up to the prisoner, one hand on his hip and the other thoughtfully massaging his chin, and, taking a long, hard look at the boy and smiling, asked him, pleasantly enough, but shrewdly, too —

"And how have you been keeping yourself, young Mr. Bertram, sir?"

"Keeping myself?" returned the child.

"Yes. Been tucking in your feed at that lodge of yours, have you? For you don't appear starved to me, no, sir. Indeed, you appear to have done rather nicely for yourself, apart from your wardrobe, which I see has been much improved upon by our worthy vicar here. I wonder who's been feeding you, then, eh? One of these mysterious friends of yours in the wood?"

"Yes."

"Not your father, then, or your mother?"

"No."

"No relations? No brother or sister there, or an uncle, perhaps?"

"No. I should like to return to my friends now, if you please."

"Ah, I see. Of course, of course. And who might these friends be, eh? Give us a hint, young Mr. Bertram, sir. This Sarah, for instance — she is not your sister?"

"No."

"Do you have any sisters?"

"I have a sister. And two brothers."

"Well, well, well — now we are getting somewhere," the Mayor exclaimed, glancing round with an air of triumph. But his bubble was pricked almost at once.

"The immediate family consists of a mother, father, two older brothers, and an older sister, all of them residing at Butter Cross," Mr. Ludlow informed the chief townsman. "This much we have been able to winkle out of him, but no more — his surname, for instance. As for why his family should have sent him into Fenshire, or abandoned him here, we haven't discovered."

This news the Mayor digested with some brushing and smoothing of his mustaches, and an abstracted contemplation of the floor; then, after a brief pause, he lifted his eyes, cleared his voice a time or two, and offered the following in response —

"Of course, of course — remember it now! Brothers and sister. Parents. Place called Butter Cross. Well, well. But to return to this Sarah of yours," he went on, addressing Bertram again. "You say you wish to be restored to your friends. This Sarah is one of your friends. And so how many more are there, exactly?"

"There is one other — the one who takes care of us," said Bertram.

"Ah! Been keeping you in your tuck, has he? And what might his name be?"

"She won't tell us her name."

"*She?*"

"Yes."

"Interesting! And why does she refuse to tell you her name?"

"She says that knowing a person's name gives one power over a person."

"Rather an odd reply. What is she like, this friend of yours?"

"She is very old and very wise, and very gifted. She can do almost anything. And she can work wonderful magic!" said Bertram, his eyes shining.

A storm of smoke blew in from the vicinity of Mr. Blathers and his pipe.

"Magic — humph! Well, I don't believe in *that*. No sir, no such thing," he declared. "Magic went out of years ago, like boar-hunting in the wood — whole centuries ago, in point of fact. Why, I'd not give you three skips of a louse for magic. But most anything can seem like magic to a child, I suppose. Funny thing, childhood — "

"What sort of magic does your friend work?" asked Dr. Chevenix. "Card-tricks, perhaps? Or can she make objects disappear?"

"She can do far more than that," the child boasted. "She is marvelous!"

"Is this white magic, or black magic?" inquired Miss Henslowe.

Bertram screwed up his brows in thought, but in the end gave no answer other than a shrug, for he had no clue as to the distinction.

"Well, give us an example of her magic, then," invited Mr. Inkpen. "Just any example that springs to mind."

"She can make all the creatures of the wood obey her," Bertram replied. "She speaks to them and they understand her, and will do as she bids them. She is wonderful!"

"Do as she bids them? Ah! Indeed. Squirrels and such, I suppose. Well, well!" the Mayor exclaimed, with a long roll of his eyes. "She flings them an acorn and they'll turn a little jig for her in the tree, is that it? Extraordinary. Come, come, young Mr. Bertram, sir!"

"She can tame any animal in the wood with a glance, or a cry," the boy insisted.

"I see. This friend of yours can subdue any beast she chooses — any marsh devil, any spotted lion — with little more than a wink. That's a very useful talent to have, I dare say. Yes, indeed. Oh, my. Well, well!" the Mayor rattled on, smiling and nodding to himself, while pacing to and fro with his hands thrust under the skirts of his coat.

"You don't believe me," Bertram said.

"Don't believe you? Come, come, young fellow my lad! What do you take us for? Clodpolls and chaw-bacons?"

"But I've told you the very truth."

The Mayor ceased his pacing and fixed the child with a stern look. "You have seen these things yourself — or have you only heard tell of them?"

"I've seen them."

"Squirrels — or spotted lions?"

"Lions, and more — teratorns even!"

A chorus of laughter filled the air. The interested persons wagged their heads, most of them, and clucked their tongues, and traded knowing glances. To think that the child's friend there at the lodge could bend the monsters of the wood to her will! It was a pleasant enough fable, they chuckled, but a fable it was all the same.

"Somebody has pulled the wool over this boy's eyes," they remarked to one another with smiling self-assurance. "Such foolishness!"

"More like it's this boy be pulling the wool over ours," opined Mr. Finlayson, the creaky little bald man with the patch — *not* of wool — on his eye.

"And she is a wizard with her bow and arrows," Bertram said, raising his voice a little so as to make himself heard above the crowd.

More laughter, more knowing glances all round; although it may be noted that Richard and Jemma and Ada had not been laughing, nor had Corney, nor the Ludlows, nor Mr. Shand, nor Sir Hector. Someone had brought down a stag with an arrow, and butchered it; and as old de Clinkers was in no condition to be firing darts at anything, this much at least of Bertram's testimony rang true. *Somebody* with a degree of skill had been bow-hunting in Marley Wood.

"What knowledge have you, young Mr. Bertram, sir, of these miscreants who have been carousing in our wood? And of a low park-keeper in a green jerkin, with a horn and quarterstaff, who threatens the sconces of innocent citizens?" the Mayor demanded.

The boy pondered for a moment. "What are miscreants?" he asked. "And what are sconces?"

"Sconces are heads," explained Mr. Shand from his seat at the table. "And miscreants are squatters."

More pondering. "What are squatters?"

"Riders, then," said the Mayor, impatiently. "Come, come, sir! These riders and their hounds — do you know something of them? Are they your friends as well?"

"They are *her* friends," Bertram replied. "She calls for them and they come to her, and together they hunt in the wood."

His answer provoked a lively discussion amongst the interested persons — one which proceeded to swell at an alarming rate, and which spurred the vicar and Sir Hector to appeal for quiet. Then Richard Hathaway got up and, walking round the table, placed himself at the small prisoner's side.

"Hallo, Bertram. You remember me, don't you?"

"Yes."

"And my sister Jemma there — do you remember her as well? You and your friend Sarah were watching her from a spinney beside the Tillington Road, one day about a week ago. My sister and our dog Snap followed you into the wood."

"Yes, they did."

"And later, it was you and Sarah who followed *them*, for mile upon mile, while they were traveling at rather a good clip in our shay-cart."

"Yes."

"Well, it's dashed curious, you know," Richard said, scratching his head and frowning, "how the two of you could have kept up such a pace as our Rosie was setting that day. However did you manage it?"

"Our friend, the lady, carried us along," Bertram replied.

"This is your friend who works the magic?"

"Yes."

"I see. You were carried along through the wood by your friend. And that is how you came to Mead Cottage as well?"

"Yes."

"So you and your friend Sarah, and your other friend, this lady, rode on horseback through the wood to Market Snailsby?"

"No."

"You were driven in a carriage, then?"

"No."

Another spirited discussion followed, its chief subjects being wool and eyes, marigold tea, the perverse nature of children in general, and the shamefulness of lying. If neither horse nor trap had carried the children along, then what?

"But Bertram, however did you follow us?" Jemma asked. "For our Rosie was laying herself out in rattling form — at the top of her speed in harness!"

"Our friend carried us along," Bertram said again.

"What do you mean she *carried* you?"

The boy seemed to be growing impatient with their lack of understanding, and with the interrogation generally; and so that particular line of inquiry was dropped for the moment.

"Tell us something about these — er — these friends of your friend, Bertram — these riders, who come when she calls," invited Mr. Ludlow. "Does she call for them in the night-time?"

"Yes."

"And why is that?"

"Because the moon must be out. Otherwise they will not come."

"Extraordinary happenstance!" the Mayor snorted.

"They do not follow the hounds by daylight?" the vicar asked.

"Never," Bertram replied.

"Ah. Well, it's true — it is only on those rare moonlit nights that the riders have made their appearance."

"But whyfor d'they leave na tracks tae be found?" wondered Sir Hector. "For 'tis a muckle great puzzlement, t'be sure."

"Ye see? Ye see? Ghosts and demons hatching plots agin us," said Mr. Finlayson. "It's jist as I've told ye, one and all. *Troublesome!*"

Bertram, who seemed not to have noticed the creaky little slodger-man until now, on a sudden leaned forward in his chair and, pointing to him, said —

"Oh, I remember you! You're Mr. Phoggie."

A hush fell over the assembly. As if on cue, all in the room turned and stared at Mr. Finlayson; then they turned and stared at Bertram, and then at Phoggie again, with mystified countenances.

Mr. Finlayson cocked his head and frowned, as if he had not heard the child aright. "Lord hoist me for a bog onion! And how d'ye know Phoggie, when Phoggie don't know ye?" he demanded, with a skeptical crunching of his brow over his good eye.

"But you do know me," said the boy. "We saw you there at the inn, my cousins and I."

"Cousins? Inn?" echoed the vicar. "Bertram, you told us nothing of this — "

"Hold on a moment," Mr. Travers broke in. "Was there not a child — a boy child — one summer, oh, some five-and-thirty years ago now — a visitor stopping in town — who went missing? A child visiting with his cousins from Dragonthorpe, and come to Snailsby to see Gaffer Goodacre, as was a relation to them. Help me here, Kitty — you remember them, don't you? Stopped a time or two at the Badger they did."

A gleam of light shone in the face of Mrs. Travers — a light which quickly spread to the faces of others there in the assembly, one by one, like candles winking on all over the room.

"True! He was with his cousins, he was. Had been sent down for a visit by his family," Mrs. Travers recalled. "Stopped for a few days with the Gaffer, and was to be posted off to Newmarsh by coach, and sent home from there."

"Aye, home, woman," her husband nodded meaningfully. "Home it was — *to Salthead town!*"

Those of the interested persons who were of sufficient age — Corney, Sir Hector, and Dr. Chevenix amongst them — remembered it now. A small boy who had disappeared, and been presumed lost in the wood, or drowned in the river, or carried off by teratorns. It had been a Snailsby fair-day, and amidst the excitement the child had become separated from his cousins. They had hunted high and low for him — round the watermeads of the river, the fishponds and draw-wells, and Snailsby Mill, in the roadside copses and berry brambles, and the old cherry gardens, and the eaves of the wood behind the Market Square — without success. By any reasonable measure it seemed impossible, but . . .

"Bertram," said Richard, watching the boy's face closely, "is this what happened to you? Were you in Market Snailsby on a fair-day with your cousins? Did you visit an old man named Goodacre, and did you become lost?"

The boy at first gave a little shrug, as if he did not recall; however, a moment's thinking on it he changed his mind, and acknowledged the truth of it.

"By ginger!" cried Mr. Blathers. He threw his horn-rims onto his brow and sprang from his seat. "A remarkable claim — remarkable — but hardly believable. And the nipper says it with his head on! Something fishy here, scientifically. Never heard such a claim in all my life. Humph! Well, a child's imagination will beat everything. Funny thing, imagination . . ."

Richard turned again to Bertram. "How do you know Mr. Finlayson here? For he says he has never met you." (This after a short pause, during which Mr. Blathers had discharged a violent sneeze into his handkerchief, the force of it hurling his spectacles into the lap of Mrs. Travers).

"Yes, yes, how d'ye know me, boy?" Phoggie demanded.

"You spoke to me at the inn, and told me of your — your slodging, I think it was," Bertram answered. "But you are so much older now, and have grown a mustache. And what has happened to your eye?"

All looked again at Phoggie, even the Mayor and Mr. Blathers, for some shred of an explanation; but the creaky little bald man had none to offer. Everyone knew that Mr. Phoglander Finlayson had worn no mustache when he was young, and that he had lost his eye in a poling mishap some ten years ago.

"How in thunder can the boy know this?" they asked.

"What are you hiding from us, old glossy-pate?" someone said.

"Hiding? I bean't hiding a thing!" Phoggie retorted.

"Then how can the boy here know you, if you don't know the boy?"

"Hoots, men, 'tis no sae vera probable," Sir Hector pointed out. "For dooms me, how can the wee-bit mannie here be the same lad as was lost sae lang syne?"

"He can't be," everyone agreed.

Here they all stopped, as a low, soft sound reached their ears. The sound came from Bertram, who, growing bored with the inquisition, had commenced humming to himself a little air.

"Why, that's the *Song of the Boats*," somebody remarked. "That's Phoggie's song!"

The creaky little bald man's eye froze into a stare of disbelief.

"How d'ye know that music, boy?" he asked, rising from his chair. "For it be a tune I sing to myself when out upon the marshes. It be music I thought up with my own brain when I was a younker."

"You taught it to me," said Bertram.

"Jumping cats!" Mr. Blathers exclaimed. He sprang to his feet again and, stepping up to the table, dealt it a level *thump!* with his fist (this to the considerable surprise of Sir Hector and the others seated there).

At one stroke the chuckles and knowing glances of the assembly had been transformed into expressions of astonishment. Mr. Finlayson, singled out as he had been by Bertram, screwed up his face and, training his goggle-eye upon the boy, studied him up and down, from the tips of his new shoes to the top of his freshly-cropped head (it was no great distance), nodding to himself the whiles and murmuring, softly at first, then more vigorously —

"Aye — aye — it *is* the lad — the very same, the visitor-child over to the Badger — I recollect it now — 'little Bertie' they called him — aye, his cousins they were — Gaffer Goodacre — Dragonthorpe — " Then, recognizing all at once the absurdity of the situation, he checked himself in mid-murmur, swallowed, licked his lips and, staring at Bertram in blank amaze, loudly proclaimed the obvious — *"But that be five-and-thirty year ago!"*

"Matter of fact!" Richard concurred.

Tremendous excitement now prevailed amongst the interested persons.

"How can this boy here have been keeping himself a boy these five-and-thirty years?" Mayor Jagard demanded. "For I think you will admit, it's preposterous."

"Aye, I quite agree wi'ye, 'tis no sae likely," Sir Hector acknowledged. "An' yet — an' yet it maun be true, for 'tis the vera same lad there as aforetimes, did ye no say, Phoggie?"

"Aye — for I did teach the boy the song," the slodger nodded.

"Yes," said Bertram. "For you were there, and he was there" (indicating Mr. Travers) "and she was there" (ditto Mrs. Travers) "but all of you were so much younger then. Why have you grown so old so soon?"

"Gracious Lud!" cried the offended listeners. "Well, of all things to say!"

"But a true thing," smiled Mr. Blathers, sending up another storm cloud. "Funny thing, the truth . . ."

Addressing the landlord and his wife, Bertram asked them if there was a little dog named Fuddle at the inn, a plucky little spaniel who had licked his face? For he should very much like to see him again.

His words brought a rush of tears to the eyes of Mrs. Travers. Fuddle — oh, how she had loved that dear little dog from days gone by! But alas, after so many years there was no longer any Fuddle at the inn. How could the boy know of him, she wondered, if he had not visited the Badger as he said, all that long time ago? Truth be told Mrs. Travers did not remember Bertram much, but she did remember the cousins and the search for the little lost boy.

But how could Bertram possibly be that boy?

"If we had the answer to that, dear lady, we should all be a good deal wealthier, not so say younger," smiled Dr. Chevenix. "For by my reckoning this child is nearly as old as Blathers there."

"Does anyone here know the name of these cousins of Bertram's?" Richard asked, addressing the group as a whole. "Does anyone recall the name of the family from Dragonthorpe?"

It was only by dint of effort, by some energetic cudgeling and straining of their collective memories, that an answer to Richard's question was plucked forth. And it was none other than Mr. Joliffe of the Mudlark who plucked it.

"Uckwatt," he announced in his slow, thoughtful way. "The family was called, I believe — *Uckwatt.*"

Accordingly, it was decided that a message should be sent to the town of Dragonthorpe, to inform whatever Uckwatts might remain there that their cousin Bertram had been found, and to come at once to Market Snailsby to claim him. A positive identification, most everyone agreed, would supply the final proof for an hypothesis that sorely needed testing.

But what of Bertram's companion, Sarah? No one recalled any such child from Market Snailsby's having gone missing. Over the years, however, there had been many round Fenshire who had disappeared in the wood; likely she had come from some other town or village on its borders. Richard questioned Bertram on this point, but he learned no more than the Ludlows had. The boy did not know the name of Sarah's family; he knew only that it was she who had showed him the lodge all those years ago.

"So it appears we have *two* impossible children here — two children who cannot possibly be children still," Richard observed. "That is the state of the case, pure and simple, and we'll have hard work to explain it otherwise."

"I dare say it's a paradox. Whatever are we to make of it?" the vicar sighed, shaking his head.

"Funny thing, paradoxes — drat 'em!" said Mr. Blathers. He threw up another cloud of smoke and sank back into his chair, thinking furiously. Here was a deep problem indeed, one for which his scientific methods offered no ready solution.

Jayne Scrimshaw, one of Mrs. Ludlow's domestics at the vicarage, was of the opinion that it was all the doing of Mother Redcap, and now made bold to say as much.

"If ye'll excuse the liberty, ma'am, but sure 'twas her what enchanted the boy and made him to vanish. Whoever else?" she asked. Then Mother Redcap herself had disappeared, gobbled up by a marsh devil most like, the which had served her right. The fact that Mother Redcap's vanishing had occurred some fifteen years *before* Bertram's did not hinder Jayne in the least, nor dissuade her from her belief that the wizened old hag who had dwelt by the mere was responsible.

"But surely Mother Redcap cannot be alive after so long a time," Corney objected. "She would be well past a hundred now."

"Very well past it," said the Mayor.

"Positively Jurassic," nodded Mr. Blathers, "and that would beat *everything.*"

"I remember one Christmas long ago, when I was a boy," Corney said. "We had been skating on the ice, my sister Lottie and my brother Jonas and I — the river had frozen completely over — when we spied Mother Redcap watching us from the bridge. It was rather a shock to see her there, as she had strange ways, you know, and never mingled. I had the sense, however, while she was watching us, that she would have liked very much to join us there on the ice; but naturally it was quite impossible. She was a bent old woman then, her course nearly run, with nothing to look forward to. It was the expression in her face that impressed me most — an expression of — of — well, of *longing*, I suppose. I have never forgotten it."

"She came to Market Snailsby to escape the folks in her town in Gloamshire, who had burned her out on suspicion of being a witch," noted Mr. Travers.

"That's Gloamshire for you," somebody snorted.

"Or so my dad did tell me once. He'd spoken with her sometimes, you know — he was one of the few who had — and would take food from the Badger out to her. She was old and lonely, he said. But he said too that he thought it a loneliness she'd brought on herself, and carried round with her and never could be rid of."

"I hadn't heard that," Corney said quietly.

"I think it's very sad," Ada declared. "Poor Mother Redcap."

"And very impossible," stated Mr. Blathers, "scientifically speaking. Well past a hundred now — yet another remarkable claim!"

"I agree," said Dr. Chevenix, who, being a physician, was the person amongst them most knowledgeable in such matters. No one but a Methuselah, he declared, could have survived to such an age as Mother Redcap was calculated to be.

"Unlessen she be a ghost or demon, and hatching plots agin us," said Phoggie.

"But what of the herbal that Sir Hector and the others found in the lodge?" Ada asked. "It was lying open on a desk, as though someone had been reading it."

"And Mother Redcap was an herbalist — a white witch," Jemma added.

"Bertram has told us that his lady friend is very old, and is able to work magic. Who can she be but Mother Redcap?"

As it happened little Sukey Shorthose had visited with Bertram earlier in the day, and it was her opinion now that he was a perfectly normal small boy, if a trifle awkward. Moreover, he was skilled in the ways of woodcraft, something he could very well have learned from Mother Redcap, and which Sarah could have learned, too.

Notwithstanding all that Bertram had told them, and the observed condition of the stables at the lodge, the children surely had a horse of some kind at their disposal. So it was generally acknowledged; it was the only means by which the two could have kept pace with Rosie and the shay-cart, or traveled all those miles to Market Snailsby to look in at the windows of Mead Cottage.

Jemma, her adventure in the wood still fresh in her mind, found herself wondering again how the children had managed to elude the horrid, snake-necked thing behind the firs. Someone clearly had been looking out for them — this mysterious "lady" friend of Bertram's, evidently. This guardian who would not tell them her name, and who could make all the creatures of the wood obey her — and who, as improbable as it sounded, could very well be the twisted old recluse of a witch of Goblin Mere.

She it must be who had made herself a new home at the lodge of de Clinkers. She it must be who had been perusing the old herbal. She it must be who had been at her spinning and sewing, and had made the children's rude garments. She it must be who had prepared their meals for them.

But why should she have abandoned her cottage by the mereside for Marley Wood?

And was it really a withered old crone upwards of a hundred who had downed a stag with an arrow and butchered it?

Perhaps these Uckwatts of Dragonthorpe, if any remained, would be able to throw some additional light on the mystery of their small cousin — a cousin who was certainly some forty years old or more if he was a day, and looking damned well for it, too.

"Enough of this, now! Come, Bertram, dear," spoke up Mrs. Ludlow, in her kindly voice; and taking his hand in hers she led the small prisoner from the dock, leaving the interested persons to ponder over his testimony. Clear as glass it was, in the well-known words of somebody or other, or something like them, that sufficient unto the day had been the questioning of Bertram thereof.

THE FOURTH CHAPTER

ALL IN A GARDEN GRAY

THE assembly in the parish rooms having adjourned, the Hathaways and Miss Henslowe took their leave and boarded the shay-cart for the return to Mead Cottage. Up the High Street they clattered, past the Market Square and Cabbage Lane, and the soaring chimneys of Goose Stacks. Before going on, however, they made a detour into Water Street, the top of which their curiosity had moved them to spend a few minutes examining.

The top of Water Street was that place where the street ended and the eaves of the wood began. But they found little of interest there — a few scattered cottages, an oast-house and rick-yard, a retired brickfield, some mossy stones, some shrubberies, and beside them the cleft tree. Likely it was at one of the cottages that the servant Bunting had been a guest on that moon-washed night, and it was from behind one of the shrubberies that the park-keeper had taken him by surprise, and warned him off with his staff, before abruptly vanishing. But like Sir Hector before them, they found nothing that might confirm Bunting's story, or refute it; and so after a while they swung Rosie about and resumed their way.

At Mead Cottage Mrs. Rudling had put a kettle on for tea, and was in the midst of preparing one of her gourmet dinners. Squash soup, smoked marsh mutton with fen lentils and turnips, saveloys, bogberries and raisins, and for dessert a chocolate bread pudding — a very square meal it was to be indeed. The valiant Snap was about somewheres, defending the grounds against squirrel raiders, while Herbert in his daily pursuit of mischief had slipped across to the Hall. Only Gerald, the stick-at-home kitchen cat, was in attendance to assist the housekeeper with her labors; although how his dozing by the fire was helpful to her in this regard is one of those mysteries for which kitchen cats are justly celebrated.

After tea the Hathaways and Ada stepped outside for a brief tour of the back-garden. Almost immediately they were joined by Snap, who had left off his prosecution of the shade-tails in favor of some human company. Rosie meantime had been turned out in the yard with Spinach, where the two were enjoying some winter hay and oats. And little Clover was there as well, in her coat of white giving a fine imitation of a lump of snow parked on the dwarf wall.

Above them hung a low sky, very dreary and gray. The garden, having yet to receive the blessings of the new spring, was like a mirror, reflecting the sky's somber tones. Beyond, a chill mist from the marshes was threatening to swallow the gazebo on its little rise above the river, from which spot Richard and his fellow-angler Corney had launched so many of their successes.

"Well, what do you make of it all? And who do you believe is back of it?" Ada asked as the trio strolled about the garden, remarking upon this bed of herbs here or those roses there. But of course her questions had little to do with either herbs or roses, or any other topic of a horticultural nature.

"Speaking for myself, I haven't an inkling," Richard admitted, after a few thoughtful draws on his pipe. (As you'll recall, his pipe helped him stave off the chill and aided his concentration. And if there was anything in Market Snailsby these days that required staving and concentrating, it was the mystery of little Bertram and what was going on in Marley Wood).

"Who else but Mother Redcap can be caring for the children?" Ada said, reiterating her stand in the parish rooms. "Not squatters, certainly — none of these 'old tramp fellows' Mr. Shand is so fond of conjuring up. Surely the evidence points to a woman — Bertram's lady friend who he claims is looking after him and Sarah."

"It's a fair assumption. There's the herbal, for instance, as you very rightly observed. But it's also true, as Corney noted, that Mother Redcap would be well past a hundred years of age today. For he remembers seeing her when he was a boy skating on the Fribble."

"But what of Bertram's words — 'she is very old'? Certainly that points to Mother Redcap?"

"And to any other daft old dear who may have chosen the lodge for her bower," Richard said, then added — "for whatever reason she may have chosen it, of course, and however she may have gotten herself there."

"An herbal would be of use to most anyone living in the wood," his sister observed, "as would certain other of the volumes as well — the cookery books, for instance."

"Perhaps Mother Redcap took them from her cottage before it was pulled down?" Ada suggested.

"Perhaps."

"It would go some way towards explaining things. At the very least we know for certain that someone besides Bertram and Sarah is living at the lodge. It isn't the children who have been poring over the old herbal, or cooking the meals, or smoking that churchwarden Richard mentioned."

"Or butchering stags in the wood," he added.

"Exactly."

"But if this is so, then why does Bertram not know her name?" Jemma asked. "Why should she wish to hide it from him? The name 'Mother Redcap' was hardly a secret; it was what everyone called her when she lived by the mere. Isn't that so?"

"Yes. But bear in mind, sis, that it was not her *real* name," Richard pointed out. "It was a nickname given to her by the townspeople, and not an uncommon one for an old dear with a fancy for scarlet kerchiefs."

"I wonder if it might be possible to look up her name? In the parish register, for example?" Ada said.

Richard worked his pipe for a few moments in thought before answering. "Not likely, I don't believe, as she was neither christened, wedded, nor buried in the parish. Still, we might inquire of the vicar — he may have the information himself. Or perhaps Travers does, as his father used to visit her. And if not he, then someone else in town who is old enough to have known her."

"Or someone with an ear for gossip, like Mrs. Locket," Jemma suggested. "It's a pity old Mr. Wackwire is not in his right mind. Likely he could have been of some help."

"Of course it may be that no one in Market Snailsby knew her name. That would accord with what Bertram had to say, and with her reputation as well. Perhaps she kept her name a secret for fear that someone would put a spell on her — a primitive notion, to be sure. I believe the ancients of Egypt were famed in that regard."

"Well, she did hail from Gloamshire, you know," Ada remarked, "and to some round here that's as barbarous a backwater as Slopshire." She paused and shook her head in frustration. "Oh, it simply *must* be Mother Redcap."

"But given her extreme age, is she likely to be a 'wizard' at knocking down stags with a bow and arrows?" Richard countered. "For that is a talent sorely out of key with what is known of her. She may have been able to work magic, but I've never pictured Mother Redcap as a tamer of spotted lions. How she could have survived for so long in the wood is a complete mystery. And of course there remains the problem of the riders and their hounds, and Bunting's park-keeper, all of whom seem to turn up only when the moon is out. Bertram claims they are the friends of his guardian, *but what does that mean?* Are they ghostly apparitions, or are they flesh and blood like the children?"

At this point the side-door of the house was opened and Mrs. Rudling appeared on the step. She tossed out a chop-bone for Snap to exercise his jaws on, the which he proceeded to do with considerable gusto.

"Perhaps Mrs. Rudling had the answer," Ada suggested, once the housekeeper had returned inside. "Perhaps it's the children who are bewitched. I say, what if Mother Redcap has nothing to do with it? What if it's a ruse on the children's part to confound the grown-ups? To put us on the wrong scent, or to gain attention, or simply for the sheer devilment of it? For I remember, when I was a child I used to make up all kinds of stories."

"Like your dream of Mother Redcap filling a sack with lies?" Jemma smiled. "Of course, as Richard says it may be some other woman who has taken up residence at the lodge, one having no connection to Mother Redcap. And there is a further mystery. Has this guardian of theirs been protecting the children for all this time — *for five-and-thirty years?* And how is it that a frail old woman can be doing this?"

"It's all so difficult to explain," Ada admitted with a sigh. "There are so many questions, one hardly knows where to begin."

"And why should Mother Redcap have given up her cottage? And how did she discover the lodge, if indeed she did discover it? And what's more, how came she there safely?"

"Perhaps she had something to guide her, like Mr. Shand's missing map. As for the lodge itself, well, it was there for her to occupy, I suppose, and so she occupied it — far grander than her old cottage, I dare say. But how she managed to find it without being set upon by beasts and monsters, and how she's managed to protect the children for these many years — well, I couldn't venture a guess." A look of sympathy came over Ada's pretty face. "Poor Mother Redcap! What Mr. Travers had to say was heartbreaking. She must have led a very lonely life there in her cottage by the mere." Then a new thought struck her and, glancing at the others, she gave voice to her suspicion — "Perhaps the children are serving as company for her?"

"Good heavens, Ada — to abduct the children for the sole purpose of gaining their companionship — why, it's not to be thought on!" Jemma cried, aghast at the very idea of it.

"I agree, it would be a dashed bad business," Richard said. "Still, we have been avoiding the most curious issue of all. If Bertram is indeed this 'little Bertie' who disappeared some thirty-odd years ago, how is it he is still a child?"

"Magic," Ada declared, without hesitation. "It's the only answer. *It is!* And this I say, Richard, in the face of any and all objections your touchy friend Mr. Blathers may have in store."

"Magical children, the both of them? Are we seriously to consider this?"

"And where magic is involved, one comes back again to Mother Redcap. Perhaps that is why she abandoned her cottage? Perhaps she discovered something magical there in the wood — some root, or herb, or mushroom — you remember, she was very fond of mushrooms — which she distilled into a potion that keeps her alive, and keeps these children young? I've heard, for instance, that the bark of the clumber pine has remarkable restorative powers. Or perhaps the children discovered it themselves? Perhaps the rest is all a fiction . . ."

"When I was a boy," Richard remarked, "I would have liked nothing better than to live in Marley Wood. I had no real conception of its dangers, you see, in spite of all the warnings from parents and friends. I thought the wood a capital place, and that living in it would have been a grand, capital adventure. Perhaps that's how Bertram felt when he was here. Perhaps his cousins told him something of the wood, and it fired his imagination and sent him trotting off to see it for himself."

"Where he met his little friend Sarah, who led him to the lodge and Mother Redcap, whereupon he was never heard from again — until now," Ada finished.

"Perhaps," said Jemma, walking slowly along with her arms folded and her eyes on the ground, "but how likely is it?"

"As likely as most any of our explanations, I expect."

"Once the boy's relations arrive we should know more," Richard said. "Still, the mystery won't be fully resolved until we discover how he has managed to remain his little self for so long — if indeed that is the case."

"But after so many years there may be no relations left to arrive. What do you know of this Gaffer Goodacre?" Ada asked.

"No help to us, I'm afraid — he died years ago, leaving no family round town that anyone knows of. A jolly-eyed old chap, as I recollect, with a fondness for beer and skittles. He was an odd-job man — a bit of this and a dash of that. If he was related to these Uckwatts, as Travers mentioned, then he was a relation of Bertram's as well."

"Perhaps the boy's name is Bertram Goodacre?"

"Or Bertram Uckwatt?" said Jemma.

"Or Bertram Somebody-or-other," Richard laughed. "At any rate, I suspect there are more than a few round here who would give their eye-teeth to know how Bertram's managed to cheat the calendar. And frankly, I'm one of them."

They had arrived in their circuit at the dwarf wall, where little Clover was sitting with her paws tucked up under her, gazing at the world through the glossy green windows of her eyes.

"Well, hallo there, little thing!" Ada sang out.

"Hallo, big thing!" said Clover.

"And what do you make of it all, then? Have you any answers to these riddles of ours?"

"I'm sure I do not, though I'll wager it's something to do with the spookies in the wood," was Clover's reply, which was delivered in the language of her kind — that is, by means of a glance, a twitch or two of her ears, a swish of her tail, and a soft *miaow*.

"It was like nothing I've ever smelled," said Snap, who was lounging nearby. He had left off exercising his jaws for a moment to reflect upon his encounter with the thing behind the firs. "And I shouldn't care ever to smell it again, thank you."

"You have no idea what it was?" Clover asked him.

"Not a glimmer. But the odd bit of it was — that although it had the whiff of an animal, it had something like the whiff of people about it, too."

Clover's ears swiveled round in surprise. "My stars! Pudding dog, you know it can be but one or the other."

"So one would *think*," Snap grunted, with an expressive wave of his paw.

Clover considered for a moment. "A mongrel, then? Some type of cross-breed? That's a new one!"

"And it gave out with the most awful, ghostly howl."

"Ghostly? Like the boom of a bittern, do you mean?"

"Ghostlier. And that whiff I had of it was even stranger. In an odd way it reminded me of Rosie and Spinach there — two of the decentest old cronies that ever trod on shoe-iron . . ."

By this time the Hathaways and Ada had resumed their tour, and were out of earshot of the animals' conversation — the which, needless to say, they would not have understood in any case.

"And how is Sir Pharnaby progressing, Richard?" Ada asked as they drew near the house. "When may we expect him to burst upon the world in the full glory of print and paper?"

"Sir Pharnaby Crust, Fenshireman," said Richard, with a thoughtful draw on his pipe, "is, I fear, not half so absorbing a puzzle these days as is young Bertram of Butter Cross."

And so the three of them went in to their early dinner of soup, marsh mutton, and chocolate bread pudding, having agreed to suspend all discussion of the puzzle that was Bertram until the arrival of the relations — if relations there were — from Dragonthorpe.

THE FIFTH CHAPTER

UCKWATTS OF DRAGONTHORPE

AND they were not long in arriving.

The message that had gone out to the town of Dragonthorpe away off to the southwestward had brought a quick response. Mr. Jeremiah Slaw, keeper of the Lizard's Head, the chief inn and posting-house of the town, knew of a family called Uckwatt whose principal member lived in the adjacent small village of Foxcote. The message being relayed to that hamlet, the startling news was communicated to Mr. Thomas Uckwatt, yeoman farmer, that his missing cousin had at long last turned up.

It was on the third day following, that representatives of the family undertook the journey by spring-cart to Market Snailsby. They had no trouble in finding the vicarage, the tall steeple of the Church of All Hallows, that well-known Snailsby landmark, serving as a most useful guide. It was mid-afternoon, and the vicar and Mrs. Ludlow were having tea with Dr. Chevenix, who had dropped in for a chat while on his physicianly rounds.

Nor was the doctor alone in dropping in, for Mr. Ingo Swain was there as well, although not for tea. The eel-trap man had delivered a handsome pair of beauties to the vicar's kitchen, and had just taken his leave when the cart bearing the Uckwatts drew up at the gate. They had come, the travelers informed him — they took him for the gardener — to see their cousin, one Mr. Bertram Longchapel, of the Longchapels of Butter Cross, and inquired if this was the home of Parson Ludlow, with whom their cousin was lodging? And so it fell to Mr. Swain to advise them that it was the very place indeed.

As you know, the eel-trap man was an amiable fellow in his way, except when pestered by bothersome small creatures like Sukey Shorthose; and that though his existence was a solitary one, that he secretly welcomed company; and so an opportunity to witness the reunion of the cousins from Dragonthorpe with their lost relative was one not to be missed. Trying not to bring undue attention to himself — it was not easy, in view of his size, his untidy appearance, his singular aroma, and the fact that he rattled when he walked — he showed the visitors to the drawing-room, and then receded into a corner to watch, and to listen.

For his part Mr. Ludlow was delighted to see the Uckwatts, but his wife, truth be told, was not. As you'll recall there were no offspring at the vicarage, and in the days since Bertram had entered the household Mrs. Ludlow had come to dote upon him as if he were her own son. The vicar knew this, and understood it, and his heart was filled with compassion for his wife; but at the same time he understood that all earthly joys were transient and must have their end.

The visitors being shown in, they were followed directly by Jayne Scrimshaw, bearing tea and buns for their comfort and refreshment after their many hours on the road.

There were two Uckwatts in the party, a man and a woman — Mr. Thomas Uckwatt, the respectable yeoman farmer of Foxcote, and his sister Phanny, the spouse of one Mr. Wilkins Maconchy, a joiner and wheelwright of Dragonthorpe. Both were in the firm grip of middle age; and it was in the similarly firm grip of their parents, as Mrs. Maconchy phrased it, that they had arrived in Market Snailsby with their cousin Bertram on that long-ago fair-day. They were anxious to see their cousin again, they said, and to learn what had become of him and how he had kept himself in the interval; for of course neither had laid eyes upon him for some five-and-thirty years.

"Ah. And — um — how is it exactly, Mrs. Maconchy, that young Bertram was sent into Fenshire, all that distance from Butter Cross, and all by himself?" Mr. Ludlow inquired.

"Yes, for you know, it is a *very* long way," his wife put in. "The vicar and I would never let a child of ours make such a journey without a companion — a governess at the very least."

"Well, first you must understand our relations, the Longchapels," Mrs. Maconchy began. She was a thin, plain-looking woman, with a freckled face, and a hint of nervousness about the eyes. Her brother, by contrast, was a big, graying man, ham-hocked and plough-horse-chested, with an enormous sling-jaw and a somber brow. The vicar, no small chap himself, recognized in the gruff, weather-beaten yeoman something of his own gruff and somewhat hard-headed farmer-father, not only in the general appearance and demeanor of the man but in the rustic broadsword that he kept vigilantly at his side.

"Little Bertie, he were the youngest of our aunt and uncle's children and, I'm afraid, to speak it bluntly, not their favorite," said Mrs. Maconchy. "They oft would send him away on visits to the houses of friends and relations. They needed to be rid of him for a spell now and then, I suppose; though now I think on it, it seems they used to send the others away, too. Our aunt and uncle, well, they didn't care particular much for little ones, I don't think. Though of course we never knew 'em all that well. We saw 'em but a couple of times in our lives, ain't that so, Tummas?"

"Ou, aye," nodded the respectable yeoman brother.

"The poor little dear!" cried Mrs. Ludlow, with a look that fairly shouted *if no one will care for the child then give him to me*. "I'll never understand how parents can be so — can be so — so — " (She wanted to say "uncaring" or "heartless," but was afraid of giving offense).

"And are your aunt and uncle still alive?" the vicar asked, coming to his wife's rescue.

"Oh, gracious me, no, sir. They passed away years ago, they did," said Mrs. Maconchy.

"Ah! I see. Well — um — as we understand it, your cousin had an older sister and two older brothers. Or so he has informed us."

"That *were* correct, sir, to the best of his knowledge, I suppose. The brothers — that's Willie and Jack — the both of 'em came to bad ends, sad to say. The older one, Jack, he were heavy in debt from gambling in the town — that's Salthead town, sir — and Willie, well, he were heavy in liquor. They perished by drownding, the one in the river and t'other in his glass. My brother Tummas has more of the particulars, if you'd like."

"Ou, aye," affirmed the yeoman, with a long face. "Kicked it they did, the pair of 'em. Right sorrowful it were, what we know of it."

"Ah. I see. Dear me. And what of Bertram's sister?" the vicar asked.

"Miss Polly? Well, sir, she it were as inherited the lot," replied Mrs. Maconchy. "Our aunt and uncle, they wasn't poor — nor rich neither, mind you, but comfortable folk — and Miss Polly, well, she's stayed a spinster-woman all her life. I think she don't want to part with so much as a shilling of the money. She were always that way, as we've gathered, though we've met her but a few times, Tummas and me."

An awkward silence filled the room. The visitors, having journeyed the many miles from Dragonthorpe to be reunited with their cousin, glanced expectantly round, wondering when he was to put in an appearance. The Ludlows and Dr. Chevenix, meantime, pondering over what Mrs. Maconchy had told them, saw fit to ponder some more. In his corner Mr. Swain scratched his cheek with a grimy fist, and rattled a little; while in the passage without, the ear of Jayne Scrimshaw maintained its tight adherence to the keyhole of the drawing-room door.

"Ah — dear me, yes," said the vicar, abruptly surfacing. He glanced at his wife; reluctantly she nodded her understanding, and rang the small hand-bell at her side. This action caught Jayne by surprise at the keyhole. In a flash she straightened, smoothed down her apron, and whisked open the door. Mrs. Ludlow, beckoning to her, gave instructions into her ear — it was the same ear that had been pressed to the keyhole — at the finish of which the maid dropped her mistress a little curtsey and a "Yes, ma'am," and obediently withdrew.

"And how do you find Dragonthorpe?" Dr. Chevenix inquired of the visitors. "It seemed a pleasant enough town, as I recollect. But that was some years ago now."

"We've lived there near all our lives, Tummas and me," smiled Mrs. Maconchy. "At Dragonthorpe and Foxcote, that is."

"Ou, aye," her brother nodded.

"Your town of Market Snailsby is a nice old place, sir, with a good mill, so it looks, and a sturdy bridge. I remember it some."

"Oh, indeed," enthused the vicar, jumping in. "And what do you think of our steeple? It's the finest of its kind in the marshlands, or so we have been told — "

At that moment the door opened again, and two small persons were led into the room by Jayne. One was Bertram, looking very fresh and bright in his new outfit. The other was that bothersome little tow-headed scrub of a little girl, Sukey Shorthose. The two placed themselves at Mrs. Ludlow's side and waited attentively, their eyes upon the visitors.

Said Mrs. Maconchy, smiling at the children in a motherly way — "And these must be your own little ones, then, Mrs. Ludlow? For certain sure, they're uncommon well-behaved. Ain't they so, Tummas?"

"Ou, aye — certain sure."

There was another awkward silence, which the vicar spent struggling to extricate himself from his chair, his hand raised in courteous objection.

"Ah — um — well, no. No. That is to say, Mrs. Maconchy — no. These are not our children, I'm afraid, though mind you we should be delighted if they were. This young one here is Miss Sukey Elizabeth Shorthose — "

In his corner Mr. Swain was grumbling to himself under his breath. What had he gotten himself into? Trapped in the vicar's drawing-room not only with that telltale of a Jayne Scrimshaw, but with little Sukey besides! *Strike me ugly,* he groaned, *what was in my mind to be so madcapped? I'd sooner have ptomaine.*

The vicar tapped Bertram on the shoulder and gently steered him towards the visitors. "And this young fellow here," he said, pleasantly enough, "is your cousin Bertram."

The silence that attended his announcement was the most awkward of all. Expressions of surprise and disbelief chased themselves across the faces of the Uckwatts. Brother and sister stared at one another in mute amazement, then at the vicar and Mrs. Ludlow, then at Dr. Chevenix, and then at little Bertram.

The brow of the yeoman farmer visibly hardened. Unfolding his considerable frame from his chair, he turned an offended eye upon the vicar and, taking a step in the clergyman's direction, one hand clenched at his side and the other fingering his sword, growled darkly —

"Here, now! What's your game, then, eh? For that's a whopper if ever I heard one!"

It was the vicar's turn to be surprised. "Game? Whopper? I'm afraid I don't understand you, Mr. Uckwatt — "

"Do you think you're funny, parading this boy before us here like a calf at auction?"

"Funny? Dear me, no, sir — "

"What is this, then — a put-up job? Here, what's your dodge?" the farmer glowered, thrusting his chin at the clergyman, not to mention his clenched fist.

"My very word! A put-up job? Mr. Uckwatt, I can assure you that — um — er — that — that — "

"Tummas, please!" cried Mrs. Maconchy, grasping at her brother's arm to stay him. "The man's a reverend gentleman of the cloth. Please to excuse the liberty, sir — "

"Now, then, no need to take umbrage, my good fellow," spoke up Dr. Chevenix. "This is no 'game,' as you call it, and certainly no 'put-up job.' This child was found in Marley Wood by the vicar here, with the aid of our good friend Sir Hector MacHector. You've heard of Sir Hector MacHector of Mickledene Hall, have you not? Ah, I thought you might have done. This boy was discovered in a ruined hunting-lodge in the wood, one built centuries ago by a man called de Clinkers. The child informed us that his name was Bertram, and that his family was from Butter Cross — a family composed of parents, an older sister, and two older brothers. Since then we have uncovered evidence that he was here on a Snailsby fair-day many years ago, in the company of certain cousins of his from Dragonthorpe, and that they had visited an elderly relation of theirs then living in our town, a man named Good-acre. It is a curious story to say the least, but one that has been borne out by a number of facts. In consequence we wrote off to Mr. Slaw of the Lizard's Head, and so the rest you know."

While the doctor was speaking, the brow of Mr. Uckwatt was observed to soften a little, and his scowl gradually relax into a frown, one more indicative of thought now than of confrontation.

"Aye," he nodded, rubbing his jaw, "it *were* Gaffer Goodacre as we'd come to see — and to see the fair, o' course." He waved his hand in a gesture of impatience. "But this here's nowt but a boy! Where be our cousin? For our Bertie, he'll be a grown man today."

"We was all about the same age, sir," Mrs. Maconchy explained.

"It's rather a mystery, we do admit," said the doctor, "but there is no means by which this child could have learned any of the particulars he has related to us. He has knowledge that can have been acquired only if he were here in Market Snailsby some five-and-thirty years ago, as he claims."

"But how can that *be,* sir?"

"To be perfectly frank, Mrs. Maconchy, I can't explain it. I'll not deny that the entire affair stumps me, but there it is. Now, then, why don't you ask Bertram a question or two? Perhaps you'll be able to draw something out of him that will persuade you."

"And it's the truth, every word of it," said little Sukey, speaking up in Bertram's defense. "I've talked to him myself. For a child will know when another child is lying, and Bertram isn't lying."

Another pause ensued, during which the visitors undertook a whispered conference a little apart from the rest.

"Ou, aye, this is a fine look-out," grumbled Mr. Uckwatt. "They've got a cheek to be telling us a yarn like that."

"But whatever for, Tummas?" his sister countered. "Why should a reverend gentleman of the cloth and his wife, and the good doctor there, be wanting to deceive us?"

"Such I can't say, Phan, though I do believe there's money behind it — reward money," said the yeoman farmer, with a knowing glance. "Ou, aye. Sure as Sunday, they'll be demanding brass of us to cover their costs. You'll see."

"Tummas, are you daft mad?"

"Look at this drawing-room — this 'reverend gentleman' of yours has a pretty soft life, I'll say. Likely he's got a wine-cellar to be stocked besides. Where do you think he gets his money, eh? From squeezing his parishioners, for a start. But sure, that ain't enough for *this* life; he'll be needing more. Ou, aye, I know these crafty parsons. This one looks like a sherry man to me — no country cider for him! There's more than bread and treacle dressing his table of an evening."

"S-h-h-h! Now, don't you be accusing, Tummas Uckwatt," his sister warned.

"And his gardener skulking there in the corner — what's he up to, eh? He's got a face that would make a cat laugh. And your 'good doctor' there's a ripe old quack, I'll be bound — "

"Mind your tongue, Tummas, mind your tongue!" snapped his sister, briskly canceling him. "I won't be embarrassed afore the parson and his wife. Why don't you ask the child there a question, like the doctor said?"

To this request the yeoman farmer grudgingly assented, if for no other reason than to persuade his sister of the rightness of his opinion.

"Well, boy," he said, fixing Bertram with a skeptical look, "your family's name is Longchapel. Come, did you know that?"

"I remember it now," Bertram said brightly. "Although I didn't remember it before, for it was so long ago. And who are you?"

"There! D'you see, Phan? He don't know us," exclaimed Mr. Uckwatt in triumphant proof to his sister.

"Well, of course he don't know us, Tummas — we was children then!" Frustrated by his stubbornness, Mrs. Maconchy overrode him and took up the questioning herself. "Tell me, little boy," she said, "do you recollect your brothers Willie and Jack?"

"Yes," said Bertram.

"And your sister Polly?"

In response Bertram made an ugly face, one which communicated to everyone present his perfect dislike of the individual so named.

"You don't care for your sister, then?"

Bertram shook his head vigorously.

"Perhaps we should send for her, boy? How would you like that? Or perhaps we should pack you off to her by coach to Butter Cross?" Mr. Uckwatt suggested, with a glance of particular meaning.

"Oh, please, sir, no, sir!" Bertram begged, wringing his tiny hands in anguish. "Not *her* — not my sister Polly! I never liked her, for she never liked me. She always hated me. She used to box my ears and call me a tiddler. She was the one who made them send me away."

"Poor dear! Whyever didn't she like you, Bertram?" said Mrs. Ludlow, her heart near to melting.

"She called me a nuisance. She never liked the other children. She wanted to be with the grown-ups. She never liked me or my brothers. She was so very selfish. She wanted the grown-ups all for herself. She wanted it *all* for herself."

"This is most extraordinary," exclaimed Dr. Chevenix. "I've never heard the like."

"Nor we, doctor," said Mrs. Maconchy.

"He's telling you the truth," Sukey declared. "He *is* your cousin. Can't you see that? He was lost in the wood, but now he's come out."

The visitors exchanged heated whispers for another few minutes, at which point Mrs. Maconchy announced —

"Tummas and me, we've decided we must think the matter out for now. We don't rightly understand how such a thing can be. For the boy's exactly correct — he didn't care for Miss Polly, but disliked her something fierce. I recollect he talked of that, and more. You remember, don't you, Tummas?"

"Aye," the yeoman farmer was obliged to admit. "Aye, that I do, indeed."

"We thank you kindly for looking after the child. We've lodgings at the Mudlark for the night, and so we must go there now and think the matter out."

"By all means," the vicar nodded. "We quite understand your perplexity. Dear me, we are all rather perplexed ourselves. Most everything Bertram has told us has been confirmed. What other answer can there be but that he is your cousin?"

As the visitors were preparing to take their leave, a small voice spoke up unexpectedly and asked —

"Where is Dandaline? Have you brought her with you? May I see her? I remember now, I gave her some carrots on the fair-day. Have you any carrots for Dandaline?"

Brother and sister froze in their tracks as if stunned. Then, like a pair of clockwork figures, they turned slowly round on their heels, their mouths agape, and stared straight at Bertram. Gone from their eyes was any lingering trace of doubt, distrust, or suspicion, all of it wiped clean away like chalk from a board.

In his corner Mr. Swain, the ersatz gardener, drew a long breath, and waited for more.

"Who is Dandaline?" the vicar asked.

"Dandaline," said Mrs. Maconchy, swallowing hard and staring, "were our father's old cart-horse when we was children. It were Dandaline as brought us from Dragonthorpe to Market Snailsby on the fair-day. And we was wont to give her carrots . . ."

Mrs. Ludlow felt the heart in her breast give a thump. "Oh, Hugh," she cried, gripping her husband's hand, "it *is* true — all of it — every word. How else can he have known?"

The visitors continued to stare at Bertram; it seemed they could not wrest their eyes from his small figure. Then Mrs. Maconchy dropped to her knees and made of him a closer scrutiny, passing her fingers lightly over his cheeks, his thatch of yellow hair, his forehead, his little nose, his chin . . .

"Lord, Phan," gulped the yeoman farmer, his brow deeply riven like a ploughed field — "Lord, Phan, how can it be?"

"I don't rightly know, Tummas — "

His sister reached back in her memory — far, far back, to those dim, long-ago days when she had been a little girl no older than Sukey, and her cousin Bertram had come down from Butter Cross for a visit. Long-vanished days they were, from the springtime of her life — her childhood days — so serene, so magical, so carefree they had been! Such glorious and wonderfully golden days — happy days, untainted by life's experience — days that were little more than a dream to her now, so distant had they grown, and so lost, and like her dear, remembered Dandaline, never to come again.

"Oh, Tummas," she exclaimed, her voice cracking — "oh, Tummas, Tummas, d'you not see it in his little face? It is Bertram — it *is* — for certain sure, 'tis our little Bertie Longchapel!"

"But, Phan! Phan! *How?*" her brother demanded.

"I don't know, Tummas, I don't know, but it surely is. You remember us, don't you, Bertie? Your cousins from Dragonthorpe? We went berry-picking over to Foxcote, we did, and then come to Snailsby to see the Gaffer, as was cousin at some distance to Mother's family. And here — here — " she plucked her brother's sleeve and drew him closer — "here be Tummas — here be your cousin, Tummas Uckwatt. D'you recollect us now? Your cousins Tummas and Phanny?"

"I believe so," said Bertram, screwing up his little face in a positive spasm of thinking. It was clear he was making a mighty effort to remember. "But you are so much *bigger* than Tummas and Phanny — you're both grown-ups! If you are my cousins as you say, why are you so old?"

It was the same question that had baffled every one of the interested persons who had gathered in the parish rooms.

Why, oh why, indeed, were they all so old?

Tears stood in Mrs. Maconchy's eyes. Here he was at last, her little cousin who had disappeared so completely and inexplicably all those many years ago. But the poor confused woman, truth to tell, had no idea now what to do with him.

What to do with a child who rightly should be a grown-up man? What to do with a child who had spent five-and-thirty years in Marley Wood doing — what, exactly? What to do with a child who to all appearances was Bertram Longchapel, but who couldn't possibly be?

At a loss for any immediate solution, she patted Bertram on his small shoulder, just as Mrs. Ludlow had come to do, and assured him that something would be worked out. Then, dashing away the tears, she rose to her feet.

"We're very sorry, Tummas and me, for doubting you, sir," she told the vicar. "My brother, he does have a temper, I know, but he ain't a churl. I'm sure he wouldn't have punched you."

"Ou, no," averred Mr. Uckwatt, shaking his head.

"Though you must see our position. As you can imagine, sir, this ain't the sort of matter as is to be taken at first hearing — "

"Of course, of course," the vicar smiled. "No need to explain, Mrs. Maconchy — we quite understand. You're perfectly in the right. Gracious heavens, you must have thought we were all cracked."

"Ou, aye," nodded the yeoman farmer.

"Tummas!" his sister warned him.

"We could scarcely believe it ourselves," Mrs. Ludlow explained. "We took him at first for a little slodger-child."

"I told you Bertram was telling the truth," said Sukey.

The visitors, despite their joy at finding their lost cousin, seemed a trifle uncomfortable now with their discovery. They didn't much care for the oddness of the situation they had been placed in, and were hankering to be off to the Mudlark. The matter needed thinking out, as Mrs. Maconchy had said, and as a result she did not want to take charge of little Bertram just yet. As for the yeoman farmer, he looked to be sorely in need of a pint and the comfort of a cozy tap-room, and as soon as possible, too.

Mrs. Maconchy informed the Ludlows that she and her brother would call again the next day with their decision. To Mrs. Ludlow she gave the address of Bertram's sister, Miss Polly Longchapel of Upper Lofting, Butter Cross, Wuffolk. In her turn Mrs. Ludlow assured her that her husband would write off to the lady as soon as possible. The visitors then bade their adieus and drove away.

After thinking it all out in the comfort of the Mudlark, the unease of the Uckwatts was multiplied tenfold. Most of their suspicions as regards the vicar had been dispelled, but in their place were new concerns. Cousins or no, they were not so sure now that they wanted to be taking responsibility for little Bertram Longchapel. They were not so sure they wanted his mysterious small self wandering about Dragonthorpe and Foxcote, frightening the townspeople, and themselves — for an object of fear the child surely would become. To take him home with them was out of the question; and so the decision was made that Miss Polly Longchapel of Upper Lofting, Butter Cross, Wuffolk, and no one else, should take charge of the boy. For she was his sister, after all, while they were merely his cousins.

His mysterious small self was a puzzle which neither of them was very keen to be working out just now; for although they were happy that their cousin had been found alive and in health, they were a little afraid of him as well.

How in the name of heaven could he still be a little boy after all these years? By what bizarre trick of nature — or supernature — had he been restored to them, and in such a fashion?

Nothing of the kind had ever happened before in Dragonthorpe, or Foxcote, or Locksley, or any other town with which they were familiar; and it had set them to wondering how anything good could be behind it, or could come of it.

THE SIXTH CHAPTER

OUT OF THE TWILIGHT

THE hour was late, and so too was Mr. Richard Hathaway, as he jogged Rosie homewards following his visit with Mr. Blathers.

The shattered lens of his new magnifying spectacles having been replaced, Mr. Blathers had invited Richard round to his bachelor quarters in Maylord Street to admire the handiwork. There, with a warm fire crackling in the grate, the two friends had spent a pleasant afternoon talking over recent events, in the genial company of their pipes and some hearty mugs of cocoa. And as it is wont to do on such occasions, the time had passed fleetly by; now it was late, and both Richard and Rosie were anxious to be home before the dark set in. A small rift had appeared in the overcast, and through it a few early stars were shining. It is the first glimpse Richard has had of an untarnished heaven since his return from Newmarsh.

As they approach the gate an exuberant Snap comes bounding out of the drive to meet them. The chimneys of Mead Cottage are smoking away right lustily in the twilight, the ruddy glow in the kitchen casements bearing witness to the activities of Mrs. Rudling at her chopping-board. Supper shortly, then another pipe, and perhaps a little music in the evening — all in all, Richard thinks to himself, it is good to be home!

"Do you suppose that's the Dog Star?" Snap asks as he falls in beside Rosie. Like Richard, both have spied the handful of stars peeping overhead.

"You think every star is the Dog Star," chuckles the mare.

"Well, what other star is as bright, or as important?" Snap says in return. "Besides which, it's the only star I've ever heard of."

"You've heard of the constellation of Pegasus, haven't you?"

"What is a constellation?"

"What about the Pole Star?"

"What is that?"

"You don't know your astronomy, Snap, that I can see," smiles Rosie. "But I suppose it's because you haven't the need to. Being a dog you're not often called upon to navigate on long drives. But we road-horses, we're regularly charged with the task — the drive to Tillington the other week, for instance, and before that to Pitchford, by Shipton-on-Lour — and so we need to know our stars and our constellations. For it's the sun and stars that a good road-horse, and other animals, too, will use to guide their way by."

"But when have we any sun in Fenshire?" counters Snap, rightly enough. "And as for the stars, well, we hardly ever see them, apart from those nights when the moon is out. And they're not so common, as you know."

"Well, you've got a point there," says Rosie, with a thoughtful bob of her head. "In any case, come by the stable some time and I'll teach you a little astronomy. We'll start with Pegasus, for it's the logical place to begin. It's the best constellation, after all."

"Thank you, Rosie. You've always been a decent one for teaching a fellow new things."

By now Richard has dismounted and is leading Rosie through the gate, when the easy small-talk between the mare and Snap abruptly breaks off. Rosie has cocked her ears and is listening hard, while Snap is trying to catch a whiff of something on the air. Without warning the mare stops short, which causes Richard, who has been striding along with the reins in hand, to experience a sudden arrest of motion.

"What's the matter, Rosie?" he asks, dropping back.

He sees that both she and Snap have gone on the alert. Something there in the murky twilight, he recognizes, is not entirely to their liking.

"What is it, Snap? What do you smell?"

Comes the distant roar of a marsh devil from out on the fens. It is a cruel, savage sound, one that sets Richard's nerves on edge. But its source lies over the river; the attentions of Rosie and Snap instead are directed at the gloomy meadow across the road, just this side of Wackwire House, behind which the tall curtain of Marley Wood can be seen looming through the mist.

The mare throws back her head and snorts through her silky nostrils. Richard, on the alert now himself, gently draws his cutlass from its scabbard. His first thought is that a beast of some kind, either devil or spotted lion, may be lurking round the eaves of the wood — or worse, may be stealing towards them through the darkened meadow. His second thought is to shut tight the gate.

"Is it a cat, Rosie? Where is it? Snap, can you smell it?" he says, reaching for the latch.

At that moment his ears detect a sound — a low rumble of hooves — and his eyes a minute flicker of light in the wood. As he watches he can see the light moving slowly through the trees, in concert with the hoofbeats, which appear to be gaining in volume.

Phantom riders!

But how can it be? For there is no moon showing, only the handful of stars, and the riders are known to be votaries of the fair Diana; even Bertram had testified to that.

Because the moon must be out, otherwise they will not come.

Richard stands waiting, his blade at the ready. What should he do? Should he alert Jemma and Mrs. Rudling inside the house? But by then the riders, if riders they be, may well have passed them by in the twilight. All in a moment he decides that he must see these visitations, ghostly or otherwise, no matter the cost; and so he swings again into the saddle, and spurs Rosie through the gate and across the road and into the meadow, with the faithful Snap trailing close behind them.

"I know that scent!" yelps the coach dog. "It's like nothing else I've ever smelled. And I'm not glad to be smelling it again — but ghostly riders it isn't, I'm afraid!"

This information regrettably he cannot impart to his master, whose knowledge of the canine tongue is scanty at best.

Slap-dash through the meadow gallops Rosie with her long, graceful stride. At the edge of the wood Richard reins her in, and there, under the soaring towers of spruce and pine, and the cold stars blinking overhead, they pause for a moment to listen.

It is unmistakable now — the thunder of hoofbeats coming steadily on. Meantime the flicker of light in the trees has grown stronger, and brighter, and clearer; for it too is coming steadily on.

"Who is it? Who can it be?" wonders Richard.

For it has become plain to both his ear and his eye that it is no company of riders that is approaching, but only a single mount, and that the light is but a single light. Horse and horseman are approaching at a good lick, however, speeding through the eaves of the wood on a course roughly parallel to the Tillington Road — that is to say, they are making straight for Market Snailsby.

They will be nearing Richard's post in a very few moments. Consequently he spurs Rosie forward a little, but she is reluctant to move. The valiant Snap, too, seems to be holding back, in fear no doubt of the thing that is coming steadily on. For Snap knows very well what is coming, having encountered it once before behind the wall of firs. But his master has not an inkling.

"You'll not want to get any closer!" he warns. "No, no, master — keep your distance from it, for goodness' sake!"

"What *is* it?" Rosie asks, scouring the air with her nostrils. "For it isn't a scent I recognize. Although it is a horsy kind of scent, after a fashion — "

"Horsy, yes, but no horse," replies Snap. "Please, Rosie — can't you do something? Can't you make him clear out of here? For we haven't much time!"

"He has a tight hold on my reins," says the mare. "And I shouldn't like to disobey him, he is such a good fellow and all — gracious, he might give me the chop!"

"What's wrong with that? I'm rather fond of chops."

"Not that kind of chop. He could sell me — send me away — then I'd be for it."

"Oh, Rosie, I'm sure he wouldn't!"

"But could you blame him? For he wants to know what it is that's coming there in the wood."

"But do *you* want to know?" Snap asks her.

"Well, not particularly . . ."

Whatever it is, it is nearly upon them now. Richard sits alert in the saddle, his heart racing, his eyes straining to pierce the gloom. All at once something breaks from the trees a short distance away, and the flicker of light can be seen for what it is — a lantern, gripped in the hand of a horseman. He is a tiny horseman, from what little Richard can see of him, and his mount an uncommonly large one, and a tall one, and rather oddly shaped.

"Hallo! Hallo! Who are you?" Richard calls out to the rider. "What are you doing here? What do you want?"

Plainly the man cannot hear him. Brighter and brighter grows the light, and louder the drumbeat of hooves, as the horse's heaving frame comes rushing, rushing on.

"Come away, master, come away!" Snap pleads, but to no avail.

Richard nudges the mare forward a step or two, but Rosie, panting and snorting, has had enough. Like Snap she doesn't care for the whiff of the thing that is coming on, or for the look of it, either. As it thunders down upon them she shies and, recoiling on her haunches, gives a wild plunge of fright. Richard, taken off his guard by her actions, loses hold of the reins and is thrown to the turf. Fortunately for him it is a springy turf; but the crash is a bone-shaker nonetheless, and jars him severely in body and brain.

"Look out, master, look out!" cries Snap — *"See where it comes!"*

At the last instant both horse and horseman catch sight of Richard sprawled upon the ground and, throwing their weight violently aside, come to a lurching halt a mere yard from his outstretched form.

Dazed, shaken, Richard lifts up his eyes, and in the glare of the lantern squints at a vision he can scarcely comprehend. The hair rises on his scalp; a strangled exclamation escapes his lips. Instinctively he rears back from it, not knowing if the thing standing over him in a smoking heat is real, or simply a trick of his jumbled brain; for it is a thing that is well-nigh impossible. He gulps, as if to swallow his heart back into its place again, and tries to make some sense of it.

Is that a little girl and not a horseman that he sees, sitting astride the animal he has mistaken for a horse? For the creature, with its powerful forelegs and immense loins and hocks, stands some twenty hands high if it stands an inch, and is unlike any horse Richard has ever laid eyes on. Suspended from its rider's left hand is the lantern; with her other she clings to the animal's thick orange mane. But is it a horse's mane she clings to or is it human hair, tumbling down in waves from the creature's human head — a human head planted atop a human torso, one furnished with a pair of lean and sinewy arms, and with a bow and quiver slung across its shoulder?

And the tiny rider holding the lantern — is she not the little girl he had seen at the window of Mead Cottage? Is she not little Sarah, the companion of Bertram?

The eyes of her impossible mount fix him with a searching look. There is something hypnotic in its gaze, something paralyzing, which is felt not only by Richard but by Snap and Rosie, too. The lips of the monster are curled back in a hideous leer, its teeth bared to the gums; an ugly growl rattles in its throat. Then little Sarah releases her grip on its mane, and as Richard watches in horrified fascination the head of the creature rises up, its neck drawn out an impossible length into a slender, flexible tube, and swoops down low for a peer at him.

Despite its extreme contortions of visage, there is something in the monster's face that resembles a woman's, just as its tumbling hair resembles a woman's flowing tresses. Or so Richard thinks, for the brief moment that his mind is clear; then the creature's head rolls sharply back, its eyes close, and from its throat erupts a horrid scream — an ear-shattering explosion that fills the whole air, and threatens to shake the very mist from the trees. It is the same weird, unearthly wail that was heard in the wood the day the survey party brought Bertram out.

The outburst concluded, the snake-like neck of the creature swiftly retracts, shortening down, and down, and down, until the head has resumed its place on the torso; at which point the monster wheels round and with its tiny rider still a-cling goes lunging off in the direction of town. And before Richard can collect his staggered wits the flicker of light and the drumbeat of hooves have been reduced to a memory, and are seen and heard no more.

THE SEVENTH CHAPTER

CONCERNING WINE, AND A WINDOW

THERE was a dinner that evening at the vicarage, with Mr. Ludlow and his wife playing host to the matronly but fashionable keeper of the beasts, Mrs. Chugwell, and Miss Ada Henslowe, and old Corney. Little Bertram, too, had been accorded a seat at the table, for Mrs. Chugwell had not seen him since she had held him in her arms on the ride back from the lodge. Mrs. Ludlow and the gossipy Jayne Scrimshaw were serving, the vicar was carving, and everyone was very keen to be eating. Absent from the feast was young Matt Chugwell, who had taken an early dinner with some friends at the Mudlark, that same establishment where the Uckwatts were busy pondering their stewardship of Bertram.

There was talk now of these Uckwatts at the vicar's table, as everyone sat down to their boiled fowl and fen-cress, cutlets, and bogberry wine, and talked over the particulars of the Ludlows' interview with the respectable yeoman farmer and his sister.

"Yes, I know something of Dragonthorpe, and of Foxcote, too," Mrs. Chugwell was saying, "but of these Uckwatts I know nothing. Are they a family of some account?"

"The lady's married name is Maconchy," said Mrs. Ludlow. "Her husband is a journeyman playwright, or something of that kind, I believe."

"Ah — um — that's a joiner and wheelwright, my dear," corrected her husband.

"Indeed? Well, I knew it had something to do with writing. I thought they were plays."

Bertram meanwhile had been quietly attending to his dinner, and showing little interest in the conversation. He had been placed between the vicar, who as per usual was at the top of the table, and Miss Henslowe. Mrs. Chugwell was seated opposite him, and was the first to address the boy.

"And what of you, Bertram?" she asked. "You have some recollection of these cousins of yours, as I hear?"

"Yes," he answered.

"And would you like to go home with them?"

"No."

"And why not, might I ask?"

"Because I'd like to return to my friends."

"Indeed?"

"You needn't ask him about his sister," the vicar put in. "I'm afraid he had a very strident reaction to the mention of her name. Evidently she treated him rather badly."

"I see. A fine family, I'm sure," smiled the mastodon lady.

"Tell us, Bertram," Ada spoke up cheerily, "would you happen to know someone called Mother Redcap?"

A hush fell over the table. No one had expected Ada to be quite so bold. But of course Miss Ada Henslowe was just the person to be bold; for, as she was quick to observe, no one as yet had questioned Bertram himself on this point they all had wondered about.

The boy chewed thoughtfully for a time before answering. "I don't believe so. Who is she, Miss Henslowe?"

"Well, young man," said Corney, with a sidewise glance at Ada, "curiously enough there are one or two of us present who suspect she may be your guardian there at the lodge."

Bertram shook his head. "Oh, no, I don't think so."

"She is not your guardian, then? The one who has no name?" said the vicar.

"I'm sure she has a name, but she doesn't want us to know it."

"But she is very old?"

"Yes."

"How old exactly, Bertram?" Ada asked.

The boy responded with a heave of his small shoulders.

"Well, give us a clue. Seventy years? Eighty? Ninety, perhaps?"

Another heave, another shake of the head.

"Perhaps a hundred, then? What do you say to a hundred years old?"

"Oh," Bertram answered with perfect seriousness, "I'm certain she's many hundreds of years older than that."

His reply sparked much fresh conversation and debate — not to say a few chuckles — of which Bertram took scarcely any notice. He was more interested in his dinner, to which he had applied himself with considerable relish, than in any further talk of his guardian; although he did reiterate his wish, for the benefit of any who had not heard, that he would rather be with his friends at the lodge. He didn't want to go to Dragonthorpe with the Uckwatts, didn't want to see the Lizard's Head, or Snailsby Mill, or any other of the manifold delights of south Fenshire. And he certainly didn't want to be packed off to Butter Cross to a sister who despised him.

"My gracious, he seems most adamant," said Mrs. Chugwell.

"Oh, indeed," nodded the vicar. "Although I'm afraid we shall be obliged to respect the decision of Mr. Uckwatt and his sister. For they are young Bertram's relations, or so it would appear, and as such are in a better position to judge what may be best for him. In any case it's a family matter."

"I expect he won't care a jot what his cousins decide," Ada predicted.

"Nor should I blame him," said Mrs. Chugwell. "Having traveled widely throughout these towns and counties, I shouldn't care to live in Foxcote myself — such a deadly dull place! — or in Dragonthorpe either."

"Our Dr. Chevenix thinks Dragonthorpe a pleasant enough town," spoke up Mrs. Ludlow. "So he told us this very day. Did he not tell us, Hugh?"

"He did," affirmed her husband.

"Well, it's each to his own taste, I'm sure," smiled Mrs. Chugwell. "As for Butter Cross, my son and I have passed through it a time or two with the beasts. An ancient small market-town, a trifle stale and mildewed, perhaps, and as cold as Christmas — colder than any spot in Fenshire, of that you may be sure. Well, it's so far to the northwards, you see."

"What else do you know of it, Mrs. Chugwell?" Ada asked.

"Not very much, as there is not much of it to know. It boasts a single inn — the Plough — and that not a particularly memorable one. The landlord is not the friendliest of sorts — not at all like your dear Mr. Travers of the Badger! As for this 'Upper Lofting' you mentioned, vicar, I cannot offer any certain knowledge. Presumably it is one of the rather modest estates lying in the hills above the town. Nor do I have knowledge of any Longchapels."

"It seems this Miss Longchapel, Bertram's sister, is head of the family now," the vicar said. "But she and Bertram don't get on — um — er — well, that is to say they *didn't* get on, years ago. He was the youngest child, and his sister and brothers were not always kind to him. At any rate, he seems not to care that his brothers are dead. They were never friends, evidently. A sad case."

"His friends live at the lodge," Ada said sympathetically, "and that is where he means to be again some day."

"Oh, Hugh — we can't allow him to go back there, can we?" said Mrs. Ludlow. Truth be told, she would have been perfectly happy had the Uckwatts presented Bertram to her as a gift wrapped up in ribbons and a bow, for she would have accepted him in a trice. "The poor little dear! Return him to the lodge? However would he survive?"

"But my dear," said her husband, gently, "from all we know he has done rather well for himself there for some five-and-thirty years."

"What of Dr. Chevenix? Has he examined the boy?" Mrs. Chugwell asked.

"Oh, indeed, and has pronounced him in the pink of health."

"Nonetheless, there has been some measles about," Corney warned. "Let us hope that we haven't exposed the boy to that affliction."

"Bertram," said Mrs. Ludlow, "have you ever had the measles?"

The child considered for a moment. "I don't believe so. What are they? A kind of vegetable?"

"No. The measles is an illness — a very serious one," Corney told him. "Small red spots appear on the skin, and there is much coughing and sneezing, and a fever. My son Phil was stricken with it when he was a boy. It can be very serious."

Bertram shook his head vigorously, declaring that no, he had never suffered from anything of the sort. In fact he could not recall ever being ill since he had come to live at the lodge.

To his credit Bertram understood that the Ludlows had only his welfare at heart in keeping him at the vicarage. He harbored no ill will towards them, and hoped eventually to be reunited with his friends in the wood — it was his home, after all. He knew that the vicar and Mrs. Ludlow were simply doing what they thought was right and proper in looking out for him.

Talk of Bertram and the lodge led inevitably to talk of the new road. Mrs. Chugwell, beaming and twinkling, delivered the glad tidings now that Angus Daintie and the drivers had broken camp at Deadmarsh, and would be arriving shortly with the beasts to commence the season's operations.

"Poor Ranger," she sighed. "He's been a bit lonely without them. Oh, it's true, he has had Matt, and there are the town children to entertain — he simply adores children! — but there's nothing to compare with one's own kind."

"I saw him in the fields behind the Badger this morning," said Ada. "The sight of a tusker, or any thunder-beast for that matter, still has power to take my breath away. I recall, when I was a child my father used to take me across the bridge to see the shaggy reds coming up the Drovers' Road from Slopshire. What a grand spectacle they all were! But the trains pass through not nearly so often now."

"That will change, my dear, once the road has been cleared," Mrs. Chugwell assured her. "Think of it — entire long caravans of beasts rumbling down from Newmarsh and Ridingham, Ardley and Bishop's Strother, Fishmouth, and elsewhere besides."

"Oh, I say, I can't wait for your tuskers to arrive!" Ada exclaimed.

"Or for the tremors as well," Corney remarked with a chuckle. "For a single tusker on the Common is earth-shaking enough, but an entire team is of wholly another order."

"And what say you, Bertram? Would you like to see a team of shovel-tuskers?" the vicar asked.

"I should like to return to the lodge, if you please," the boy replied.

"Do you know," said Ada, "that none of us has a clue how Bertram has managed it? Well, I for one should very much like to find it out. It will be one fewer mystery on our plate."

"What has Bertram managed, dear?" Mrs. Ludlow asked.

Once more Ada was about to surprise them with her boldness.

"Bertram," she said, in an easy, conversational manner, "how is it that you've remained a little boy for so long? For you know, if you and your cousins are to be believed, you've been rattling around in that lodge of yours for a good many years now. Well, it's awfully hard for us to fathom. How is it that you've not grown up?"

Bertram creased his brow, and meditated over the problem for a spell.

How silly that no one had thought to ask him the key question they all had been asking one another! They had deemed him either too young, or too small, or too ignorant to know the answer — which of course was absurd. It was the reverse of that question which Bertram himself had posed to certain of the interested persons, and to the cousins from Dragonthorpe — why, oh, why had they grown so old?

"It was so long ago, I can't rightly remember," he said presently, "but it may have had something to do with the drink she gave me."

"A drink?" echoed Ada.

"When I was first brought to the lodge, I was given a drink from a silver cup by the lady there. It was a very thick and slimy drink, and tasted very bad."

"By 'lady' do you mean your guardian, the one who works magic? She is the one who gave you the drink?"

"Yes. She called it a — a — a *posset*, I believe. Yes, a posset. She said it was very good for me, and that it would protect me, and that I should never after want for health."

"Do you recall what was in the drink?"

Bertram shook his head. "I'm very sorry, Miss Henslowe. Although I do remember, the lady told me it had some of her blood in it."

Another hush descended upon the table.

It had some of her blood in it — that was not very reassuring. What could it signify? Mother Redcap's devotion to witchcraft, perhaps? Was this drink the magic elixir that Ada had postulated might be keeping Mother Redcap alive, and the children young — or was it something more sinister, something devilish? Or was it something else entirely, of which they had as yet no inkling?

Needless to say, no one knew quite what to make of the revelation.

"In all my travels," Mrs. Chugwell stated, "I have never heard the like."

"Nor I in my duties," said Corney, the retired magistrate and J.P. for the county.

Ada frowned, wishing almost that she had not broached the subject. "I expect this will be one for Mr. Blathers," she said, dryly. "I believe we have quite enough now on our plate! Sufficient unto the day — eh, vicar?"

In an effort to shake off the mood Bertram's words had cast them into, the vicar smiled, rubbed his hands together briskly and, glancing round the table, declared —

"Yes, I dare say it was a most unusual concoction, this posset of Bertram's. As for the bogberry wine you are enjoying tonight, well, I fear I must apologize for it. It is not of the finest, although it is much superior to our last few bottles. Is that not so, my dear? But I'm afraid it's the best one can do under the circumstances."

"Not to worry, vicar — it's not so dreadful," Corney assured him. But the retired magistrate and J.P. for the county was lying through his peg-like teeth. He had barely managed to stifle a grimace upon sampling this latest vintage. The wines on offer at the vicar's table were famously bad — everybody knew it — but Mrs. Ludlow's dinners were well worth the trouble. Corney, however, was too much the guest and a gentleman to be finding fault, or to give utterance to anything so uncharitable as the truth.

As for the present dinner, it was a modest composition but a tasty one, and in the opinion of Mrs. Chugwell *perfectly splendid.*

"One thing I am very much looking forward to, once the road has been completed, is an Ogghops sherry," the vicar remarked. "For you know, they're very hard to come by round here. One must travel to Ridingham or Newmarsh to find a bottle — that is, of course, if there is a bottle to be found. For even in the north there is precious little Ogghops to be had."

"What is an Ogghops sherry?" Bertram inquired.

"An Ogghops? Ah! Well, young man, an Ogghops is a very nice wine, yes, indeed. Very dry, and rather distinctive in appearance, so far as sherries go — it's a faint shade of green — and highly prized as a result. Oh, yes, an Ogghops is very nice."

"Why do you ask, Bertram?" said Ada.

"Would you like to have one now?" Bertram asked the vicar. "For you and Mrs. Ludlow have been so kind to me, giving me these new clothes and looking after me here, that I should like to do something for you in return."

"Like to have one — ?" the vicar echoed, not quite understanding.

"An Ogghops sherry."

Amused expressions all round, save for Miss Henslowe, whose intuition was telling her that something unusual was about to happen.

"Well, it's very nice of you, dear," smiled Mrs. Ludlow, "but I'm sure the vicar can wait for his sherry. He has more than a few wines left in his cellar."

"Yes, and a cellar of wine is a very comfortable thing in a house," her husband noted.

"Where can one find an Ogghops in Market Snailsby?" wondered Corney. "Perhaps Joliffe at the Mudlark — "

"I don't see how it can be possible," "Most unlikely," "Amusing child," were some of the remarks that went round the table.

But no such remarks passed the lips of Ada, who had been watching Bertram closely. She saw him shut his eyes now and wrinkle up his little brow, as if steeling himself for some vigorous exercise of mind. Seconds later he began speaking quietly in a strange, low voice. The words were rather difficult to make out; to Ada and the others they sounded something like a child's nursery rhyme. After about a minute of this, he opened his eyes and reached a hand towards the vicar's glass of bogberry wine. Concentrating very hard he swept his hand over the glass with a vaguely circular motion — once, twice, three times. This activity he concluded with a brief flutter of his fingers, followed by a sudden, sharp snap.

Immediately something stirred in the glass. As all watched, the rich, deep, violet color of the wine began to fade: paler and paler it grew, changing from violet to red to pink before their very eyes, then growing paler still until it was almost entirely clear, before assuming a final, faintly greenish tinge.

With a smile Bertram nodded towards the glass, as though inviting Mr. Ludlow to partake.

The vicar touched the wine to his lips — albeit a trifle hesitantly — and tasted it. Great was his astonishment at the result. His eyebrows flew up like wings; and holding the glass off, he stared at it in disbelief.

"God bless my soul," he exclaimed.

"What is it, dear?" his wife asked.

"Look at the wine, my dear — look at it! It's green. It's — it's — it's an Ogghops sherry!"

"But how can that be?"

"I poured it out myself from a bottle of bogberry, and it *was* bogberry, not many minutes ago. But now it's Ogghops!"

"But, my dear, we have no Ogghops," his wife reminded him.

"Of course we don't, but now we do — half a glass of it, at any rate. Dear me, dear me . . ."

The vicar sank back in his chair, thunderstruck.

"Oh, I say!" Ada exclaimed. Her delight at this little show of skill on Bertram's part — and so neatly done, too — was unbounded, and so wholly genuine, and so exuberant besides, that she clapped out loud. *If only Richard were here,* she thought, *he'd be jiggered!*

All eyes were on Bertram as he turned to the vicar and asked — "How do you like it?"

"How is this possible, Bertram?" said Mr. Ludlow. "How are you able to make an Ogghops from bogberry wine? How are you able to make anything from bogberry wine?"

"As I'm alive, sir," said Jayne Scrimshaw, who had been watching from the door in growing alarm, "the boy's enchanted!"

"As I remember, Mother Redcap was said to have performed illusions of this type — transmuting one substance into another," Corney remarked. "Most maintained it was a charlatan's trick for cozening the gullible, effected by quite ordinary means. But *this!*"

"And what's to be next, sir, if ye'll excuse the liberty?" Jayne asked. "Rhubarb from cabbage stalks? Purple apple pie? Or is the sky to rain hickory nuts?"

"In all my travels never once have I seen such a thing," Mrs. Chugwell declared. "My gracious, vicar, it's certainly no trick, for the wine never left your glass. And the glass was never moved."

All eyes bore witness to the truth of her statement, so much so that the vicar was reminded, in an odd way, of a certain hoary proverb of Pliny's — *in vino veritas.*

"Bertram," he asked, "who taught you how to do this?"

"She did."

"Whom do you mean, your guardian? The one you call the lady?" Bertram nodded.

That clinched it — the twisted old recluse of a witch was alive, even if Bertram was unaware that her name was Mother Redcap!

"This is no charlatan's trick but a very real thing. It's nothing short of magic," Ada said. "Mother Redcap was renowned for her knowledge of potions and elixirs. Perhaps she was a kind of alchemist, as well as a conjuror?"

Now that his stated aim of doing something for the vicar had been achieved, Bertram's attention began to wander. At one point he rose a little in his chair, and was noticed to be gazing intently at one of the latticed windows across the room. Moments later there came a shriek from the maidservant, followed by a loud crash of china. All but Bertram leaped from their seats in alarm.

"Goodness, what has happened?" the vicar exclaimed.

Jayne Scrimshaw, the shattered remains of several cups and saucers lying at her feet, stood as if frozen before them, staring in open-mouthed horror at the same window that had drawn Bertram's interest.

"Whatever's the matter, Jayne?" Mrs. Ludlow cried, her face near as white as her broken china.

"As I'm alive, ma'am — ghostly faces in the dark — peering in!"

All of them but Bertram rushed to the window. True, the window *was* dark, as Jayne had stated, for it was night outside; but of ghostly faces there was no sign. There was in fact no sign of anything there, apart from the reflected light of the dining-room candles. This particular window was on the north side of the house, hard by the vicar's garden. The clergyman, for want of any better idea, drummed his fingers on the pane, thinking it might attract the notice of whoever was out there. It didn't.

"Are you sure it was not a marsh devil?" he said to the maid.

"No, sir, no devil o' *that* sort — a child's face, sir — a little girl — and — and — and something else, sir — something *monstrous* — something neither beast nor man, or both — something as can't rightly be described — "

"At last, they've come for me!" Bertram was heard to exclaim from his place at the table.

Came a noise from the enclosure beside the garden — a low grunting and snorting kind of animal noise. It was Hortense, the vicar's pet glypt, giving warning of a trespasser in the area.

Boldly the vicar declared his intention to step outside and have a scout round for the intruder. His wife, horrified at the idea, strove to dissuade him; but he was bent upon it.

"If the girl is Sarah, my dear," he explained, patiently, "we simply must bring her in. Don't you agree? Good. Not to fear! Are you prepared for it, Corney?"

To allay Mrs. Ludlow's fears, Mr. Oldcorn had volunteered to join her husband on the mission. (Truth be told, the vicar was himself rather glad of the company).

"Shall I assist you, gentlemen?" Mrs. Chugwell offered. As a driver of mastodons and commander-in-chief of an extensive road-building operation, she was accustomed to danger and the vicissitudes of circumstance. But neither the vicar nor Corney would hear of it.

Plucking up their courage they crept out onto the step, the vicar bearing in hand some lights from the dining-room, and Corney a kitchen poker. For a brief minute they stood in alert silence, watching and listening. The cold air sprang at them from the darkness; fortunately, nothing else did.

Cautiously they descended the stairs and, stealing round the corner, peered into the shadows that lurked in abundance there. But they found nothing save for a brick wall, behind which Hortense's anxious grunting could be heard as she waddled about her enclosure.

The vicar swung his lights the opposite way.

"Look there!" Corney whispered, seizing his friend's arm and pointing with the poker.

In the soft ground beneath the dining-room window lay a trail of hoofprints. They were the prints of a very large horse, one wearing no shoes. They showed that the animal had approached the window from the direction of the churchyard, before retreating into the nearby Vicar's Walk. Of the little girl, however, there was no trace.

After some further minutes of searching, without result, the gentlemen withdrew indoors. There they found little Bertram in high spirits, Mrs. Chugwell in close talk with Miss Henslowe, and poor Jayne begging grievous pardon of Mrs. Ludlow for annihilating her china.

Faces at the window, the bogberry that was now an Ogghops, the enigmatic guardian of Bertram's who was hundreds of years old, an elixir composed of human blood — it was all rather too much for Mr. Ludlow. The puzzle that was Bertram had entered upon a new and entirely unforeseen chapter. In the end all the poor bewildered clergyman could manage was a crunch of his big brow, a rub of his chin, and a long, slow shake of his head.

"Dear me," he sighed, glancing again at the dark in the window, "but the Lord does move in a mysterious way . . ."

PART FIVE

THE FIRST CHAPTER

TOUCHES ON MAGIC, WHICH WENT OUT YEARS AGO

IN the morning Richard awoke to find himself in a perfect state
of shivers.

Upon opening his eyes the first thing that met them was his
own breath, rolling forth as if in the open air, like steam from
a geyser. Glancing at the casement he saw that the windows were ajar,
and swaying a little on their hinges. This unpardonable lapse he attrib-
uted to that general clouding of the brain he had suffered as a result of
his adventure in the meadow. The trying nature of the experience had
sent him to roost at an early hour, after a warm drink and a brief re-
counting of events for his sister and Mrs. Rudling. Fortunately his
room was at the very tip-top of the house, and nothing of a brutish
disposition had found its way in through the casement during the
night.

To rise early in frigid weather, particularly in the wintry gloom of
a Fenshire morning, is an exercise requiring no small exertion of effort.
But rise he must, and rise he did, if for no other reason than to shut
the casement. Adding to his discomfort was the absence of a fire in the
room. Probably his sister, wishing for him to have a good lie-in after
his bad experience, had instructed Molly Grime not to disturb him until later.

A quivering body, a shock-head of unruly hair, benumbed fingers,
a chilly grate, frozen towels, a ewer full of water turned to ice — all
these things greeted him as he rose and dressed. Once on his feet he
had been quick to discover that his right arm was a trifle sore after his
plunge from the saddle. What distressed him most, however, was the
cold in the grate; and hearing the maid's tread now in the passage, he
stepped to the door and threw it open.

"Hallo, Molly!" he exclaimed, still looking a sight, for he had yet
to brush down his hair. "A crisp m-morning, is it n-not?"

"Aye, uncommon brisk, Mr. Hathaway, sir," Molly agreed. "'Tis
for sure, the days they ought to be milder now — " She gazed with a

wondering look at the steam rolling from his lips. "And 'tis especial brisk in *this* room, sir!" she cried, peeping inside.

"Left the dashed window open," Richard explained, with an embarrassed wave towards the casement. "Please, Molly, could you get a fire blazing in here? There looks to be neither kindling nor turf — exhausting evening, you know — or so I suppose you've heard — "

"Ou, aye, that I have — and at once, sir! And some hot water," said the maid. (She had observed not only the roiling fog of his breath, but the ewer of ice as well).

In short order the materials for the fire appeared, together with a steaming jug of water from the kitchen. While Molly was tending to the grate, Richard poured the water into a basin and warmed his face and hands, in preparation for shaving.

"Capital blaze! Thanks awfully, Molly," he said as she withdrew. "And would you tell my sister I'll be down presently?"

"Ou, aye, that I will, sir."

Richard approached the razor — how cold it felt in his hand now, how edgy, and how hard — with a degree of trepidation. The arm that pained him was his shaving arm, and he did not entirely trust it to wield the blade. By now the fire had cast a comforting glow over the room, and the water had removed the chill from his fingers. Came the steady *clip-clop* of the razor as it was sharpened, followed by the tinkle of his shaving-brush in its lather-mug. Stooping before the glass he managed to shave the face in it without causing undue injury. After taming his shock-head of hair, he changed into a clean shirt and waistcoat, settled his neckcloth, drew on his coat, and with his pipe in hand went whistling down the stairs to the kitchen.

There he was met by the women of the house, who welcomed him with expressions of sympathy. The two cats, Gerald and Herbert, who had been dozing on the hearth-rug, woke up briefly, in sign to their master that they too approved of his good health this morning; then, their duty discharged, they resumed their slumbers.

Richard went first to the tobacco-jar to fill his pipe, then dropped down onto a chair and surrendered himself to his housekeeper. A bowl of oatmeal porridge, an enormous slab of bread and jam, a dish of mulberries, a sizzling rasher of bacon and some griddle-cakes, a fragrant cup of coffee — all made their appearance before him, as if by magic; and he wasted no time in putting their reality to the test.

"Mrs. Rudling, you have surpassed yourself!" was his verdict.

The housekeeper, her face glowing pink under her sugary hair, accepted the compliment with her usual grace.

As he fell to with an appetite, Richard's thoughts returned, as inevitably they must, to the events of the previous day. He knew jolly well that what he had seen there in the twilight was no figment of the imagination. As for what it was exactly that he *had* seen — well, all he had had to see it by was the dim cloud-light, and the glitter of a few frosty stars, and the gleam of the lantern in the rider's hand. He was positive, however, that the rider had been little Sarah; as for her mount —

"You know very well what it was," his sister told him. "It was that creature Snap and I met with on the drive from Tillington. It was the snake-necked monstrosity, which, from your description of it, appears to bear some resemblance to a horse."

"And rather a large horse at that, one with a grotesquely human-like countenance, and a tangle of orange hair — and packing a bow and arrows!" said Richard, between mouthfuls of bread and jam. "Moreover, I sensed an intelligence in its gaze — an intelligence far more human than animal. But by then Rosie had shied and laid me as flat as this flapjack. I've an idea it was this creature that was tracking us from the shadows during our survey of the new road."

"Perhaps the bow and arrows belonged to Sarah?" Jemma suggested.

Richard frowned at the chunk of bacon impaled on his knife-point, and shook his head. "Afraid I'm inclined to disagree with you, sis. This creature, although it resembled a horse, was like no animal I have any knowledge of. It was as different from Rosie and Spinach as chalk is from cheese. No — the bow and arrows, I suspect, were the creature's own."

"The fact that Sarah was astride the beast may explain why she and Bertram were not harmed by it. Plainly they exercise some mastery over it."

"That would seem to be the case."

"But where were they off to so hurriedly last night, do you think? And why?"

The answer to this, of course, none of them knew; nor had they any notion, despite two encounters with it now, just what the snake-necked creature was or from where it had sprung.

A couple of friendly barks from Snap, outside in the garden, announced the arrival of Corney. He entered the kitchen in a state of quiet excitement, and proceeded to describe for his neighbors all that had transpired the evening before at the vicarage. Great was their surprise on hearing of Bertram's feat of magic, and the mysterious faces in the window. By the time he had finished, Mrs. Rudling and Molly were visibly shaken, Jemma was burning to see Ada, and Richard — true to Miss Henslowe's prediction — was jiggered.

"Goodness, the child is bewitched," the housekeeper declared. "The pair of 'em, most like. It's just as I feared — the stories my grandmama did tell me of such conjuring — "

"Ou, aye," Molly agreed. "Bogled and bedeviled they are — 'tis for certain sure now, Mrs. Rudling. *Spookish!*"

"And what is your view of it, Corney?" Jemma asked.

Mr. Oldcorn, like Ada, was of the opinion that the magic was very real — there had been no question of trickery — as were the faces in the window, which had been seen by both Jayne Scrimshaw and Bertram, and which the child afterwards had identified as belonging to Sarah and his guardian.

Then it was Corney's turn to be surprised, as Richard told him of his adventure in the meadow, which had taken place shortly before the vicar's dinner. It was clear now what it was Richard had seen there in the twilight — it had been Sarah and the children's guardian riding out of the wood in search of Bertram.

At last, they've come for me, the boy had said.

The evidence appeared to support Richard's belief that the horse-like creature, whatever it was, was rather more human than horse. It was plain now why the children had not met a grisly end behind the wall of firs — for the creature which Jemma had deemed a beastly monstrosity was in fact their caretaker!

"Well, that's put paid to a few theories," Richard remarked.

But what sort of creature was it, they wondered, this guardian of Bertram's? And why was it looking after two children in the wood? And more importantly perhaps, who was minding the guardian? Was there in fact another, more shadowy figure, a mysterious keeper of the lodge, lurking behind it all?

Perhaps these secrets, Jemma suggested, and that of Bertram and his feat of magic, lay at the ruined lodge in the books of Mother Redcap. The herbal, no doubt, had belonged to her; and there had been more books as well, as Richard and the others had testified. In those volumes likely lay the secret of the posset of blood, the elixir that had prolonged Bertram's childhood. *And it was this snake-necked creature that had prepared it for him!*

But what, then, had become of Mother Redcap? For it was no bent and withered hag who was protecting the children, it was the creature — Bertram's friend, whom he called "the lady," and who he believed to be many centuries old. It was the creature that had dropped the stag with an arrow and butchered it. It was the creature that had carried the children through the wood, enabling them to keep pace with Rosie and the shay-cart. And it was this creature whose lifeblood was part and parcel of Bertram's magic posset.

No room for Mother Redcap there, Jemma thought. Might she be then the shadowy keeper who lay back of it all?

That is, unless — incredibly — the snake-necked monstrosity and the bent and withered hag were one and the same . . .

Corney told them now that plans already were being made for an expedition into the wood, as soon as the tuskers arrived from Dead-marsh, to look for Sarah. It was impossible to know for how long she had been a prisoner, but likely she had been taken by the creature just as Bertram had. What remained inexplicable, to Corney's understanding at least, was the creature's motive for taking them.

There was another outburst from Snap as the postie, Mr. Murcott, came breezing through the gate on his daily round. The hard-working young fellow was shown into the kitchen, where he delivered the cottage mail into Richard's hands. Overhearing the name of Mother Redcap in the conversation, Mr. Murcott declared how unfortunate it was that poor Mr. Wackwire was *non compos mentis*, for more than likely he could have told them something about the old woman.

"When my dad was a boy, running errands for the butcher," he related, "he often called at Wackwire House with deliveries. I recollect his saying how the old gentleman's gardener, Moses, him as died some few years back, would take to grumbling now and again about somebody he called 'Miss Crouch.' A 'pariah' he said she was, and a 'foreigner,' a 'slave of Old Harry,' and a 'stain on the parish.' One day the laundress told my dad that Miss Crouch was Mother Redcap — aye! Told him Moses had complained more than a few times to the master about her, but that Mr. Wackwire didn't hold with superstition. My dad never did learn if 'Miss Crouch' was her real name, or one perhaps Mr. Wackwire himself had given her. Most like it was the former, as this was many years ago, when Mr. Wackwire was yet a lucid man."

Nowadays of course Mr. Wackwire was anything but lucid, and had given people such as Mrs. Locket more names than one could shake a stick at, none of them making any sense.

"My dad told me Mr. Wackwire had had some family once, years back, away down in Gloamshire. And Mother Redcap, she was said to come from those parts," Mr. Murcott added.

And having delivered these choice bits of news, along with the mail, the postman tipped his hat to the company and went his way.

Perhaps Mr. Wackwire's family had been known to Mother Redcap all those years ago, they thought? Perhaps that was how she had come to dwell in Market Snailsby? It was even possible that she and Mr. Wackwire could have been related . . .

It was decided now that a call on the vicar was in order, to apprise him of Richard's encounter with the snake-necked creature that resembled a horse but wasn't, and of Jemma's as well, which hitherto she had refrained from disclosing for fear of being labeled a hare-brain.

Little Gerald, sensing a commotion, opened his eyes and looked about him. "Where are they going in such a rush?" he asked.

"I think it has something to do with magic," Herbert yawned.

"But magic went out years ago. Isn't that what that fellow Blathers is always saying?"

"It's a mystery to me, brother."

"Well, I'd like to see a little magic round this kitchen today. There's been no grub in our bowl for *hours*. I wish we had a magic bowl that would fill itself — then I'd show you how the cow eats the cabbage! And we shouldn't need to rely on these people so much for our grub."

"You don't need to rely on people. Why don't you catch your own food like a regular chap?"

"Tut, tut," Gerald sniffed, his spoiled little pink nose in the air. "Too much bother, brother — too much bother. The hunting game's not for this cat. I'd rather be lounging."

"Oh, poof! Whatever's the use?" Herbert grunted. Fully awake now he rose and stretched, and spent some minutes washing his face and paws, before scampering out the door in search of mischief.

Meanwhile in the stable-yard Rosie was being put to the shay-cart; and so off to town she went with her mistress and master, leaving Snap to the company of Corney, Mrs. Rudling, Molly, and Gerald (whose empty bowl had been replenished, magically enough, by the housekeeper while he slept).

As they rolled through the High Street, the Hathaways were treated to the spectacle of Sir Hector MacHector at the river wall, his silver-mounted pipes filling the air with their deafening blasts. Across the river at Clopton Stair, Mr. Ingo Swain could be seen on the low pier, inspecting his traps. Nearer the bridge they caught a glimpse of Ranger over on Snailsby Common, his lofty back and shoulders rising up, mountain-like, behind the mossy tiles of the Broom and Badger.

They arrived at the vicarage in time for tea with Mr. Ludlow, who had already another caller, a paunchy fat man with a heavy mustache — it was Mr. Shand, the fen-reeve. The conversation of the two men had been concerned with the events of the previous night, and so both were deeply interested — and deeply shocked — to hear of the Hathaways' experiences. They were even more astonished to learn that the snake-necked monstrosity was in fact Bertram's guardian, and that it was this creature's blood which had fortified the magic posset.

Absorbed in their thoughts they sipped their tea for a spell, until Jemma, glancing out the window, saw Ada riding past on Spinach; and getting to her feet she went to the street-door to call to her. As she swung open the door she saw Dr. Chevenix pull up in his dog-cart at the vicarage steps. The doctor was visibly agitated, and his face wore an anxious look — an uncharacteristic state for the dapper and delicate little physician. As he was shown into the drawing-room, all could tell that some matter of excitement was brewing.

The doctor declared that there was something in Yocklebury Great Croft — a derelict farmstead lying about a mile off to the southwestward — which required their immediate presence. He had been returning home from his morning's call on a patient, he told them, out on the Dragonthorpe Road, when he had heard something in the Croft. To his untutored ear it had sounded like a choir of voices, singing. Knowing the Croft to be long abandoned, the doctor had investigated, and in so doing had discovered something quite extraordinary — something quite unnerving — something downright alarming, in fact — which he insisted the vicar and the others simply must see for themselves, otherwise they should not believe it. And it was urgent that Sir Hector MacHector see it too, he declared; and upon learning that the knight was presently at the river wall, the doctor hastened away to fetch him.

Shortly afterwards the company set off at a brisk pace for the Croft — the Hathaways in the shay-cart and Ada on her stout little riding-horse, the vicar and Mr. Shand on their hunters, and Dr. Chevenix in his dog-cart with Sir Hector, the doctor's black bag stowed away with the Laird's black sticks in the louvered boot under the seat.

What could the doctor have found there in the Croft, the others wondered? What could have so disturbed the calm, clear-eyed physician and dapper dispenser of medicines, and made him so uneasy in his mind?

"I smell an adventure in this," said Spinach, looking quite the dapper gent himself in his green-and-white headstall and shiny new snaffle-bit. "I wonder what it can be?"

"We'll find out soon enough," Rosie replied, as she jogged along beside him.

"By the by, Rosie — did you apologize to your master for spilling him last night?"

The mare hesitated. "Well, after a fashion . . ." she began.

"Was he terribly cross?"

"Not particularly."

"He hasn't taken you off your bran mash for the week?"

"No. Not yet, at any rate."

"Well, he seems a decent enough fellow. Chin up, Rosie! It wasn't your fault. When your master's off his guard, he's off his guard."

"I suppose so," Rosie nodded. Still, she felt terribly bad about it. She knew very well that she was the apple of her master's eye, and she had failed him. She had let him down — all too literally.

"I wonder what we'll find in the Croft?" said Spinach, his eyes scanning the way ahead.

"I've no idea what we'll find," the mare replied, half to herself, "but whatever it is, I'll lay odds it has something to do with those two children and the horsy thing that's no horse — and little Clover's spookies in the wood!"

THE SECOND CHAPTER

THE HORROR IN THE CROFT

THE company put their horses into a trot and went on for a mile or so, past the turning that led to the new road, and beyond that the disused windmill and the lonely stretch of meadow that rolled away behind it.

On their left stood a wide expanse of broken ground dotted with scrub and peat, and some patches of bog myrtle, and here and there a crumbling stone wall or heap of tumbled masonry. It was all that remained of Yocklebury, a farming hamlet that had vanished from the maps of Fenshire a couple of centuries ago. It had gone almost without a trace, but for a few foundation walls, and its ancient fish-pond, now dry, and the Croft, the rambling gardens of what had been the manor-house. But the gardens had gone all marshy, and the manor-house the way of Mother Redcap's cottage — like the old woman herself, it had long since disappeared.

It was a raw, cold day, as Richard had so uncomfortably discovered. The sky was in full dreariness, and ominous of rain, or snow, or sleet, or perhaps all three. An air of lonely silence pervaded the Croft, where once smallholders had tended their plots, and servants had bent to their labors, in those bygone days when our cheeky ancestors had led their colorful lives and were not so fearful of the world.

"There! Do you hear it?" Dr. Chevenix said aloud.

They had reined in their horses and were listening intently. At first the others heard nothing; then, by degrees they became aware of an odd sound that had grown upon the quiet — a distant chorus of voices. But Yocklebury Great Croft, as all knew, was bereft of inhabitants, and had been so since long before anyone could remember.

"From where is it coming?" asked Mr. Shand, his eyes under his wide-awake sweeping the Croft like a lighthouse-beam.

"From that knot of trees there," the doctor indicated.

"Aye, 'tis sae — 'tis those ower yont, by ma reckoning," nodded Sir Hector. "But wha' be the cause of it, doctor? Gangrels an' scaff-raff? But there be no sae mony o' the like hereaboots. An' sure there be na

kirk 'twixt here an' there for croonin' in! 'Tis a muckle great puzzlement, t'be sure."

"As for the answer to that, Sir Hector," said Dr. Chevenix, "it lies
before us. Come along, everyone."

They approached by way of the old carriage-road which in former
times had served the manor-house. As they came near the trees, however, the horses in a body turned restive and refused to go on. Spinach
and Rosie, the pair of hunters, the doctor's nag — all began snorting
fiercely and stamping their feet, and throwing their heads in the air.
Some backing and sidling then followed, the animals so resisting every
and all efforts to urge them on as to make further progress impossible.

"They're nervous as witches," exclaimed Mr. Shand. "This is not at
all like my hunter — "

The Laird suggested that they tether the horses in the Croft and
continue on foot, an expediency to which the others readily assented.
Before setting off, however, Richard drew his cutlass from the shay-
cart, and Mr. Shand his sword from its scabbard, and Dr. Chevenix his
steely blade from the boot. Sir Hector, in the absence of his fighting
claymore, took from his belt his trusty *skene dhu*, or dagger, of good
Scotch steel.

"Shall we?" the doctor invited, pointing the way with his sword.

The odd sound grew steadily upon their ears as they approached
the trees — voices, sounding for all the world like a choir, chanting in
a brisk but monotonous rhythm that resembled singsong. And the
closer the doctor and his companions got to the trees, the plainer it became that the voices — high-pitched and so sweetly singing — were the
voices of children.

But where were these children? Were they hiding behind the trees?
Were they hiding *in* the trees?

There was not a lonesomer spot in the country round than Yocklebury Great Croft, nor a more unlikely one, to be hearing the voices
of children in song. It was a spot more suited to the beastly cries of
marsh devils on the prowl, for which ever-present threat every eye in
the company had been keeping a wary watch.

The doctor singled out one tree in particular amongst the group —
a venerable pumpkin oak, one every bit as gaunt, gnarled, and knotted
as those ancients in Marley Wood which, to Jemma's mind, had suggested the hands of buried giants thrusting up from below.

From the branches of the tree hung an array of glass bottles. There must have been four or five dozen of them at least, all glowing with an eerie blue light. The voices appeared to be emanating from the tree; and yet there was not a single chorister to be seen. In point of fact there was nothing to be seen save for the pumpkin oak and its crop of ghostly, glowing fruit.

"By St. Poppo!" exclaimed Sir Hector.

"What in thunder is this?" growled Mr. Shand, pushing back his wide-awake.

"What is it they're saying?" Jemma asked.

They cocked their heads and listened closely. Once accustomed to the pitch of the voices and the cadence of the song, they were able to decipher the words with relative ease.

> *Keep away*
> *Keep away*
> *Keep away from the wood.*
> *Your meddling there*
> *Will do you no good.*
>
> *Keep away*
> *Keep away*
> *Keep away from the wood.*
> *Why risk your souls*
> *In that neighborhood?*
>
> *Keep away*
> *Keep away*
> *Keep away from the wood.*
> *Your Heaven's no help*
> *Nor your Holy Rood.*
>
> *Keep away*
> *Keep away*
> *Keep away from the wood.*
> *Your warning's clear —*
> *So clear off you should!*

"'Tis gway uncanny," declared Sir Hector, with a thunderous stare. "Dooms me, mayhap 'tis mair than uncanny — mayhap 'tis a thing ridiculous!"

"Is this more of that boy's work, I wonder?" murmured Mr. Shand. "Changing bogberry wine into an Ogghops — and now this?"

"But Bertram is home at the vicarage," said Mr. Ludlow. "He is entirely blameless in the matter."

"Perhaps it's Mother Redcap's doing?" Ada suggested. "Perhaps this is some of her sorcery?"

Was the old woman indeed still alive and in command at the lodge? Perhaps the snake-necked monstrosity — the horsy thing that was no horse — like the two children was in her thrall, and forced to do her bidding?

"Have a peer at those bottles," Dr. Chevenix directed, "and you'll understand why I summoned you here. But careful, now."

His companions, heeding his advice, crept warily beneath the outstretched arms of the tree. The bottles were something short and squat, as bottles go — they were rather like Mr. Shand in that respect — and had been suspended from the branches by lengths of thin cord tied to their necks and finger-holds. The most remarkable thing about them was the bluish glow, which appeared to arise from some strange, inner light. The bottles contained no liquid that anyone could make out; as for what they did contain, however —

"Gracious heavens!" the vicar cried, reeling back in horror. "This is — this is monstrous — the poor wretches — "

"Hoots, man, an' there's a fact," Sir Hector nodded grimly. "'Tis an unco' devilish thing, an' a right bluidy piece o' work. Wad that ma gillies were here tae behold the sight!"

Every bottle hanging from the tree was filled with a weirdly-glowing human head.

Imprisoned behind the glass of each was a dead-looking human face. Gruesome, swollen, ghastly-looking things they were, like heaps of overripe figs, crammed into the space inside the bottles — horrible, ghoulish-looking things, like the faces of executed criminals, the sort whose bodies in ruder times had been hung from the old gibbet-irons for public scorn.

The dead eyes in each face were rolled far back in their sockets, as though gazing on heaven, while their dead lips moved in concert with the chanted words of the song. And yet the voices issuing from their dead throats were the voices of children.

Icy shivers raced down the spine of the Laird and his companions. The hair on their scalps tingled, save for that of Mr. Shand, whose scalp under his wide-awake was rather shinier than most.

"This is a trick, in my estimation, Sir Hector. This is perfect nonsense!" the reeve declared. So said he; but even as he said it his voice betrayed him. It was thin and unconvincing — anything but reevish, in fact — and did little to inspire confidence. Uneasy with the notion of phantom riders on his patch, he had phantom heads to contend with now as well.

"How can this be a trick?" Ada asked. "It all looks very real to me. Surely this is more magic?"

"We'll have dashed hard work to explain it otherwise," Richard said.

"They are demanding we stay out of Marley Wood. Perhaps it's to keep us from looking for Sarah?" Jemma suggested.

"Or to keep Mrs. Chugwell from her work," said Mr. Shand, with a manful tucking-down of his hat-brim (this to compensate perhaps for his thinness of voice). "Well, we needn't search very far for a candidate in that regard. No farther than Fore Street, in my estimation."

"Hallo! You don't mean Erskine Joliffe?" Richard returned.

"I'll not accuse, Mr. Hathaway; but in my office I am obliged to weigh all possibilities. Already a fistful of this town's money has been laid out upon Mrs. Chugwell, and we can ill afford to have wasted it."

"Well, that's just daft," said Ada. "Mr. Joliffe of the Mudlark? Not a tinker's chance!"

"Aye, 'tis an unco' deal o' money, an' muckle gude money forbye," noted the Laird. "Howsomeffer, I'm no sae sure 'tis trickery here as ye claim, Willie. Mayhap 'tis magic indeedy. For how should ye explain it itherwise?"

"Perhaps it's slodgers' work, then, Sir Hector," returned the reeve. "Or some cracked rustic's notion of a joke. Or the doing of some old tramp fellows, to keep us from the lodge . . ."

They were so absorbed in the debate, they hardly noticed that the eyes in the dead-looking faces inside the bottles had rolled down, and were glaring at them now in a show of spectral frightfulness. Nor had they noticed that the heavenly expressions on the faces had turned to

black scowls, or that the chanted song had risen dramatically in ve-
hemence and volume.

Keep away! Keep away! Keep away from the wood!

Then in words it chilled the reeve and his companions to hear, the
singing assumed a more ominous, and a distinctly more personal tone.

> *Lub-a-dub-dub, three men in a rub,*
> *And who do you think they be?*
> *There's the doctor, the brewer, and the Laird MacHector —*
> *Chuck 'em out, they're fools all three!*
>
> *Lub-a-dub-dub, three more in a rub,*
> *The Hathaways and a Henslowe we see.*
> *Two came by cart, one came by saddle —*
> *Chuck 'em out, they're fools all three!*

As they watched, the bottles began to swing slowly to and fro, to
and fro, as though brushed by unseen winds. Meanwhile the ghostly,
glowing heads inside them were growing brighter, and the voices louder, and louder — all children's voices still, but in chorus risen now to
such a din that even Sir Hector, he of the deafening bagpipe blasts, was
forced to stop his ears.

> *Keep away!*
> *Keep away!*
> *Keep away from the wood!*
> *Your meddling there*
> *Will do you no good!*

"Come, we must leave this place," Dr. Chevenix urged. "The noise
— it will harm your hearing!"

Nobody controverted the doctor's learned opinion; indeed it struck
them all now as excellent advice. Together they legged it back to the
horses and, surrendering the Croft to its ghostly inhabitants, galloped
home to Market Snailsby as fast as they could go.

They arrived at the vicarage in a breathless state — the horses, too
— and with faces as troubled as Dr. Chevenix's when he had pulled up
at the steps in his dog-cart. By now a drizzle of something like sleet
had begun leaking from the overcast. The vicar escorted his compan-

ions indoors where it was warm and dry, and where they found, to their surprise, that the day's excitement was not yet over.

On entering the hall they were met by Jayne Scrimshaw, followed by a very distraught Mrs. Ludlow. The good woman's hands clutching her handkerchief were trembling; her eyes were red; tears streamed down her cheeks.

"Oh, Hugh, he's gone, he's gone!" she sobbed. "Our poor little dear is gone!"

"He's been taken, sir," stated Jayne, rather more calmly.

"Taken? Who has been taken? Bertram, do you mean?" inquired Mr. Ludlow.

"Yes, sir."

Needless to say, the vicar and the others were much concerned.

"There, there, dear. Not to worry now. How did this happen?" the clergyman asked, trying his best to soothe his wife, and winkle out some facts in the process.

"Jayne — Jayne will explain," the good lady blubbered through her tears.

All eyes turned to the maidservant.

"She came for him, sir — the little girl, Sarah — the face in the window!" said Jayne. "'Twas she as come and took him away by the back-stairs."

"The temerity!" exploded Mr. Shand.

"Where did she take him?" the vicar asked.

"Over churchyard way, sir — by the mossy stones and across the church fields — to Marley Wood," the maid replied.

It seemed that Bertram had contrived to distract the women while they had been at their work in the kitchen. They had made him some pancakes, and were tending to some kidneys frizzling on a hot-water dish, when Bertram had suddenly closed his eyes and begun speaking again in that strange, low voice, and making odd motions of his hand over the flapjacks.

"It was just as with your Ogghops, dear," Mrs. Ludlow managed to whimper out. "Wiggling his tiny fingers and muttering to himself — something about boodle and doodle, or noodle, or something or other — "

Then Bertram had snapped his fingers, and the pancakes had risen into the air above the heads of the startled women.

"Oh, I say!" Ada exclaimed, her eyes alight with admiration — I dare say she couldn't help it.

"Not rhubarb from cabbage stalks, Mr. Ludlow, sir — nor hickory nuts, nor purple apple pie — but magic pancakes!" said Jayne. "As I'm alive, sir, 'tis the very truth."

The two of them had been thrown into such confusion, she explained, that they had known not what to do; and in the squeezing of a lemon, as she put it, the boy was through the scullery and out the door and dashing across the churchyard with Sarah.

"Ah, was there any evidence of — um — er — anything else?" the vicar asked.

"The monstrous thing as was neither beast nor man, sir? No, sir. And then, sir," Jayne continued, a trifle embarrassed to relate it, "as we watched the pancakes floating in air — 'twas after the boy had run out and was gone — if ye'll excuse the liberty, ma'am — the pancakes, they did fall down plop upon our heads — "

"Magic children — magic wine — now magic pancakes," Richard remarked. "Who would have believed it but a few short days ago? Well, I for one am properly jiggered."

"Aye, Dickie, an' fair amazed at it I am," nodded Sir Hector.

"But Hugh, our poor little dear — out there in the freezing cold!" said Mrs. Ludlow, wringing her hands. She was as heartbroken at the loss of Bertram as if he had been her own son — the which for a brief time he had been, or so it had seemed — and sought consolation in the arms of her husband. As for Jayne Scrimshaw, she was observed to breathe more than a few sighs of relief. Plainly she was happy that the mysterious, magical small boy had gone.

They conducted a *pro forma* inspection of the back-stairs, and of the shrubbery path that led to the churchyard and Bury Street, and in the moist earth had little trouble identifying the footprints of Bertram and Sarah. But of course, at this late hour there was nothing to be done.

Small wonder, now that the sleet that had been dripping from the overcast was turning, not to hickory nuts, but to snow.

THE THIRD CHAPTER

IN THE PARISH ROOMS

TWO days went by, and another assembly was convened in the parish rooms. This gathering, unlike that held earlier to discuss the finding of Bertram, was called chiefly to discuss his loss, and the circumstances surrounding it, and what steps ought to be pursued as a result.

Matters of late had taken an unfavorable and, to many, a downright sinister turn. The curious incident of the bottles stuffed with glowing heads was the talk of the town, persons of no less rank and credit than Sir Hector MacHector, Dr. Chevenix, Mr. Shand, and Vicar Ludlow having borne witness to it. Someone had gone to a great deal of trouble to warn them off — to warn not only Sir Hector and his companions, many felt, but the entire population of Market Snailsby. None doubted but that it was the same mysterious someone who had been keeping Bertram a prisoner at the lodge for lo these many years.

And yet the paradox of it was this: that to all appearances the boy was a willing captive. Had he not been telling everyone that he wished to return to his "friends" at the lodge? Had the incident in the Croft been not only a warning, but also a ruse to aid his escape? For as regards the latter, there many there in the room, like Sir Hector, who held that it was vera likely, aye, an' plain eneugh too, by St. Poppo.

And so the question before them now was — *what to do about it?*

The late snowfall had been a surprise, but the weather that had brought it had been relatively tame, and the snow had failed to stick. Indeed it had departed almost as suddenly as it had arrived, leaving behind it the usual blanket of dull gray mist and cloud. But there was a touch of something like mildness in the air now, which boded well for the season to come.

Not so, however, for the assembly.

The room was filled near to bursting, many of those in attendance being concerned not so much for Bertram perhaps as for their own skins, in light of the threats that had been made against them. Most of the usual regulars were present. Others attending included Lady Mac-

Hector, looking very handsome in a violet gown that mirrored her eyes, and Mrs. Locket — not so handsome, and with a face so bright with powder it might have glowed, had it been placed in a bottle and hung on a tree — and pretty Miss Alice Pingle, the schoolmistress. The slodgers were represented by Phoggie Finlayson, and the staunch yeomen of the marshes by the brothers Doughty and Farmer Dillweed. Tweedy Mr. Joliffe of the Mudlark was there as well, and Mr. Ingo Swain, and the gillies of Mickledene Hall. Altogether it was a mixed and a motley company, one representative of every class of folk from the town and country round.

Absent from the gathering were Mrs. Chugwell and Matt, who had driven Ranger out onto the Drovers' Road to meet the tuskers coming up from Deadmarsh. The team was overdue, and it was thought by some that the snow perhaps had delayed them; that is until Mr. Inkpen reminded everyone that nothing under the sun could stop a thunderbeast. But as there never was any sun to speak of in the whole wide county of Fenshire, the relevance of his remark was open to question.

The tea and sundries having been laid on, the vicar rose to address the assembly. He then called upon Mayor Jagard, who rose in his turn and, strutting to the fore in all his magnificence — luminous pink cravat and fancy-striped waistcoat, yellow gold watch and chain, tail-coat of parsley green, and brandy-colored trousers — announced, in a voice befitting his lofty position, that threats against the citizens of Market Snailsby, be they prominent citizens or be they humble, would not be tolerated. (A ripple of applause).

Further to that, the Mayor went on, with a grave stroking of his mustaches, it was not in the character of fenlanders to be yielding to threats. (Applause and cheers).

"Here in the fen country," the Mayor declared, wagging his finger in the air at an imaginary antagonist, "we don't knuckle under to scoundrels and miscreants." (More cheers). "Come, come, what do they take us for? Hopeless wet-shods?" ("That's telling 'em, Walkie!")

As for what should be done to counter the threats of the unnamed scoundrels and miscreants to whom they would not knuckle under, the Mayor, like most men in his lofty position, was disappointingly vague. (Cheers giving way to frowns and questioning looks).

In point of fact the Mayor and several others, including Mr. Blathers, had the day before traveled — through the *mire* and *snow*, as Mr. Jagard had not hesitated to mention — to view for themselves the reputed horror in the Great Croft. They had found the old oak with the bottles suspended from its limbs, but try as they might they could find no glowing heads inside them, only a vile, sticky substance that looked and smelled like rotting figs. Although most were willing to accept on faith the testimony of Sir Hector and the other witnesses — and such estimable witnesses they were, too, representing as they did some of the oldest and most prominent families in the town — some privately deemed it a "queer mad tale," and were uncertain what to make of it.

As for Mr. Blathers, he had had no comment with respect to the alleged horror, other than to say that rotting figs in bottles hung on a tree in Yocklebury Great Croft were funny things. As for the claim of magic, the evidence had left him unmoved, despite the statements of his worthy friends Richard Hathaway and Sir Hector. It was not that he doubted their word; it was simply that he had seen nothing to convince him. A well-regulated mind such as his needed proof — solid, absolute, indisputable proof — and he had none. Without proof any claim of magic was, in his opinion, unscientific, and little better than hearsay; and Mr. Blathers could not take hearsay for evidence, no matter the source.

"Although if true," he added, by way of qualification, "it would beat positively *everything.*"

As the discussion went forward, it became evident that there were two competing factions amongst the people there. There was one faction whose members, like the vicar's wife and Mrs. Travers, were keen to be rescuing Bertram from the shackles of his imprisonment. ("Hear, hear!" from their supporters). And then there were others, those with a contrary view, like the Ludlows' Jayne Scrimshaw, who feared the consequences of any such action. They were more than glad that Bertram had decamped, and didn't care ever to see his small face round Fenshire again. ("Not our concern!" was their rallying-cry).

What cause had anyone to be "rescuing" Bertram, the Scrimshaws asked, when it was clear that the boy himself had not wanted to be rescued? As had been pointed out numerous times, he had managed perfectly well for himself for some five-and-thirty years without their interference, thank you. Mrs. Locket was counted amongst this faction, as were Farmer Dillweed, the lanky old yeoman who thought Mr. Shand's squatters to be back of everything, and the Doughty brothers, who were equally sure that evil goblin-hounds scouring the wood for human souls were to blame, and oh, aye, they certainly wanted no part of *that*.

"Not looking for trouble!" the brothers declared, with identical grim expressions on their identical gingery-whiskered faces.

Like their colleagues, they were afraid what another incursion into Marley Wood might bring down upon them. They feared that the expedition would make a mess of things, and further enrage the mysterious keeper of the lodge — then they should have more than ghostly blue heads in bottles to worry about! Even more, perhaps, they were distrustful of Bertram himself — bewitched, bedeviled little Bertram — and were uneasy at the thought of his walking the streets and lanes of Market Snailsby unfettered.

As if this were not objection enough, there was the small matter of the boy's origins. For Bertram was without question a *foreigner*, from round Salthead way in the county of Wuffolk. What was Wuffolk to Market Snailsby, the Scrimshaws asked, or to Fenshire, or to Slopshire for that matter? ("Hear, hear!") What had Wuffolk ever done for the south counties? Nothing, nowt, not a whit. ("That's giving it to 'em!") As for the magic elixir that had prolonged Bertram's childhood, the dissenters asked what good it was to any of them now, since they already had seen their own childhoods wither and die years before?

"Well, what of your children, then, and your children's children? Would you not wish them to drink of this wondrous potion in the silver cup?" said the Bertramites.

"And who would be wanting children to remain children forever?" was the opposition's reply. "For sooner or later we must all grow up and look after ourselves. As parents and grandparents we shan't want to be looking after children to the end of our days — we haven't the strength for it! Besides, how many of you are keen to have your own small ones drinking the blood of a horrid, snake-necked monstrosity?"

And so it went. Each argument produced a certain measurable response, which was countered by a dissenting argument of equal and opposite effect.

Pretty Miss Pingle stated that because Bertram and Sarah were children — or something like children — it was the obligation of the adults to care for them in the absence of their parents. Naturally she would say this, because caring for children was her life's work; but her reasoning swayed few to her side.

Everyone was reminded then of the fact that Vicar Ludlow already had written off to Bertam's sister, Miss Polly Longchapel, of Upper Lofting, Butter Cross. Suppose that Miss Longchapel should respond by asking that her little brother be returned to her? How was Mr. Ludlow to explain that they had mislaid him *a second time*? In the view of both the Mayor and Mr. Inkpen, it was a situation that would reflect very poorly on the citizens of Market Snailsby.

"And I, for one, abominate poor reflections," the attorney declared. "For we are backwatered enough here as it is. We must present a more competent face to the world."

The opposition in answer declared boldly that it was fine, let it reflect! Everybody who was anybody in south Fenshire knew the worth of Snailsby townsfolk. But who in Fenshire had ever heard of Miss Polly Longchapel of Upper Lofting, and what was she to them?

So ran the arguments which were being batted to and fro like shuttlecocks by their supporters, amidst periodic outbursts of indignant fuming, and cries of "Vanilla!" "Milksops!" "Bossy-boots!" and "No backbone!" At one point emotions rose to such a pitch that Vicar Ludlow, struggling to maintain civility, found himself drowned in his own calls for "Order, order!" Even Sir Hector's respected presence and his demand to "Haud yer tongues!" were insufficient to restrain the bolder spirits in the crowd.

So insistent were the supporters on each side, and so brisk in their defiance, that it was left to someone like Phoggie Finlayson to restore that order for which Mr. Ludlow and Sir Hector had been clamoring. His patience at an ebb, the creaky little bald man hopped to his feet and, glaring round him with his single eye like a Cyclops, called loudly upon his fellow citizens for SILENCE!

"Listen, listen, ye fen-frogs!" he scolded them. "I bean't sure if it's ghosts or demons as be hatching plots agin us, or squatters, or magical younkers; but whatever it be, it's marsh devils and spotted lions as remain the more troublesome for Fenshire folk. The boy remembered Phoggie and others of ye from five-and-thirty year ago, and very kindly, too; and for that 'tis only proper we should remember *him*."

"Weel spoken!" nodded Sir Hector, his voice booming above the sudden quiet. "'Tis no right nor juist tae be keepin' the wee-bit lad frae his clan an' family, d'ye no say? A muckle great mystery he may be, like the wood itsell, but dinna let that fash ye, for the troth will oot.

Sae cock yer bonnets the noo an' bide a wee. Hae trust i'the troth, an' ye'll needna fear."

In the end it was agreed that a small party of volunteers, to be led by Sir Hector, would attempt to rescue Bertram — and Sarah too, if possible — once Mrs. Chugwell's team had established their camp in the wood. Whatever force it was, demonic, ghostly, or otherwise, that had drawn Bertram back to the lodge — whether it be a mysterious keeper, or a snake-necked monstrosity, or phantom riders, or Mother Redcap, or squatters even — did not signify. Every effort would be made to get to the bottom of the mystery, and quickly, too, the which Sir Hector had every confidence would be achieved.

Mr. Blathers expressed his entire readiness to brave the perils of the enterprise, and examine with his own eyes any evidence of magic that might be uncovered. His statement was met by ironical cheers, and cries of "Splendid!" and "Good luck to you!" from the defeated faction. Some of that ilk declared it was all foolishness, and nobody's business what Bertram was getting up to in the wood; for if it were not the wish of Providence that he be getting up to it, as Mrs. Locket argued, then it would not be so.

Mr. Shand, hearing this, frowned deeply into his jowls and, rising, stated that it might be so, but that in his estimation it was nothing to the point. He believed that not only he himself, as an elected official of the parish, but the entire town had been dealt a grievous insult in the Croft. The brewer, a gentleman normally given to conviviality and compromise, did not appreciate being called a *fool* by anyone, least of all by a pack of glowing blue heads in bottles slung from a tree. Why did those in the opposition not see that?

Truth to tell, not everyone in attendance believed that the threats, couched as they had been in such enigmatic terms, bore any connection to the new road, but only to the snatching of Bertram from the lodge. In his position as fen-reeve, however, Mr. Shand could ill afford any uncertainty. He was resolved that the town should not beggar itself by laying out cash on Mrs. Chugwell, only to be frightened off by anonymous squatters and trespassers, the road left unfinished and the money gone for naught.

As for Mayor Jagard, he too was in favor of the expedition — "for the preserving of civic and moral dignity," as he said, "and in the interests of the public weal." Sadly, the many obligations incumbent upon his office precluded him from joining the volunteers; but he pledged to establish a headquarters down in the tap-room of the Broom and Badger, and keep abreast of events from that locale.

"Still, it's silly going after these children, who plainly belong in the wood and wish to remain there," declared the more obstinate amongst the Scrimshaws. "At any rate, we know what the boy's cousins from Dragonthorpe think of him — *not bloody much!*"

Indeed. For a verdict had been brought in the day previous by the Uckwatts — the respectable yeoman farmer and his sister — informing Vicar Ludlow that they had no interest in taking charge of their small cousin (assuming he could be gotten out of the wood again), or in affrighting the people of Dragonthorpe with his magical presence. The Uckwatts had heard and seen enough. They had heard of the magic Ogghops, the flying pancakes, and the glowing blue heads in Yocklebury Great Croft, and had seen fit to put three and three together. That being the case, and with the snow having largely melted away, they had set off home for Dragonthorpe, their duty discharged, their consciences clear, and the puzzle that was little Bertram left behind them in the wake of their flying spring-cart.

"You see? His own relations care not a whit for him, and so why should we? What is he to us but a burden, and an uncomfortable one at that?" challenged the Scrimshaws. "Let his sister look for him!"

"Cowards!" snorted the Bertramites.

"Busybodies!" shot back the opposition.

"Infantine!"

"Swinish!"

"Miserable objects!"

"Stinkers!"

Cheers from the one side invariably were met by jeers from the other; and so the uproar waxed afresh.

"God bless my soul — no rancor, please — it will not avail us — everyone — dear me — my good people, I beg of you," implored the vicar, trying as best he could to appease each side and prevent a real-life Punch-and-Judy from breaking out in the parish rooms. "We shall see what response my letter brings. I dare say we'll hear something in another few weeks — "

The vicar was so absorbed in his imploring, and appeasing, and his general preservation of the peace, he failed to note that the tea in his cup was shaking — that is until his ears informed him of the fact when his cup and saucer began to rattle. At about the same time he detected a subtle movement of the floor beneath his shoes. In an instant everybody in the room ceased their squabbling, both the Bertramites and the Scrimshaws, and gazed wonderingly at everybody else. For their own cups and saucers were rattling as well, and the boards under their feet had grown similarly unsteady.

"Gracious Lud!" they cried.

"I say!" Miss Henslowe whispered. "Corney, do you think — ?"

"Oh, yes, indeed," nodded Mr. Oldcorn, exchanging glances with her, "I believe we know very well the cause of it . . ."

They rose and went at once to the window, where voices could be heard exclaiming in the street below. The vicar quickly joined them and threw up the sash, while the rest of the assembly gathered round behind.

There were some children at play outside by the gently-lapping river. Amongst them was little Sukey Shorthose, she of the red cheeks and plaids and beaver bonnet. Like her fellows she was jumping gleefully up and down and clapping hands, and looking off to the southwards across the Fribble towards the Drovers' Road. A general barking of dogs had broken out all over town, and people were calling and shouting to one another, and crossing in their numbers over the stone bridge to the Broom and Badger.

Even more curious were the odd rumblings and trumpetings that were rolling like distant thunder on the gloomy air, and whose echoes could be felt in the subtle shaking of the boards underfoot.

"Are they here? Have you seen them?" the vicar called down to the children.

In answer little Sukey pointed to the opposite shore, where a line of steely-gray forms the size of mountains was emerging, one after another, from the mist of the Drovers' Road. They were traveling in close column up the highway, their long heads nodding, the cabs atop their shoulders swaying, their powerful limbs hammering the earth of Fenshire with a rhythmic *tramp! tramp! tramp!* Just back of the Badger they had turned out of the road and were marching in stately procession onto the wide, open expanse of the Common.

"My very word," said Mr. Ludlow.

"It's tuskers, vicar!" Sukey exclaimed with a flourish. "Tuskers in the road!"

THE FOURTH CHAPTER

THERE BE MONSTERS

TREMENDOUS excitement now prevailed in Market Snailsby.

At last the team of shovel-tuskers had arrived, with its company of drivers, sawyers, and navvies, its string of pack-horses, its caravans and supply wagons, drays, and transport vans. Several riders on horseback, posted at intervals within the train, were holding aloft tall poles from which bright red flags were waving. These were the well-known flutter-sticks, whose pennants thunder-beasts of every stripe had been trained from their earliest infancy to follow, and which were used to guide them on long journeys.

Of the beasts arriving there on the Common, one above all was observed to tower over the rest. It was Ranger, of course, that most stupendous of tuskers, and bearer of the Chugwells. Sharing the cab with the good lady and her son was a lanky, bespectacled young man, ready of smile and twinkly of eye — Mr. Angus Daintie. He was Matt's chief lieutenant, who had been left in command at Deadmarsh while the Chugwells were conducting their survey of the new road.

Miss Ada Henslowe was but one of many in the town who were thrilled to see the beasts again. These were not the shaggy red mastodons of overland transport, however, which in her childhood her beloved father had taken her across the bridge to see — no, they were a thing even more spectacular. The steely-coated tuskers were no mere thunder-beasts of burden; they were skilled engineers and excavators, diggers and dredgers. It was they who had carved out the coach-roads which were extending their reach throughout the length and breadth of the realm. And it was by dint of their efforts that Mrs. Chugwell's promise would be fulfilled — trains and coaches speeding through the wood to Ridingham in under four hours!

It was on the Common that they would make their camp for the night, before the start next morning for Marley Wood. As a result Ada and the others had but the few brief hours intervening to come out and see them; and come out and see them everybody did.

The assembly in the parish rooms having adjourned, Mr. Erksine Joliffe ambled across the bridge with the others, then took the short stroll down Fore Street to the Mudlark. There, beside the back-stairs of his establishment, he stopped for a while, pipe in hand, to view the tuskers as they trimmed sails and hove to on the Common like a fleet of steely galleons in harbor.

It was not long before he was joined by other admirers of the species, namely the Hathaways and Miss Henslowe, and Sir Hector Mac-Hector.

"Inty, tinty, tethery, methery . . ." the Laird was heard saying as he took count of the galleons, his Balmoral bonnet nodding in concert with his reckoning of each vessel.

"There are fourteen of them, I believe," said Mr. Joliffe, quietly smoking. "Magnificent, are they not?"

"Capital!" Richard exclaimed.

"O' that there's na gainsayin', t'be sure," declared Sir Hector, "an' a muckle great horde they be as weel."

"I think they're beautiful," said Ada.

"Quite so," nodded the landlord. "Indeed, what would our lovely Fenshire be without its roving fogs, its solitary marshes, its booming bitterns, and its thunder-beasts?"

"It would be Grimshire," Jemma said with a smile, in allusion to an ancient adage, one which remains common round the fenlands to this day.

"By the by, Mr. Joliffe, have you heard the news?" Ada asked.

"News, Miss Henslowe?"

"We had it from Mrs. Chugwell and Matt a short while ago. There were teratorns spotted in the Drovers' Road, not more than a mile from town. All of the drivers saw them."

"That is a bad sign."

"Dashedly so," Richard agreed.

"And there have been marsh devils prowling round the outskirts — and in Yocklebury Great Croft," Jemma added.

The landlord paused in his smoking and frowned. "The creatures are grown very bold this year. Perhaps it has some relation to this warning that was given in the Croft?"

Richard's eyes narrowed briefly at the remark. He recollected Mr. Shand's suspicions as regards the keeper of the Mudlark; but he could not believe that this serene, contemplative man, who preferred his sedgy streams and lonesome marshes, his dear land of fen and flood, to the grimy world of commerce, had any knowledge of the sinister doings in the Croft and Marley Wood.

Anything for a quiet life — was that not Mr. Joliffe's well-known motto? To what extremes, Richard wondered, might their tweedy townsman go in his pursuit of this ideal? Had not Mr. Joliffe been "gowked" on April Fool's Day last, and by Sir Hector and Dr. Chevenix no less? And although he had celebrated the joke with a hearty laugh and a round of drinks, might that have been simply a charade? Given Mr. Joliffe's stated opposition to the new road, might not that incident have served as the final straw? And yet, opposed or no, was he not clearly, and always had been, an admirer of shovel-tuskers, the very instruments by which that new road was being constructed?

"Goodness me," Richard said to himself, "whatever am I thinking? It's quite impossible. I've known Erskine Joliffe all my life. He's a gentleman and a publican. It's utterly daft — sheer lunacy!"

And straightway he dropped the idea from his mind, as wholly and completely as if he had dropped it off the edge of the earth. Besides, he thought, they should be discovering the truth of the matter soon enough, once the expedition had succeeded in making its way to the lodge.

That evening at the vicarage, Mrs. Chugwell and Matt were told of the plan that had been formulated to rescue Bertram from his captivity. It would be necessary for them first to establish their camp at the terminus of the road. One of the shovel-tuskers then could be dispatched to Market Snailsby to escort the volunteers into the wood. Once arrived at the camp, the expedition members would then proceed on their own with the search for Bertram.

The mastodon lady and her son listened attentively, weighing each element of the plan with careful deliberation. The atmosphere in the room was one of grim resolve. There had been nasty things afoot in the wood of Marley since before the year dot; if one wished to avoid them, one simply steered clear of that dreadful, dark domain. Now, however, someone there had made specific and calculated threats against the town and its citizens.

This likely was the same someone who had lured two small children away from their families, and given them to drink a magic elixir that had prolonged their childhood. It was an extract derived in part from the blood of the horrid, snake-necked monstrosity, the children's guardian, and summoner of the ghostly riders and their hounds. Now this same someone had threatened interference, or so it appeared, with the clearing of the road.

Not unexpectedly, the Chugwells voiced some concern as regards this latter prospect. They had triumphed over many an obstacle in the practice of their profession, in the years since Phrank Chugwell had established the team. Obstacles were part and parcel of the job; mere obstruction itself was nothing unusual. But Marley Wood was shaping up to be a singular case. The team had confronted its share of spotted lions, marsh devils, short-faced bears, and other savage beasts; not once, however, had the Chugwells run up against a ghost or demon, phantom rider, or evil goblin-hound. Nor had they seen or heard tell of a creature resembling the children's guardian, the reality of which nonetheless was beyond dispute.

There looked to be no alternative now but to take action; and, so deciding, mother and son lent their wholehearted support to the plan.

Next morning the tuskers were assembled again into a train and driven one by one over the old stone bridge. The people of Market Snailsby, watching in awe, held their collective breath, as they always did; but the bridge and its piers successfully weathered the strain, as *they* always did, and afforded the beasts a safe crossing over the Fribble. Turning into Holy Street, the procession, with Ranger at its head, its horses, caravans, and wagons trailing behind, and its flutter-sticks rippling on high, set off for Marley Wood.

As the train went rumbling past the Church of All Hallows, the clock and chimes in its tall landmark of a steeple began to sound the hour — *of thirteen.*

"There's another bad sign," thought Mr. Joliffe, who had been observing from his inn across the river. He took a long whiff of his pipe and shook his head. Another bad sign, like teratorns in the Drovers' Road, and marsh devils in the Croft, and glowing blue heads in bottles, and who knew what more yet to come.

"I must see to that," the vicar said, craning out for a glimpse of the clock from his study window. He turned round and called to his wife — "Dear, we must see to that!"

"I shall send for Tom Trot," said Mrs. Ludlow, who had been viewing the spectacle from the next room, in the company of Jayne Scrimshaw.

The vicar paused. "But Tom Trot knows nothing about clocks," he said.

"Yes, but he's very good with bells, dear."

"Strange, very strange," the vicar murmured — in reference to the church clock, not his wife's answer. "Thirteen hours. It's rather like that old long-case in the lodge of de Clinkers — the one with thirteen hours on its face. Can this be more magic, I wonder? Dear me!"

In the street outside, Mr. Blathers had been observing the parade through his horn-rims when the clock struck the impossible hour.

"An error in the mechanism," he nodded to those around him, all of whom were remarking on the oddity. "Perhaps our holy man has received a judgment from his employer. Humph! Funny thing, mechanisms — and judgments."

"Aye," nodded Mr. Swain, who was one of those standing nearby. Like most of his fellow-citizens, the eel-trap man had left off his toils for a spell to view the departure of the train. Then he sighed and, throwing his heavy brow into folds, murmured darkly — "Lord bless us, what can come of this? Nowt to the good, I'll be bound. 'Tain't swamp-lights be ketching dead men's sconces in bottles hung on trees — 'tis something worse. Woe betide us!"

"That may be so, my iron-headed friend," remarked Mr. Blathers, overhearing him, "but it's hardly proof of cause and effect. Ghostly lights in the wood and figgy bottles on a tree do not a scientific case make. We've proof of nothing yet. Funny thing, proof. But most anything can seem like proof to an ill-ordered mind."

"Bothersome!" grunted Ingo. Clearly he was not a champion of the owlish little man in spectacles. "Strike me ugly," he muttered under his breath, "if not half so ugly as ye! And so what else be in this fellow's ordered mind today?"

All of Market Snailsby had been shaken to its core — literally — by the train and its retinue as they rumbled through Holy Street and out onto the Dragonthorpe Road. Along the route crowds on the footway and at windows and in the waterside fields were clapping and cheering, and urging on Mrs. Chugwell and her team with cries of "Godspeed!" and "Bring us to Ridingham!" Women were waving handkerchiefs, men were giving overhead handclasps, bands of schoolchildren were shouting, and the noise was tremendous.

With a slow and stately tread the tuskers thundered past Blossom's Court and the old cherry gardens, at which point the ghostly mist from the marshes began to close in about them. One by one they were swallowed up by it and so became ghosts themselves, leaving behind them only the echoes of their departing trumpet-calls.

A week went by, during which time the party of volunteers was settled upon — Sir Hector and the gillies, Mr. Shand, Richard Hathaway, Vicar Ludlow, Dr. Chevenix, and Mr. Blathers. From the outset Richard had refused to heed his sister's pleas to join them. But she had persisted; and then Ada had demanded that *she* be allowed to come as well; and although Richard and the others had kept up a spirited protest throughout the week, it was of no avail. There simply was too much at stake, too much curiosity about Bertram and Sarah and the elixir of youth, and the snake-necked guardian, and the lodge and its shadowy keeper, for the women to be denied.

Then, late one day, the earth of Fenshire trembled again, and a lofty colossus blowing jets of steam came striding out of the mist of the Dragonthorpe Road. It was the mighty Ranger himself, with Matt Chugwell at the helm. The volunteers' escort had arrived.

The expedition set out the next morning at daybreak. The ladies, followed by Vicar Ludlow, Dr. Chevenix, and Mr. Blathers, scaled up the cord-ladder to join Matt in the cab. Amongst those on horseback, Sir Hector as usual assumed the lead on his favorite gelding. Behind him came Mr. Shand on his hunter, and Richard on Rosie, and the gillies on their sturdy cobs. And trailing in their wake was the majestic figure of Ranger, who it was the horses' constant challenge to outpace, so as not to be trampled underfoot by the tusker's mighty stride.

There were a number of dogs in the company as well, among them Snap, who had known for days that an undertaking of momentous import was in the works. He hadn't wanted to be left out, and had attached himself to the leash of hounds which Sir Hector had brought to sniff out Bertram's scent. Although the Hathaways were conscious of the risks inherent in the enterprise, both believed that the formidable presence of Ranger would provide sufficient safety for the coach dog, and for Rosie as well.

The expedition by now had turned out of the Dragonthorpe Road, and was passing the old gallows with its creaking gibbet-irons. Before them rose the tall curtain of Marley Wood, its peaks soaring steeply into the mist like a range of gloomy cliffs. Snap and Rosie, meanwhile, had been jogging along together and talking over the merits of the adventure, and the mystery of little Bertram, and the reports of magic wine and magic pancakes, and glowing blue heads in bottles, and the cowardly cousins who had fled from it all to Dragonthorpe.

"Why do you suppose they call it Dragonthorpe?" Snap asked.

"There was a dragon's fossilized skull uncovered there," Rosie explained. "It's on show now at the Lizard's Head, which is the principal inn and public house of the town."

"How do you know that, Rosie?"

"I know it, because I've been there," the mare answered, with a little conscious pride. She was a road-horse who had seen something of the world — well, of the south Fenshire world at least. Poor Snap had not traveled so much; the excursion some weeks before to Tillington had been one of his few in recent years. And never had he been so far from home as Dragonthorpe.

"And that is why the inn is called the Lizard's Head? Because of this dragon's skull?"

"Yes. Although it wasn't actually a dragon or a lizard, but what the professors call a Megalosaurus, which was a type of saurian — a huge reptile, from bygone days. It was bigger even than a shovel-tusker. But its kind has gone succinct."

"Gone where?" Snap asked.

"Succinct. It means they died out — disappeared — long ago."

"How long ago?"

Rosie shook her head. "I don't know; I don't believe anyone does, not even the professors. I'm afraid paleontology isn't my long suit. Astronomy is more my bag of oats, as you know."

Poor Snap looked confused. "What have your oats to do with it, Rosie?"

"It's just an expression, Snap — gracious, you needn't take everything so literally," laughed the mare.

They continued on in silence for a time. Meantime the looming fortress of the wood was growing ever larger, ever darker, ever more sinister as they drew near its bodeful precincts. Even Rosie the traveled road-horse had to admit to a slight case of nerves at the sight of it. But only to herself did she admit it; not a whisper of it reached the flop-ears of the coach dog trotting beside her.

"Were there other such monsters in bygone days?" Snap asked.

"Of course. The world was full of monsters then, and it's full of monsters still. Marsh devils, spotted lions, megatheres and mylodons, teratorns, thunder-beasts — they're all monsters of a sort. And there's that horsy thing that's no horse, as you've termed it."

"That *was* a monster!" Snap yelped, shivering at the memory of it, and of its curious, odd whiff.

"Agreed. We'll be fortunate not to meet up with a marsh devil on this trip — if our luck isn't entirely out."

All the spots in Snap's coat suddenly went very pale.

"A marsh devil in the wood? You're not serious, are you?" he asked, worriedly.

"Of course I am. There's danger in this undertaking — didn't you know that? And we'll be in it up to our fetlocks."

Snap pondered for a moment. "But I haven't got any fetlocks," he said.

"Well, you've got dew-claws, haven't you? It's the same principle. Heigh-ho," sighed the mare, with a little toss of her head, "once again, Snap, it's just an expression."

"What of the ghostly riders and the goblin-hounds? Might we meet up with them as well?"

"Not to worry, that's why Ranger is here — to protect us from whatever befalls. And there's an entire regiment of tuskers awaiting us at the end of the road, to guard against marsh devils and spotted lions, and glowing heads in bottles, and horsy things that aren't horses."

"But first we must reach the end of the road, in order to be guarded," Snap pointed out.

End of the road! He didn't like the sound of that. He was feeling distinctly ill at ease at the moment, and unlike Rosie he was not afraid to admit it. He may not have been *the* most valiant of valiant coach dogs, but he was brave of heart, if not of deed. He was not so sure now that this undertaking of momentous import had been such a good idea. Truth to tell, he would rather have been chasing shade-tails in the back-garden at Mead Cottage, or gnawing on a good chop-bone, or exchanging pleasantries with little Clover. To his credit, however, Snap plucked up his courage and soldiered on, as he joined the hounds in sniffing the wind.

The mighty limbs of Ranger continued to pound the road at the horses' heels, while his shovel-tusks swung to and fro in the air overhead, his every sense on the alert. Soon the ancient gallows and its creaking irons had been left far behind — gone, dissolved, vanished in the mist, and the whole wide, dreary expanse of south Fenshire with them.

Onward they jogged, towards the opening in the gloomy fortress of evergreens and oaks — which opening now, to Snap, looked uncomfortably like a mouth gaping wide to receive them — onward along Mrs. Chugwell's plank-and-gravel road, and through the gaping jaws and straight down the throat of Marley Wood.

PART SIX

THE FIRST CHAPTER

SCATTERED!

A S they went along, the vicar and the others riding with
Matt learned that there had been trouble at the new camp
in the wood, and of a more worrisome kind than in prior
seasons.

The strange flittings amongst the trees, the tracking movements, the
sensation of eyes studying them from afar — all were there again as before. But now a new element had been added: thievery. Already in the
short week that the team had been in the wood, mauls, axes, felling-
saws, and other implements had disappeared from the camp. Wheels
had been removed from some of the vans and wagons, rendering them
inoperative. Some spare pieces of the tuskers' equipage — bridles, sur-
cingles, tug-lines, cruppers, and the like — had gone missing, as had all
the flutter-sticks. As for the beasts themselves, they had grown increas-
ingly restless, and had taken to casting frequent looks about them as
they worked, and sniffing the air for clues.

And, as before, the tracks of an unshod horse had turned up wherever the thieves had struck.

The feeling of unseen eyes watching was upon the travelers even
now as they neared the terminus of the road. There had been the usual
beastly roarings in the wood since they had set off, which had made
the horses nervous, and the hounds, too. At one point an immense,
sinewy shape had been glimpsed striding through the shadows beyond
the verge — a spotted lion. It had kept pace with them for a while, but
had been driven off by a couple of threatening movements from Ranger, and a ferocious burst of trumpeting. For what was a mere spotted
lion, or a marsh devil for that matter, to such a kingly creature as the
shovel-tusker?

The hours had sped by, and now at last they had arrived at their
destination. The stand of trees that had blocked the survey party's way
had been removed; in its place lay a strip of cleared ground stretching
off into the wood. A few caravans and a supply wagon were resting at

the side of it, some hundred feet or more ahead, where a company of workmen was directing a tusker in grading and smoothing its surface. Beyond them other beasts could be seen clearing the new ground, scooping up whole mountains of it in their jaws and hurling it aside. At their heels another tusker was drawing a sledge, to stir up the soil, while a second was tamping the earth to firm it. Others were making use of their powerful trunks to remove felled timbers to the verge, while still more were breaking large stones into fragments for inclusion in the new roadbed.

Already many of the felled trees had been cut into planks, and laid down over stretches of the new ground and sealed with pitch. A layer of stones and coarse gravel mixed with lime was being spread over the planks, to be followed by a wearing-surface of fine gravel and asphaltum. On either side of the road shallow ditches were being excavated to provide drainage. And farther on, well out of sight of Matt and the others, the rumble of operations could be heard echoing through the wood — the noise of the workmen cutting and sawing, the sound of mighty trees falling, of tuskers grubbing up roots and clearing ground, of sledges being towed through the soil, all of it in concert with the bantering cries of the navvies and the spirited trumpeting of the beasts.

What a wild, splendid, craggy scene it was! The new roadbed growing forward of the old, cleaving the darksome wood in twain. It was proof how much could be accomplished by the diligence and skill of the Chugwell team even in one short week.

And at the far northern edge of the wood, where the road one day would break free of its gloomy confines, Ridingham and Newmarsh awaited.

"An' sae we'll be gangin' the noo, Mattie," said Sir Hector, as the volunteers were making final preparation for their ride to the lodge. "The gude God be thankit for safe journey through the wood, an' yersell forbye, and yont muckle great beast. Aye, an' a right braw an' a bonny great beast y'are, Ranger ma lad! Gang whaur ye will through town an' country, there be no a finer beast tae be found in a twelvemonth."

"Perish me, Laird, 'tis the vera troth," agreed the fiery Haggis. "By ma certie, 'tis plain as a packsaddle."

"Aye, 'tis juist as ye say, Laird," nodded Jorkens.

"Indeed," chimed in the vicar. "We all have been greatly blessed by Ranger's presence. Now, let us pray for a safe and successful conclusion to our errand."

From on high, Ranger's soft brown eyes gazed down upon the tiny band of adventurers who were making ready to brave the hazards of the wood. Did he pity them, I wonder? Did he admire them? Or did he know something — some deep and wondrous secret, perhaps — that they and the others did not?

Some horses had been procured from the Chugwells' string, for the use of the volunteers who had ridden in the cab with Matt. Meanwhile Sir Hector had taken charge of the dogs and put them on the scent. All of them looked stout, level, and uncommonly fit to go. And so too did the expedition members, who offered their thanks and farewells now to Matt and his mother. The Chugwells in their turn assured them that they would post Angus Daintie at the terminus with one of the beasts, in the event their assistance might be required.

Through the chill and gloom of the sinister, soaring trees the riders took their way, with Sir Hector and the gillies in the advance, and the hounds and Snap scouring the ground before them. After only a brief period of searching, however, the dogs began milling about, whining and fretting, and rolling over one another, in a clear sign of confusion. Evidently they had picked up Bertram's scent, only to lose it, then had picked it up again, and lost it again. It was much like the trouble the survey party had encountered when tracking the unshod horse. Meantime the riders, on the lookout for the elusive clearing wherein lay the ruined lodge, again were feeling the burden of hidden eyes upon them.

But that was not their most pressing concern.

"By St. Poppo, 'tisn't this ridiculous," exclaimed a frustrated Sir Hector.

They had reined in their mounts in the loom of a clumber pine. Peering round its massive trunk the riders beheld, about a bowshot distance off, not the gates of the ruined lodge — but the terminus of the new road.

They had come round full circle to their starting-point.

"What manner of trickery is this? This is — this is nonsense!" complained the reeve, glancing about him in bewilderment.

Trickery and nonsense? Some cracked rustic's idea of a joke? Squatters? Erskine Joliffe of the Mudlark? But if one of these, how in the devil's name had it been accomplished?

"Not trickery, sir — magic," Ada declared.

"More clock magic, perhaps?" the vicar wondered aloud. Then the significance of it struck him, almost as forcefully as his church clock's striking thirteen. "Goodness! The thirteenth hour — and is this not the thirteenth day of the month?"

Richard snapped his fingers. "Hallo! As a matter of fact it is. A dashed curious thing, is it not?"

"How else are we to explain it?" said Ada. "Surely this is more magic by Bertram's keeper, to prevent us from reaching the lodge?"

"Aye, 'tis vera likely," opined Sir Hector, with a thoughtful scrape of his chin. "For there's naught else, I'm thinkin', can fule this gude gelding o' mine, an' Willie's hunter there, an' the hoonds forbye."

"Nor have I any other explanation," Dr. Chevenix admitted, shaking his head.

"Nor I," said Richard.

"Well, here is some proof for you now, Mr. Blathers," smiled Ada, with a little show of triumph. "What do you make of this predicament of ours? Here our horses have been carrying us along to the lodge, and yet we've returned to the very place from where we set out. How does your science explain that?"

But Mr. Blathers was not a man easily dissuaded of his views. "No magic here," he stated confidently.

"Think ye? Hoots, man, what mair proof wad ye hae?" returned the Laird. "Maist everything aboot this wood be a boggle an' a mystery. An' sae whyfor no magic, eh?"

"I'll admit, there may be something fishy here," said Mr. Blathers, with a noisy clearing of his voice, "but I'll *not* admit that it lies beyond the bounds of rational thought. Most anything can seem like magic if sufficiently cloaked in nonsense. In my view we have simply been misled by these dense forest aisles — these ill-lighted passages, treacherous thickets, and cloistered, canopied domains. Hardly more mysterious than that. Humph!"

So declaring, the little bachelor-man in black proceeded to sneeze up a storm into his handkerchief, the echoes of it reverberating loudly through his forest aisles and cloistered, canopied domains.

"So that is your answer? We have simply lost our way?" returned Dr. Chevenix, in some amazement. "By your leave, sir, I think you're rather wide of the mark. What of Shand's hunter there? It's a well-known fact that horse has a nose like a compass. And what of the hounds? For they've had the boy's scent to follow."

"And what of our Snap?" Jemma added. "He can sniff out a millet seed in a marsh meadow if given half a chance. Isn't that so, Richard?"

Her brother, torn between his friendship for Mr. Blathers and his duty to his sister and his loyal coach dog, relented, acknowledging that her assessment was fundamentally sound — an assessment, by the by, with which the loyal coach dog heartily concurred.

"And if magic went out years ago, Mr. Blathers," Ada continued, "how is it that the vicar's bogberry was made into an Ogghops before the very faces of his startled guests, mine included? And that flying pancakes crashed down upon Mrs. Ludlow's head?"

"Yes, how does your science explain these away, Mr. Blathers?" the vicar was interested to know.

The owlish little man had hard work to conceal his annoyance. A resounding "Humph!" was his initial response to these attacks upon his well-regulated universe. He folded and re-folded his arms, and grunted, and cleared his voice again. Such tiresome questions! Explaining rational thinking to some people was like feeding peanuts to a marble clock — no result. For want of any useful retort he simply looked away, his arms defiantly crossed, his quick, bird-like gaze darting about his forest aisles and cloistered, canopied domains.

The others carried on with the discussion for several minutes more. As for Mr. Blathers, he took little notice of it, owing to the look of horror that had suddenly come into his face. Straightway he froze into a statue in the saddle, as motionless as the marble of his marble clock, his eyes fixed upon something in the shadows not far off.

The others soon noticed his odd posture. "Is it Angus Daintie and the tusker?" they wondered, recollecting the Chugwells' promise. But the eyes of the little man in black were looking in the opposite direction.

"What is it, Mr. Blathers?" Ada asked him. "For you look peculiar." (*More peculiar than usual*, she nearly said).

Mr. Blathers licked his lips and swallowed, but otherwise made no sign that he had heard. All the blood had drained from his face; tiny beads of moisture could be seen popping out all over his brow.

"Whatever is the matter, Mr. Blathers?" said Jemma.

The owlish eyes behind their horn-rims had grown to white balls, their gaze locked with a fearful intensity upon — what?

"Perhaps he has suffered an attack?" said Mr. Shand. "What think you, doctor? Is he apoplectic?"

The doctor was about to respond when Mr. Blathers, substituting dumb show for words, lifted a trembling hand and pointed.

"Jumping — c-c-cats!" was all he managed to stammer out.

As words go it was an unfortunate choice, if an accurate one. In the same instant the horses threw their heads, snorted wildly, and began backing and sidling away. All the dogs were growling, and gnashing their teeth, and staring in the same direction as Mr. Blathers. Like the horses they had caught a whiff of something very bad, and now they had caught sight of it as well.

A huge, dark form lay a-crouch amongst the shadows, its flaming yellow eyes fixed balefully upon them. Beneath the eyes two long, steely canines could be seen projecting from the monster's upper jaw. Slowly the creature lowered its head, its ears flat, its upper lip turned back in a savage smile, its coat of tawny velvet rippling like a sea of wheat. It was a vicious, evil-looking thing — a gigantic carnivore, bristling with horrid fangs and ripping claws. To a Fenshireman there was no mistaking what it was.

"Marsh devil," whispered Sir Hector.

"Gracious heavens!" the vicar gasped.

Swift as light Sir Hector's claymore sprang into his hand. As he worked to steady his horse, the gillies, struggling to control their own frantic cobs, drew their whingers.

"Here's a fine lookout, by — !" swore Mr. Shand, tucking down his wide-awake.

"Richard, what are we to do?" Jemma said in appeal to her brother, who had drawn his cutlass and was nerving himself for the defense of the women.

"A hasty retreat is in order, I dare say," he replied — a view with which no one could have disagreed. (*Or we shall certainly be butchered* he nearly added, but caught himself in time). Rising in the stirrups, he bent over Rosie's neck and spoke to her in a low, quiet voice. Bravely the mare neighed her understanding; then, patting her shoulder, Richard nudged her gently towards the road. "Let us draw back now," he said to his companions. "This brute will not dare challenge the tuskers at work there in the road. Snap, come here at once — "

"It's a monstrous specimen, and a speedy one, by the look of it," warned Dr. Chevenix, "and there is not much ground for it to cover."

Mr. Shand and the Laird grimly nodded their concurrence. As for Mr. Blathers, he had no opinion, and no recommendation. His face had turned into a mask — a deathly shade of pale. *Scared blue* he was, or so, I believe, is the medical term for it.

What followed took place with striking speed and suddenness.

The dirk-tooth, having worked itself up to charging pitch, sprang from the shadows and bounded towards them. (How swiftly the devil-faced demon could cover that ground Dr. Chevenix had spoken of!) At the same time the riders wheeled their mounts about and rammed in their spurs. The horses, madly voicing their eagerness to be gone, took the bits in their teeth and, as one animal, turned tail and fled.

It was clear at once that not all would make it — the lightning-like speed of the dirk-tooth and the angle of its trajectory would see to that. Those nearest the clumber pine beat away ferociously for the road; those behind them, however, seemed destined to become victims of the great cat, which would be upon them in a few more mighty bounds.

These poor, doomed souls — Richard and Jemma, Ada, the vicar, and Dr. Chevenix — seeing they had little hope of reaching the road, would be forced to take some other action if they were to avert disaster. It was Richard who took it. Calling to his sister and the others to follow, he jerked Rosie aside and lunged off into the wood, guiding his companions round a dense growth of firs, and through a stand of oaks, and across a noisy brook, and down a gloomy row of forest aisles. Having spurred the mare into a gallop, he abruptly swung her to the right, then to the left, and then to the right again, then drove her full-tilt through the pines and thick clumps of spruce, and up and over a grassy flat towards a maze of timber and berry brambles, very cool and dark. A fast goer was Rosie, most everyone in town was agreed — a regular clipper — but never before had she laid herself out in such form as in those few critical, desperate minutes in the wood. It was all the other horses could do to keep up, and the valiant Snap as well.

Mere seconds after the riders had departed the grassy flat, a horse-like creature came racing onto it from the trees. Lurching to a stop directly in the path of the charging saber-cat, it thrust out a hand towards the monster, barring the way. There was a small child astride the creature's back, clinging by his tiny fists to its bright orange mane. A wild, unearthly scream, ghastly enough to freeze the blood of most anything alive, burst from the creature's throat. Its eyes — such haunting, hypnotic eyes they were — fastened themselves upon the cat with an expression that was at once proud, commanding, and terrible.

The dirk-tooth arrested its spring and stood panting, riveted to the spot by the creature's mighty gaze. For a long moment it glared at the beast and its tiny rider; but there was something in those proud and terrible eyes, some eerie, mesmerizing force, overwhelming and unopposable, which insinuated itself into the brain of the marsh devil and took hold there. Before long its entire attention was in the grip of that strange, hypnotic glance, as irresistibly drawn to it as iron to a magnet.

Then the creature shook its head slowly from side to side, and with a steady finger pointed the cat away. The dirk-tooth, faced with something even more powerful than its own dread fangs and ripping claws, lowered its eyes and its short brush of a tail, and obediently slunk off into the trees, its menace deflected by a look.

Neither Richard nor his companions were witness to any of this, of course, as they already had fled deep into the maze of thicket and timber.

For several hours they wandered about, searching for another way to the road but not finding it, and looking for the way to the lodge, but not finding that either. They had managed to elude the marsh devil — or it had given up the chase, they did not know which — but there were fearsome noises enough in the forest stronghold to keep them in mind of the dangers that threatened. They were tired and hungry after their long day's ordeal, and now the light in the wood, dim as it always was, was growing steadily dimmer. Slowly the night with all its attendant perils was drawing on.

It was nearly dark when Snap, his nose to the ground, let out a yelp and bolted into the underwood. Richard called after him, demanding that he return; but then, thinking the better of it, he spurred Rosie on to follow.

He and the others were upon them before they knew it — a couple of stone columns, cracked and moldering, and between them a pair of rusty gates leading to the railed causeway of the lodge. Nothing of the clearing beyond, or of the lodge itself and its ramparts, was visible in the fast-gathering gloom. Even the causeway was merely a darker lump of darkness in a swirling twilight of mist and fog.

They found Snap excitedly sniffing round the foot of the gates. It was plain he had caught a whiff of Bertram's scent.

"Is this it?" Ada asked, straining her eyes to see. "Is this the old lodge?"

"It is indeed," the vicar replied. "The fabled hunting-seat of Godfrey de Clinkers!"

They all were very much relieved, and gave thanks to heaven for their good fortune; but Richard for one wasted little time over it.

"Now that we've found it, we must hurry across," he urged, "for the lodge is the only safe bit of ground in this dashed unfriendly neighborhood."

There was no argument on that score, Dr. Chevenix remarking he hoped there might be some food on offer in the place, for he was as hungry as a mouse in a barley-sack.

Quickly they dismounted and led the horses across. Only after he had shut the second pair of gates behind them did Richard allow himself the faintest sigh of relief.

They secured the horses in the fog-shrouded courtyard. The air was cold and still, and the darkness all but complete save for a ruby gleam of firelight shining in some windows nearby. Richard, seeing to which part of the lodge those windows belonged, instructed his sister and the others to follow him there. Importantly he ordered Snap, under threat of chop-bone prohibition for life, to remain as quiet as the doctor's mouse in its barley-sack.

Noiselessly they stole across the yard, and then up the steps and into the lodge through the tall double-doors. Once inside, the vicar led the way — for he too had recognized which part of the lodge it was — to a long and lofty chamber, one with a row of windows down the side of it, and skylights piercing the roof, and a tiled floor. It was the great hall or banqueting-room of the lodge.

The ruby gleam originated at its farther end, where a fire was blazing away in the massive stone hearth. Like flitting ghosts the intruders glided silently across the tiles. As they drew near the chimney, the sound of a voice quietly speaking reached their ears. It was a woman's voice — a low voice for a woman, to be sure, but by no means an unpleasant one, and with something of a musical ring to it.

> *Simple Simon met a pieman,*
> *A-going to the fair.*
> *Says Simple Simon to the pieman,*
> *"Have you no pies to spare?"*

In a body they crept forward towards the screen that stood near the fire, blocking their view; and having gathered behind it, they peered stealthily round its edge.

On the ancient oak settle beside the chimney sat Bertram and a little girl — it was Sarah. Both were listening attentively to the rhymes as they were read out, their eyes a-shine, the light from the fire playing across their faces, its quivering shadows adding weirdness to what was, already, one of the weirdest of scenes.

Seated on the hearthrug before the children was the horsy creature that was no horse — the hideous, snake-necked monstrosity. Its long neck, however, had been withdrawn into its torso, allowing Richard and the others to see the creature now for what it was. Much of its body was composed of a horse's frame — and a most massive and powerful frame it was indeed. At the moment it was sitting with its horse's muscular limbs drawn up under it. Above its forelegs the creature was not horsy but very human, and very female. A bodice of rustic design adorned its torso, and its orange mane — actually a shower of tresses flowing down from its very human head — had been gathered neatly at its back and tied with a ribbon.

On its nose was perched a pair of spectacles, which it was using to read to the children from a book it held in its very human hands.

> *Hey! fiddle, fiddle!*
> *The spit and the griddle,*
> *The sow jumped over the loom;*
> *The little frog laughed to see such sport,*
> *And the mop ran away with the broom.*

"God bless my soul," the vicar whispered.

"You know what that creature is, don't you, Richard?" Jemma said.

"Matter of fact!" her brother nodded.

"That is the creature from the Tillington Road."

"Indeed, and the same one that nearly ran me down in the twilight. But I'm dashed if I can believe it, sis. To be perfectly frank, I'm jiggered!"

THE SECOND CHAPTER

THE SECRET OF THE LODGE

I N some respects the creature resembled a very proper-looking governess, with its bookish spectacles and its book, and its long hair drawn neatly back, and its bodice trimmed with fur, which clung to its shapeliness snugly, but modestly. But the bodice, it was observed, was made of the same rude stuff as the clothing Bertram had worn, and the garments little Sarah was wearing now — hardly proper attire for a governess of credit (except perhaps in Slopshire). Indeed in most respects the creature on the hearthrug was anything but proper in any human sense whatsoever.

"My gracious," Ada whispered, "it's a Centaur!"

"Most extraordinary!" said Dr. Chevenix.

"And, if I am not mistaken, a female Centaur to boot," Richard remarked. "Or, more correctly, a *Centauress* — rarest of the rare!"

"But how came she here?" wondered Ada. "And why is she reading to the children?"

"And where is the keeper of the lodge? And the phantom riders?" dittoed the doctor.

Unfortunately Snap chose that time to voice a little nervous growl — evidently his master's injunction concerning the chop-bones had slipped his mind — and it was this small sound that betrayed them.

Alerted to their presence, the Centauress cocked her head and sniffed the air. Cautioning the children to silence, she laid by her book and spectacles and, rearing up onto her hooves, turned her proud and terrible gaze upon the screen. Being partly equine — that part of her that was uncommonly massive and powerful — she was rather tall, and the human part of her made her even taller. Higher and higher she rose as she gained her feet, her mighty figure soaring above all else in the great hall. The firelight playing upon her anatomy sent her inky shadow flowing up the wall and wainscot, adding further miles to her height.

Then her long neck came out and sent her head shooting towards the screen. It slid over the top of it and, hovering there, gazed fiercely down at the strangers crouching beneath. Snap, smelling that thing he had wanted never to smell again, and seeing it now, too, could not help himself. He was a coach dog, after all, and what he did next was only natural — he growled at the angry, staring object afloat in the air above him, and burst out in a fit of yelping.

"Away with you!" he commanded. "My master has his sturdy cutlass drawn, and he'll soon sort you out. And my good friend Rosie is in the courtyard — Rosamond is her name — a famous road-horse, I'm sure you've heard of her. She's no duffer, and will give you what for. So you'd better clear out of here!"

O brave-hearted pudding dog! O guardian of so much more than the mails!

The response of the Centauress was immediate, and unequivocal. Frowning horribly, she rolled back her eyes, opened her mouth, and gave vent to as awful, unearthly, and hair-raising a scream as ever was heard in all the vast, wide county of Fenshire. It rang and echoed and reverberated throughout the great hall — indeed throughout the entire length and breadth of the lodge — bounding and rebounding from the walls and windows, from the glazed tiles of the floor to the airy rafters, and set the blood of the strangers to curdling.

Then the angry, staring thing withdrew from above the screen, the long neck shortening down and down, and down, and so dropping the head into place again on the torso. The Centauress then took in hand a great, curved bow that lay at her side, nocked an arrow on the string and, rising up with her arms at full stretch, took threatening aim at the intruders behind the screen. Little Sarah meantime, fearful of the strangers, and over Bertram's objections, had clambered to safety atop the Centauress's broad back.

Having not a moment to waste, Bertram dashed round in front of his guardian and interposed his small self between her bow and the screen.

"No, no! They are the ones you spared in the wood!" he cried out. "They are the ones who were so kind to me, especially the vicar, Mr. Ludlow there, and his wife. I'm sure they've not come to harm you. They've come looking for me."

"Likely she's a dead shot," Richard whispered to the others as they peered round the screen. "Can there be any doubt it was she who dropped that stag in the wood?"

"Of course, of course!" said the vicar. "The Centaurs of old were renowned for their skill in the hunting-field — "

Bertram's plea appeared to have had the desired effect. Cautiously the Centauress lowered her bow. Then she withdrew a few paces, her unshod hooves clattering noisily on the floor-tiles, and stood glowering at the strangers, her face twisted into a hideous scowl.

"Hallo! Hallo there!" Richard called to her, craning out, his hand raised in a sign of truce. One by one he and the others stepped from behind the screen. Immediately Snap began growling again, but a sharp word from Jemma put a period to *that*.

"Dashed sorry to intrude," Richard went on, in as easy a voice as he could muster under the circumstances. He had sheathed his cutlass, and the doctor now followed his example. "Yes — well — at any rate, Bertram is quite correct. We have come looking for him, to be sure, and for the lodge as well. It's dangerous out there in the wood, particularly at night, and much safer behind these walls."

The Centauress was unmoved. She continued to glare at them, her scowl as black and stormy as the summit of a thunder-crowned peak. They could feel the hypnotic tug of her gaze, which Richard and Snap had experienced once before upon a certain evening at twilight. It was a gaze with strength to charm the most feared predators of the wood. One glance at those proud and terrible eyes and the visitors understood how the children had survived for so long in the wild.

"The Centaurs are thought to have had power over the beasts of nature," the vicar whispered. "Oh, yes, it's in all the texts — "

The Centauress maintained her angry stare, even as Richard was doing his utmost to explain to her the odd particulars of the situation. Meanwhile Sarah had slipped down from her back and taken her place again at Bertram's side. Evidently she had recognized the Hathaways and was no longer afraid.

In the end Richard's words appeared to satisfy the children's guardian, for the time being at least. Gradually her scowl subsided, restoring her features to their more tranquil and governess-like appearance. They were regular features, the visitors noted; indeed they were rather handsome and elegant features, beautiful even, when not disrupted by one of her ghastly contortions of visage.

The Centauress extended a hand in invitation to Richard and the others, then motioned towards the ancient oak settle, and towards the leather-bottomed chairs ranged about the dining-table. Some of the chairs being drawn up by Richard and Dr. Chevenix, the company sat down together by the fire, which Bertram and Sarah had stoked with some fresh wood and turf. The children then took their places on the cushioned settle beside Jemma and Ada, while the gentlemen occupied the chairs, with Snap lying at the feet of Richard, and with their hostess, restored to her position of authority on the hearthrug, presiding over all.

It was an awkward and precarious few minutes that followed, with the visitors not yet at their ease, and not knowing what to expect or how exactly to proceed. There was not the slightest doubt in their minds, however, that the Centauress, like the marsh devil that had pursued them, was a deadly dangerous customer.

The vicar was the first to find his voice. "Ah!" he said, rubbing his hands over his knees and smiling. "Bertram, I must say you are looking well. We have all been very concerned, and my wife, Mrs. Ludlow, particularly so. She misses you a great deal."

"It was my wish to return to the lodge," the boy explained, "and so Sarah and the lady came for me."

"And the lady's name is — ?" said Dr. Chevenix, his glance straying to the formidable figure of authority on the hearthrug.

"To know the name of someone," declared the Centauress, in her low voice with its faintly musical ring, "is to have power over someone. No one ever shall have power over *me.*"

No one within earshot could have had the least cause to doubt her sincerity on that score. Having settled herself comfortably by the fire, the Centauress had taken in hand a long-stemmed churchwarden pipe — Richard and the vicar recognized it from their prior visit — which she had filled and lighted, and was quietly smoking. It really was the most extraordinary thing, the doctor reflected — the sight of this fearsome, majestic, astonishing, hideous, lovely, and altogether impossible creature, seated there in their midst, smoking a pipe and discoursing by the flicker and hiss of a turf-fire in the great hall of the storied lodge of de Clinkers!

"And who is the keeper of this place, may I ask, dear lady, and where might he be?" he said. "For indeed it has been quite a mystery to us."

Puzzled looks crossed the faces of the impossible creature and the children.

"Keeper?" the Centauress repeated. "I am the keeper of this place."

"What! You alone, and no other?"

"There is no one else. There are only myself and the children."

"Extraordinary! And for how long have you been here?"

The Centauress shrugged, as one might who had no concern for the days or their passage, and as a result took no pains to keep track of them.

"And what is that — that odd business with your neck?" Jemma asked, half afraid to broach the subject, yet curious beyond all belief to know.

"It is to frighten the creatures of the wood," said Bertram, his eyes alight with admiration for his protectress. "She is marvelous at it. She can tame them with a glance. It is more of her magic!"

The Centauress took a long whiff of her pipe. "It is harmless," she said, "but effective. And the cry is a stunner, don't you think?"

"It was you who frightened me that day in the wood, when I was trying to rescue the children," Jemma told her.

"The children did not need rescuing, that day or any other. I am the only guardian they require," the Centauress said sternly.

An uneasy silence followed, one that went on for several minutes while their hostess busily worked her churchwarden, and the visitors their brains.

"And how — er — how do you find your spectacles?" the doctor said at length. "I ask it out of professional interest, of course."

"Indeed, doctor, I did find them, just as you say, in an upstairs apartment of the lodge. They were the property of a dear friend who once lived in this place. I am older now, you see, and not so keen-eyed as before. The lenses are of help to me in my reading and sewing."

It turned out that the Centauress, despite her native ferocity, was of a learned and studious disposition, in keeping with certain others of her race. There had been Chiron, for instance, son of Cronos the Titan. Widely esteemed for his knowledge and wisdom, it was Chiron who had first grouped the stars into constellations — something which Rosie would be interested to learn — and who had been tutor to such figures as Jason and Achilles. The Centauress herself was a prodigious reader of books, not only for the children's sake but for her own enjoyment as well. These books she obtained from an extensive library which was housed in an adjacent wing of the lodge.

"Hmmm. Descended from Hylonome, I should think," the vicar whispered to his companions.

"Hylonome?" queried Ada.

"Oh, indeed. The most celebrated of the female Centaurs of antiquity. She was said to be very intelligent, and very beautiful — dear me!"

"Do you recall, vicar, what Bertram said of his guardian that evening at dinner? He told us that she was very old — hundreds of years old, in fact."

"I do remember it."

"I say, how old do you think she can be?"

No one dared hazard a guess; and so Dr. Chevenix, his professional curiosity aroused again, cleared his voice and inquired of their hostess, in as tactful a fashion as possible, how long a Centaur might reasonably be expected to live?

"For some two thousand years, perhaps three," she replied, gazing at the fire and smoking. "But I devote no thought to it. I abandoned all such folly when I passed my thousandth year. As a race we retain most of our youthful faculties for the balance of our lives. My eyes, however, as I've told you, are no longer so keen as they once were."

"Never heard the like!" the doctor exclaimed. "And might I say, dear lady, that you appear to be in very fine trim, professionally speaking, for someone who has passed her tenth century."

"Capital trim, to be sure!" Richard nodded.

The Centauress accepted the compliments for what they were — smilingly, and with a gentle inclination of her head — before resuming her churchwarden. She was clever in the arts, a student of literature, skilled at woodcraft, and a wizard with her bow and arrows, with which she provided food for herself and the children. She even had made their clothes for them. And despite her professed shortness of sight, her gaze remained daunting enough to freeze the fiercest marsh devil in its tracks.

Her care of the children notwithstanding, it seemed she was not so well disposed towards most others of their race. In her view the ages-old hostility between the *Kentauroi* (as the Centaurs were known in ancient times) and humankind had not abated one jot. It never would, she declared, and never could.

"Oh, dear," thought the vicar, "whatever does one say in answer to *that?*" Unsure how to counter her argument, the reverend gentleman chose not to, saying instead — "So it is you who has haunted Marley Wood for all these many years?"

Their hostess acknowledged that it was so.

"And for how many of those years, exactly — that is, of course, if you have kept a reckoning?" Richard asked.

Again the Centauress shrugged; she could not rightly say.

"I had been gravely wounded," she explained. "Some men had been endeavoring to capture me, when I sought concealment in this vast tract of woodland. To my surprise, I was aided by a gentleman — a rarity amongst your species, I must say — who in time became a great and loyal friend. He was the first to have shown kindness to me. He brought me to this lodge of his, where he and his good wife cared for me until my health was restored. Despite our lengthy lives, those of my race have little resistance to injuries of the flesh. So long as we are not physically harmed, however, we are immune to most of those infirmities to which others are subject, until our very last years."

"My very word," the vicar exclaimed. "Do you mean to say that it was Godfrey de Clinkers himself who saved you?"

"Yes. And sheltered me."

"But that was in the old days — three hundred years ago — God bless my soul!"

Another shrug from their hostess, another whiff of her pipe, another glance at the fire. What were three centuries, the visitors mused — what, indeed, was Time itself — to a being who reckoned her life's span in millennia?

"After my recovery, the gentleman invited me to hunt with him and his followers in the wood. There we enjoyed many a noble day's sport seeking stag, antelope, and elk, and galloping to covert for the powdered fox, and routing flat-heads from their dens. The gentleman's devotion to the hunt was nearly as great as mine — as keen a rider he was as ever trailed a pack of hounds. Those of my race were the first in the hunting-field, as you know, just as we were first in the arts and medicine."

"Medicine?" blinked Dr. Chevenix.

"Indeed, doctor. Do you not recollect that Chiron was the first physician, and that your venerated Aesculapius was his pupil?"

"The chase — scouring the wood for venison and swine — so much dash and variety in the old days — what colorful lives our fathers led!" enthused the vicar. Horses and hounds, stirrup-cups and horns of stingo, powdered foxes and flat-head boars — such sport they had had in those old days, and in such a field as Marley Wood! How much more stirring than his own daily morning's trot on the Snailsby gallops!

"What became of your gentleman friend? What became of Godfrey de Clinkers?" the doctor asked.

"A riding mishap — fallen on by his horse. Was that not so?" the vicar said to their hostess.

A shadow darkened the Centauress's handsome features. Her eyes, gazing on the flames, seemed to be staring through them into another time, another age, another world.

"Yes," she answered. "I myself was with him when he breathed his last. A true and noble friend he was, as good-hearted as he was good-humored. When his wife, the lady Isobel, died, not many years after, this lodge of theirs was given up. No one, it seemed, cared any longer to hunt in Marley Wood. The gentleman's followers and servants all drifted away — all but myself, of course. Then came the great sundering . . . " Her voice trailed off.

"And what of the others of your kind?" Jemma asked. "What has become of them?"

"Ours has ever been a secretive race. Our traditions hold that we arose in Thessalia, in old Hellas, and flourished there. But our numbers have dwindled, with precious few left now to carry on. Indeed I myself may be the only one, for since the sundering I have had no news of the others. And so this forest has become my retreat and sanctuary. Since the beginning my kind have exercised a measure of control over the lesser orders; thus I have had naught to fear from the dirk-tooths and spotted lions that inhabit the woodland. I am safe here, and this safety I have extended to the children. But now this safety of ours is threatened."

"How do you mean? By whom?" Ada asked.

The Centauress abruptly left off her smoking, and turned her angry scowl again upon the visitors. "By this loathsome road that approaches from your town! It will bring strangers here — human strangers — outsiders — men from the cities, who will come to capture me, or to kill me. It is a thing from which I have enjoyed relative freedom for these many years. The good gentleman who lived here sheltered me from the evils of his race. For centuries this lodge has been my home; now it is being menaced by you and by these others who will come. Why are you doing this? Why do you bring shovel-tuskers into the wood to pull down our beloved trees and fill the air with clamorous trumpetings? Why do you dig your road so near the lodge? How have I or these children harmed you that you would do this to us?"

The visitors were quite taken off their guard by the charge. After revolving it in their minds for a spell, however, they could see something of the logic of their hostess's position. They then made a valiant effort to explain to her their own logic in clearing the road, which was intended to improve the welfare of the town and its citizens. No one had set out to violate her sanctuary, they told her; indeed, until now no one had had any idea she was there. Certainly, they argued, some fair and equitable accommodation could be reached?

The suggestion was met with another thunderous scowl. "No accommodation! Men from your cities will come for me as soon as they hear of me. It is the way of your kind. It has been the way of your kind since before I was foaled, and it remains your way still. That is the hard lesson I have learned."

The visitors endeavored to assure her that this was not so, that the times and people were different now, and that a few bad hats did not a haberdashery make; but she refused to believe a word of it. Her distrust of humans and their ways was complete. The doctor then struck in, bringing up the subject of Mrs. Chugwell — a very dear lady, he said, much like the Centauress herself — who had charge of the tuskers, and who certainly harbored no ill designs against the keeper of the lodge; none indeed, for she was a keeper of sorts herself. But it was of no avail. The Centauress, after her long years of exile in the wood, could not see how much humanity and the world had changed.

Or had they?

Regardless, a change of some kind was in order now — a change of topic certainly, for it was clear that the Centauress was not about to be persuaded to their view.

"What of this magic we have seen Bertram perform?" Ada asked, her curiosity brimming over. "For he claims he learned it from you."

To their very great relief, the Centauress's manner towards them slowly relaxed. "Indeed he did," she answered proudly. "He is a quick study, as is my Sarah there. Not only have my race power to charm the lesser orders, but we have our magic as well."

"The Ogghops sherry? The flying pancakes?"

"And our church clock, perhaps?" the vicar chimed in.

Taking the pipe from her lips, the Centauress exchanged knowing glances with the children — sly, mischievous glances I might even call them — which set Bertram and Sarah to giggling, just as they had done when spying upon certain travelers one day in the Tillington Road.

"Most are simple conjuring tricks, which have been known to my race since time beyond recollection," the Centauress explained. "Some, however, were taught to me by others — as for example the bottles stuffed with glowing figs. Tell me, did you find them effective?"

A very sober expression came into the vicar's face at the mention of this horror. He glanced round at his companions, and they glanced at him; at which point he frowned, cleared his voice and, screwing up his courage a notch, made bold to address their hostess, albeit hesitantly, and as delicately as possible —

"Pray, if you'll excuse the liberty, madam — um — er — well, it wasn't so nice a thing, you know, to threaten us in that way. It was an enormously cheeky thing, in fact, if I may so observe. There are those in our town who were rather — um — er — well, shall we say *disturbed* by your warning — indeed, they were very much angered and affronted by it. Well, they're really very cross with you! No one much enjoys being called a fool, you know. Dear me, do you know how provocative it was?"

The visitors felt their hearts give a collective thump. All held their breath, not knowing how the vicar's words might be received. Even Snap could sense the tension in the air, and edged himself a little nearer his master's feet.

For an instant a spark of that proud and terrible gaze flashed in the eyes of the Centauress; then it passed. Instead the impossible creature folded her arms, and threw up her chin — and with it an enormous cloud of smoke from her pipe — in a gesture of defiance.

"It is you and your vaunted Mrs. Chugwell who have provoked *us*, by threatening our safety and our way of life," she responded, with deadly coolness. "I have done only what I must, no more and no less, to protect myself, my home, and these children, who have become like my own offspring and for whom I alone am responsible. They are safe and settled here. I have fed them, I have clothed them, I have read books to them. I have played music for them, taught them cards and cribbage, the secrets of our magic — "

"But none of us has harmed you or the children, or has any wish to," the vicar broke in, earnestly. "Is that not so, Bertram? Have we not shown you every kindness?"

The boy affirmed that it was true.

"Perhaps you have; if so, then I grant you are not like most others of your race," the Centauress answered. "But no matter — *it changes nothing.*"

Again all talk came to a stand. There was another uneasy quiet, while the visitors were left pondering over their hostess's words. Her objective, it was clear, was to chuck them out of the wood — the lot of them. With each season as the road had grown closer to the lodge, the Centauress had grown bolder in her actions. Now the lodge had been discovered. What might this proud, imperious, and wholly implacable adversary not do to preserve herself, her children, and their sanctuary?

"And what of Bertram?" the vicar asked. "We know that his full name is Bertram Longchapel — his cousins from Dragonthorpe identified him — and that he is from a place called Butter Cross, and that he disappeared in Marley Wood on a Snailsby fair-day some five-and-thirty years ago. He was but a child at the time. How is it, might I ask — um — er — that he remains a child to this day?"

"Ah!" the Centauress exclaimed, managing to look boastful, angry, aggrieved, and delighted, all at the same time. "That, sir, is an example of some of our finest magic. Although alas I cannot claim sole credit for it."

"Bertram told us that he was given something to drink from a silver cup — a posset he called it," said Ada.

"That is true."

"And that it would protect him, this posset, and that he should never after want for health."

"True as well."

"And he told us further that it had some of your blood in it."

"It did — a good deal, in fact."

A new thought had struck Ada, and, true to her nature, she boldly pursued it. "You say that you were taught some of your magic by others, and do not claim sole credit for the posset. Did you learn of it, perhaps, from a woman called Mother Redcap?"

A guarded look crossed the face of their hostess. She darted a quick glance at the children. To all appearances they seemed to have no knowledge of the withered old recluse of a pig-faced crone, who, like Bertram himself, had vanished years ago in the wood.

"I did," the Centauress answered slowly, "if by that name you refer to the old woman who lived by the black pool."

"I thought as much!" Ada exclaimed in triumph.

"There was an herbal here in the lodge. In fact it is at this moment lying on that table there. Did it by any chance belong to her?" Richard asked.

"It did, as did certain other books in the library which she was good enough to share with me," the Centauress replied. "She was in a bad way when I found her — collapsed under a tangle of bogberries on the edge of the wood, short of breath, and her heart all a-patter."

"She went out one morning to gather roots and mushrooms, and was never seen again," Jemma recalled.

The Centauress shook her head. "I'm afraid that is only partly true, Miss Hathaway. It had been a bitter cold night, and the dirk-tooths were everywheres about, scouting for their breakfast. She had not gone to look for roots and mushrooms that morning. She had gone into the wood to die."

"Gracious heavens!" gasped the vicar.

"It was all up with her, or so it appeared. She had been ill for some months, and believed her time to be short. She loved this wood and its treasures nearly as much as the children and I do, and was looking to pass her final hours in it."

"And did she?" Ada asked.

"No. She was brought here to the lodge, and in time recovered her health. In the interval we became friends. One day I collected some of her books for her from her cottage. Amongst them was an ancient formulary, of a kind much prized by your human sorcerers and enchanters. Amongst the formulae there was one in particular which called for Centaur's blood. Of course she had never before compounded the mixture, as she had never had that scarce ingredient at her dispose.

"For as long as any can remember, Centaur's blood has been a prized constituent of remedies of many types — and therein lies the chief cause for the slow dwindling of my species. The posset may be compounded only sparingly, as it calls for a good deal of blood; and those of my race are greatly weakened when our blood is let. Much time is required for the blood elements to replenish themselves, and each bleeding shortens our life's span by a measurable sum."

"And why was Bertram chosen to receive this great gift?" the doctor asked.

The Centauress, smiling, took a little whiff of her pipe and gazed fondly upon her adopted small ones. "It was my Sarah there. She had been with me for a few years, and was wishing for a companion of her own age and kind. Well, it was only to be expected. One day we came upon Bertram hiding in a thicket by Snailsby town. He had run away from his cousins, he said, and wanted nothing more to do with them. They were sending him off home to a sister who hated him. He meant to disappear in the wood, which his cousins had told him something of, and where they should never find him. And as Sarah at the time was seeking a little friend, well — the solution was clear."

"It was Sarah who showed me round the lodge, after she and the lady brought me here," spoke up Bertram.

"In truth it was rather a lonely stretch after the good gentleman and his wife died," the Centauress related. "Then the children came to me. Since then none of us has wanted for company."

"Dear me, it has all been rather a puzzle," the vicar sighed, shaking his head. "Well, you do certainly keep the hall here in good order — everything so trim and tidy! But however do you fill in your time? For you have had so much of it . . ."

"Bertram has told us of some acquaintances — friends of yours, he called them — horseback riders, who hunt the wood by night in the company of their hounds," spoke up Jemma.

"And there is a park-keeper as well," said Ada. "A rude fellow in a green jerkin, with a quarterstaff and bugle-horn."

"Indeed. Who are they, might I ask? For Bertram has said that they come at your bidding, but only when the moon is out, and that you join them in their hunts."

"And by the by," the vicar put in, "just what does one hunt in Marley Wood in the night-time?"

The Centauress carried on with her smoking as if nothing had been asked of her; but she had heard it all well enough. Her glance drifted to the line of windows running down the side of the great hall, and to the skylights overhead, through which the fog was shining with a dim and ghostly radiance.

"It is nearly the hour," she announced.

Hearing this the children shouted joyfully and clapped their hands, and were all smiles and enthusiasm.

The Centauress laid by her pipe and rose to her feet. "Watch now," she commanded the visitors, "and see what else some Centaur's blood and a little magic can do."

THE THIRD CHAPTER

MAGIC UNDER MOONLIGHT

TOGETHER Bertram and Sarah joined to assist their guardian in her undertaking, whatever it was: for the visitors had been left wholly in the dark as to its nature or objective.

From a corner of the hall the children retrieved a small brazier of antique design, mounted on a tripod of hammered iron and bronze, and placed it beneath the skylight nearest the chimney. An old oak sideboard then was rolled out and stationed beside it. Next some candles in standing brass sticks were lighted and ranged atop the board. From its drawers and cupboards the children began removing an array of vials, tins, jars, bottles, and other receptacles. Each vessel was opened, and a small sample of its contents laid in the pan of the brazier, in a precisely-ordered sequence. As each item was applied to the pan, its identity was called out by the child who placed it. The Centauress herself took no active role in the exercise, but stood quietly by, her breast a-swell with pride at the skill demonstrated by her adopted small ones in its execution.

The ease and speed with which this ceremony was gone through showed that the children were no strangers to its performance. It was in effect a recital of the ingredients of a baffling concoction that was gradually taking shape in the brazier, one whose purpose the visitors for the life of them could scarcely comprehend.

> *Eye of toad and knee of spider,*
> *Pinch of gold from bishop's miter.*
> *Gristle of dirk-tooth, hair of fox,*
> *Chestnut, beechnut, butterbox.*

> *Spice of mummy and stew of pear,*
> *Deadly nightshade — oh, do beware!*
> *Tongue of hart and hoof of elk,*
> *Yolk of egg and fletch of whelk.*

Squat of flat-head and scute of glypt,
  Ossicle from megathere snipped.
Hemlock, houseleek, holly, and yarrow,
  Foxglove, mistletoe, moss, and marrow.

Pinch of snuff and fill of shag,
  Brain-dust from a stenching hag.
Tail of lizard, slick and nimble,
  Drop of purl in a tailor's thimble.

Tooth of zeug and bill of bittern,
  Tallow scraped from a slodger's kitchen.
Marshberry, bogberry, in the pan,
  And a smidgly crumb of marzipan.

Lard of porker and rheum of drudge,
  Gorge of miser and bile of judge.
Wormwood, bogwood, turf, and treacle,
  Bark of fir and horn of beetle.

Colewort, stinkwort, lemon-peel,
  Smack of grease from elver eel.
Brimstone, moonstone, horse's fodder,
  Gizzard dipped in dragon's water.

Slime of cricket and fenny slug,
  Eye of murphy from Fenshire dug.
Quicksilver, march root, such good stuff,
  Wolfsbane, wallpepper, pocket fluff.

Mix in the land of fen and flood,
  And sprinkle o'er with Centaur's blood.

Of necessity this final item was supplied by the children's guardian.
Taking in hand a small knife she dipped the blade in a flame, allowed
it to cool, and pricked the flesh of her wrist. Five drops of her life's
blood she allowed to trickle onto the pan. Five drops was not so
much: very little, in fact, when compared to what was needed for the

magic posset. The operation accomplished, she stanched the flow with her thumb and bound up her wrist with a handkerchief.

Next she struck a light and applied it to the brazier. The flame spurted, the fire took hold, and a blue column of smoke began to rise from the pan. The Centauress went through a little recital then of her own, one delivered in a tongue unfamiliar to the visitors (although the vicar, who knew his Latin and a bit of Greek, thought it a dialect of the latter). As she proceeded she slowly lifted up her eyes, spread wide her arms, and trained her mighty gaze on the skylight overhead.

Scarcely had she commenced her incantation than the heavy fog without began to dissolve. The dim glow in the skylights and windows grew brighter, and brighter, until the chill, misty heaven over lodge and wood had cleared entirely to black. Stars could be seen blinking and staring in the sky, where — wonder of wonders — a gibbous moon as white as bone was rising over the lodge. The courtyard was suddenly awash in a flood of light, which tipped the roofs and timber-tops and, streaming in through the windows, filled the hall with the splendor of its silvery radiance.

The slanting beams as they poured into the room fell hard and strong upon the sculpture that covered the opposite wall. It was the magnificent carving in bog oak of Godfrey de Clinkers and his followers on horseback, the hounds at their feet, riding to the chase. The peat-stained wood shone like ebony in the moonlight, its sculpted forms standing out in the very boldest of bold relief. Had they not been made of bogwood they could easily have been mistaken for their historical originals, so vivid and lifelike was their rendering by the nameless craftsmen of old.

The Centauress and the children having turned their attention to the carving, the visitors followed their example. Hardly had their eyes lighted upon it than something rather odd began to happen. All across its surface the sculpted timbers had begun to stir, had begun to squirm, had begun to rustle. It was no illusion of the dazzling moonshine, but a very real thing. Before the visitors' astonished eyes the figures in the carving, one by one, were coming alive, all of them tugging and straining at their shackles of bog oak as they labored to free themselves. Then all in a moment it was done; and as the vicar and his companions looked on, spellbound, the entire party of horsemen, horses, and hounds stepped forth from its prison of bogwood onto the tiled floor of the hall.

The effect was indescribable. The visitors were profoundly shocked, and for some minutes found themselves bereft of speech. Their scalps tingled, their eyes bulged, their mouths gaped; to their credit, however, they managed to stifle their next (and very natural) impulse, which was to leap out of their shoes.

At the head of the party was Mr. Godfrey de Clinkers himself. Long-booted, silver-spurred, rapier-girded, he was the first to dismount from his horse. He was attired in a close-fitting doublet trimmed with lace, leather breeches, and a handsome jerkin belted with a buff girdle, from which hung his tuck and a pair of daggers. A short cape or mantle of russet-brown, riding-gloves, and a hat sporting a gorgeous plume, as befitted his rank, completed the picture of his grand and noble person.

His retinue of followers wore dress of a similar vintage, though less splendid in design, and like de Clinkers himself were well-provided with weapons. In short, they were armed to the teeth: broadswords, cutlasses, claymores, halberds, and falchions all were in generous supply. Several of the men carried tall lances with fearsome speared points, the purpose of which was clear — the routing of flat-heads from their dens. A number of the hunt-servants in addition bore small lanterns in hand, which they were setting about to light.

The horses — magnificent chargers every one — looked eager, clean, and well-groomed. There were blacks and roans, buckskins and paints, chestnuts and grays, all with shapely heads, arched necks, and slender fetlocks, and all smartly caparisoned for the chase. The hounds, meantime, having been alerted to the presence of Snap, were proceeding to respond in that way that hounds will. The valiant coach dog returned their salutations with a few choice growls of his own, but for the time being remained at his master's feet; for, like Richard, he too had been taken aback by the sudden and utterly unlooked-for transformation of the bog oak.

"Hallo! Have we gone daft?" wondered Jemma, scarcely crediting the evidence of it herself.

"There are your phantom riders, doctor," said Ada. "It's more of that magic that went out years ago, I dare say."

The physician shook his head disbelievingly. "It has quite taken my breath away, Miss Henslowe — most extraordinary — never seen the like — I can't explain it, but there it is!"

"And look there! There is that churl of a park-keeper. Oh, my — is he not exactly as Bunting and Mrs. Crumbey described him? Look at that sour expression, as if he'd just swallowed a dish of bogberries. And is he not staring at us uncommonly hard?"

"Dear me," worried the vicar, "he doesn't seem very pleased to see us, does he?"

Arrayed all in green with his forester's cap on his head and a bugle-horn at his side, the park-keeper was standing amongst the lesser hunts-men, his quarterstaff — a heavy wooden pole some eight feet in length — planted on the ground. A long, lean man, like his staff, rough-hewn and coarse-featured, he was regarding the strangers through eyes darkly swarming with suspicion.

Amidst all the stir and bustle there in the hall, Godfrey de Clinkers himself made approach now with a jingle of spurs and a clink of steel. Having received a merry welcome from the Centauress and the children, he turned a curious eye upon the visitors. He was a stout man of middling height, graying at the temples, who bore himself with an air of frankness and liberality. His face was a study in contrasts: an eccentric, slightly whimsical face it was on the one hand, with its jolly lip and museful brow, and yet a staunch and a commanding face it was as well — the face of a man with boldness enough to have constructed a hunting-lodge in Marley Wood. In short, he was the dead image (as it were) of the Godfrey de Clinkers in oils upon the wall, and of the painted plaster bust staring at them from amongst his hunting-trophies.

"Prithee, good friends," he said, speaking aside to the Centauress and the children, "who be these strangers yonder, and what do they seek here? Are they to bear sword and hunt with us?"

"They are my own good friends, sir," answered Bertram. "The vicar, Mr. Ludlow there, took me into his home in Market Snailsby and looked after me there. He and Mrs. Ludlow gave me this new suit of clothes and much good food from their kitchen. They were both very kind to me. Mr. Ludlow and his friends have come to visit us, and to meet Sarah and the lady."

"Hah! These be Snailsby folk, then?" exclaimed de Clinkers. "Odds-fish! Excellent gentlemen all three, I'll warrant — and a brace of fair ladies to boot."

So saying, he paid his *devoirs* to Jemma and Ada with a courteous bow — as courteous a bow as his stoutness of figure could manage — and a graceful flourish of his hat with the plume in it.

"Come, we bid thee welcome, worthy friends, to this our fair seat. Godfrey de Clinkers is my name in the flesh. Men roundabout call me de Clinkers, or Sir, or what they will; as for my dear wife, she calls me to supper! Nay, do not fret — we are more than glad of thy company. Prithee, what is thy name, good sir?"

This latter was addressed to Richard, who, having made answer, took it upon himself to present his sister and Ada.

"And the good clergyman yonder — the Reverend Ludlow, is it? A noble name, sir, and an honorable one in the county of Fens," smiled de Clinkers. "Ah, and here a worthy French doctor of physic as well. Prithee, doctor — what? Welsh, say'st thou? Zookers! Have we then a Glendower amongst us? 'The earth did shake at my nativity, and the front of heaven was full of fiery shapes,' as old Will Shakespeare says. Marry, now we shall have fine sport indeed with a Welshman in our ranks. Welcome, doctor. Travelers from Snailsby town, friends of our good friends — we give thee welcome all!"

It was plain he was hugely delighted to see them. The visitors, exchanging glances, did their utmost to put on an easy demeanor, and thanked the phantom of bogwood who called himself de Clinkers for his generosity.

"What think'st thou of this lodge of ours, its quirks, its oddities, its treasures? Hast mounted its staircases, cast open its doors, challenged its galleries? Hast counted the hours on yonder long-case clock? Hast fathomed out *The Answer to Everything?* Such merry pranks have we had here, so many jolly hours have we passed, in all manner of entertainments! Think'st not this seat of ours the handsomest, and the cleverest builded, before or since, in all this vasty wide shireland of Fens?"

"Bless my soul," exclaimed Mr. Ludlow, wholly entranced, "it *is* Godfrey de Clinkers — he of the old days — in the flesh — and his followers!"

"I shouldn't expect so, vicar," Richard cautioned him. "It seems impossible that these can be the same gentlemen — *dashed* impossible, in fact. First we've had two impossible children to account for, and now a party of impossible huntsmen wrested out of bog oak."

They looked to the Centauress for an explanation. After a brief word with de Clinkers, who left them then to mingle with his followers, she drew the visitors aside and proceeded to initiate them into the mysteries of moonlight, braziers, and bogwood.

The origin of it, she explained, lay in another of Mother Redcap's magic formulae. The Centauress's great and noble friends, Godfrey and Isobel de Clinkers — they who had rescued her from certain death in the wood — had themselves been dead and buried for these past few hundred years. Their loss had touched her to the quick, and she sorely longed for their company. One day, through the aid of Mother Redcap, she discovered a means by which she might revive de Clinkers and his followers, if only after a fashion. It required the varied mix of ingredients which the children had applied to the brazier, and five drops of her precious blood, and a flame, to summon the moonbeams from the sky. And it was the magic of those beams falling on bogged oak, and the incantation the Centauress had recited in her native tongue, which had brought the carving — one commissioned by Godfrey de Clinkers himself — to life, of a sorts.

"So it is you who has been the cause of this bright moonlight over town and country, when by day we have had nothing but cloud?" said the vicar. Then a light of another kind flashed upon him. "Of course! For that is when the riders have made their appearance — the flash of lanterns in the wood — the whoops and hollows of the huntsmen, the winding of horns, the baying of hounds — "

"I believe you've winkled it out, vicar," Jemma nodded.

"The influence of the spell extends for some distance beyond the lodge in every direction — to the southwards easily as far as Snailsby town," the Centauress explained.

It was on those curious, moon-washed nights that the hunt was up and the field mounted, just as it had been in days of yore when the Centauress and her gentleman friend and his followers had scoured the wood for venison and swine — save that now their meets of necessity were held in the light of the fair Diana's silvery beams.

This mystery explained, the Centauress proceeded to take up her bow and quiver in readiness for her night's turn in the hunting-field.

"Shall it be stag or flat-head this evening, I wonder?" Richard mused, half aloud. "Or a bit of this, perhaps, and a dash of that — "

"Aye, and a proper killbuck she is, too," nodded de Clinkers, as he came jingling up. "By this fair moonshire, a good and kindly friend, and true as steel. For her good stewardship of us and ours, her assiduous care of this our seat, making all things seemly and shapely upstairs and below, and of these children, we would fain have made her keeper of our abode in her own right. Marry, how we should'st have fared without her in years gone by I know not."

The expressions of mutual trust and accord which were exchanged between these two impossible beings — a creature of ancient legend on the one side, and one of resurrected bogwood on the other — bore testimony to the strength of that friendship that had existed between the Centauress and the grand and eccentric de Clinkers, of whom the phantom of bog oak was, in the end, but a pale imitation.

"He is not Godfrey de Clinkers in the flesh, as he says, although he believes himself to be," the Centauress confided to the visitors. "These whom you see before you are but reflections of those who have been. In truth my dear good friend, his wife, and followers remain asleep in their narrow beds beneath the churchyard loam. Even the magic of the ancients of my race has no power to raise that which has crumbled to dust."

Again the shadow came across her face, and the Centauress, looking away, stood absorbed for a time in her memories of days long past and done. The children waited silently by; but though they gave no voice to it, their sympathy for her was writ large in their eyes. The visitors were greatly moved. Little had they comprehended how deep were the feelings of the children for their beloved guardian and keeper of the lodge.

Yet surely bog oak was preferable to memories, was it not? It was like having her old friends restored to her, for a brief while at least; and for that brief while the Centauress was thankful. For once the fair Diana had dropped from the sky and was gone, Godfrey de Clinkers and his followers would be gone as well — would fade gently, quietly into the night, and so be returned to bog oak once more.

"Wilt hunt with us, then, good friends? Wilt take up the chase?" said the ersatz de Clinkers.

The visitors, after a brief, whispered conference amongst themselves — it was for form's sake — politely declined the invitation. The grand and eccentric man could not hide his disappointment. His expression fell, and some of the light went out of his eyes. Nonetheless he strove to put a courteous and a gentlemanly face on.

"Be it so," he said, the regret all too evident in his voice, as he bowed his farewell to them.

"But they are to quarter with us for the night, sir," the Centauress interjected hastily, to boost his spirits, "as they cannot return to Snailsby town until the morrow."

Her words immediately put new heart in him. His brow rose, and a joyful grin split his boggy face from ear to ear. "Ah! So say'st thou? Is't true? Marry, then, has the pantry bread? Has the buttery ale? So we are well-victualed tonight — much wine, and much wit also! Withhold nothing. Let them have all, good lady, for we keep a jolly household," he exclaimed, rubbing his hands and chuckling. "Prithee, good friends, dost know these my followers here? Marry, they be stout and gentlemanly folk to be sure, from families of good account, every man jack of 'em. Sure thou know'st Tom Delancey and Giles Hawking, both of Snailsby town? And this be Algernon de Worde of Tillington, and this good William Barley of Strood. And here be Thomas Hyde of Hyde — Phrank Mulciber of Yocklebury — and here sturdy Monk Mason, the pride of Festermouth — young Morgan Johns of Pitchford — Lionel Chickpea of Eelworth — "

Each man in his turn stepped forward, some dozen of them in all, crisply, as their names were called out, and flourished their hats in salutation. Gentlemen all they were indeed — some short, some tall; some sober of mien, some merry; some gray as iron, some pink as mutton; some mustachioed and bewhiskered, some with cheeks as smooth as pumpkins; some well-favored in shape and countenance, and some not. Altogether they were as honest, manly, and respectful a contingent of followers as it warmed the heart of Vicar Ludlow to see.

All, that is, but the frowning park-keeper, who had drawn his quarterstaff and was standing on his guard.

"How now, Mr. Green Jerkin? How now, our man of bolts and bucks? By the moon and stars, Jack Poins, certain thou art dreadful out of sorts tonight," said de Clinkers, stern of tongue, but with mirth dancing in his eyes. "Do retire that villainous countenance of thine, Jack, or we shall take thee for a marsh devil."

"Sir," returned the aforesaid Poins, eyeing the visitors distrustfully, "these here be strangers — trespassers — poachers, most like. Aye, marry, sir! For these I have seen, and others like them, skulking round the park here, and yonder by Snailsby town, in fashion most suspect, as does encroach upon thy rights and prerogatives — "

"By the Mass, Jack, thou art an antic fellow! Thou art keeper of waif and stray, vert and venison, and yet but poor keeper of thine own tongue," chuckled de Clinkers, delivering a good-natured cuff to the other's shoulder. "This I do advise thee — to sheathe thy staff for the nonce, and cast off thy devilish frown. These be not poachers; these be Snailsby friends of our good lady there who are to quarter with us this night. Troth, Jack, thou would'st do well to give thy respects and compliments to these our honored guests."

The park-keeper, so admonished, colored up to his eyes, and applied fingers to the shock-head of hair beneath his cap, for the purpose of scratching it. Visibly humbled — not to say a trifle embarrassed — the servant retired his staff forthwith, and obligingly paid his *devoirs* to the said honored guests.

"Now, by this hand, I believe thou art our worthy Jack Poins once more. Zookers! The time wears late. *Festina lente*, as 'tis scribed 'pon yonder clock-face. Come, gentlemen," de Clinkers called to his followers, "shall we go a-sporting?"

Instantly a tremendous cheer went up, as with one voice they chorused their assent.

The lanterns being now a-light, the party of phantoms — phantom horses and horsemen, phantom hounds, phantom park-keeper — the whole ghostly, phantom lot — proceeded towards the tall double-doors which issued onto the courtyard. The keen, wistful looks in the eyes of the hounds, the eager faces of the huntsmen, the chargers gnawing at their bits — all was as it had been in glorious days of yore, and as it was to be played out again this night by these impostors of bogwood.

"Prithee, good gentlemen, see you stay your mounts in the yard," the Centauress called after them. "The children and I shall follow along directly."

"See you tarry no jot of time," smiled de Clinkers, with a goodnatured wag of his finger, as he led his men to the doors. "Up hearts, gentlemen, and hie thee to the courtyard! For we have hope of excellent sport tonight."

The doors flew open, as if by magic (which of course it was), and horsemen, horses, and hounds were on the point of sallying forth, when a startled cry rang through the hall. Immediately all sallying came to a stand, as all attention was trained on Miss Ada Henslowe — for it was she who had cried out.

She had been standing a little apart from the others, and from curiosity had picked up the ancient herbal of Mother Redcap's which lay nearby. Glancing over its pages, she had come across something that had left her breathless with excitement. In truth it had done more than that — it had downright shocked her, nearly as much as had moonbeams falling on bog oak. It had caused her eyes to fill with wonder, her pretty cheeks to pale, and her jaw to drop. Looking up, she stared in amazement at the children, and then at Jemma and the others.

"Oh, I say!" she exclaimed. "You'll not believe it. You'll not guess what I've discovered, never in a thousand years. So many questions we've had, and yet the one answer was so plain. It was Corney who hit upon it, although he little knew it then, nor did we. Don't you see? The solution to the mystery — Mother Redcap — it has been before us the entire time!"

THE FOURTH CHAPTER

PARADISE REGAINED

A S herbals go it was a rather ordinary specimen, of a type that had been commonplace in centuries past, examples of which might be found in any antiquarian's library. It was a hefty volume, its binding of tooled leather showing considerable wear. Many of its leaves were spotted with age, and it was one of these that had stolen Ada's breath away. It was in fact the title-page, the composition of which was unremarkable, and wholly of its period:

A COMPLEAT

HERBALL

TREATING OF

All sorts of *Herbs, Plants, Vegetables, &c.*
How rightly to know them, and how they are
to be used in *Physick*; with their several *Doses,*
for the most part *Simple,* and easily
prepared: Useful in families, and
very Serviceable to Country People.

Written in *Latin,*

BY THE LATE

Rev. Dr. ZOZIMUS BING,

And *Englished* for the first time,
through the Care & Learning of

Charles Thomas Mangrove, Dr. of Physick

Goforth: Printed by *Isaac Alleyn,* for *Edward Smallcoats,* and are to
be sold at the Sign of the *Gull and Grapple,* Slaughterfields
16——

Bing's herbal had been widely popular in its time, especially, as it was claimed, "amongst the apothecaries and such old wives that gather herbs." What had captured Ada's interest, however, was not the title-page *per se*, but the name in faded ink that was inscribed upon it, along its upper margin, in a woman's flowing hand — *Sarah Crouch*.

"What was it young Mr. Murcott told you?" she said to Jemma. "About his father's calling at Wackwire House, years ago as a butcher's boy, and hearing the old gardener's complaints about a 'foreigner' woman?"

"Yes. A 'pariah' he called her, a 'stain on the parish,' and a 'slave of Old Harry.' We think it was Mother Redcap who was meant," her friend replied.

"And the name of the woman was Miss Crouch?"

"It was. And Mother Redcap had come from Gloamshire, which to some qualifies as foreign territory, and where it's believed Mr. Wackwire had family once."

"They may have been distant relations," Richard explained. "Likely that is why he dismissed the gardener's grumbles. Though he still may not have wanted his connection to the daft old dear bruited about."

"But what has this Miss Crouch to do with matters here?" the doctor wanted to know.

For answer Ada passed the herbal round to him and the others. It required but a moment for the significance of the name inscribed upon the title-page to register its effect. As soon as it had, the visitors in a body turned their gaze upon little Sarah.

Wide blue eyes shining sapphire-bright, ruddy apple-cheeks and lips, a pert nose, and hair clipped evenly round on the bowl-cut principle — such was the portrait of youthful innocence that presented itself to view. For her part Sarah said not a word, but returned their wondering looks with bashful glances. She appeared not to understand the cause of the visitors' sudden interest in her.

Then and there Ada knew that it must be true; but confirmation must come from the children's guardian.

"This child — little Sarah — she is Mother Redcap?" Ada asked her.

The Centauress, her expression very sober and reflective, did not respond straight away. She seemed to be weighing in her mind the consequences of her answer — its pros and cons, its rights and wrongs, its potential repercussions; and so, having weighed them, she gave leave to make her decision known.

"Indeed she is," she replied. "My little Sarah there is the woman who once lived by the black pool."

"Matter of fact!" Richard burst out.

The vicar's eyebrows flew up in surprise. "Gracious heavens," he said, clapping a hand to his forehead. "Young Sarah is Mother Redcap? I should never have believed it — dear me — my very word — "

"But how is it possible?" asked Dr. Chevenix. "We understood it was this elixir or 'posset' that had preserved Bertram's youth. Do you mean to say it can restore it as well?"

"It is, in point of fact, just what you and your friends have termed it, doctor — an elixir of youth," the Centauress replied. "For Bertram, who was but a boy at the time, it acted to prolong his childhood. For Sarah, who was an old woman and nearing the end of her days, it restored her to her former state of innocence."

"And how did this come about? For Sarah, that is?"

"One day, while she was recovering here at the lodge, she took me into her confidence and told me of her most fervent wish, which was to be a child again. She had grown weary of her solitary life, and of her struggles against her many infirmities, and had sought to put a period to her existence by walking into the wood. But as the formula for the posset was there in her book, I offered her the needed sample of my blood, which was the one ingredient she lacked."

"Surely you remember, everyone," Ada said. "It was Corney's recollection of one Christmas long ago when he himself was a boy. He'd been skating on the ice with his brother and sister, and had seen Mother Redcap watching them from the bridge. The expression of longing in her old eyes, the memory of which he'd never shaken — that was the clue! It wasn't simply that she had wanted to join him and the other children on the ice; she had wanted to *be* one of those children."

"Many years before Sarah walked into the wood, my great and noble friend de Clinkers had saved my life when I lay dying there," the Centauress explained. "It was to my immeasurable grief that I was unable to save his, when the time came, or that of his good wife. Thus, in recompense, I offered my blood to a sad old woman so that her dream might be fulfilled, and the thread of her life spun out to years beyond her wildest imagining."

To the visitors it seemed impossible that little Sarah — she of the sapphire eyes, ruddy cheeks, and turned-up nose, and one of the gigglers in the Tillington Road — could be the old pig-faced woman who had disappeared those many years ago in the wood. Sarah the withered hag! Sarah the twisted old crone of a witch who had dwelt by the mereside, and whose ripe and rotten old age, as Mr. Swain had phrased it, had been turned back as easily as the hands of a clock!

The vicar, as startled as the others by this revelation, was at a loss at first what to say to her. It was all so very awkward, and quite without precedent. How to address Mother Redcap — witch, recluse, herbwoman, pariah, and slave of Old Harry — whom they had thought dead for fifty years, and who had been returned to them in the shape of this small child?

"So you are Miss Sarah Crouch?" he smiled, taking one of her little hands in his. (It was a decent enough beginning, as she did not withdraw the hand). "Well, well! I am — er — um — very pleased to know you, Miss Crouch. I am Vicar Ludlow of All Hallows Church. Do you remember our church? It has the finest steeple in the marshlands, so they say. And this is Miss Hathaway, of Mead Cottage. I believe you are — um — already acquainted with her. And this is her friend Miss Henslowe. And here is Miss Hathaway's brother Richard, and here our town's physician, Dr. Chevenix. Dear me, we have heard much about you for many years, and from many quarters. You have been — um — er — well — rather a puzzle, as it were. Oh, yes, indeed. As it happens we know a distant relation of yours — a Mr. Jervas Wackwire. Leastwise we *believe* him to be a distant relation — "

But his efforts to draw her out proved fruitless. His every query and remark was returned with an uncomprehending look, or a mystified glance at her guardian. The vicar for his part seemed as baffled as Sarah. What possible cause could she have for not responding to his overtures?

Unable to make any headway, the reverend gentleman and his companions turned again to the Centauress for an explanation.

"I'm afraid that my little Sarah does not understand you," she told them, "for indeed, she knows nothing of what you speak."

"Ah! And why is that? Has she suffered an illness?" inquired Dr. Chevenix.

The Centauress shook her head gently. "No, doctor, it is nothing of that sort. It is merely the natural result of her condition. In taking the posset she has been restored to that childhood self from which her mature being had sprung. As a consequence she has assumed not only the physical form she possessed as a child, but as well the demeanor and thoughts appropriate to it. For that is what it means to be a child again, does it not?"

Her fervent wish, it seems, had been to return to the simple joys of that time, and its simple glories, before she had been trodden on by injustice and misfortune. In her old age she had yearned again for that bright, unsullied, morning view of life, for that dewy sparkle and freshness that is the world as seen through the eyes of the young. In drinking from the silver cup she had lost all memory of her life's experience beyond her earliest years — *for that is what she had most wished to lose.*

"So you see," the Centauress concluded, "my little Sarah does not remember that she was this Mother Redcap of yours. She knows nothing of such a person — and neither indeed does Bertram."

For the visitors it was another stunner. It was astonishing to think that the child had not the slightest notion of who she was, or had been some fifty years before. No recollection of Mother Redcap and her potions and her mushrooms, no recollection of her cottage by the mere, or of Market Snailsby, or of Mr. Wackwire — no recollection indeed of anything beyond a child's ways and a child's blissful vision of existence.

For how much longer would this condition of Sarah's persist, they wondered? And would she not eventually, at some time in future, become Mother Redcap again?

"She will age, but at a Centaur's stately pace," their hostess replied. "Assuming she suffers no grievous injury, she will live out her span of some two thousand years, perhaps three, before the inevitable decline overtakes her. Until then her youthful bloom will remain largely undiminished. It is the gift of my race."

"Do you mean to tell us she will be just as she is now — a little girl — for all that long time?" said Dr. Chevenix.

"That is what I mean to tell you, doctor — and have."

"But that's extraordinary — it seems impossible — a child — for thousands of years!"

"Then I myself am impossible," smiled the Centauress, her arms folded calmly upon her breast, "but am I not here before you?"

"I'm afraid she has you there, doctor," Richard remarked. "But two thousand, three thousand years — that's a dashed tall stack of calendar to be cheating. And we were cudgeling our brains to know how Bertram had managed his five-and-thirty."

By venturing into the wood, Miss Sarah Crouch — Mother Redcap — had succeeded in regaining the lost paradise of her childhood, the which little Bertram never had surrendered. To all intents and purposes, Time stood still now for the both of them. Richard recollected how as a child himself he had yearned to live in Marley Wood and fathom out its secrets. He remembered how the wood had ignited his imagination, and recalled the sense of wonder it had planted in his soul. He had thought the wood a capital place for exploring in; but, like most everyone else in Market Snailsby, he had come to feel otherwise as he grew older.

"We never want to leave this place," Bertram declared, "nor do we wish to leave the lady who has cared for us for so long."

Exactly how long "long" had been, Bertram little comprehended. Like most children, neither he nor Sarah had any real notion of time or its passing. The fact that they themselves had not aged since drinking from the silver cup was all unknown to them. For they were but children, after all, unrecking of the wider world, and untarnished by it — and yet had all of its time at their dispose.

Such lucky, lucky children! Who amongst us in that wider world would not gladly have exchanged places with them?

"As for this magic you have learned, Bertram — Sarah has learned some of it as well?" Ada asked.

"Oh, indeed," the boy replied.

"Like Bertram, Sarah is very clever," the Centauress said proudly. "Allow her to perform for you one of her favorite transformations. It will take but a moment."

She bent down from on high and whispered something in Sarah's ear. In response the children took up the brazier and carried it to the opposite side of the hall, where the marble bust of some august personage in a huge, full-bottomed peruke was sitting on a pedestal, beside a disembodied suit of chain-mail. The magic moonlight was shining full-force upon the bust from both skylight and window, its rays drenching the august personage in a shower of molten silver.

With the residual smoke from the brazier rising beside her, Sarah began speaking in a low, quiet voice, her eyes shut and one small hand uplifted towards the bust. When she had finished her incantation she glanced briefly at the Centauress, then gave a little wave of her hand and snapped her fingers.

Instantly the eyes of the bust rolled down in their sockets and fixed themselves upon her. A smile spread over the sculpture's marbly countenance, from lofty brow to jutting chin, and enveloped it like a halo, like the wig that enveloped its head. Then it glanced up, the visitors

and the party of horsemen having come to its notice, and — oh so im-
probably — burst forth in voice.

"Company, adad! You'll pardon me for not bowing, all of you, but
as you can see it's a trifle difficult. Embarrassing, is it not?"

The children giggled.

"How are you tonight?" Sarah asked.

"Exceeding well, Miss Sarah," answered the august personage. "And
how is your fine self, then? I observe we have guests this evening. A
jolly-looking lot — ha, ha, ha! Have you been practicing your charades?"

"Yes, I have, sir."

"Outstandingly wonderful. We shall have a jolly time, then, just as
soon as you and Master Bertram have returned from your little excursion. We'll kick up a real shindy — ha, ha, ha! For as you know, Miss
Sarah, a good game of charades always puts me on my mettle — or is
it marble? Ha, ha, ha!"

"Yes, sir."

"I must confess, I've not practiced so much of late, for as you can
see I'm stuck here on this bloody pedestal. But you young folk, you're
as lively as crickets — ha, ha, ha! Let me think, now. Have you or
Master Bertram seen my hat? For I appear to have mislaid it."

"But, sir, you don't wear a hat."

"Not wear a hat? Adad! Like as not that's why I can never find it.
Well, it's nothing short of a scandal. Perhaps some day I shall have a
hat; at the very least I have hopes in that direction. Until then I shall
remain as I am, a mere carcass of a man, shut up in this bloody rock
like a buttoned boot. Heigh-ho! Well, where's the old squat, then?"

"Whom do you mean, sir?"

"Why, de Clinkers, of course. Ah — there he is, fussing again with
his horse's buckle. Splendid! Well, good hunting to you this evening,
Miss Sarah. And you, too, Master Bertram. Safe excursion! We'll have
a good chin-wag, just the three of us — ha, ha, ha! — and charades
once you've returned. I very much look forward to it."

"Yes, sir," Sarah replied; at which point she turned round and confided to the visitors, out of earshot of the bust, that the august personage was "a bit of a rattle, but a good chap all the same."

"And this is hardly all," extolled her guardian, the demonstration
having met with success. "The children have a wealth of friends here

at the lodge whose existence is all unknown to you. Have a look behind you now."

The visitors complied, and to their surprise beheld several small, whiskered cat-faces peeping shyly from around corners and behind the furniture. A misty gray, a calico, a mackerel tabby, and a tortoiseshell were counted amongst them. Immediately the ears of the valiant coach dog went up, and he uttered a little plaintive whine.

"Hallo! Where did *they* pop from?" he yelped. "This looks rummy to me. Why couldn't I sniff them out? More of Clover's spookies in the wood, I'll be bound!"

And there was more still. There was a wicker-basket that cracked bad jokes; oil paintings of noble ancestors that came magically to life, and discoursed upon tenants and timber; ghostly rappings in the wainscot; grinning clock-faces that told the time when asked, and sometimes when not.

"As you may observe, the children suffer from no lack of companionship," said the Centauress. "They have their small animal friends there, and others whom I have tamed in the wood. And they are able to create new friends for themselves from most anything through the medium of magic. And of course they have their cards and cribbage, and backgammon, and the books in the library. They have warmth and shelter, and plenty to eat, and much to occupy their imaginations. As well they have my guidance and protection, and the gift of their childhood for centuries to come. What more, as children, could they possibly require?"

What more indeed. It was a question for which the visitors, even the reverend clergyman, had no answer; and so they wisely held their tongues.

Meanwhile the followers and hunt-servants of de Clinkers had been chafing at the delay. "We are some time behind the hour now, and the horses grow restive — as do we," they complained. "We must hie to the chase!"

The grand and noble gentleman himself raised a hand in signal to the Centauress. The children, seeing this, sprang eagerly to their places on their guardian's back, and there clung to her long, tumbling shower of orange hair which she had loosed from its ribbon.

"Await us here. We shall return in due course," the Centauress instructed the visitors. (Actually, it was more than an instruction — it was a command, one delivered in a stern ring of voice, and whose meaning was only too clear to them). She and the children then joined de Clinkers and the hunting-party; and with the men leading their horses by the reins, and the hunt-servants striding along with their lanterns in hand, the hounds gamboling round their feet, they sallied forth at last.

The double-doors closed magically behind them as they exited onto the courtyard. There, in the vivid glare of the moon, the party of phantoms with de Clinkers at its head swung astride its phantom chargers, its phantom servants on foot beside them, and marched in all its spectral glory towards the causeway. The horns were bugling, the men were singing, the hounds were yelping; and with the Centauress and the children square in their midst they swept out through the gates and over the causeway, and were quickly lost to view.

The visitors, watching from the windows, were feeling a trifle overwhelmed by all they had seen and heard. What they had witnessed that evening in the great hall of the lodge was entirely impossible — and yet there it was. There was no denying the reality, such as it was, of the phantom riders; just as there was no denying the reality of the bust of the august personage, which for some minutes had been smiling and nodding at them from its pedestal, and batting its eyes at them, as though seeking to gain their acquaintance. This was making the visitors a bit ill at ease; so to counter its advances they lingered for a while at the windows after the hunters had departed, gazing out at the courtyard awash in its flood of moonlight.

"It really is quite beautiful," Jemma remarked after a time.

"Yes," agreed Dr. Chevenix, "and quite unusual, to be sure."

A brief interval of silence followed, punctuated by the sound of the doctor's abstracted tapping on the window-pane.

"She may be the last of her kind, but she really is a frightful hypocrite, you know," he said at length.

"How do you mean, doctor?"

"She complains about her people's being hunted to extinction for their blood, to be made into potions. And yet what is her own favored sport? *Hunting!*"

"True, doctor. But are you prepared to contest the point with her?" Richard asked.

The doctor drew a long breath and smilingly shook his head. "Ah — not I, sir, not I!" he answered with a chuckle.

"It's simply the way of her kind, I suppose," said Ada.

They relapsed again into silence, their eyes tracking the moon on its flight above the timber-tops. The only sounds were those of the fire crackling and snapping, and the long-case ticking and tocking, and a steady, low-voiced stream of chatter emanating from the august personage. (Unable to procure an audience with the strangers, he had procured one instead with his august self, whom he was entertaining with stories he had heard a thousand times). It was the long-case clock that eventually broke the spell, by proclaiming the hour — the which, as it happened, was *not* thirteen.

"In any event she seems a decent sort, all things considered," Richard remarked.

"What do you suppose she has in store for us?" the doctor asked.

"How do you mean?" said Jemma.

"Well, to be perfectly frank, Miss Hathaway, we're in more than a spot of trouble here. Do you suppose our hostess will give us leave to depart these premises now that we know of her existence?"

"What do you think she means to do with us? Boil us in a copper?" Ada said lightly.

"Or make us into pies?" Jemma chimed in.

The two friends enjoyed a merry laugh over it; but the doctor did not share their amusement. However French he may have appeared on the outside, the doctor was a Welshman through and through — a Hoddinott from the old Welsh marches — and his offhand, gently-mocking exterior concealed a brooding spirit.

"Perhaps something worse," he suggested, darkly.

"Oh, I doubt that," the vicar smiled; although it seemed to the doctor like a forced smile. "I dare say young Bertram would never permit it."

"Perhaps old Marblehead there knows a thing or two in that regard," Richard suggested, meaning the bust.

"Please, Richard, do not ask him," begged his sister, "for I've a suspicion we'll not hear the end of it."

"Well, she certainly can't keep *you* here, doctor. Whatever would people in Market Snailsby do without you?" Ada said, hastily adding — "oh, and you as well, vicar, of course."

"We have no choice. We must persuade her of the usefulness of the new road," the vicar declared, "and that we do not mean to disturb her life here or that of the children. Perhaps Mrs. Chugwell could be of some assistance in this?"

"Ah, but our hostess has made it quite plain she resents having her trees grubbed up," Dr. Chevenix reminded him, "and are not Mrs. Chugwell and her team the guilty grubbers?"

"*Her* trees? But is this land not parish land? What of Mr. Shand and his authority?"

"It's a futile argument, vicar, and a futile exercise as well — one that would be wholly to our cost. Who amongst us, for example, is to be the one to turn her out?"

The doctor had a point — who amongst them, indeed? None of them seemed particularly keen to volunteer, and the doctor suspected that no one in Market Snailsby would be, either.

"What do you suppose will happen, come daybreak?" he asked. "Will she be rid of us, do you think?

The answer to this none of them knew, although the women and Vicar Ludlow remained skeptical that any harm would come to them. Hence there was nothing for it now but to wonder, and to wait, the vicar remarking that it all was still such a puzzle — the wood, the lodge, the Centauress, the children, the magic, the lot.

Presently Ada, her mind returning to that spell of the children's that had drawn the moonbeams from the sky, addressed herself to Dr. Chevenix.

"By the by, doctor," she asked, "where does one obtain 'brain-dust from a stenching hag'?"

The doctor smiled and shook his head again; but this time he did not chuckle.

"I shudder to think, Miss Henslowe," he answered.

THE LAST CHAPTER

TELLS WHAT CAME OF IT

THE years rush by us like the wind. Season follows season, and the springtime of our grandparents, like the events recorded here, has long since passed into history.

What eventually happened, you may ask, as regards the Centauress and her guests, and the children, and the new road? A question altogether right and reasonable, and one I shall answer by saying that things fell out pretty much as you might have supposed.

Firstly, the visitors were *not* treated to a grisly end by being boiled in a copper or made into pies, as Dr. Chevenix had worried; on the contrary, they were treated rather well. Ultimately, after a good deal of discussion, the Centauress was prevailed upon to meet Mrs. Chugwell, with a view to working something out in the matter of the road. It was stipulated beforehand, however, that no particulars of their interview ever should be divulged, not so much as an iota; indeed, the very fact that it took place at all was kept a dead secret. Even young Matt Chugwell never knew the cause of his mother's abrupt disappearance for a day. It was the day she was escorted by Richard Hathaway, the vicar, Dr. Chevenix, Rosie, and Snap to the great hall of the lodge — where, at the end of that day, it was Mrs. Chugwell who prevailed.

It was her amiable character, her twinkling eyes and crinkly smile, and her talent for negotiating agreements and forging good relations — all of which she employed to great effect — which persuaded the Centauress that the road would cause no harm, either to herself or to the children. Its sole purpose, Mrs. Chugwell explained, was to convey passengers and cargo from northwards of the wood to south Fenshire, and vice versa. No sensible individual ever would dream of venturing into the dark domain beyond the verge, given its roster of fearsome inhabitants; indeed, the speedier the passage through the wood the better it was for all concerned. It was a different world today than in ages past, and it was futile to stay the tide of progress. Hence, so long as the Centauress and the children did not show themselves in proximity to the road, no one would be any the wiser.

Further, Mrs. Chugwell assured the keeper of the lodge that as few trees as possible were being pulled down to clear the road, and that the boles and branches of those few were being made good use of by incorporating them into the new roadbed. It was a guiding principle of Mrs. Chugwell's that nothing should be wasted — a view and a sentiment with which the Centauress was in deep philosophical accord.

The interview went on for a good several hours there in the hall, with Mrs. Chugwell sipping her tea and the Centauress calmly working her churchwarden. All in all the two of them got on remarkably well. The Centauress was much impressed with Mrs. Chugwell, a fellow representative of the fair sex who, like the Centauress herself, had made her way in the world, and who was as proud of her son Matt as the Centauress was of Bertram and Sarah. Coincidentally the mastodon lady's natural good humor, her honesty, and her girth had put the Centauress in mind of her old friend from bygone days, the grand and eccentric de Clinkers. More importantly, perhaps, the Centauress trusted her, and came to understand that an assurance from Nan Chugwell of Deadmarsh was worth its weight in wormwood, bogwood, turf, and treacle.

A condition of their pact was that the Centauress should return the items she had taken from the workers in the road; this she did. Further, she agreed to the simple expedient of directing the ghostly riders deeper into the wood, as she had in years past, and where the lights and sounds of the chase would attract no notice. Fortunately, the power of her magic would continue to benefit the townspeople in the matter of moonlight; for had it not been for the Centauress, two children, and a brazier there would have been hardly any moonlight over Market Snailsby at all.

As I have said, the circumstances of their interview were never to be made known by the parties involved. It was a secret most zealously kept, and has remained so to this day — or so it was thought. It appears that my grandfather Snap, the brave-hearted coach dog of Mead Cottage, had felt himself to be under no such obligation. Or perhaps he simply forgot; knowing my grandfather, I'm inclined towards the latter theory. And that is how I came to have this tale from him, when I was a youngster, and now am passing it on to all of you, my kin and cousins.

"Grandpup," my grandfather said to me one dark and wintry afternoon, as we were lazing on the rug before the kitchen fire, "I've got a story to tell you. It's a rather fantastic story — indeed it's like nothing else you've ever heard — but it's a true story nonetheless, every word of it. Do you understand me?"

"Yes, sir," I answered him.

My grandfather was a funny old fellow, who enjoyed gnawing on a good chop-bone now and then, and ousting shade-tails from the back-garden, and eavesdropping on the conversations of human folk. I have had no cause to doubt him, insofar as the truth of this story is concerned; but of course with funny old fellows one never knows. Like Mrs. Locket my grandfather had a gift of the gab, and a lively imagination. He was always well thought of in dog society, however; and although he never mastered the science of astronomy, he remained, in the view of Rosie at least, one of the decentest pudding dogs who ever barked. In his later years he adopted Mr. Erskine Joliffe's motto, "anything for a quiet life," and led a retiring existence. Nonetheless, let all hearers of such stories beware: for the truth, as they say, is in the ear of the listener.

Normality soon returned to the lives of those at Mead Cottage. Mr. Richard Hathaway returned to his rods and flies and his violin, and Miss Jemma Hathaway to her duets with Miss Henslowe. Mrs. Rudling returned to her housekeeping, and young Molly Grime to her maid-of-all-working, and the estimable Rosie to her — well, to her being Rosie, the joy of the stable and apple of her master's eye. Her master's treatise on Sir Pharnaby Crust, Fenshireman, eventually saw the light of print, being brought out by no less a firm than the university press at Salthead, and did tolerably well amongst a small circle of enthusiasts.

All in Market Snailsby remained curious how the adventurers had escaped the charge of the marsh devil, and what they had discovered subsequent to it; but their lips, like those of Mrs. Chugwell, remained firmly sealed. Not one word ever was peeped concerning a Centauress in Marley Wood. The two children were nevermore seen round its eaves, or in the Tillington Road, or anywhere else for that matter. They were presumed lost; and so in time people forgot about them, as people often will.

Mr. Blathers, having recovered from his fright, had seen nothing to convince him of the reality of magic, and never did; although Richard dearly yearned to enlighten him. Mr. Joliffe of the Mudlark was found to have had no connection to the recent strange events, including the horror in Yocklebury Great Croft. The latter eventually was dismissed as an anonymous prank by an anonymous crank, someone more to be pitied than prosecuted, and in time was forgotten as well.

As for Mr. Jervas Wackwire, he knew nothing of these matters, and so had nothing to forget; although he might have shed some light upon them had he been more soundly in his wits. We shall never know for certain the nature of his relationship to Mother Redcap, although it was rumored that certain cousins of his down in Gloamshire on his mother's side had been Crouches. Coincidentally it was this same side of the family that had produced a beadle, a Lord High Chancellor, an atheist, and a patent-medicine man.

After one further season of work, Mrs. Chugwell and her team at last broke through the northern eaves of the wood. There the new road was joined to the highway leading to Ridingham and Newmarsh. The citizens of Market Snailsby rejoiced; finally they had their road, and their traffic. The tradesmen turned handsprings and threw somersaults to express their delight. Life in the town, and in south Fenshire generally, entered upon a new chapter, and attendance on Snailsby fairdays picked up with surprising dispatch.

Mayor Jagard, Mr. Shand, and the vicar were very much pleased. So were Sir Hector MacHector and the gillies, by St. Poppo, and Mr. Blathers and Lawyer Inkpen, and Mine Host of the Broom and Badger, Mr. Travers, and his plump little badger-wife. Mr. Richard Hathaway too was pleased, as it speeded his travels to and from the Municipal Library, and thereby expedited the completion of his treatise (which nonetheless took several years longer than anticipated). And Mr. Philip Oldcorn was pleased as well, almost as much as his father Corney. Young Phil, having sat his terms at Clive's Inn and been entered upon the honorable roll of solicitors, had been engaged by Mr. Inkpen as the junior partner in his firm — the which, as I lately hear, is flourishing.

Mr. Ingo Swain was one citizen, however, who was not so happy, and who performed no somersaults in celebration of the new road (an exercise which in any case his considerable bulk would have precluded). Being a solitary sort, and an eel-trap man, he found the traffic disturbing to both his ears and his eels. But it was not all bad; for with so many new visitors in the town to occupy her attention, Miss Sukey Shorthose no longer pestered him so much as before, thereby relieving him of a good deal of annoyance.

As for Dr. Chevenix, he remained staunchly of two minds in the matter of the new road. Like my grandfather and Mr. Joliffe, the doctor preferred his quiet life there amongst the misty marshes, and in time adopted for himself the motto of young Herbert Hathaway — that there was nothing in this busy world worth taking seriously.

Mr. Ludlow began receiving regular shipments of his Ogghops from vintners in the north, and so dinners at the vicarage became even more festive. His wife eventually recovered from the loss of Bertram; and though I rather suspect that the vicar renounced his vow and told her all, Mrs. Ludlow, being the gentle, quiet, useful soul that she was, and a good person, never let on.

I've only to add that a letter arrived one day by the morning post, while the vicar and Mrs. Ludlow were having their tea. It was brought by young Mr. Murcott, and delivered into the vicar's hands by Jayne Scrimshaw. What follows I had from Miss Hortense, the glypt, who happened to be munching on some celery beneath the vicar's window when the postie came striding up.

The vicar unfolded the epistle and read it over quietly to himself. Little did he anticipate the shock he would receive from that small scrap of gilt-edged writing-paper, on which were traced the following lines —

"Upper Lofting,
Butter Cross.

"SIR. Immediately on receiving your note, my first thought was to burn it for the hoax and cheat that it is. A few words with my solicitor, however, served to convince me that a darker motive was at work. In consequence I have taken some time in answering, and have taken some pains in crafting that answer, and that answer is — *you can't fool me.*

"I shall have nothing to do with you and your preposterous claim to have found my lost brother, which is nothing more than a ruse *to extort money* from me and my family. Be assured, sir, that it *will* fail — most deciduously so. Even were this child of yours my brother, he *could not be,* for my brother would be near his 40th year of age today. Your arithmetic is far wide of the mark, sir, as is your honor and your mortality.

"In no way can your claim account for my brother's disappearance. They said at the time he had been *eaten by beasts,* and as no sign of him or his pluck ever was found, then it must be so. He *was* eaten, and by beasts; and so he cannot be walking around. But no matter. He was a beastly little creature himself — dirty, disobedient, disagreeable, and a nuisance. I never liked him; I never knew anybody who did.

"If you are indeed a parson as you say — *the which I sincerely doubt* — may you blush with shame. Yours is no honest business, sir, and you are no gentleman, not the least a reverend one. Undoubtedly you think yourself a clever fellow — no matter. If you persist in this *transparent* and *miserable* effort to extort money from my family, I shall have no recourse but to instruct my solicitor, Mr. Swindle, of the house of Dodge, Swindle, and Lynch, to take VERY FIRM MEASURES — you understand me. You shall be in more trouble than you can imagine. You may be spinning your web now, but it is your head soon that will be spinning, and I and my family spared the mercenary connivances of a scoundrel.

"Be assured, sir, there is no extremity Mr. Swindle will not make you feel, should you persist in your machicolations.

"If you think this letter a warning, then take it as you will. I shall not expect to hear from you again.
"Yours sincerely,
"POLLY LONGCHAPEL."

The vicar read the letter over a second time, as if not believing what had passed through his eyeballs, and thereby doubled his astonishment.

"*God bless my soul!*" he exclaimed, and fell back in his chair, his spectacles thrown onto his forehead.

"I'm sure He will, dear," said his wife, patting her husband's hand. "Now, then, won't you have another bun with your tea?"

THE END

ABOUT THE AUTHOR

Jeffrey E. Barlough was born in 1953, and holds a Doctor of Veterinary Medicine degree from the University of California, Davis, and a Ph.D. from Cornell. He has published some seventy research and review articles in scientific journals, and has edited several small-press publications of minor and archaic English works. His "Western Lights" series of fantasy-mysteries, begun in 2000 with *Dark Sleeper*, has been widely praised for its imaginative setting, eccentric characters, droll humor, and unconventional storylines.

To learn more about Jeffrey E. Barlough and
the Western Lights series visit

www.westernlightsbooks.com

Dark Sleeper
(2000)

"Are you pleased with your station in life, man?"

So asks the dancing sailor, before unscrewing his own head and handing it over to a very startled Mr. John Rime, the cat's-meat man, one foggy night.

Mocking laughter pierces the dark sky. An enormous brindled mastiff is seen in the streets, walking upright like a human being. A little lame boy with red hair and a green face haunts the corridors of the Blue Pelican public house — eighty years after he died there. A sunken ship rises from the ocean bottom and comes sailing into the harbor. A manlike creature with great leathery wings is seen clinging to the spire of St. Skiffin's Church.

Such are a few of the mysterious apparitions afflicting the ancient city of Salthead. What do they mean? Who is responsible for them? And what of the marvelous glowing metal that looks like gold but isn't, and the exploded statue in a remote chapel crypt?

In a frigid world shattered by a cometary collision, where saber-cats prowl the mountain meadows and the old mastodon trains are fast disappearing from the land, something wicked has been released. Join Professor Tiggs and Dr. Dampe as they search for answers and uncover a 2,000-year-old menace threatening all that remains of earth.

The House in the High Wood
(2001)

It looked to have been once a very picturesque little market-town, but had fallen into decay. Signs of neglect and disuse were everywhere evident, in the general disrepair of the houses, in the tattered casement-windows and tottering chimneys, the disarticulated doors, the extensive overgrowth in the churchyard and gardens and village green. Over everything lay a ghostly pall of silence.

"Driver," I called out, "what is this place? This hamlet below us?"

"Shilston Upcot," replied the coachman, then added, slowly and enigmatically — "or more rightly *was.*"

"Who lives there?"

"None what has a decent brain, sir," answered the guard. "Though there might be some — some folk as yet at the great hall, up there in the wood. But none takes to the village now, sir, unlessen they be off the latch. Crackers I mean, sir. Daft!"

What frightful secret lies hidden in the dismal ruined village high in the mountains of Talbotshire? Where have the inhabitants gone, and why have they gone there? Who — or what — lives now in the old mansion-house atop Skylingden point?

"There's deviltry here," said the guard. "The village, the mansion-house, the woods, the black waters — mischief — devil's work — "

"Aye," nodded the coachman. "The kind as don't bear thinking of!"

Discover for yourself the startling answer to the mystery of Shilston Upcot, in this second volume of the Western Lights series.

Strange Cargo
(2004)

She opened the case and from one of its compartments removed a lady's hand-mirror. The mirror itself was not of glass but of polished bronze, which reflected but poorly.

She turned the mirror over in her hands, examining every aspect of it with a mixture of fascination and dread. But nothing untoward happened, and so she returned the mirror to the dressing-case. She was about to close the lid when she heard it.

It was a noise like a hissing whisper, and it came from the mirror. A slithery, slippery thing it was, that whisper, dark and sinuous, like an evil vapor rising from a caldron.

"Djhana," it said.

A cold breath of fear raced up her spine, chilling her to the marrow.

"Djhana of Kaftor," said the mirror.

"I do not hear you," she answered, "no, no, I do not hear you — "

"Djhana of Kaftor," said the mirror again.

"No, no," she said, her head turning slowly from side to side and her eyes shut tight. "No, no, no!"

"Our mighty lord the earth-shaker commands you. Return — *or beware the Triametes!*"